DOUBLE

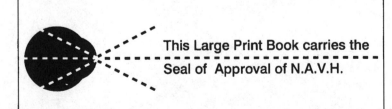

This Large Print Book carries the
Seal of Approval of N.A.V.H.

DOUBLE

Marcia Muller
and
Bill Pronzini

Thorndike Press • Waterville, Maine

Copyright © 1984 by the Pronzini-Muller Family Trust

All rights reserved.

Published in 2003 by arrangement with
Dominick Abel Literary Agency, Inc.

Thorndike Press® Large Print Paperback Series.

The tree indicium is a trademark of Thorndike Press.

The text of this Large Print edition is unabridged.
Other aspects of the book may vary from the original edition.

Set in 16 pt. Plantin.

Printed in the United States on permanent paper.

Library of Congress Cataloging-in-Publication Data

Muller, Marcia.
    Double / Marcia Muller and Bill Pronzini.
      p. (large print) cm.
    ISBN 0-7862-5174-3 (lg. print : sc : alk. paper)
    1. McCone, Sharon (Fictitious character) — Fiction.
    2. Nameless Detective (Fictitious character) — Fiction.
    3. Women private investigators — California — San Diego
    — Fiction.   4. San Diego (Calif.) — Fiction.   I. Pronzini,
Bill.   II. Title.
PS3563.U397D68 2003
  813'.54—dc21   2002044839

DOUBLE

1: McCone

The Casa del Rey Hotel gleamed white in the afternoon sunlight. With its peaks and gables and round turrets at each corner, it looked like something straight out of a Gothic novel. It was, I thought, as unlikely a setting for a convention of private investigators as I'd ever seen.

I steered my beat-up red MG around the circular driveway — where I was pointedly ignored by the valet parking attendant — and into the lot at the side. Getting out, I glanced over at the well-tended grounds that stretched toward the ocean. A couple of people were walking across the lawn, probably heading for the little white bungalows that nestled among the tropical gardens, but otherwise it was deserted. The heat was fierce, even for August, and any sensible person would have been at the beach or pool.

Taking my purse from the convertible, I

turned toward the hotel. The Casa del Rey, on the Silver Strand south of Coronado Island, was a San Diego institution, as was its counterpart, the Hotel del Coronado, on the island itself. I'd been coming to the Casa del Rey all my life — first for Easter egg hunts in the formal gardens, then for high-school proms, and finally for the wedding receptions of old friends. For as long as I could remember, it had belonged to a prominent La Jolla family; in fact, during the 1920s, one of them had hanged himself in the east tower — reputedly over a blighted romance — and after that the place had been said to be haunted. Then, two years ago, it had been bought by a Japanese conglomerate. Somehow I doubted any grieving ghost still walked the Casa del Rey's corridors; the Japanese, with their high-tech approach to business, were too pragmatic to permit *that* sort of thing.

Of course, other things had changed too. The hotel and its beautifully landscaped grounds had once stood in splendid isolation. Now it abutted a group of high-rise buildings — apartments or perhaps condominiums — called the Coronado Shores. Once chauffeured limousines had waited in the circular driveway; now tour buses disgorged hordes of passengers. The accepted mode of dress had become less formal, and probably the service was less gracious. Changes — I'd found them everywhere during this visit to San Diego, my old hometown.

I climbed the wide front steps and went into the chill of the air-conditioned lobby. There were lines at the registration desk, luggage heaped all over, and bellboys in the hotel livery running back and forth. The people didn't look like conventioneers. Probably they were tourists from one of the buses parked outside. I tried to squeeze past a particularly noisy group with cameras, and when they wouldn't budge, I shoved a luggage cart aside and went around them. Ahead was a bulletin board telling convention members to go to the mezzanine.

It was quieter up there, although the buzz of voices rose from the lobby. At the far end, next to a circular staircase that led up to the formerly haunted east tower, was a registration table staffed by the same fussy, officious types who are always behind registration tables. It was backed by a red-and-gold banner that said WELCOME, NATIONAL SOCIETY OF INVESTIGATORS. I got my badge and an information kit — fat and doubtless full of papers describing seminars and panels, lectures and films — and went, as directed, into a large room at the right.

There was a bar to one side and on the others were manufacturers' booths that apparently displayed the latest in electronic surveillance equipment. Quite a few people were already milling around and talking, some clutching plastic cups of wine. They ranged in age from the early twenties to the sixties; the men were dressed in everything from formal summer suits to golf clothes; some of the women wore jeans like me, others had on colorful floor-length dresses. It might have been a roomful of life-insurance agents, and I smiled as I looked around for someone I knew, thinking of how this crowd could explode once and for all the stereotype of the private eye.

I headed for the drink table, listening to snatches of conversation as I went.

". . . which parts of the program are you planning to attend?"

"I don't know. They all look awful to me."

"What about the seminar on 'Interpersonal Relationships with Law Enforcement Officers and Government Officials'?"

"Christ!"

Personally I agreed. I'd learned all I needed to know about interpersonal relationships with law enforcement officers during a two-year affair with a homicide lieutenant.

". . . terrifically high airfare down here. Why didn't they schedule this thing when the airlines were having that special deal last winter?"

". . . brought Marie and the kids along. It's the closest thing we'll get to a vacation this year."

". . . ethics, ethics, ethics! Why are all these panels about ethics?"

I finally reached the bar and got some wine. Sipping it, I continued to scan the room for a familiar face and eventually spotted Elaine Picard, a striking woman in her late forties who had been my supervisor when I worked in security for Huston's Department Store some ten years ago. I'd heard she'd recently come to Casa del Rey as head of security, and wondered if she'd been instrumental in bringing this convention to the hotel. I began weaving through the crowd toward her, but stopped at the sight of a second familiar figure — this one skulking by a display of wiretapping equipment.

It was a fellow investigator from San Francisco, the one the newspapers had dubbed "the last of the lone-wolf private eyes." He was a big Italian guy in his fifties, sloppy in a comfortable sort of way, and right now he looked far from happy. In fact, he was eyeing a voice recorder as if it might bite him.

I was delighted to see him there. Besides being the kind of investigator I could look up to, he was a gentle man with a wry sense of humor and a somewhat jaundiced way of looking at the world that was often at odds with an idealism he did his best to hide. We'd met while testifying on the same court case a few years ago, had discovered a common intolerance for abuses of the justice system, and since then we'd kept in touch. A couple of times, I had called him to kick around ideas on a case, and I'd found the price of a few beers would buy me a great deal of expertise.

Moving up behind him, I stuck my forefinger against his back like a gun. He started and turned around. "Hi, Wolf," I said, using my nickname for him.

"Sharon McCone. Well, this is a surprise."

"I can say the same."

"That cheap outfit you work for send you?"

"Not exactly." He was right in his assessment of All Souls, the legal cooperative where I work; they are as tight as they come. "San Diego's my hometown, and it's a good chance to visit my family. I paid for the gas driving down, All Souls picked up the registration fee."

"You ought to get a better job, Sharon."

"I know, but what better outfit would have me?" I glanced over at Elaine Picard. She was talking to a heavyset man in a loud red shirt. "What about you? I didn't think you went in for stuff like this."

His face became even more gloomy. "I don't usually. I let Eberhardt talk me into it."

I nodded. Eberhardt was his partner and had been a cop on the San Francisco homicide detail for many years. I studied my friend. "You're looking svelte, Wolf."

"Yeah. I took off about twenty pounds."

"How'd you manage that?"

"Lots of eggs. Rabbit food. And I gave up beer."

"What!" I couldn't imagine him not drinking beer. It was all he drank, but he was very fond of it. "No beer at all, even now?"

"Well, just the light stuff. It's beer-flavored water, but it's better than none."

I wondered how much his lady, Kerry Wade, had had to do with this new image, and was about to ask him when a fat woman in a Hawaiian muumuu pushed between us. I was enveloped in a cloud of her sickly

13

sweet perfume and moved back, grinning helplessly at Wolf. Someone bumped into me from behind, and my wine sloshed over onto my hand. Then two men in business suits began elbowing between me and the fat woman, complaining loudly about the lack of a full bar.

It seemed hopeless to try to continue the conversation, so I called, "Let's have a drink sometime this weekend."

"Sure. I'll be around."

By the time the men moved, he had been swallowed up in the crowd. I turned and went to find Elaine Picard. On the way I stopped at a couple of tables displaying video equipment, picked up some brochures — wistfully, since All Souls would never spring for that sort of gear — and chatted with an extremely good-looking lie-detector salesman. When Elaine saw me, her face lit up and she waved.

All in all, it looked like this was going to be a great weekend.

2: "Wolf"

The Casa del Rey wasn't at all what I had expected. With a name like that, it should have had stucco walls and red tile roofs and courtyards full of yucca plants and Spanish mosaic tile. Instead it looked like something you'd find on the English moors: big white Gothicky affair, lots of gingerbread trimming, round open-sided towers poking up on all four corners of the main building, flags flying like medieval pennants. There were also gardens full of palms and tropical flora, an acre of bright green lawn, and some quaint little bungalows for those folk who liked their privacy. Out behind the complex, a silvery strip of beach and the deep dark blue of the ocean glittered under the hot summer sun.

I took my airport rental car past the expensive-looking Glorietta Bay Marina, diagonally opposite the Casa del Rey on the bay side of the Silver Strand highway, and turned in to the hotel parking area. This is a hell of a place for a convention of private eyes, I thought as I bypassed the valet and parked the thing myself. Makes it seem as if we're all getting fat off our clients, rolling in big bucks.

Maybe the rest of them *are* rolling in big bucks, I thought.

I managed to work up a pretty good sweat in the walk from the parking lot to the front entrance; it must have been a hundred degrees, and I have never dealt well with heat. But as soon as I stepped inside the plush lobby, the air conditioners froze the sweat and left me feeling chilled. I have never dealt well with air conditioners either.

At the desk, a clerk who looked as if he'd come out of an *Esquire* fashion ad took in my shiny suit and my wrinkled shirt and my paisley tie and gave me an Oh-you're-one-of-*those* look. But all he said was "You're with the convention, sir?" I said I was, and he found my reservation, and I signed myself in. But I didn't get a key until he had satisfied himself that I'd paid for my three days in advance and that my check hadn't bounced.

A uniformed bellhop insisted on conducting me and my bag up to my room. It was on the third floor and about the size of a walk-in closet, and it had a nice view of a big building farther down the coast that bore the words HEADQUARTERS OF NAVAL SURFACE FORCE, U.S. PACIFIC FLEET — part of one of the military installations in the area. Obviously this was one of the luxury accommodations reserved for famous detectives like me. I decided to forgo the luxury for the time being and left when the bellhop did. On the way down in the elevator, I asked him where I went to sign up for the convention, and he told me the mezzanine. So that was where I got off.

The first thing I saw was a big red silk banner that said WELCOME, NATIONAL SOCIETY OF INVESTIGATORS in gold letters. Under it was a registration table, and behind that was a guy wearing a name tag that said he was a Society vice-president from an agency in Kansas City. I told him my name, and he asked me twice to spell it before he got it straight; then he gave me what he called an information packet and a name tag of my own. The badge thing was supposed to be pinned onto your shirt or coat; I hid it in a pocket instead. Then I went where the guy told me, through a doorway into a big room filled with people and booths and an open bar and plenty of noise.

Most of the people were men, but there were more women than I'd expected, even considering that some of them would be wives and girlfriends. A lot of both sexes looked young, too young to have had much experience as private investigators. And not many of them *looked* like detectives, either: there wasn't a trench coat or an underarm bulge in the place. Hawaiian shirts and muumuus, and one guy in a pair of Bermuda shorts. Except for the booths, and the displays of equipment inside them, it might have been a gathering of tourists waiting for a luau.

I took a deep breath and went in among them. Nobody paid any attention to me. And none of the faces was familiar. I hadn't been to one of these conventions in fifteen years, but I knew a fair number of people in the business; there should have been *somebody* around that I recognized. A roomful of strangers. It made me feel old and out of touch and probably out of date.

The stuff in the booths definitely made me feel out of date. The latest in electronic surveillance equipment, everything from large scanners to the famous martini-olive bug invented by Hal Lipset, San Francisco's richest P.I. Equipment for home, automobile, and personal use. Voice recorders, video recorders, bugs, wiretaps. Cameras, both conventional and of the spy variety. Home and business computers. Even a lie detector and a guy to demonstrate how it worked. At one of the displays, two earnest types were talking about a "worblegang veeblefetzer," or something like that, in a language that sounded like English but might have been Serbo-Croatian for all the sense it made to me.

I stopped at another booth and stared at a jumble of wires and other apparatus that a sign said was "the latest in ultramodern multidirectional voice recorders." I thought that if I had to learn to operate one of those things in order to conduct my business, I would retire and raise vegetables for a living — and somebody poked something into my back and made me jump a little.

When I turned around I was looking into the smiling face of somebody I knew, finally: Sharon McCone, one of the women who had come into the profession in the past few years and who also worked out of San Francisco. It was an attractive face, with high cheekbones and a dark complexion and a framing of long black hair that testified to her Shoshone Indian blood. She had a nice figure, too, but she was twenty years younger than me and I didn't want her to think I was a dirty old man by staring at it. Besides which, she brought out latent paternal feelings in me for some reason. Maybe part of it was that I knew she'd been in some tough scrapes in the past and was lucky to be alive. I'm hardly a male chauvinist, even though my lady, Kerry Wade, accuses me of it sometimes; I think women ought to be and do anything they damned well please and get paid equal money for their efforts. But that didn't stop me from feeling protective toward McCone.

She waggled her finger at me — the thing she'd poked into my back — and said cheerfully, "Hi, Wolf."

I tried not to wince. Wolf. She'd got that from a newspaper story that had appeared a few years ago in which some smart-ass yellow journalist had referred to me as "the last of the lone-wolf private eyes." Other people called me that and I got annoyed and told them to cut it out. But with McCone I couldn't seem to muster up the effort. I just grinned and took it like a nice old papa.

But I was still glad to see her, so my answering smile was genuine. "Sharon McCone," I said. "Well, this is a surprise."

"I can say the same."

"That cheap outfit you work for send you?"

"Not exactly. San Diego is my hometown and it's a good chance to visit my family. I paid for the gas driving down, All Souls picked up the registration fee."

All Souls was a legal cooperative she worked for that undertook cases for people who didn't have much money, some of whom had backgrounds that were questionable at best. It was an aboveboard operation, but that couldn't make it any more pleasant to work for.

"You ought to get a better job, Sharon."

"I know, but what better outfit would have me?" She glanced away for a moment, as if someone in the crowd had caught her eye. Then she said, "What about you? I didn't think you went in for stuff like this."

"I don't usually. I let Eberhardt talk me into it."

She nodded. And then gave me an up-and-down look, as if she'd just realized that there was less of me than the last time we'd seen each other. She said approvingly, "You're looking svelte, Wolf."

"Yeah. I took off about twenty pounds."

"How'd you manage that?"

"Lots of eggs. Rabbit food. And I gave up beer."

"What! No beer at all, even now?"

"Well, just the light stuff. It's beer-flavored water, but it's better than none."

She started to say something else, but a fat woman in a muumuu that looked like a paint-factory explosion got between us. McCone backed up, and somebody bumped into her and spilled the plastic cup of wine she was holding, and somebody else got in my way. Conventions. Crowds — I hated crowds. Somebody was always shoving his way into your space.

McCone called, "Let's have a drink sometime this weekend," and I said, "Sure. I'll be around," and then two more guys, both of them wearing suits, blocked my view of her and I said the hell with it and went away to find a quiet corner to grumble in.

"Why not go to the convention?" Eberhardt had said when the Society's flyer came in the mail. "Talk to some other private cops, get a different perspective on things. It'll be good for you and good for the agency. I can take care of business here for three days."

"I'd love to go to San Diego," Kerry had said later, "but you know I can't get away that weekend. The new Bowzer Bits dog-food commercial is being filmed on Friday and Saturday and I've got to be there in case they want any last-minute changes in the promo material. But you go ahead. It'll do

22

you good to get away for a few days, be among people in the same profession."

So here I was, among people in the same profession — people who wore hideous muumuus and Bermuda shorts and looked like tourists from Cincinnati and talked about worblegang veeblefetzers. I felt like a guy who had just stepped off a time machine, or maybe into another dimension. I felt like an anachronism. I felt obsolete.

This, I thought, is going to be a *lousy* weekend.

3: McCone

Elaine Picard was as slender as ever, her sleekly styled dark hair frosted with the lightest touch of gray. She wore an impeccable beige linen suit and tasteful gold jewelry, and, as I remembered, exuded an air of control and confidence. Strangely missing, however, was the impression of bursting health and vitality that she usually conveyed. There were tired lines around her mouth and dark circles under her eyes; she looked almost haggard.

She smiled at me, though, and said, "I'd hoped you'd be here, Sharon. How are you?"

"Fine. And you?"

"Quite well, thank you." She studied me, faint amusement in her eyes. "I see you haven't grown up yet."

I glanced down at my tailored blouse and jeans. "Good Lord," I said, "and I even wore high-heeled sandals for this occasion!"

"They're very stylish, but the general impression remains the same." There was no censure in her voice. When I'd gone to work for Elaine just after graduating from high school, she'd realized there was no way a true child of the sixties would be believable in the suburban-housewife pose that Huston's female security guards usually assumed. So she'd encouraged me to wear the bell-bottoms and Indian cloth blouses that were popular then, to go barefoot and let my long hair hang free. The costume had worked, placing me beneath the suspicion of shoplifters; and as I'd lurked among the racks of clothing with a walkie-talkie in my macramé bag, I'd become one of Elaine's most effective operatives. It was also to her credit that she didn't attempt to hold her people back; she had been one of the first to suggest I might be wasting my time by not going to college.

The big man in the red shirt whom Elaine had been talking with earlier was still standing next to her, holding a drink that looked like whiskey. He must have brought his own bottle or got it from the hotel bar, because all they had at the drink table here was wine. He shifted his weight from foot to foot and cleared his throat.

Elaine said, "Sharon, I'd like you to meet Jim Lauterbach, one of our local investigators. Jim, this is Sharon McCone, from San Francisco."

Lauterbach extended his hand. He was about six-two, overweight, and nondescript. Although there was no obvious reason for it, the phrase *down at the heels* flashed through my mind. I shook his hand briefly.

"Great convention, isn't it?" he said. "Lots of good people, and these manufacturers' tables are terrific." He motioned at the booths displaying electronic gear. "All the latest equipment, better even than a lot of the stuff I've got."

Elaine said, "Jim was just telling me that he recently moved here from Detroit." Usually you couldn't sense much of what Elaine was thinking or feeling; she had a very polished and polite surface manner. But something about the way she spoke told me she didn't like Lauterbach. Maybe it was the heavy sprinkling of dandruff on the collar of his shirt — that would offend a fastidious woman like Elaine. Come to think of it, it offended *me*.

"How do you like California?" I asked him.

"Oh." He gave me a lopsided grin. "Compared to Detroit . . . well, there's no comparison. Detroit's a depressed area. Very depressed. So many out of work. And the winters . . . well, you can't imagine the winters." His words were slightly slurred, as if he had been drinking for some time.

"Do you have your own agency here?"

"Yes. I took over a friend's. An old Navy buddy, Jack Owens — the Owens Agency, on Sixth Avenue, downtown. He couldn't take the grind anymore, so I'm running the business for him. And believe me, since I've been at it things are looking up."

I glanced at Elaine and saw she was staring off in a preoccupied way. When I caught her eye, she moved her head slightly in the direction of the door.

"Well, I've enjoyed meeting you, Jim," I said. "I'm sure we'll be running into one another again this weekend."

"Yeah, sure." He nodded curtly, clearly annoyed at the dismissal.

Elaine took my arm and steered me toward the exit. "God, what a dreadful person," she said. "He's been boasting and breathing booze at me for what seems like hours. Let's go downstairs and get a drink. The smoke in here is starting to get to me."

I set my plastic cup on a nearby table and we went out onto the mezzanine. The air out there was definitely clearer.

"At least the bar has proper ventilation," Elaine said. "And we can put it on my expense account."

"I'll drink to that." I followed her down the wide staircase to the lobby. "An expense account — my, my. I have one too, but every time I turn in a report, it's like the Spanish Inquisition before they'll reimburse a dime."

Halfway across the lobby, we encountered two men standing close together, in an apparent conference. The one facing us put out his hand and stopped Elaine. He was slim and elegant-looking in a light summer suit, and had thick blond hair. The man with him half turned, and I saw he was younger, maybe thirty-five to the other man's fifty, vaguely effeminate, and appeared to be of Mexican descent.

"Elaine," the first man said, "the security at the bungalows—" He stopped, looking at me.

Elaine removed her arm from his grasp and said, "Sharon, this is Lloyd Beddoes, manager of the Casa del Rey." Now her tone, under the polite words, was cold.

Lloyd Beddoes nodded and shook my hand.

"And Victor Ibarcena, our assistant manager."

Ibarcena bowed slightly. "How do you

do," he said in accented tones.

"Sharon," Elaine added, "is one of my former employees from Huston's Department Store — and a private investigator herself now. She's here for the convention."

Beddoes's eyes flicked to me. They were sharp and assessing. "One of your protégées, Elaine?"

"You might say that." Her tone was even more frosty. I glanced at her, but her face was set in its usual cordial mask. "Now, what about the bungalows, Lloyd?"

"Never mind," he said. "I can see you're busy. Victor will handle it."

"If it's a security problem—"

"No problem, Elaine. Just a nuisance that will be taken care of." Beddoes motioned to Victor Ibarcena, and the two went off across the hotel lobby toward the reception desk.

Elaine watched them, her eyes narrowed, then said, "Let's get that drink now."

The bar was at the back of the hotel, overlooking a terrace with white wrought-iron furniture, the beach, and the ocean. Spacious and dimly lit, the lounge was furnished with old-fashioned red plush sofas and chairs grouped around low mahogany cocktail tables. The bar itself was a mammoth carved affair that, I recalled, had been imported years ago from some European castle. Elaine signaled to the waitress and led me to a window table. The waitress followed and took our orders.

While we waited for our drinks, I gazed out at the ocean. The water sparkled in the late-afternoon sun, as if to prove the peninsula's claim to the name Silver Strand. When I looked back at Elaine, her face was pensive, and once again I noticed the lines of tension and the dark circles under her eyes that belied her relaxed, assured manner.

Probably the new job was taking its toll, I thought. Nothing much in Elaine's background had prepared her for the task of dealing with guests of a hotel such as Casa del Rey — or with the delicate problems that could come up there. Although her rise in hotel security had been rapid in the five years since she'd left Huston's, she'd previously supervised a small staff of twenty-five whose primary responsibility had been apprehending shoplifters. And before that she'd been merely a saleswoman in the cosmetics department, a brighter-than-average employee who had been pulled from the ranks and thrust into a management-training program.

The waitress returned and placed our

glasses of wine — white for me, red for Elaine — on the table. Elaine raised hers to me and sipped.

I said, "How's the new job going?"

She shrugged. "Like any job, it takes some getting used to."

"What's Lloyd Beddoes like to work for?" I wanted to explore the tension I'd sensed between them, to see if perhaps it was the cause of her haggard appearance.

"Lloyd?" She picked up her glass again and drained off a good third of it. "Lloyd's an arrogant, officious bastard — but I can handle him."

Well, that hadn't taken much probing. "And Victor Ibarcena?"

"He's Lloyd's whipping boy. He takes what Lloyd dishes out and smoothes everything over when he starts getting to people." She sipped her wine more slowly this time. Seeing the concern on my face, she added, "Oh, it's not all that bad. I've taken on more than I can handle lately — a new job and a new house in Chula Vista all at the same time — and I tend to dramatize my difficulties. But what about you? How's the job with the law co-op?"

"It's pretty good, actually. A lot of the time the work is routine and boring, but I've stumbled onto a few big cases over the years.

And I like the people there — they're casual and easygoing."

"Like you."

"Like me, yes. Every now and then I think of going out on my own, but . . ."

"But the law co-op is security."

"Well, security on a low economic plane. I did manage to scrape enough together to buy a house this year, though."

"Ah, another homeowner. What's the place like?"

"Peculiar. It's one of the cottages built by the Relief Committee after the earthquake of '06. Only it's been added onto and improved — somewhat. I redid the living room because the ceiling was about to fall in, and now I'm contemplating the bathroom. It's a top priority, since the toilet's currently in a cubicle on the back porch, and that's going to be mighty cold on some of those winter nights."

Elaine smiled and signaled at the waitress for another round of drinks. "I take it you haven't married," she said.

"No. Somehow I don't think a wedded state is compatible with being a private eye. I've got a boyfriend, though." Just saying it gave me warm glow.

"You look like you're in love."

"Yes, I guess I am. I know I am."

The drinks came, and Elaine raised hers in a toast. "Here's to love, then," she said with an odd note in her voice.

I sipped my wine. "What about you — any interesting males in your life?"

A barely perceptible shadow crossed her face. "No one worth mentioning."

I remembered how reticent about her private life Elaine had always been. A number of the other security guards at Huston's had speculated that she existed only for her work, but I had never bought that theory. She was too good-looking and vital not to have attracted someone equally dynamic and successful. Still, she had to be forty-seven by my reckoning, and she'd never married or — as near as I knew — even lived with someone.

"Tell me about this boyfriend," she said.

I grinned broadly, always glad to talk about Don. "His name's Don Del Boccio. He was a disc jockey in Port San Marco, where I met him while I was working on a case there. Last spring he moved to San Francisco. He's still a d.j., but in addition he has a talk show, interviewing celebrities."

"It sounds serious, him moving up there."

"As serious as I'm about to let it get right now."

"He doesn't live with you?"

"No. He lives with a baby grand piano, three thousand records, a set of drums, and a full complement of gourmet cooking equipment."

"My God, what an assortment."

"He claims it's all absolutely essential to his health and well-being. In college he trained as a classical pianist. And he's an excellent cook — Italian, primarily, as you can tell from the name."

"Ah, yes. Lasagna. Veal parmigiana . . ."

"You've got it."

Elaine sipped her wine, looking pensive once more, and I had the feeling that she was suddenly far away. I glanced over in the direction she was staring and saw a few occupied tables, but no one notable at any of them.

Finally she said, "I take it you're staying with your family?"

"Of course. All Souls certainly wouldn't spring for the Casa del Rey when I had free bed and board available. Actually, it's good I am staying there — as usual, there's a crisis."

She smiled. She probably remembered the McCone family crises, which involved anything from grease fires on the stove to my two older brothers' frequent scrapes with the San Diego cops. "What now?"

"Oh, John — that's my oldest brother —

is getting divorced. He's decided he wants custody of the kids, even though his wife is willing to give him very reasonable visitation rights. My mother has tried to talk him out of it — *she* knows who would end up raising them — and tensions are abuilding."

"And you think you can ease them?"

"I can try. John and I have always been pretty close." I looked at my watch. "And speaking of that, I have to be going. There's a big family barbecue tonight, in honor of my presence, and it starts in an hour."

"Are you coming back for the program tonight?"

"Later, if I can."

"Good. But please don't wait for me now. I'm going to have another drink, and then I have some work to catch up on."

"When can we get together again? I'd love to see the security setup here."

"I have a breakfast meeting in my office tomorrow — the executive committee of the San Diego Professional Women's Forum — but then I've got an hour free before I have to chair a panel."

"Which panel?"

She smiled wryly. " 'Modern Techniques of Hotel Security.' Eleven o'clock. It's on your program. Why don't you come by the office about ten? I'll give you the grand tour."

I agreed, thanked her for the drinks, and left. On the way out, I noticed Wolf seated alone at the bar with a beer and the convention packet spread open in front of him.

"Hiding in dark bars already?" I said in passing.

He looked up and I waved at him in the back-bar mirror.

4: "Wolf"

I got out of the convention room before long; the damned place, with all those people and all that electronics stuff, gave me claustrophobia. A cold beer was what I needed and a cold beer was what I went looking for.

The hotel bar was off the lobby, at the rear. A sign over its entrance said that it was called the Cantina Sin Nombre, but like the rest of the place it didn't have much of a Spanish motif. Heavy dark wood paneling and furnishings, with a bank of windows at the far end to admit some natural light. The windows looked out on a terrace strewn with white wrought-iron furniture, and the beach beyond, and the ocean beyond that. It was cool in there, but not an icebox like the lobby, and not too crowded, and I thought that I would probably be spending a good portion of the weekend tucked away in here.

I was halfway to the bar and beer when I noticed that I wasn't the only conventioneer who'd fled to this sanctuary: Sharon McCone was over at one of the tables near the windows, deep in conversation with a stylishly dressed older woman I'd seen earlier in the convention room. Well, at least *she'd* found somebody else to talk to. I considered going over and joining them, but they seemed to be enjoying each other's company, and I had never been any good at rolling in as a third wheel for polite chitchat. I kept on going to the bar and plunked myself onto a stool and ordered a Miller Lite from the barman. It came ice cold, along with a frosted stein. Score one for the Cantina Sin Nombre.

While I worked on the beer, I decided I might as well see what the convention had to offer, so I opened up the information packet the guy at the registration table had given me. Lots of great events, all right. All guaranteed to insure a fun-filled, informative "weekend in the sun," as the Society's flyer had put it.

Tonight, for example, after the usual welcome speeches, I could go to a pair of stimulating panel discussions: "Questionable Ethics and Practices of Private Detectives" and "The Investigator and Group

Dynamics: A Sociological Overview." I could also attend the first of several product demonstrations, put on by an L.A. supplier of handguns and other self-defense weapons. Tomorrow morning I could attend a film dramatization called *A Day in the Life of a Typical Investigator.* Or a seminar on "Interpersonal Relationships with Law Enforcement Officers and Government Officials." Or two more provocative panel discussions: "Modern Techniques of Hotel Security" and "Electronic Eavesdropping: Morality Versus Legal Admissibility."

Then on Sunday, if I was still thirsty for more knowledge, I had my choice of two films on various investigative techniques, some demonstrations involving computers and electronic surveillance products, and/or a fifth and final panel, sure to be the most stirring of all, entitled, "Seidenbaum's Method of Directive Interrogation: A Creative Debate." And *then* — the high point of the convention — the Society's annual awards dinner Sunday evening, at which no less than two politicians and six interpersonally relating law enforcement officers, government officials, and private investigators would speak, no doubt in great depth and detail, and handsome little ebony plaques would be presented to those members of the Society who had "distinguished themselves in the field of investigative service" during the previous calendar year. I looked for my name among the nominees, but it wasn't there. The only one I recognized was a guy from Boston; I knew him and his methods, and as far as I was concerned he was a wisecracking, borderline psychotic who operated under a moral code that was anything but and who ought to have been tossed in jail a long time ago. But then what did I know, really, an ordinary slob like me?

But that wasn't all. Oh no. The Society and the Casa del Rey weren't about to let the rest of the evening go to waste. There would be a postprandial cocktail party in the Marimba Room, featuring free champagne, and after that there would be dancing "until the wee hours" to the Latin melodies of Pedro Martinez and his world-famous Mexican Bandit Band.

I closed the information packet. I drank the rest of my beer. I thought: God, what if my heart can't stand the excitement of it all? What if I keel over right in the middle of one of the Latin melodies of Pedro Martinez and his world-famous Mexican Bandit Band?

I ordered another beer. And I was trying not to cry into it when a familiar voice said behind me, "Hiding in dark bars already?" I glanced up into the back-bar mirror, and it was McCone sailing by on her way out; she waved when she saw me looking at her. By the time I thought of something clever and unfatherly to say to her, she was gone and I was alone again.

McCone, I thought, if you keep disappearing all weekend, who the hell am I going to talk to?

Well, I had one other prospect, anyway — one guy I had never met but with whom I had corresponded and spoken to on the telephone and who shared a couple of common interests. He wasn't a private investigator; he didn't have anything to do with the convention, even though he would probably come and hang around for most of it. His name was Charley Valdene and he was a painting contractor who lived in Pacific Beach, up the coast a way. I had traded pulps with him off and on over the past several years; he collected mystery and detective titles, as I did, but more selectively — only those that contained stories about private detectives. He also collected anything else written or drawn or aired that involved the exploits of P.I.s. He'd cheerfully admitted that he had a private-eye fixation. Always dreamed of being one, didn't have the brains or the courage for the job — his self-analysis — and so he'd devoted himself to the species vicariously.

I could understand that sort of obsession all too well, because I'd had — still had — one something like it myself: it was the pulps I read as a youth that had led me to become, first, a cop and then finally to hang out my own shingle. And I had never forgotten that early desire to emulate the pulp-detective heroes of my youth, even though I never would, never could, because the world they'd inhabited was a make-believe world, and their era was long gone. But I kept trying. I would go on trying, too, until the time came to plant me somewhere. So what if I was obsolete? To hell with seminars and panels and electronic surveillance equipment and group dynamics and Seidenbaum's Method of Directive Interrogation. You are what you are.

I poured more beer, and when I lifted my glass I happened to glance into the mirror again. McCone's stylish lady friend was still sitting at the table by the window. Somebody else had joined her — a handsome wavy-haired guy in a Madras jacket and white slacks — and the two of them appeared to be having an argument of some kind.

It wasn't any of my business. But then I'm a detective, and detectives are curious types, and I was bored besides; so I kept on watching them. The woman seemed pretty upset. She said something to the man in a low angry voice, and he sat there relaxed, one leg crossed over the other, and laughed at her. Her voice got louder when she spoke again, so this time I could hear the words.

"Goddamn you, Rich, stop bothering me like this. I'm warning you — leave me alone!"

People at nearby tables were looking at them. The woman was aware of it; she said something else, lowering her voice, and got up out of her chair. The wavy-haired guy got up too and blocked her way when she came around the table. She tried to push past him; he caught her arm, not gently, and held her.

Well, I don't like scenes like that; I don't like men putting rough hands on women in public. I swung around and got off my stool and went toward them. Nobody else in the Cantina Sin Nombre moved at all — except for the bartender, who was heading for the telephone.

"Let go of me, Rich," the woman said to the guy. Her tone had a cold deadly edge to it.

He said, "You're making a scene," as if he was amused by the idea.

"No, *you're* making it. I'm head of security at this hotel, remember? I'll have you arrested, I mean that."

"Do you, Elaine? You wouldn't want me to start telling tales out of school, now, would you?"

She was paper white, and she looked frightened as well as angry. She made an effort to pull away from him; he hung on, hurting her because she winced. And that was when I got to them. I clamped my hand onto his shoulder, not too hard but not too lightly either, and arranged my mouth into a smile as I spoke.

"Some trouble here?"

The guy turned his head to look at me. There was no anger or hostility in his expression; it was just a look, shadowed with vague annoyance. He was in his late twenties, the wavy hair was dark brown, and he had funny eyes — gray-blue, with small pupils and little lights that burned down deep in them, like secret fires.

He said, "Let go of my shoulder."

"Sure. As soon as you let go of the lady's arm."

"This is none of your business."

"You let go, I let go. How about it?"

The funny eyes crawled on my face for about five seconds. Then he smiled — secret amusement to go with the secret fires — and released the woman's arm. When I took my hand away from his shoulder, he brushed at the place where it had lain as if he were afraid I might have somehow contaminated him.

The woman was rubbing at her forearm, where his fingers had left dark red marks. "Get out of here, Rich," she said to the guy. "And don't come back, do you hear?"

"Oh, of course," he said lazily. "Sure thing." He straightened his jacket, winked at me, smiled at her, said, "See you soon, dearheart," and took himself away across the room. Some people at one of the tables gawked at him as he passed, and I heard him say to them, "Nothing to worry about, folks. Just a little spat between lovers. Enjoy your drinks and have a nice day." Then he was gone.

When I looked at the woman again she was making gestures to the bartender, who still stood behind the plank with the telephone receiver in his hand; asking him tacitly if he'd called anybody. He shook his head and put the receiver down. He might have been throwing a switch, too, because the hush that had fallen over the room broke just then and the customers started whispering to each other and shifting around in their chairs.

The woman brought her attention back to me. Her anger was gone, but some of the fright still clung to her expression. She was nice-looking in a severe sort of way, with sculpted, close-cropped brunette hair frosted with gray and a well-preserved figure; she could have been anywhere from forty to fifty. One of the convention name tags was pinned to the front of her beige suit coat: *Elaine Picard — Chief of Security Operations, Casa del Rey, San Diego.*

"Thank you for stepping in," she said. "It really wasn't necessary, but thank you anyway."

"Well, I don't like to see women being mauled. Especially a friend of a friend."

"I'm sorry, I don't—?"

"I noticed you talking to Sharon McCone a while ago," I said. "Sharon's a friend of mine."

"Oh, I see. Yes, she and I used to work together. Are you with the convention too, then?"

"Yep. Also from San Francisco."

I told her my name and she nodded, but she was only half listening to me. Her thoughts were elsewhere, probably on the guy named Rich. She was still rubbing at her forearm.

I said, "Did he hurt you much?"

"What? Oh, my arm. No, it's all right."

"The way he was hanging on, he might have broken something."

"I doubt that. He always stops short of committing a felony in front of witnesses."

"Does that mean he's bothered you like this before, in public?"

"Yes. He's a nuisance."

"Old boyfriend?"

"No. Just . . . an acquaintance."

"Maybe you ought to get a restraining order to keep him away from you."

"Restraining order?" She smiled faintly, almost painfully, as if something had struck her funny in a macabre sort of way. "No, he's not dangerous. I can handle him." She paused, as if the conversation was making her uncomfortable, and then said, "Well. If you'll excuse me?" and gave me her hand.

"Sure. Nice meeting you, Miss Picard."

"Yes. Same here. I'm sure we'll see each other again during the convention."

Before she left, she detoured to the bar and told the bartender to pour a round of drinks on the house and to tear up my tab. So I nursed a third bottle of Miller Lite — Kerry wouldn't have approved, but what the

47

hell, I had to get *some* pleasure out of this weekend — and when it was gone it was almost five o'clock and the Cantina Sin Nombre was filling up with thirsty conventioneers. I fled to my walk-in luxury closet upstairs.

The bed was soft, at least. Hard beds play hell with my back, and I don't care what anybody says about them being good for you. I sat on it and picked up the telephone and called the Bates & Carpenter ad agency in San Francisco. And, wonder of wonders, Kerry was not only in but available.

"Well, I'm here in San Diego," I said when she came on the line. "Safe if not sound."

"That's good. How was the flight?"

"Okay. They gave me a clunker to drive at the airport, so I'm right at home on that score. But the hotel's too fancy. I feel like I ought to be using the service entrance. Besides, I can't figure it out."

"Figure what out?"

"The hotel. It looks like Wuthering Heights but it's got a Spanish name and so does its bar and nightclub, and the band that plays here is called the Mexican Bandit Band. What do you think that means?"

"I don't even want to guess," she said. "How's the convention so far?"

"It hasn't started yet. But I met a blonde

with a forty-two-inch bust who wants me to come up and service her later. I guess I might as well do it."

"What kind of service?" Kerry said. "The Private-Eye Special — in at ten, out at ten-oh-five?"

I sighed. "I hate snappy comebacks," I said.

"That's because you can never think of one yourself."

We went on like that for a while, bantering the way lovers do, and by the time we said good-bye I was pining away for her. Who needed a blonde when you could run your fingers through rich red hair as soft as velvet? Who needed a forty-two-inch bust when you could snuggle up to seven inches less around the chest but a whole lot more elsewhere, all of it slender and smooth and—

Cut it out, you horny old fart. It's only Friday and you just got here.

I tried to call Eberhardt, to find out if any business had come our way during the day and to tell him what a terrific time I was having so *he'd* want to go to next year's convention; that way I could get even with him. But he wasn't at the office. And he wasn't home yet either.

Which left me with nothing much to do except to read one of the pulps I'd brought along as trade items for Charley Valdene. At six o'clock I got up, not without great reluctance, and combed my hair and put my suit coat back on and rode the elevator down to the mezzanine.

The convention was in full swing. Hundreds of people milling around and chattering and fondling voice recorders and wiretaps and each other; a riot of swirling color and half-naked flesh and name tags and plastic wine cups and glistening machinery. I stood outside the elevator for a time, taking it all in and marshaling my courage. And then, like a soldier on a suicide mission, I girded my loins and gritted my teeth and plunged into the midst of it with no hope at all.

5: McCone

As I drove back to my parents' home in the Mission Hills district of the city, a kind of low, flat mood stole over me. I had spent very little time in San Diego during the past ten years, and now that I was here for what might be an extended visit, nothing felt right.

The city had changed, of course. Where there had once been a funky auto ferry from Coronado Island to the mainland, there was now a white soaring expanse of bridge. New, tall buildings lined the downtown streets. And the town limits had spread, shopping centers and housing tracts obliterating what had once been wild canyons.

But the biggest change was really in the people. I looked at my mother and father and saw they had more wrinkles and tired easily. My sister Charlene, down from Los Angeles for the week with her four kids, was pregnant again, and her poor color and lack of appetite told me this time things weren't going so well. John, naturally, had his troubles. Joey, my other brother, was still trying to decide what to do with his life, but his willingness to try everything and settle on nothing wasn't as charming as it had been five years ago. Patsy, my littlest sister, wasn't even here; she lived on a farm up near Ukiah, and Lord knew when I'd ever see her again — or if we'd have anything to say to each other when we did.

And then there were my old friends. I'd come down two days ago and, since my mother had spread the word, the phone had immediately started ringing. The calls led to a gathering the next night at my friend Donna's house, out in an area of expensive homes near San Diego State. And that had been a disaster.

First there was Donna, who had married a guy from our high-school class. He had done well in computers. They had a four-bedroom house with a pool; two children, a boy and a girl, well behaved as far as I could tell; country club membership; boat at a Mission Bay marina; twice-yearly trips to Hawaii.

And Donna was scared to death of me.

She had perched on the edge of the couch

waiting for the others to arrive and asked polite questions — how was my family, was I settled in my new house yet, was I glad to be back in San Diego? And all the time she watched me, nervously, warily, as if she expected me to do something peculiar. Then the others had arrived: Tina, a new embittered divorcée; Janey, still teaching school, still looking for Mr. Right; Connie, now a bank vice-president, married to "another professional"; Amy, wife of a professor at State, looking comfortable and sloppy as ever.

And they were all afraid of me too.

To ease the tension, we had had some wine, and then some more wine. And when the questions started to flow, I realized what was wrong. Despite the fact they were all different from one another, I was more different yet. In fact, to them I was strange. After all, I was a detective. I consorted with underworld characters, I carried a gun, I had — for God's sake — even shot a man to death. The questions went on and on; I could see the vicarious excitement gleaming in their eyes; and when I finally couldn't take it anymore, I had escaped early.

I didn't like to put much stock in old adages, but now I saw the truth in the one about not being able to go home again.

The street was crowded with cars when I pulled up to my parents' home at the end of the cul-de-sac. Getting out of the MG, I spotted their next-door neighbor, Mr. Murphy, and realized some things never change. He was sweeping his sidewalk, pushing the dead leaves and twigs down onto the walk in front of my parents' house. And when he saw me, he leaned on the broom and glared.

"Hi, Mr. Murphy," I called, and waved.

He glowered harder and turned his back. I smiled and went up the front walk. You'd think he'd have mellowed with the years, but no, Mr. Murphy, along with the pyramids of Egypt and a few other immutables, would go on and on. He'd never forgive the McCones for their too numerous kids and cars and parties that sometimes brought the cops. He'd never forget the night that John and Joey had toilet-papered the trees in front of his house. Mr. Murphy would go on glaring and sweeping as long as there was breath in his body.

And somehow that pleased me. It gave me the stability that had been missing during the last two days.

I pushed open the front door and went in, dumping my purse on the table in the hall. The place was a big, rambling ranch house.

Originally it had stood on an acre of land, but as more kids had arrived and more room was needed, it had expanded until it sprawled haphazardly toward all four lot lines. Bedrooms had been added in one direction, and in the other the kitchen had been moved twice, until it was now at the extreme end of the house. From year to year nothing had ever been in the same place; in a way it was like moving without ever having to pack.

Ahead of me was the old living room, which had been converted into a playroom, and beyond that what was left of the backyard — the part with the pool. The pool had been there when Ma and Pa had bought the house, but it had later been cracked by a sonic boom from the fighter planes at Miramar Naval Air Station. My parents had sued the Navy, but had never been able to prove their case, and since they couldn't afford to repair the pool, eventually they'd had a couple of loads of dirt hauled in, filled it, and turned it into a vegetable garden. We'd always had plenty of zucchini and corn and melons, and since we hadn't been raised to expect luxury, it was no hardship to drive to the beach for a swim.

I went through the playroom, stepping carefully over stuffed animals and games, and went outside. The brick barbecue was going full blast, but no one was to be seen. Taking a shortcut around the grape arbor, I entered the kitchen by the side door.

My mother stood at the center chopping block, making hamburgers. Her long hair, red streaked with gray, was fastened on the top of her head with a couple of barrettes, and beads of perspiration stood out on her forehead. When she heard me close the door, she turned and said, "Aha! There's the prodigal daughter. Did you get registered at the convention all right?"

"Yes." I grinned at her and then at Charlene, who leaned heavily against the refrigerator, her shape reminiscent of the back end of a Volkswagen Beetle. She was a curly haired towhead, like the rest of my siblings. Although there is an eighth Shoshone Indian blood in the McCone family, I'm the only one it came out in — a genetic accident unkindly labeled a "throwback." I've taken plenty of abuse in my time because of that label.

My Uncle Ed was at the opposite counter, wrapping ears of corn in tinfoil. I went over and hugged him; his shiny bald head came exactly to my chin. "Where's Aunt Clarisse?" I asked. "And where are the kids?"

"Clarisse took them off to the bedroom so Charlene could get some peace," Ma said. "She's telling them stories."

"Uh-oh." I glanced at Charlene, and she shrugged. Aunt Clarisse was a good story-teller, but she had a lurid imagination. The kids would probably be unable to sleep tonight, after being regaled with tales of witches, ogres, and dismemberment.

"And Joey?" I asked.

"Picking up his date," Charlene said.

"A date?"

"Her name's Cindy."

"A new one, of course." Joey changed ladies as quickly as he changed careers.

"Yes." Charlene grinned companionably at me. "This one's a computer program-mer."

"My, he's coming up in the world."

"Don't scoff," my mother said. "Programmers make good money. Maybe she'll marry him and support him."

"And where, while all this preparation is going on, is Pa?"

"The garage, of course. You can fetch him when you put the corn on."

"And John?"

Ma patted the last hamburger into shape — none too gently — and slapped it down on the plate. "Your brother John has taken

57

himself off into the canyon — with a six-pack."

"Hmm."

She turned from the chopping block, wiping her hands on her apron. "Sharon, I wish you'd talk to him. At least make him join the party. You always could talk to him better than any of us." The vertical lines between her brows deepened, and her mouth turned down woefully.

"I'll see what I can do, Ma." I patted her arm and went to take the platter of corn from Uncle Ed. "You want to help me with these, Charlene?" I said.

"Sure." She pushed away from the fridge and waddled out the door after me. "God," she said when we were out of earshot of the kitchen, "Ma's as bent out of shape as John is."

"Well, it's not easy being asked to raise two more kids at her age — especially after what she went through with us."

"I know."

I set the platter down on the edge of the barbecue and looked for the tongs. As usual, they had fallen off into the dirt. I brushed them off on my jeans and started putting the corn on the coals. "Even with Nicky leaving you alone as much as he does," I went on, "you've never come down here from L.A.

and dumped your kids in Ma's lap." Nicky was Charlene's musician husband; he had a pattern of getting her pregnant and then going out on tour with his country-and-western group. As soon as the baby was born, he'd return and work at local gigs until the next rabbit test came up positive.

"Yeah, that's me — good old self-sufficient Charlene." Her mouth twisted bitterly.

I looked sharply at her. "Now what did I say wrong?"

"Nothing. It's not you. Maybe I'm just tired of always being the dependable one."

"Don't *you* go causing problems now! It's bad enough with—"

"Don't worry." Her wonderful smile lit up her face and, with her mop of curly hair, she looked just like her three year old. "I'll be good."

"You better. I'm going to find Pa now."

The garage was at the extreme side of the lot, beyond the bedroom wing. As I approached, I could hear my father's guitar, and his reedy voice raised in song.

"But if there be dishonesty
Implanted in the mind,
Breeches nor smocks nor scarce padlocks
The rage of lust can bind. . . ."

59

I stopped, listening. The song was a new one. For years, my father had concentrated his musical talents on Irish folk ballads, but my mother had informed me in one of our weekly phone calls that his interests had expanded recently to American songs — and the bawdier the better.

"Whores will be whores, and on the floors,
Where many have been laid. . . ."

Quickly I knocked on the side door of the garage. The guitar issued one last plaintive chord and fell silent.

"Enter, if you must," Pa called.

I entered. He was seated on his workbench — a big man with a full head of snowy-white hair. When he saw me, his ruddy face broke into a smile.

"You caught me at it, Shari," he said, using the pet name only he called me.

"What's this with the dirty songs, Pa?"

He stood up and laid the guitar on the bench. "A man's got to have an interest in life — that's mine."

I looked around the garage, with its lathes and drills and sanders. Ever since he'd retired after thirty years in the Navy, Pa had been a cabinetmaker. "I thought your interest was carpentry."

60

"That's my work; there's a difference." He came over and put an arm around me. "You're not going to begrudge your own father a little pastime, are you?"

"No, Pa. Sing all the dirty songs you like — I'll even join in."

He gave me a mock-pained look. "Please don't. You know you can't sing worth a damn. I suppose your mother sent you for me."

"Uh-huh."

"Frankly, I'd rather stay out here. Parties, family gatherings . . ." He shut off the light and followed me outside.

"Frankly, Pa, I'd rather stay here with you."

"What, you don't like your family?"

"I love my family. But I think it's going to be kind of a hectic evening."

"What other kind do we ever have?" He stopped, his eyes studying my face fondly. "Your mother asked you to talk to John, didn't she?"

"Yes." I felt a sudden flash of resentment. Here I was, home two days, and already the burden of family responsibility was being heaped on me.

"See what you can do, Shari," Pa said, his face suddenly lined. "He needs help, and it's something he can't accept from the rest of us. Maybe he can from you."

"Maybe," I said somewhat ungraciously.

"Try it."

"All right, all right!" I turned and went toward the rear of the property where it backed on the canyon.

This part of the city was full of little finger canyons that stretched behind what looked like ordinary square lots. The canyons were overgrown with scrub oak, eucalyptus, and Torrey pine, and all kinds of animals, from chipmunks to coyotes, lived in them. For a time when I was small, we had had ducks in the yard, but one by one they fell prey to coyotes that would hop the fence at night. Finally one had even got our proud black cat, Gilroy, and after that my mother had said no more pets.

I took off my high-heeled sandals and stepped over the place where the rough rail fence had been pushed down ever since my childhood. There was a series of stone steps that my father had set into the side of the hill so his kids wouldn't break their necks climbing down. I followed them deep into the canyon, toward the ruins of our treehouse.

My mother had been right — John had taken himself into the canyon. He sat on a log under the oak that held the shell of our abandoned aerie, drinking a beer. Ma had been wrong about the beer, however; it was not one six-pack, but two.

He heard me coming and looked around, his fine blond hair falling against his forehead. With a shock, I saw how much the last few months had aged him: there were worry lines like my mother's between his eyebrows, and his blue eyes were peculiarly without light.

"Welcome." He gestured with the beer can. "I take it this means supper is almost ready."

"Not yet. I just wanted to escape the crew up there."

"Ma sent you."

I'd never been able to fool my older brother. "Yeah, she did."

"Poor Ma. She worries too much. Have a seat. You want one of these?" He reached for the six-pack.

"Sure."

He pulled a can from the plastic holder, cracked it, and held it out to me. It was a Schlitz, the brand Wolf drank before he got svelte and switched to beer-flavored water. "Thanks."

"What does Ma want you to do, talk me out of the custody fight?" John asked.

"No, just talk you into joining the party."

"I'm not in much of a party mood."

"I can understand that."

"She did tell you about the custody fight, though."

"A couple of weeks ago, on the phone."

"Is that why you came down here?" His responses to those around him had become the self-centered ones of a person in pain.

"No, I came down for a convention of private eyes."

He laughed harshly. "That must be something to see."

"What do you mean?"

"I can picture you all, comparing notes on the best place to buy your deerstalker hats."

I smiled faintly. "I think that was Sherlock Holmes. Private eyes are supposed to wear slouch hats."

"Do you?"

"No."

"Does anyone?"

"Probably not."

We were silent for a moment, sipping beer.

Finally I said, "John, are you really going to go through with this custody suit?"

"Yes."

"Do you stand a chance of winning?"

"Maybe. I've got to try. They're my kids, and they belong with me."

"Ma said you've been offered reasonable visitation rights."

He crumpled his beer can and tossed it down the hillside into a clump of manzanita. "It's not the same thing, Shar. I want to be with my kids every day, the way Pa was with us. I don't want to see them every other weekend and a month in the summer. I want to be there, to teach them things, to help them when they have problems, not—"

"I understand how you feel."

"Do you?" He turned to me, and I saw that in spite of his anger, his eyes were still oddly dead. "I don't think so."

"Why not?"

"Because you were the smart one of all of us. I don't mean it as something against you, Shar. I admire you for it. You didn't fuck up. You got a good job after high school and then you went off and put yourself through college, and then you got another good job. You own a house, you've got a life of your own. You never got married and had kids and put yourself in a position where you could lose everything — and everybody."

"You make me sound pretty cold."

"No, but you play it safe."

Did I? I wondered. I thought of Don, and of how I could lose him — in so many ways, at any time. Not being married was no guarantee against shattering loss.

John cracked another beer and took a swig. "A few months ago I thought I had it all. I'd gotten my contractor's license, bought a house — hell, I hadn't even had so much as a speeding ticket in a year. I thought it was all together, and then that bitch comes to me and says get out. 'Get out, you don't meet my needs anymore.' Meet her needs! I thought I was meeting them, working eighteen hours a day. But no, I don't consider her needs, don't listen to her. There's no one else, the bitch says, but she doesn't want me around anymore."

He wasn't going to refer to his wife by her name. I remembered Tina, the embittered divorcée at the party the night before; she'd called her ex-husband "that bastard" the whole evening.

"So you want to punish her by taking the kids away?"

"No! All I want is my kids. And I'm going to have them." He looked off over the canyon, his jaw thrusting forward in deter- mination. "There's no reason a man can't be as good a parent as a woman."

"I guess not."

"There isn't."

"I agreed with you."

He laughed bitterly. "Yeah. You give it lip

66

service, like Charlene does, and like Patsy did when I talked to her on the phone last week."

"But?"

"But you don't really believe it. Underneath, you're just like Ma."

"John, all I think you should do is consider what you're getting into. You don't even have a job now."

"I could go back to housepainting, I guess. That's what I did before I got the contractor's license."

"And then what? You'd be working hard, then coming home and cooking, and getting them ready for bed. Helping them with their homework, doing laundry. There'd be doctor's appointments, P.T.A. . . . . Good Lord, *think* of it."

"Lots of women do all that. And more."

He was right. But some people — male or female — are equipped to cope, and some aren't. I knew my brother; he'd always been a little bewildered by the world of day-to-day reality.

John waited. When I didn't respond, he said, "Ah, hell, I knew you wouldn't understand. Why don't you just go back up there with the rest of them." He motioned toward the house.

"John—"

"Just go."

This discussion wasn't getting us any-place, so I went.

Halfway across the yard, I turned and looked back at the canyon. The sun was falling behind it, and the shapes of the bushes and trees were twisted and elongated in the shadows. I'd never liked that canyon since our proud black cat had disappeared into it — and I liked it even less now.

6: "Wolf"

Charley Valdene was a character. And then some.

He showed up at the convention wearing a belted trench coat and a slouch hat, which caused quite a stir among all those muumuus and party dresses and Bermuda shorts. They wouldn't let him into the convention room, because he wasn't a registered member of the Society, but he hung around out on the mezzanine gawking at people and introducing himself and generally acting like a kid in a toyshop. Some of the conventioneers were put off by him — I heard one call him a "buffoon" and another say snootily that the image he presented was "just the kind of idiotic stereotype our profession is trying to live down." But most of the people seemed to find him charming and refreshing. It was a good thing I did too, because he latched onto me first thing — I

69

was hanging around the mezzanine myself, where it wasn't so crowded — and peppered me with questions and comments.

He was about fifty, pudgy, crackling with energy and enthusiasm; bald as an egg under the hat, as I found out later, except for a thin dangly fringe of sand-colored hair. He had fat red cheeks and a fat red nose like Santa Claus, pale blue eyes full of candle-power, and a voice so deep it sounded as if it were coming out of a well. Or maybe out of a geyser: his words seemed to erupt from his mouth, tumbling over each other and wet with spray.

After about an hour he insisted on taking me to dinner. But not at the hotel, he knew a much better place, did I like cannelloni, sure he knew I would because I was Italian, a *much* better place, cannelloni and garlic bread and sour red wine, that was their specialty, it was out near his house in Pacific Beach and I'd come there afterward of course, see his collection of private-eyeiana. I said okay; anything was better than sitting in on a sociological overview of the private detective and group dynamics.

The restaurant he took me to was a little place with about a dozen tables. The cannelloni and garlic bread and red wine lived up to his advertising; it was the kind of fare that

70

would have brought smiles and approving nods in any kitchen in San Francisco's North Beach. We had espresso afterward, and homemade spumoni ice cream. And throughout the meal, he kept asking questions about this or that case of mine — the more public ones, because damned if he hadn't studied up on them through back issues of the S.F. newspapers on file in the San Diego Library.

The one he was most interested in had involved another convention a couple of years ago, that one in San Francisco and devoted to the pulps, featuring a gaggle of former pulp writers who had called themselves "The Pulpeteers" and who were being reunited for the first time in thirty years. ("I wanted to go myself," Valdene said, "and I would have but I had a rush job up in Carlsbad and I just couldn't get away.") The gathering had degenerated into homicide and then, later on, multiple homicide, and I had been involved. It had worked out all right, though, primarily because it was at that convention that I'd met Kerry: both her parents, Cybil and Ivan Wade, were writers and had been members of the Pulpeteers.

"Maybe there'll be a murder at *this* convention too," Valdene said at one point. "Wouldn't that be something?"

"Yeah," I said, "it sure would. But nothing like that is going to happen here."

We left the restaurant finally, and went to Valdene's modest little house on a modest little street. But when I stepped inside it was like walking into the past — into the dark but still gaudy world of the Depression thirties and war-torn forties.

The furniture was straight out of a 1935 Sears Roebuck catalogue, right down to the fringe on the lampshades and the big console Philco radio in one corner. The walls were papered with old movie posters: *Meet Nero Wolfe*, *Fog Over Frisco*, *Lady in the Lake*, *The Maltese Falcon*. There were shelves stacked with plastic-bagged pulp magazines, by far the most prominent title being *Private Detective*. There were cabinets jammed with rows of videotapes, each one neatly labeled; other cabinets with old radio-show tapes: "The Adventures of Sam Spade"; "The Fat Man"; "Pat Novak for Hire"; "Martin Kane, Private Detective." In other rooms were shelves of hardcover and paperback books, among them a section of soft-core and hardcore porn items with private-detective protagonists.

Valdene gave me a guided tour of all this, complete with running commentary, and his pride at what he had amassed here was evident and justifiable. The tour ended in a basement workroom, where he had a table of duplicate pulps that he had set out for my inspection. Among them were seven issues of *Dime Mystery,* four of *Dime Detective,* four of *Clues,* one of *G-Man Detective,* and one of *Crimebusters* that I didn't have. The total was more than I had brought with me for trade, but Valdene insisted that I take all of them anyway; we could work out something later on.

He got beers for us — Pabst Blue Ribbon, in honor of Mike Hammer, he said — and we sat in the living room and talked for a while. About eleven-thirty, in the middle of a second beer, I began to get drowsy. Valdene noticed it; he noticed everything about me, it seemed. You could almost see him making mental notes, filing them away in his storehouse of material on private eyes, real and imaginary.

"You must be pretty tired," he said, "plane flight and the convention and everything. I'll run you back to the hotel so you can get some sleep."

"Thanks, Charley."

"Wish we'd had more time, though. I've got a good print of *Sleepers West,* with Lloyd Nolan as Mike Shayne. You ever see that one?"

"Long, long time ago."

"Great flick, one of the best of the B private-eye films. Nobody knows it today; you hardly ever see it on TV anymore. But I guess you can't make it another night?"

"Well . . ."

"Or maybe Sunday afternoon, before the banquet?"

He sounded so eager and hopeful, like a puppy with its leash in its mouth, that I didn't have the heart to refuse him. Besides which, I *wanted* to see that Lloyd Nolan film.

I said, "You know, I think Sunday afternoon might work out fine," and he beamed, and I thought: And if Sunday afternoon slides into Sunday evening, and it gets too late for me to make the banquet, why that'll be just too bad. No rubber chicken, no boring speeches, no postprandial champagne, and no all-night hoofing with the Mexican Bandit Band. Yeah, that sure would be a shame.

We went out and got into Valdene's coupe and headed south to the Casa del Rey. It was after midnight when we got there, but the place was still lit up pretty good and the parking lot was still half full. Valdene turned in to the lot and swung up one of the rows toward the circular drive in front. And after about thirty yards the headlights picked up something ahead that made me sit up and take notice.

Valdene saw it too. He said, "Hey, look at that! Somebody's on the ground over there."

Somebody was. The driver's door to one of the parked cars — a ten-year-old Ford — stood open; the dome light inside was on, and the bulky figure of a man was half sprawled between the door and the seat.

"Stop the car, Charley."

He came down on the brake, and I opened my door and was out before the coupe came to a full stop. I ran around the rear and over to where the guy was kneeling on the pavement with his head against the seat and one arm flung over it. I squatted beside him. But there wasn't any crisis. Hell, there wasn't even any emergency.

Behind me Valdene said, "He hurt or something?"

"Drunk," I said. Parboiled might have been a better term; the smell of liquor came off him in near-palpable shimmers on the hot night air. He moved when I touched him, made grumbling noises in his throat. I turned him a little, so I could get a better look at him. Big guy, heavyset, not much to look at. Wearing a red shirt that now had a fresh decoration of vomit on it. Also wearing a convention name tag, and in the domelight I could read what it said: *Jim Lauterbach — San Diego, CA.*

"He's a private eye, huh?" Valdene said.

"One of the alcoholic variety, apparently."

"Must be a lousy one if he can't hold his booze. What should we do with him?"

"Leave him in his car to sober up," I said. "If this *is* his car."

I leaned over Lauterbach and the clutter of stuff on the seat beside him — a small wire recorder, some other electronic stuff, and a scatter of brochures, all of which said that he was one of the computer-age investigators. I opened up the glove box, poked around among the papers inside, and found the registration: the car was his, all right. Valdene helped me hoist him up and lay him out across the seat. Lauterbach grumbled and grunted some more, and then he said, clearly, "Dumb son of a bitch." But he wasn't talking to either of us. To himself, maybe. After that, he was quiet.

The keys were on the pavement outside, where he must have dropped them after he got the door open; he'd passed out right on top of them. I put the keys in my pocket. Then I got my notebook out and wrote on a clean page: *Drunk driving is a felony. You ought to know that, Lauterbach. You can pick up your keys at the hotel desk.* I signed it *A fellow P.I.,* and put the note on the dashboard where he'd be sure to find it when he got his senses back, such as they were.

In the row of parked cars beyond Valdene's coupe, somebody gave several sharp blasts on a horn. I glanced over there as I shut the driver's door on the Ford. A guy in a suit was standing alongside what appeared to be a light-colored Cadillac, looking impatient; then, when neither Valdene nor I ran to do his bidding, he came stalking toward us. I got a look at him as he passed through the glare of the coupe's headlights. About my age, midfifties, with a stiff military bearing, brush-cut iron-gray hair and a matching mustache. Fancy three-piece suit, a diamond stickpin in his tie. I knew it was a diamond because other kinds of jewels don't throw off that kind of reflected dazzle.

He said something as he neared us, but the words were lost in the roar of an airplane passing overhead: one of the Navy patrol planes that were constantly taking off and landing at the North Island Naval Air Station nearby. He looked up in annoyance, waited for the noise to fade, and then said, "What's the idea of parking your car in the middle of the lane? If you don't move it instantly, I'll call the police."

"I'll move it," Valdene said. "We were just trying to—"

"I don't care what you were trying to do. There's no excuse for blocking the lane this way."

"Look, mister, we maybe just saved your life."

The rich type blinked at him. "What was that?"

"The guy in this Ford is drunk, drunk as hell. We hadn't come along and spotted him and my friend here took his keys away, he might've woken up and started driving. He might've run right up your fat tailpipe."

A sputtering sound came out of the rich guy; he didn't know what to say. For about five seconds, anyway. Then he said, "Move your car," huffily, and stalked off to the Cadillac.

"Asshole," Valdene said.

"Lots of them around these days, Charley."

"That kind's one of the worst. Damn politician."

"You know him?"

"Seen him on television. His name's Henry Nyland. Used to be in the Navy. Now he's running in a special election for the San Diego City Council. One of those Let's-

Nuke-the-Commies nuts, big on religion and all hot for censorship. That type sets my teeth on edge, you know?"

"Yeah," I said, "I know."

We walked back to the coupe, not hurrying, and Valdene drove around to the hotel entrance. I gathered up my pulps, we shook hands, he told me again how great it was to meet me and not to forget Sunday afternoon and *Sleepers West,* and we said good night.

The plush lobby was empty when I entered. But as I started across to the desk, to get my key and to turn over Jim Lauterbach's car keys for safekeeping, the doors to one of the elevators whispered open and Elaine Picard came out. She passed within ten feet of me, and I said hello, but she either didn't hear or chose to ignore me. She looked tired, preoccupied; the skin across her forehead was drawn so tight it had a waxy look.

I watched her walk out through the front doors. Odd lady, I thought. Not as odd as that guy Rich who'd been bothering her this afternoon, but odd enough. Maybe it came with the job. I had yet to meet a female P.I. of any variety who wasn't strange in some way, and that included McCone.

Not to be sexist, though. Women didn't have a corner on the oddball P.I. market;

this convention was proof positive of that. Look at Jim Lauterbach. Look at the guys who held earnest discussions about worble-gang veeblefetzers.

Hell, look at *me*.

7: McCone

When I arrived at ten the next morning, the Casa del Rey's lobby was much less crowded than it had been the afternoon before. Guests sat around on the heavy Victorian furniture; a few of them wore convention badges; some of them looked hung over. A Japanese family with two little girls in fluffy pink dresses posed for a photograph in front of — strangely enough — the rental-car counter. Otherwise all was quiet.

I stopped a bellboy and asked the way to the hotel offices. He indicated a door marked PRIVATE to the left of the registration desk. I crossed the lobby and went through it, finding that all luxury stopped just over the sill.

The carpet was gray and institutional, the walls devoid of pictures. The only furnishings were a bank of steel file cabinets and a secretary's desk. An unkempt young woman sat hunched over a typewriter, dabbing white correction fluid onto the paper. When I asked for Elaine, she motioned wordlessly at one of the doors in the opposite wall. I went over and knocked, and Elaine's voice called for me to come in.

She and two other women were seated at a cloth-covered table from room service, the remains of breakfast in front of them. Elaine immediately got up and fetched me a chair. She told the others who I was, then said, "Sharon, these are fellow members of the Professional Women's Forum executive committee — Karyn Sugarman and June Paxton."

Karyn Sugarman, a willowy, long-haired blonde, nodded at me. She lounged in her chair with a fashion model's grace, her black sleeveless dress reinforcing her stylish appearance. The dress completely eclipsed my crisp white pants and blue silk blouse that had seemed very sophisticated when I'd put them on at home. If I'd been alone in the room with her, I'd probably have felt like a teenybopper, but as it was, June Paxton neutralized Sugarman's effect.

Paxton was probably in her midfifties — at least fifteen years older than Sugarman, I guessed — and everything about her was round. She had a plump

82

little face, china-saucer eyes, and a roly-poly body. Her hair was nondescript brown, done up in tight little curls, and she wore bright turquoise polyester that must have come straight off the rack in a bargain basement. When she smiled, though, it was with genuine friendliness, and her blue eyes sparkled.

"Sit down," Elaine directed me. "Can I get you something to eat?"

"No, thanks. I'll take some coffee, though, if you have any."

She poured coffee from a silver pot, and I watched her closely. Although she was as immaculately groomed as ever — wearing pale pink today — there still were dark circles under her eyes that spoke of a bad night, and her hand shook as she passed me the cup. I frowned, wondering what was wrong in my friend's life; if I could get her to talk about it, maybe I could help.

"Are you sure you don't want something to eat?" June Paxton asked in a motherly way. "I think there's a croissant left over."

"Really, no. I'm visiting my family, and my mother forced a big breakfast down me."

"It's just as well," Karyn Sugarman said. "The croissants were tough. How on earth can this hotel make a croissant the consistency of shoe leather, Elaine?"

Elaine merely shrugged — wearily, I thought.

"Probably made them with margarine instead of butter," Paxton said, reaching for the object under discussion. "If no one else wants it?"

We all shook our heads.

I said to the table in general, "So what has your executive committee been deciding?"

"Nothing earthshaking," Sugarman said. "We just went over the program for next week's dinner meeting. It's to be held here at the hotel."

"How often do you meet?"

"Once a month for dinner, although we have occasional breakfasts with speakers," Elaine said.

"What kinds of speakers?"

"Oh, anyone whose talk might be beneficial to the membership. Time-management people, financial planners, small-business consultants . . ."

Sugarman took up the conversation. "Once we even had a color consultant come in — one of those people who charge you a couple of hundred dollars to tell you what color clothes to wear."

"When you could figure that out for free by holding the clothes up to your face,"

Paxton said. "If you turn green, it's no go. Otherwise—"

"Well, June, some people like to be told." The way Sugarman looked at Paxton's bright polyester dress clearly said she thought she could benefit from such a consultation. "Anyway, the speakers aren't the real purpose of the Forum. It's more social, in a business sense, of course."

"How do you mean?"

"Networking." When I looked blank, she went on. "The men in this country have always had old-boy networks — from the Jaycees on the small-town level, right up to the president's buddies who get the Cabinet positions or the fat defense contracts. Now that women are moving into the professions and going into business for themselves, we need that kind of thing too. The Forum helps us establish the necessary connections."

"I see."

Sugarman's mouth twisted sardonically. "Of course, we don't go in for it on the same level the men do. For instance, none of us feel compelled to take off on a retreat like the Bohemian Club members. Running around in the redwoods and putting on skits wearing the opposite sex's clothing is not for us."

Paxton popped the last piece of croissant into her mouth and said around it, "Don't be such a stuffed shirt, Karyn. I've always wanted to see someone like Henry Kissinger dressed up in heels and a miniskirt."

Sugarman snorted.

"Well, *I* wouldn't mind hiding out in those redwoods — there's no telling *what* you might see."

"That's racy talk for a widowed grandmother of three."

"The old urges don't give out when you get the first gray hair, Karyn."

"Ladies, please." From Elaine's expression, I gathered this sort of bantering went on all the time.

"Anyway," Sugarman said, "the networking concept really works. Take me — I'm a psychotherapist. Suppose I have a patient who — in addition to all sorts of weird hang-ups — needs to get his financial records in shape. I send him to June, who's a C.P.A."

"Yes," Paxton said, "and when the tax auditor comes to look at the guy's books, I recommend he stay at the Casa del Rey."

"And," I said, picking it up, "when the tax auditor runs amok in the flower beds here, and Elaine has to apprehend him, she sends him to Karyn for therapy."

Paxton beamed at me. "It's simple, you see."

"Well, it sounds like a fine idea to me."

"It is." Sugarman nodded emphatically, tossing her mane of tawny hair. "It's time we took advantage of the same methods men do. We've got a lot of catching up to do."

I studied her, wondering how she would be as a therapist. Maybe my brother John could benefit from a few sessions with her . . . but no, John would never put up with it. He was like the rest of us McCones, preferring to let our private demons rest undisturbed deep in our psyches, in the hope that if they went unmolested, they wouldn't surface.

Glancing at Paxton, who was picking through the croissant flakes that remained in the bread basket, I decided it was easier to picture her going about her chosen profession. I could see her with her ledgers, placing neat round figures in long straight columns, and telling her clients — between explanations of debits and credits — about a perfectly divine recipe she'd tried the night before.

I looked back at Elaine, about to ask when we would start the grand tour she'd promised, but saw that she was far away again, wrapped up in some private worrisome thoughts of her own. Elaine, I wondered, are *your* private demons becoming restive?

The door opened suddenly, and the hotel manager, Lloyd Beddoes, stuck his head in. "Elaine?"

She started and looked up.

Beddoes came into the office. He wore a crisp vanilla-colored suit that accented his slim waist and broad shoulders. "I need to talk with you. There was a security problem out at the bungalows last night. Drunks traipsing around after midnight and annoying the guests."

"Of course, Lloyd." She got up slowly, as if not fully awakened from her reverie. "We were just winding up."

Karyn Sugarman was gathering her purse and briefcase, ignoring Beddoes. June Paxton, however, was staring at him in open admiration. She put a hand to her hair and patted her curls.

Elaine looked at me. "Sharon, I'm sorry, but I guess the tour will have to wait."

"That's okay. There's plenty else I can do."

Beddoes said, "I'll see you in my office, Elaine," and went out.

Paxton stood up. "My goodness, every time I see that man I can't help thinking what a truly fine figure he cuts!"

"June, for God's sake." Sugarman rolled her eyes.

"Well, he does. Like I said, the old urges . . . Elaine, he's not married, is he?"

"No."

"I'd sure like to get to know him better. Couldn't you arrange an intimate little gathering for some of your good friends?"

"I don't think you'd like Lloyd," Elaine said curtly.

"Oh, you just say that because he's your boss and he gives you a hard time."

"Come on, June," Sugarman said. "Let's get out of here so Elaine can go to her meeting."

"But—"

"She's right, you know. You wouldn't like Lloyd."

"Why not?"

Sugarman exchanged a look with Elaine that could only be termed guarded. "Lloyd has some . . . strange interests."

"Interests?"

"Hobbies."

"Like what?"

Sugarman hesitated.

"Like what? You brought it up — now tell me."

Sugarman gave a resigned sigh. "Like pornography. Among other things."

"Oh, that. A lot of people are into that."

"Maybe so, but it's not your cup of tea."

"You Jungians think you know it all."

"We certainly do." Sugarman caught Paxton's arm and moved her toward the door. "Nice to meet you, Sharon. Elaine, I'll escort June to her car. That way, Mr. Beddoes will be free to run his hotel in peace." She paused, looked back at Elaine, and added, "And remember, we have to talk about that other matter soon."

Elaine nodded wearily. "Yes, I know."

They went out, Paxton's voice chirping good-natured protests.

Elaine smiled wanly at me. "I'm sorry about the tour."

"That's okay. Your job comes first."

Her drawn face showed real dismay, however, and I smiled reminiscently, remembering the days when I'd worked for her at Huston's. Elaine had been more a big sister than a boss — always there for those on her staff, always ready with the word of advice, the listening ear, or simply the commiserating pat on the shoulder. She'd helped me through numerous family crises; she'd counseled others about their love lives; she'd loaned money, given rides home, and gone to bat with management when an employee's performance had been adversely affected by personal problems.

I would never forget the night when, leaving the store at ten-thirty, I'd encountered her in the cosmetics department where she'd once been a saleswoman. One of the new clerks was in tears over an enormous cash shortage, and Elaine was sitting beside her on the floor, calmly going through the cash register receipts. The other woman was doing more snuffling and crying than helping, but Elaine was unperturbed. She kept saying in soothing tones, "It's all right. We'll fix this if it takes all night. *I* know you didn't steal the money."

That was Elaine; she'd cared deeply for the people around her. And I suspected, in spite of whatever might be troubling her, that the same concern and consideration persisted to this day.

Now she asked me, "Are you planning to come to my panel on hotel security?"

"I wouldn't miss it."

"Good. I'm sure to be finished with Lloyd by then."

At the mention of Beddoes, I wanted to ask her if it was true about him being interested in porn, as Sugarman had indicated. Somehow it didn't fit with his elegant appearance. But time was running short, and we'd have an opportunity to discuss that later. "In the meantime," I added, "I'll stroll up to the mezzanine and see what's happening."

It was quiet up there, with no one staffing the registration desk and only about a dozen people wandering through the displays in the room behind it. I spotted the good-looking lie-detector salesman and remembered he'd promised me a demonstration, so I went over to his display and he cheerfully consented to hook me up to the polygraph apparatus.

Soon I was seated beside the table, the sensors attached to my arms, watching the steel pens chart my truthfulness. A small crowd gathered as I answered such questions as how long I was in town for, was I married, and would I be interested in dinner at a little seafood restaurant on Coronado.

I lied, saying, "forever," "yes," and "no," and the pens zigzagged all over the chart.

8: "Wolf"

Saturday morning I went to the movies.

One of the meeting rooms off the mezzanine had been outfitted as a theater: rows of folding chairs, a big portable screen, and a 16-millimeter projector at the rear. I took a chair in the back row near the door, as I used to do at Saturday matinées when I was a kid so I'd have quick access to the snack bar. The room filled up rapidly to capacity; I looked for McCone, but she wasn't there. Neither was the big drunk in the red shirt, Jim Lauterbach.

They closed the doors right at ten o'clock, and one of the Society's officers got up and told us what the movie was about. It was about a day in the life of a typical private investigator, which was the title of the thing, so most of us, being trained detectives, could have figured out the essential story line by ourselves. But that didn't stop the guy from doing a five-minute monologue, four and a half minutes of it boring. Finally he sat down and they shut off the lights and the projector began to grind.

The film was in color; after ten minutes of watching it, that was the only positive thing I'd found to recommend it. The print was sort of fuzzy and the sound was too loud and a little out of sync, so that people's lips started moving a second or two before you heard them say anything. It was a dramatization, which meant that it had actors; but these were not ordinary actors. No, these were special actors, with special talents — all of them awful. The guy playing the typical investigator whose life this was supposed to be a day in was so bad that when he walked it was in funny little stiff strides, like a toddler with a loaded diaper; and when he spoke it was with great concentration on the proper enunciation of his words, which required exaggerated shaping and reshaping of his mouth, which got to be pretty funny after a while because of the sound being out of sync — as if the actor were chewing up his words for a second or two before spitting them out.

I wanted to laugh, but nobody else was laughing; it was a very well-behaved audience, very serious about all of this crap. I

wanted to laugh about the story line too —
most of all about that. If this was the life of
a typical private detective, I was glad I was
an untypical private detective, I would have
lasted maybe a week at this guy's job before
I went bonkers.

He worked for a big agency in an un-
named city. He came into the office in the
morning, to the accompaniment of some
voice-over narration, and had a consultation
with his boss on his current assignment:
something to do with industrial espionage.
The exchange of dialogue bulged with electronics jargon and buzzwords that I didn't
understand. Then he went to his desk, which
happened to have a computer terminal on it.
But the first thing he did was make a couple
of telephone calls, some of each conversation we got to listen in on while the rest was
obscured by more voice-over narration.
Then he plugged in his computer, or whatever it is you do with the things, and the
camera moved in for some nifty closeups of
the screen — orange letters on a black background — and there was a lot more stuff
printed there that made no sense to me.
Then he got up and left the office —

— and I got up and left the theater.
Popeye said it best: I can stands so much, I
can't stands no more.

I went downstairs and through the lobby and outside. It was another hot day, cloudless, windless. The ocean was glass-smooth except where powerboats made clean white slashes across its surface; farther out you could see the shapes of some barren, rocky islets and a naval vessel, probably a destroyer, drifting past. The beach was already crowded, mostly with kids and young adults. I went along a path under some palm trees, to the seawall that adjoined the terrace bar, and ogled some bikini-clad women for a while. Which was a hell of a lot better than ogling a black-and-orange computer screen; even Kerry would have agreed with that.

All that calm blue water looked inviting, too, and I thought that pretty soon I would go upstairs and haul out my trunks with the hibiscus flowers on them and have myself a swim. Back before I took off weight, I might have been leery about exposing my flab to the public eye; but I didn't look too bad in swim trunks these days. "A fifty-four-year-old Italian god," Kerry had said to me a while back, kidding the way she does. But what the hell, there were a lot of guys my age who looked worse than I did with their clothes *on*.

I wandered off through the gardens that paralleled the beach. The bungalows were down that way, half a dozen of them built to resemble thatched-roof English cottages, with little enclosed gardens at the rear and easy beach access. Fronting them were several interconnecting paths that wound among palms, banana trees, stands of bamboo, jacaranda and oleander shrubs, and other kinds of tropical flora that I didn't recognize; the paths also passed over a couple of little wooden bridges spanning a tiny creek. There were sections of formal gardens, too, that you might not think would blend in with the tropical stuff but did. Plus wooden benches where you could sit and read or contemplate your sins or whatever. Plus a little glade with some picnic tables in it.

There were three or four acres of grounds, and it was cool and kind of soothing among all that greenery. At least it was when one of the Navy patrol planes wasn't zooming by overhead. I saw some people at one of the bungalows, and a young couple holding hands, but nobody else for a ten-minute stretch. Then I came around a turning in the path, not far from the last and most secluded of the bungalows, Number 6, and there was a kid about seven years old sitting by himself on another of the benches.

He was a big kid, blond and fair-skinned,

wearing a pair of Levi's and a blue cotton pullover. He hadn't had a haircut in a while; the shaggy look of him made me think of a bear cub. A lost bear cub, at that: he looked kind of lonely and forlorn sitting there, staring at nothing much and picking the bark off a twig.

I went his way. He jumped a little when he saw me, as if he might be afraid of strangers. Or afraid that I was somebody he knew. But then he saw me smiling, and he relaxed and stayed where he was.

"Hi, guy," I said.

"Hi. Who are you?"

Because kids like nicknames, I said, "You can call me Wolf, if you want."

"Wolf. That's a funny name."

"I think so too. But a lady I know likes to call me that, and you can't argue with a lady."

"No," he said solemnly. "I guess not."

"What's *your* name?"

"Timmy."

"Are you staying at the hotel, Timmy?"

He looked down at the twig in his hand. Then he pointed toward Bungalow 6 and said, "Over there. But pretty soon I'm going to see my dad."

"Your dad's not here with you, huh?"

"No."

"Just your mom?"

Timmy was silent for a few seconds. "I don't like my mother," he said finally.

"No? Why not?"

"She makes me afraid. I don't want to talk about her."

"Okay."

He brightened. "My dad lives in Mexico. Have you ever been there?"

"A few times. How about you?"

"One time. But I don't remember it."

"How come?"

"I was a baby, I guess."

"Where in Mexico does your dad live?"

"In a town on the water with monkeys in it. I'm going to—"

"Timmy! Timmy!"

It was a woman's voice, calling from over by Bungalow 6. The kid cringed a little; a kind of caught look came into his eyes and he went nervous, twitchy. For a moment I thought he was going to hop off the bench and run. But he didn't do it; he just sat there, squirming.

The woman called again, and there were thrashing sounds in a group of oleander bushes nearby. Then she came around the oleanders, saw the boy, and said, "Timmy, damn it—" before she got far enough along the path to spot me sitting on the other end of the bench.

Her mouth clamped shut and she stopped and stared at me. "Who are you?" she demanded. "What are you doing with Timmy?"

"We were just having a talk," I said.

"Talk? Talk about what?"

"Nothing much. Are you Timmy's mother?"

"If it's any of your business, yes." She was a brunette in her midthirties, slender, pretty enough except for the suspicious scowl she wore and some heavy fatigue lines around her eyes. A tough lady, I thought, all bone and sinew and bubbling juices. Nice at the core, maybe. And maybe not. "And you?" she asked. "Who are *you?*"

I told her my name and that I was also a guest at the Casa del Rey. "Timmy was sitting here when I came by," I said, "so I sat down to pass the time of day." I gave her my best smile. "I'm not weird, if that's what you're thinking."

She didn't have anything to say to that. She looked at the boy and said, "Timmy, what are you doing out here? Why did you disobey me again?"

"I'm sorry. I just wanted to come outside for a while, that's all."

She went over and took hold of his arm and urged him off the bench. If she had tried to swat him one, I would have interfered; it was none of my business, but I don't like to see kids abused. But she didn't hit him and she didn't manhandle him either. Just hung on to his arm, holding him close to her in a protective way. Timmy didn't struggle; he wore a vaguely embarrassed look now, as if it were unmanly for me to see his mother threatening him this way, like a little kid.

The woman's eyes were on me again. She said, "What did Timmy say to you?"

"About what?"

"About anything. What were you talking about?"

"Why?"

"Because I want to know, that's why. Timmy tells stories sometimes. I don't like him telling stories."

"What kind of stories?"

"He makes things up. About . . . well, about me."

Timmy said, "I don't. Honest, I don't!"

"Yes, you do. Now be quiet."

I said, "He didn't say anything about you, Mrs. —What did you say your name was?"

"I didn't say. Didn't Timmy tell you his last name?"

"No, he didn't."

She hesitated as if she were going to say something else to me. Instead she turned abruptly and took the boy away toward Bungalow 6. He glanced back just before they disappeared beyond the oleanders; his face was scrunched up, the way a kid's gets when he's fighting back tears.

I sat there for a time after they were gone. The little episode with the boy's mother had left a bad taste in my mouth and I didn't quite know why. She hadn't done or said anything that indicated she might be mistreating Timmy, and neither had he. And yet, there was some kind of tension there, something that carried the vague unpleasant smell of fear.

None of my business, I thought again; and nothing I can do about it even if it was. Forget it.

But I couldn't forget it; it kept worrying around inside my head. I went down by their bungalow, but there wasn't anything to see — the front windows were shuttered and hedges obscured the entrance — and there wasn't anything to hear either.

I headed back toward the hotel. Out on the beach, some young people had started a game of volleyball and were making a not unpleasant racket. The gardens were still deserted. Nuts to the convention, I thought. I'll go for a swim, I'll have some lunch, then maybe I'll come back out here and wander around some more. Not because of Timmy and his mother. Just because it's a nice place to be.

I came around a clump of bamboo, and straight ahead there was open space and I could see most of the east side of the hotel. The tower jutting up on that corner caught my eye: it had open arches on four sides with waist-high railings in them, so that people standing up there could take in the view in all directions. I saw movement inside — one person, maybe two. I couldn't be sure because of the angle: the inside of the tower was a blend of light and shadow.

Overhead, the droning of two or three approaching Navy planes began to build in volume. I glanced up at them briefly, then looked back at the tower.

And somebody appeared at the rail, came flying *over* it like a person diving off a high board — a woman dressed in something pink, arms clawing at the air, screaming.

She screamed all the way down, a death cry that was barely audible above the pulsating roar of the planes. Something moved up in the tower, a suggestion of someone there in the shadows peering down. Or maybe it was just an illusion; I couldn't be sure of that either, because I was already running by then, with that sense of shock something unexpected and frightening always instills in you. There were fifty yards separating me and the hotel when the falling woman hit and the screaming stopped. But even with the noise of the planes I swear I could hear the sound of impact — that melon-splitting sound of bones breaking and tissue ripping that you can never forget once you've heard it.

I ran through some shrubs, across a square of lawn, between a couple of palms. A few people on the beach had also seen the woman fall and were just starting to come out of their own frozen moment of shock. I plowed through a bunch of tropical flowers, and there she was, lying broken on her side on a section of cobblestone path. Dead — you could see from a distance that she was dead. Part of her skull had cracked open; there were streamers of bright blood already trailing away from it.

Five paces from her I stopped, panting, feeling sick to my stomach. I had seen a guy who'd jumped from a fifteen-story window once, but it was no worse than this — and she'd only come down four stories. Several people were milling around behind me; somebody yelled, somebody else began to shriek. Overhead, more planes picked up the roar of the ones that had just gone by. All I could do was stand there staring, because I recognized the woman and that made it even worse.

McCone's friend, the Casa del Rey's security chief — Elaine Picard.

9: McCone

When he'd unhooked me from the poly-graph, I thanked the salesman — whose name was Wally — for the demonstration, gave him my parents' phone number so we could make a date later on, and stared out toward the mezzanine. I didn't feel guilty about planning to have dinner with him; after all, neither Don nor I was a particularly possessive individual. I liked to think that what we had together was too strong to be disrupted by jealousy.

The movie must have ended, because the room was now crowded with people looking for someone to talk to. I chatted with a woman named Kinsey Millhone, who had her own agency in Santa Teresa, then tried once again to go outside. Halfway to the door, a fellow from New York named Miles Jacoby stopped me, pointing to the *San Francisco* on my name tag, and asked me if I knew Wolf. It turned out Jacoby was a big admirer of his and knew all about his pulp collection, so we talked about that for a while. Finally I made my way to the mezzanine, where the crowd was thinner.

I went over to the railing and leaned on it, waiting for it to be time for Elaine's panel and enjoying the comparatively smoke-free air. Out here I could hear the drone of planes taking off and landing at N.A.S. North Island, and a couple of them went over with a great roar that actually shook the hotel. It, as well as the del Coronado, had been built before the base and now was right in the flight path. I wondered how the guests managed to get any sleep with the patrol planes coming and going at all hours, and decided to ask Wolf about it.

A couple of minutes later, I noticed a commotion down in the lobby. I had almost decided it was Japanese tourists rioting to see who would be first to get his picture taken with the rental-car counter, when I noticed that a lot of people were hurrying outside to the formal gardens.

Because I am a very curious person and anything was better than killing time up here, I went around to the stairs and started down. A few of the other conventioneers fell in behind me, and I had the absurd feeling that we were participating in an impromptu field trip. In a line, like little ducks following their mother, we crossed the lobby and went through the big French doors to the garden.

A good-sized crowd was gathered there, tourist types and some conventioneers, including a guy in a slouch hat and trench coat who looked like someone the hotel might have hired to publicize the convention. I spotted Wolf, standing to one side with Victor Ibarcena, the assistant manager. They both looked nervous and upset.

Next to me, a young woman in a bikini said, "My God, what a horrible thing. Did you see it?"

"No," a man wearing a convention badge said. "I was in the lobby. Jesus."

"Could you hear her scream? She must have screamed."

"I didn't hear anything. Couldn't. Right about the time it must have happened, those bombers — or whatever they are — went over."

What *had* happened? I thought. Who had — or hadn't — screamed? I scanned the garden and saw an open area everyone seemed to be avoiding, close to the foot of the east tower. On the cobblestone path lay a bundle of pink splashed with red. . . .

I stopped moving and the person behind me banged into me. My hand went to my mouth and cut off a gasp. Feeling a rush of apprehension, I started forward again.

It was Elaine, lying there on her side, her arms spread out and her legs askew. Inside the pretty pink dress, her body looked broken and bloody. Lifeless. And her head . . .

Sickened, I looked up at the east tower. She must have fallen from up there, I thought, to do that much physical damage.

Quickly I started through the crowd toward Wolf, pushing around clumps of people who were conversing in low murmurs. He had his back to me and was staring at the ground. I grabbed his elbow. "Wolf, for God's sake, what happened?"

He looked around, his face stricken. "I don't know. She fell from up there."

"By accident?"

"I don't know."

Lloyd Beddoes came hurrying through the crowd and took Ibarcena by the arm, turning him away. They conferred for a time. The voices of the people around us rose as a couple of uniformed deputies entered. Beddoes went over and spoke to them, and then they took charge. I had no more chance to talk to Wolf, not then.

A little while later, three white-coated

men hurried out from the hotel lobby. County coroner's men. They would be followed by lab technicians and homicide investigators from the San Diego County Sheriff's Department. Since we were outside the city proper, the sheriff would have jurisdiction. And his homicide men came out on all violent deaths.

This was the kind of scene I'd witnessed many times — far too many, even for a person in my profession. Tears sprang to my eyes, and I lowered my eyelids, forcing the tears back. Who was I crying for, anyway? Elaine? We hadn't been close friends, not really. Maybe I was crying for myself. Poor Sharon; she has to go through this again.

I got myself under control and caught Wolf's eye; he looked at me with an understanding expression. Then his gaze moved toward the lobby door, and mine followed, to a brown-haired man in a matching brown suit. Instantly I knew he was a detective; he had that look about him. Wary, braced for anything — they all get it after they've seen enough death. They're expecting the worst, and most often they find it.

The plainclothesman joined the coroner's men by Elaine's body. He looked around, spoke with them for a time, then went to where Beddoes was standing a few yards away. They talked and then joined Wolf and Ibarcena. I inched closer, heard the brown-haired man introduce himself as Lieutenant Tom Knowles of the San Diego County Sheriff's Department.

"Which one of you found the body?" Knowles asked.

Wolf said, "I did," and introduced himself.

"Will you describe what happened, please."

"I was walking in the gardens, back there." He motioned behind him. "And I happened to glance up at the tower. There was movement up there, but I didn't see anybody. Then she came flying over the railing. She must have died as soon as she hit those cobblestones."

Knowles nodded. "You say she came flying over the railing. She wasn't standing at it, then."

"No. She must have been back behind the archway. She came out pretty fast, as if she'd taken a run at the railing. . . ."

As he spoke, Wolf looked up at the tower, and my eyes followed his gaze. Beyond the curving archways was a shadowy area, where shafts of light played. Involuntarily I shivered, thinking that this was the east tower, the one that was supposed to be haunted.

"Was she alone up there?" Knowles asked Wolf.

"Well . . ." Wolf paused, his eyes still on the tower. A slight frown passed across his face. "I think so."

"You think so?"

"I thought I saw movement after she fell, but I can't be sure. And I didn't *see* anyone."

Lloyd Beddoes, his face pale and beads of sweat standing out on his forehead, spoke for the first time. "Surely, Lieutenant, you don't think Ms. Picard was pushed from the tower."

Knowles turned to him. "I don't think anything yet, Mr. Beddoes. I take it you were acquainted with Elaine Picard."

"She was our chief of security."

"I see. Do you have any idea what Ms. Picard might have been doing in the tower?"

Beddoes glanced at Ibarcena, who shrugged. "None whatsoever. We had just completed a meeting in my office, and Ms. Picard was due to moderate a panel for the convention, in one of the meeting rooms off the mezzanine. When I last saw her, she was getting ready to go up there."

"The private investigators' convention?"

"Yes. The panel was on hotel security."

Knowles looked around the garden; his eyes rested on the man in the trench coat and slouch hat, and the corner of his mouth twitched derisively. He controlled it and turned his bland gray eyes back to Beddoes.

"Where in the hotel can you gain access to that tower?"

"There's a stairway to each tower in each corner of the mezzanine."

"And they're left open?"

"Yes. The guests use them for looking at the view, picture-taking."

"Was there any official reason for Ms. Picard to have gone up there? A security problem, for instance?"

"None that I know of. Perhaps something came up after I last spoke with her."

Knowles nodded as if he were filing that away in some mental folder. "Getting back to this meeting you had with Ms. Picard, how did she seem? Was she in good spirits?"

"She was . . ." Beddoes hesitated and glanced at Ibarcena again. "Lieutenant, are you implying that she killed herself?"

"I'm not implying anything," Knowles said patiently. "Please answer the question."

"She was . . . well, she was distraught," Beddoes said. "I had the feeling her mind was not on what we were discussing. Isn't that so, Victor?"

"Oh, yes." Ibarcena nodded.

"In fact," Beddoes added, "she has been in quite a state for some time now."

"What kind of 'state,' Mr. Beddoes?" Knowles asked.

"Distracted. Not herself. She seemed worried, depressed."

"Do you have any idea what might have caused this?"

"None at all. Ms. Picard was not one to confide in her coworkers. Isn't that so, Victor?"

Ibarcena nodded again. "Ms. Picard kept very much to herself."

Knowles looked back to where the body lay. The medics and lab crew appeared to have finished and were obviously waiting for him. "I'll need more detailed statements from the three of you," he said, "but that can wait until later. In the meantime, if you'll stay close by and make yourselves available to us, I'd appreciate it." He turned and walked over to the technicians.

I glanced at Wolf. He was staring up at the tower again, a puzzled expression on his face.

As I had before, I looked at the tower, too, wondering why Elaine had gone up there. She'd been in a meeting, and her panel was due to start momentarily. Unless some security problem had arisen suddenly . . . But a security problem would have involved other people, and Wolf had said he hadn't seen anyone, only movement. . . .

I wanted to ask him about that, so I started over to him again. Beddoes and Ibarcena had moved away, and were conferring with one another near the French doors. After a moment, Ibarcena hurried off into the lobby.

From Knowles's questions, I knew the sheriff would treat this as either an accident or a suicide. And the surface facts definitely pointed that way. But I remembered Elaine from our days at Huston's; she was as sure-footed as they come. One time we'd had a saleswoman who'd just been fired threaten to commit suicide by hurling herself off the roof. Elaine had gone out there, walking on a ledge with precision balance, and talked the woman out of it. She was not the sort to slip and fall.

We'd also talked a good bit about suicide after the incident, and I'd found Elaine strongly opposed to it. She felt it was a reprehensible act, a nasty piece of emotional blackmail that only a coward would inflict on friends and family.

And one thing I knew beyond a doubt: Elaine Picard had been no coward. She might have been worried, as I'd seen. She might even have been distraught, as Beddoes had claimed. But she had definitely not been afraid.

10: "Wolf"

When the sheriff's investigators decided they didn't need me anymore, and the coroner's assistants moved in with their body bag, McCone came up and caught my arm and said she wanted to talk to me. She had been hanging around the whole time, listening in on conversations, looking pretty upset.

I suggested the Cantina Sin Nombre, because I needed something alcoholic and it looked as if she did, too, and she agreed. We went there and got our drinks — beer for me, a bourbon for her — and sat near the terrace windows, at the same table she and Elaine Picard had occupied yesterday. There wasn't anybody on the terrace now, and only a few people on the beach. The pleasure boats were still out, but the ocean had a hard brassy look under the noonday sun — not an inviting place to be right now.

McCone took a slug of bourbon, ran a nervous hand over her black hair. "Did it really look to you like Elaine jumped?" she asked.

"Well . . . she went over the railing in a kind of dive. People don't fall that way if they trip accidentally."

"People do if they've been pushed."

"Yeah," I said.

"I heard you tell Lieutenant Knowles you might've seen somebody else up there with her."

"I can't be sure if I did or not. I wasn't paying that much attention before she fell — and while she was falling . . . I didn't want to but I was watching her."

"Did you look up at the tower again after she landed?"

I nodded. "But I didn't see anybody. No movement then at all."

McCone was silent for a time, her dark eyes fixed and unblinking — turned inward, I thought. At length she said, "Elaine didn't kill herself, Wolf. It just isn't possible; she wasn't the suicidal type."

"Are you sure of that? How long had it been since you'd seen her?"

"Years. But that doesn't mean anything. People like Elaine don't change."

Some people do change, lose some part of

themselves for any one of a hundred reasons, lose their taste for living; but I wasn't going to argue with her about it. I said, "Maybe there'll be a note. Would that convince you?"

"It might," McCone said. "But I don't think there'll be a note. And if there is, it'll probably be a fake. Dammit, Wolf, I think she was *pushed*."

"By who? For what reason?"

"I don't know — yet. But something was bothering her, and I could see it getting worse in just the short time I've been here."

"You mean she seemed despondent?"

"No. Very preoccupied about something. Upset. Worried, somehow."

I remembered seeing her leave the hotel last night; that was how she'd impressed me too. I asked, "Do you know a friend — a former friend — of hers named Rich?"

"Rich who?"

"I didn't get his last name. He might have been a boyfriend once, although he seemed younger than her by several years. Handsome guy, wavy brown hair, gray-blue eyes with a peculiar look to them."

"I've never met anyone like that," McCone said. "And Elaine never mentioned him. How do you know about this Rich?"

I told her about the little altercation here

in the bar yesterday. McCone's eyes narrowed; her mouth and jaw took on a determined set.

"I don't like the sound of that," she said. "Grabbing her arm, hurting her . . . and she told you he'd done it before?"

"Bothered her in public before, yes. She didn't say if he was in the habit of putting his hands on her. She didn't seem to think he was dangerous."

"What did you think?"

"Well . . . maybe. I didn't like those eyes of his."

"Did Elaine say he was an old boyfriend or what?"

"No. I asked her if he was and she denied it, but I got the impression she might not be telling the truth. And he said something to some customers on the way out, something about a little spat between lovers."

McCone did some more nibbling at her bourbon. "Did you tell Knowles all of this?"

"Sure."

"What did he say?"

"That he'd look into it."

"Well, so will I. Just in case he doesn't look very hard."

"Sharon . . ."

"Elaine was my friend," she said. "I'm just not going to sit by and let the sheriff's department treat her death as an accident or a suicide."

"If it was anything else, they'll find it out. Don't go messing around in it, stirring things up."

That made her angry. She said, "I hate it when people start lecturing me. I'm not a little girl, Wolf. I'm a grown woman and I know what I'm doing."

"I just don't want you to get into trouble."

"What makes you think I'm going to get into trouble?"

"Well, you've done it before, for personal reasons."

"And you haven't, I suppose?"

I didn't say anything. She had me and she knew it. And I *had* been about to lecture her, like a father trying in his stumbling and bumbling way to explain the facts of life to his daughter. Why did I have to turn paternal with McCone every time I dealt with her? The last thing in the world I needed was a daughter who packed a .38, and the last thing in the world she needed was an old curmudgeon like me for a papa.

She finished her drink. When she put the glass down, her anger was gone and the look she gave me was softer. "I'd better be going," she said.

"Going where?"

"My business, okay?"

"Yeah. Okay."

She reached over and patted my arm. "Don't worry," she said. "I'll be all right. This is just something I have to do. You know how that is, if anybody does."

"Too damned well," I said. "Sharon, if you need me for anything . . ."

"Thanks, Wolf. I'll remember."

When she was gone, I felt kind of low and empty. In a corner of my mind I could still see Elaine Picard falling, that terrible, futile clawing at the air; still sense her screams like after-echoes just beyond the range of hearing. I debated having another beer, decided against it, and got up to leave.

A bunch of people came in just then, among them Charley Valdene — minus his trench coat and slouch hat, as if the sudden entry of death had put an end to his role-playing. He saw me and detoured in my direction. Watching him approach, I remembered what he'd said to me last night at dinner, jokingly at the time but words that might have been a kind of prophecy: *Maybe there'll be a murder at* this *convention.*

Valdene was subdued. He said, "It's a hell of a thing — an awful thing. You saw it happen, huh? That must have been a shock."

122

"It was," I said. "Be glad you weren't there."

He seemed to want to talk about it, but I didn't; I put him off until later. "Sure," he said, "sure, I understand," and I left him and went out onto the terrace, down onto the white sand beach.

I walked a ways, with the sun hammering down on my head and neck. I wasn't going anywhere in particular, just drifting — or so I thought until I noticed the thatched roofs of the bungalows half hidden among the tropical vegetation. And then I found myself thinking again of the little boy, Timmy, who'd said his mother made him afraid; and of the brunette woman with the suspicious frown and the odd reaction to strangers talking to her son. And not long after that, I was back in the gardens and on my way to Bungalow 6.

I had nothing in mind for when I got there; this was just a little scouting expedition, because the incident with Timmy and his mother still bothered me and because I needed something to take my mind off Elaine Picard. Maybe I would have done nothing more than wander by in front of the bungalow, just to find out if there was anything worth seeing or listening to. Or maybe I would have gone up to the door and knocked and made some excuse for showing up again, so I could have another chat with Timmy or his mother or both of them. But I didn't do either of those things. When I came within sight of the bungalow, there was a maid's cart on the front walk and somebody was coming past it in quick angry strides. The alcoholic local detective, Jim Lauterbach.

He was wearing a flowered shirt today, and nursing a bad hangover; you could see it in the slack pouchy flesh of his face, the red-veined whites of his eyes. He still smelled of liquor too — or, more likely, he'd had some hair of the dog to brace himself for the day. He gave me a scowling glance as he passed by, but without recognition: he'd been too drunk last night to remember much of anything that had happened.

What's he doing here? I wondered. I turned to watch him hurrying off among the tropical greenery. Then I shrugged and went down the path around the maid's cart.

The front door of Bungalow 6 was standing wide open. Inside, a heavyset black woman in a crisp blue uniform was busily opening windows. There was nobody else in the bungalow that I could see. And no sign of habitation, either — no luggage or personal effects of any kind. I rapped on the door panel, poked my head and shoulders through the opening.

"Excuse me, miss."

The maid jumped a little, startled. "Another one," she said when she'd had a look at me. "Well?"

"I'm looking for the woman and her little boy who—"

"What woman? What little boy?"

"The ones staying in this bungalow."

The maid shook her head in an emphatic way. "What's the matter with everybody today? I told that other man — ain't nobody in this bungalow. Just me, here to air it out and get it ready for guests coming tomorrow."

"What?"

"Nobody staying here," the maid said. "No woman, no little boy. This here bungalow's been empty for a week now."

11: McCone

After I left Wolf, I looked up Elaine's address in the telephone directory and then headed south on the Silver Strand and crossed over to Chula Vista. All the way there, I kept thinking about Rich, the man who had bothered Elaine in the Cantina Sin Nombre. A boyfriend? A former boyfriend? The "no one worth mentioning" in Elaine's life? Who?

Wolf had said that Rich was a good bit younger than Elaine. Would she really have become involved with a younger man? I wondered. Elaine was so self-possessed and successful that a younger man would have had to have been someone special to attract her. And a man who roughed up a woman in a bar didn't sound very special to me.

The house was a ranch-style on Hilltop Drive, not far from downtown Chula Vista. It was an older area of nice homes on reasonably large lots. Elaine's was shaded by pepper trees, and a line of willows shielded it from its neighbors to the right. A tall redwood fence provided privacy on the left.

The sheriff's department, of course, would check out Elaine's home eventually, but I doubted they would be here this soon. Still, I drove by slowly, looking for official cars, before I parked a couple of doors down the street. I walked back up there, glancing around to see if there were any nosy neighbors, but saw no one. The street was quiet for a Saturday afternoon; in this heat, probably most of the residents had taken off for the beach.

I went up the walk, tried the front door, and, as I'd expected, found it locked. A little graveled path led around to the side. I followed it to the backyard, where there was a patio with redwood furniture and a thatched structure — called a Tiki Hut — which I remembered as being popular in the early sixties. Glass doors opened onto the patio, the kind whose locks are fairly easy to slip.

As I took out my Mastercard to loid the lock, I felt a twinge of conscience. I knew what Wolf would think of this. He was so damned ethical, played everything to the letter of the law. But then Elaine had been my friend, and, from things I'd heard, I suspected Wolf had stepped outside the law when his friend and partner, Eberhardt, had been shot a while back. I was only doing what I had to, and — should he find out, which was doubtful — Wolf would understand. I went to work on the door latch.

In minutes I was standing in a fair-sized dining area off an immaculately clean kitchen. I waited, listening, but all I could hear was a fly buzzing in the greenhouse window over the sink. The heat in the closed-up house was oppressive.

I'd have to work fast and get out of here before the sheriff's men arrived. Quickly I went into the living room at the front of the house. It was furnished in light wood and tasteful blue upholstery; the only jarring note was a wall of mirrored squares that probably had already been there when Elaine bought the house. I caught sight of myself behind their tacky gold veining — bedraggled, nervous-looking, and clearly depressed.

So much for your terrific weekend, I thought.

There was a hallway off the living room, probably leading to the bedrooms. I turned, about to go that way, when there was a crashing noise near the front door. Whirling, I got ready to run.

One of the mirrored squares lay on the

floor of the little tiled area near the door. The heat, of course, had softened the adhesive that held it to the wall. Smiling weakly, I remembered when my sister Charlene had decided — in a fit of teenaged worldliness — that she had to have the same sort of squares on the ceiling above her bed. My parents, adopting the attitude of letting us live out harmless fantasies, allowed her to do it; my father even helped her affix the squares to the ceiling. The fantasy, which involved a lot of posturing and risqué talk from Charlene, lasted until the first hot spell. Then, in the middle of one torrid night, the entire thing had come down, right on Charlene's rear, scaring hell out of her. The next day, the squares had been dumped unceremoniously in the trash.

Leaving the square on the entryway floor, I hurried down the hall to the farthest door. The room contained a brass bed with a fluffy comforter and many pillows, a dresser, and a walk-in closet. The bedside table yielded Kleenex and aspirin and calcium lactate. Evidently, Elaine had not been much of a reader, because there were no books in evidence.

Next I started through the closet, which was full of conservative suits and dresses and pants and tops — all in good taste and of excellent quality. I worked left to right, toward the back, where a number of items were jammed together as if they were things she never wore.

And I could see why. There was a bright red party dress with a plunging neckline; a black number with a slit that must have extended all the way up the thigh; pants in a shimmery fabric that were cut to be skintight; see-through tops designed to be worn over sexy bras. The clothes were not Elaine, not her at all.

So what was she doing with them? Did she actually go out in public dressed like that? No, more likely she — like my sister Charlene — had had her fantasies. Nothing wrong in occasional dressing up in front of a mirror.

Or for a male friend, someone special.

I gave up on the closet and went through the dresser quickly, coming up with only standard serviceable lingerie and jewelry items, plus a whole collection of security gear — three pairs of handcuffs and some leather thongs with loops at the ends — tucked under some sweaters in a bottom drawer.

Why bring all that stuff home? I wondered. Probably because it was her own property and she didn't want anyone at

Casa del Rey appropriating it. After all, handcuffs don't come cheap, and Elaine hadn't been on the job long enough to know if she could completely trust her coworkers.

From the bedroom I went across the hall to a room that had been fitted out as a combination TV and exercise room, complete with a stationary bicycle and a small set of weights. I opened the closet and saw it was what my mother called a "crazy closet" — crammed with things too junky to display but too full of sentimental value to get rid of. There was a doll with a chipped china face, a white tulle creation that might have been Elaine's first prom dress, a large box of photographs, several scrapbooks and high-school yearbooks, stacks of old 45 records, an incredibly ugly beer stein, three stuffed animals, and a sorority paddle. Curiously I picked up the paddle and looked at it. It was one of those wooden ceremonial things inscribed with the Greek letters and crest — in this case, Mu Omega Sigma. I was surprised because I hadn't known Elaine had gone to college. Nor had she seemed like a sorority type.

I put the paddle back and left the room. There was another door off the hall, and I went through it into an office. It contained some shelves and filing cabinets, and a desk with a bunch of folders stacked in the center of the blotter. I went through them, finding insurance papers, income tax records, and a simple will leaving everything to a nephew, James Picard, in Lemon Grove. There was a note clipped to a homeowner's policy indicating she planned to increase her coverage.

Does a person who is depressed enough to kill herself worry about liability and loss from fire or theft? I asked myself. It didn't seem likely.

Inside the bottom folder in the stack there was the carbon of a typewritten letter, dated two days ago, to an Alan Thorburn, Esq., at a downtown address. The first paragraph mentioned a meeting next week with Thorburn and someone named Hugh — probably a C.P.A. — to review Elaine's tax situation. I was about to put the letter back in the file when the second paragraph caught my eye. I skimmed the rest of it, then sat down in the desk chair and reread it more slowly.

As I mentioned on the phone the other day, I've uncovered a disturbing situation at the Casa del Rey. I am taking this opportunity to go on record about this, and ask that you date-stamp this letter and place it in your safe, in

132

case I should need evidence of my lack of involvement in this situation at some future date.

At this point, I can't say exactly what is going on, although I'm quite certain that the hotel is being used for illegal activities. I am also fairly certain that the parent company, Yamana International, is not involved.

Should these activities come to the attention of the police, I would naturally be suspect as chief of security. Therefore I need this letter and the attached clipping on file as proof of my noninvolvement.

You cautioned me to be careful, Alan, and I assure you that I will be, although I definitely intend to get to the bottom of this matter.

Please don't worry; I will proceed very cautiously.

Looking forward to seeing you and Hugh next week, with all best wishes,

Elaine's name was typed below the closing sentence.

I sat staring at the letter, then looked for a copy of the clipping she'd mentioned, but didn't find it. Then I stuffed the letter into my purse.

A wastebasket stood next to the desk. I pulled it over and began going through its contents. There was a draft of the letter to Thorburn, a bunch of junk mail, some crumpled Kleenexes, an empty paper-clip box, and a wadded-up ball of blue paper. I smoothed the blue paper out on the desk and saw it was written on in bold felt-tip printing. With a slight sense of shame at further invading my friend's privacy, I read what appeared to be a love note.

I know that you have been avoiding me and I can guess the reasons why, but I think we are both aware that this thing that has started between us is totally beyond our control. Ever since that night at the club, I have been unable to get you out of my mind. And although you claim otherwise, I know you feel the same way too. Please don't turn a cold hand to me, Elaine. There have been others for me, but never anyone like you. I wait for your reply.

The signature was a scrawled letter that could have been an *H* or an *R* or a *K*, or perhaps even a *B*.

So she'd had a lover after all — one who sounded pretty devoted, if not downright lovelorn. *H* or *R* or *K* or *B?* Or possibly a stylized *S* or *P?* I was willing to bet it was *R*. For Rich.

There was a red purse-sized address book on the desk. I picked it up and went through it, looking for someone named Rich. There were two, along with someone called Rick. A few of the other names I recognized — Karyn Sugarman, Lloyd Beddoes, Alan Thorburn — and others were totally unfamiliar. I glanced through the entire book, and put it and the love note in my purse with the other letter. Hastily I checked the desk drawers, found them almost empty, then left the office and went down the hall to the living room.

What about the situation Elaine had uncovered at Casa del Rey? I wondered. And what had been in the clipping she'd sent with the letter to her lawyer? Since it had only been written on Thursday, I doubted she had been able to find out much more in the interim.

Or maybe she had. Maybe that was why she'd died.

This new information made Lloyd Beddoes and perhaps his assistant, Ibarcena, look very bad. I tried to picture them as they'd stood with Wolf in the garden that morning after Elaine's fall. They'd been nervous. Nervous and upset. But guilty-looking? Perhaps. I'd been plenty upset myself, and my memory wasn't too clear on the fine points.

I was so preoccupied by the matter of Beddoes and Ibarcena that I simply walked through the living room to the front door, turned the dead bolt, and stepped outside onto the porch. And as soon as I did, I realized I'd made a big mistake.

A sheriff's-department car was parked at the curb, and Lieutenant Tom Knowles was coming up the walk toward me.

12: "Wolf"

The clerk on the registration desk was the same one who'd checked me in yesterday. Young, spiffily dressed, polite in an aloof way. And as adamant as the black maid I'd talked to a few minutes ago, if a little more patient.

"You must be mistaken, sir," he said. "Bungalow Six has been empty for over a week."

"You're sure of that?"

"Yes, sir, of course I am."

"All right. A woman about thirty-five, brown-haired, slender, fairly attractive. A little boy, seven or so, on the hefty side; fair-skinned, blond hair. His first name is Timmy — I don't know hers or their last name. Maybe they're staying in one of the other bungalows?"

"No, sir. Only three of the bungalows are occupied at the moment and I know all of the guests. None of them is a woman such as you described. And certainly none is a little boy."

"Here in this building, then?"

"Not to my knowledge, sir. If you could give me their last name . . ."

"I told you, I don't know their last name."

"Then I'm sorry, I don't know what I can do."

"You can let me talk to the manager."

"Mr. Beddoes isn't available."

"No? When will he be available?"

"I don't know, sir."

"How about his assistant?"

"Mr. Ibarcena has left for the day."

"And you don't know when *he'll* be available either, right?"

"No, sir, I don't."

I gave it up; this wasn't getting me anywhere. And none of it made any damned sense. Timmy had as much as told me he was staying in Bungalow 6; his mother had come from there when she was calling him, had dragged him back in that direction when they'd left me. Now they were gone, and nobody would admit that they'd ever been here. Why? What the hell was going on?

Well, maybe the drunk, Jim Lauterbach, had some answers. He'd been there at the bungalow; he'd talked to the maid just before I had. Personal interest in Timmy and his mother? Or professional interest? That was another question that kept nagging at me.

I took a tour of the lobby and the Cantina Sin Nombre, but Lauterbach wasn't in either place. There was some activity on the mezzanine, and I went up there and the convention was still going on — people milling around, waiting for another panel or product demonstration to start, talking and drinking wine, a couple of them laughing. It surprised me a little and it shouldn't have. There was no reason for the Society to cancel the rest of the convention just because one of its members had died suddenly. No reason for the Casa del Rey to curtail its normal operations, or for its employees to show any apparent signs of sadness or grief, just because its security chief had tumbled out of the east tower and cracked herself open like Humpty-Dumpty. Just clean up the remains, clean up the blood, pretend none of it had really happened, and then it was business as usual.

It annoyed me — all these people, all that pretense. Because Elaine Picard had been a human being, and she had died badly, and I had seen and heard her die, and death was not something that ought to be ignored or treated with indifference. But there was another reason, too: Timmy and his mother. Something peculiar was going on around here, and that also ought not to be ignored or treated with indifference.

Some of the conventioneers tried to buttonhole me, but I knew what they wanted and I brushed them off. Lauterbach wasn't anywhere to be seen. Either he was still out roaming the hotel grounds or he was long gone.

I left the building again, made my way back through the gardens to Bungalow 6. No Lauterbach. The black maid had vanished too; the place was shut up tight. I tried the door, the windows in the front wall, but there was no way in short of felonious breaking and entering. And after the maid's visit, I had a feeling that there wouldn't be anything to find even if I did get inside.

Fifty feet of landscaped ground — scrub palms, jacaranda, some other vegetation — separated Bungalow 6 from Bungalow 5. But the foliage wasn't dense enough to obscure completely the view of anybody looking out of Number 5's side windows toward the front of 6. I followed the path over to 5 and knocked on the door.

Nobody answered immediately. I thought

that maybe this was one of the allegedly deserted bungalows and started to turn away — and the latch clicked and the door edged open and I was looking at a tiny woman somewhere in her seventies. A tiny *bald* woman: except for a few strands of wispy red hair, the whole top of her head was barren. She saw me looking at it, showed me her dentures in a pleased way, and said, "Never saw anything like it, did you, young man?"

"Ma'am?"

"My bald spot. I'm bald as an eagle."

"Uh, well . . ."

"Been that way for years now. Started getting the bald spot when I was sixty-two, along with my Social Security. At first I wore wigs, you know. Then I turned seventy and I said phooey on that. When you get that old you don't mind people staring at you. It's better than no attention at all."

"Yes, ma'am."

"You woke me up," she said. "I was taking a nap. I always do in the afternoons. Old people need naps, same as kids." She squinted at me out of bright blue eyes. "Are you with the hotel?"

"No, ma'am. I'm a guest here too."

"What do you think of the place?"

"Well . . ."

"Used to be a first-class hotel — not any-more. Some conglomerate bought it. Japanese, I believe." She paused. "That's funny, don't you think?"

"Ma'am?"

"A Victorian hotel with a Spanish name owned by Japanese."

"It does seem kind of odd."

"The Perkins family built it and they had a sense of humor. Called the place their Spanish Victorian. They knew how to run a hotel too. Now . . . well, the service is ter-rible. I had to call the desk three times to get clean towels. *Three* times. And I've been coming here thirty years, with one husband or another."

"Yes, ma'am. I was wondering—"

"Drunks," she said, "that's something else we never had to put up with in the old days. A bunch of rowdies last night, whooping it up like Indians. One of them puked in the rhododendrons out front. I complained about *that*, I'll tell you."

"Did you happen to get a good look at these rowdies, Mrs. . . . ?"

"Andersen. But it's Miss. I took back my maiden name when my fourth husband died. Oh, yes, I saw them. Nasty specimens. Never did like a man who couldn't hold his liquor."

"Was one of them a big guy in a red shirt?"

She nodded emphatically. "He was the loudest one."

"Did he go next door, this man?"

"Next door?"

"Bungalow Six."

"I didn't see him if he did. When the big fat one puked in the rhododendrons, I went straight to the phone to call the manager."

"What about the people staying in Bungalow Six, Miss Andersen? Have you seen them in the past day or two?"

"I didn't know anybody was staying in that bungalow, not until this afternoon."

"Oh? Then you *did* see them — a little boy about seven, a brown-haired woman in her middle thirties?"

"That's right. Why are you so excited about that?"

"I'm trying to find them," I said. "They seem to have disappeared. You wouldn't have any idea where they went?"

She shook her bald head. "Not a clue. They went away with that Mexican fellow."

"What Mexican fellow is that?"

"I can never remember his name. He's the assistant manager, I believe."

"Ibarcena? Victor Ibarcena?"

"That's him," Miss Andersen said. "I'm

not nosy, you understand; I'm too old to be nosy. Only reason I saw them was that I was getting ready for my nap and I like the window open when I sleep. I chanced to look out just as the woman and the boy and the Mexican fellow were leaving. He was carrying their bags."

"Did you see which way they went?"

"Out to the highway. I expect they had a car parked there. That's the way Hank and I always used to come and go. Hank was my fourth husband. He hung himself."

"Ma'am?"

"Hung himself. Left a note saying there wasn't much use to go on living when he couldn't get an erection anymore and had a bald wife besides."

She said that with a straight face, but there was a twinkle in the blue eyes and I had the feeling she was pulling my leg at least a little. She was some little old lady. She'd probably mowed the men down pretty good in her time, and not just a field of four husbands.

I thanked her, and she said, "Don't mention it, young man," and I went straight back to the hotel. All right, now I had confirmation that Timmy and his mother *had* been staying in Number 6. And now I knew that Victor Ibarcena had hustled them away this

144

afternoon. But there was still a lot I didn't know, a lot that was still puzzling. Like, where had Ibarcena taken them? And why in such a hurry? And why had the desk clerk and the maid both lied to me about them being registered?

In my room I dragged the San Diego telephone directory out of the nightstand. With Ibarcena away somewhere, and Lloyd Beddoes "unavailable," the best lead I had to some answers was still Jim Lauterbach. There was only one J. Lauterbach listed in the directory, with an address in National City; but when I dialed the number and let it ring a dozen times, there was no answer.

I sat on the bed, brooding. And wondered *why* I was brooding — why I was doing all this work. Maybe it was just restlessness and boredom. For all I knew, there was nothing the least bit sinister about this thing with Timmy and his mother. No danger to them, no fancy intrigue. It was none of my business, in any case, just as Elaine Picard's death was none of my business.

Sure. But private detectives are as curious as cats, and meddlers besides; that's the nature of the beast. McCone knew that and accepted it and didn't worry about it, but I always had to go around grumbling and rationalizing. So why didn't I just cut it out? I knew damned well why I was mixing into this thing, and it didn't have much to do with restlessness or boredom. It was the way Timmy had looked there on that bench, and afterward as his mother was dragging him off: scared and trying not to show it. Brave little kid harboring secrets, on his way to see his dad in some town in Mexico that had monkeys in it. . . .

The telephone rang. Now who the devil is that? I thought. I snagged up the receiver and muttered a hello.

"Wolf, good, I caught you in. This is Sharon."

She sounded relieved — and a little odd, a little nervous. "What's up, Sharon?"

"Well, I need a favor."

"What kind of favor?"

"A small one. Two small ones, actually."

"Uh-huh. What are they?"

"Um, first I need you to come and pick me up."

"Pick you up. What happened, your car break down?"

"No. I'm downtown — not too far from the hotel."

"Where downtown?"

"The second favor," she said quickly, "I sort of need you to vouch for me. For my integrity as a private investigator and all that."

146

"What?"

"They won't let me go otherwise."

"What?"

"Wolf, I'm in jail."

"What!"

"Well, not really. They haven't booked me yet."

"Booked you for *what?*"

"I got picked up in Chula Vista, at Elaine's house. For, um, breaking and entering. That cop you talked to, Knowles, showed up just as I was coming out and he dragged me all the way back here to the sheriff's department and if you say I-told-you-so, I think I'll scream."

I didn't say anything. I just sat there holding the receiver and thinking: Why me, Lord?

"Wolf? Are you still there?"

"Yeah, I'm still here. But I wish I wasn't."

"There's nobody else I can call," she said. "Except my family, and I'd never hear the end of it if I did that. Will you come? Right away?"

Go directly to jail, I thought. Do not pass Go, do not collect two hundred dollars. I sighed. "So tell me how to get there," I said.

13: McCone

I was sitting in the hallway on one of those uncomfortable molded plastic chairs when Wolf came out of Knowles's office. He looked at me, his expression a mixture of disapproval and concern, and nodded at the bank of elevators. I got up and followed him over there. He punched the down button impatiently.

"Doesn't Knowles have anything else to say to me?" I asked.

"He seems to think it's all been said."

"Yes, I guess it has." The lieutenant had told me I was lucky he wasn't going to book me for breaking and entering; he'd told me to keep my nose out of his case. On the other hand, I was to report anything I heard or remembered about Elaine Picard immediately; and I was to let him know if I planned to leave San Diego. He hadn't expressed appreciation for my cooperation, even though I'd done my damnedest in that quarter.

Wolf made an annoyed noise and punched the button again. The doors of the nearest car slid open and we got on. In silence we rode to the lobby and went through the main door to C Street. Wolf led me around the big pinkish building that housed the sheriff's department and onto Union Street, where a clunky-looking Chevy Monza was parked in front of a bail bondsman's office. The car was pale yellow, with plenty of dents and scrape marks. Leave it to Wolf to rent the most scabrous vehicle in the airport fleet.

We got into the car and he started the engine. It wheezed to life like a wino waking up after a particularly bad night. Wolf said, "Where to?"

"Go down here and get on the freeway to Chula Vista. I'll tell you how to get to Elaine's house. My car's still parked near there."

Immediately I regretted mentioning Elaine. Wolf's brows came together in a frown as he eased the clunker out of the space and turned toward the waterfront, where the freeway entrance was. "You really got yourself into it this time, didn't you?"

"Listen, I know what you're going to say,

and I'd rather not hear it, if you don't mind."

"Well, it was a dumb thing to do."

"I know."

"You can lose your license—"

"I know!"

We drove in silence for a couple of blocks.

I said, "Anyway, I cooperated with Knowles. He can't fault me on that."

Wolf was concentrating on his driving, trying to get over toward the freeway on-ramp.

"I found some evidence in Elaine's house and turned it over to him right away." Actually, I'd turned it over to him when he'd announced his intention to search my purse.

"What kind of evidence?" Wolf guided the car into the stream of southbound traffic on Highway 5.

"A letter from Elaine to her lawyer, saying she suspected something illegal was going on at the Casa del Rey." Briefly I outlined its contents for him.

When I finished, he was looking thoughtful. "Well, now," he said. "Maybe that ties in with something I've discovered that doesn't seem to be strictly aboveboard."

"Oh, what?"

"Guests who were staying in one of the bungalows, but weren't registered."

"Who?"

"A woman and a little boy. They were at the hotel this morning, then gone suddenly this afternoon. Another guest saw them leaving with the assistant manager, Ibarcena. But when I asked about them at the desk, the clerk said they'd never been there. One of the maids denied it too."

"Hmm. It's illegal not to register guests, but that can't be all of it. I wonder what's going on. They didn't seem to be there against their will, did they?"

"No. The woman seemed nervous and suspicious, though."

"What about the kid?"

"Quiet and scared. He said his mother made him afraid."

"That's not good. Well, maybe Ibarcena's giving free room and board to his relatives."

"They didn't look Mexican. And that's hardly something that Elaine would get upset about."

"Or not be able to figure out. She'd just have complained to Beddoes, and that would have been the end of it." I stared out the window at the industrial section of National City.

"There's another thing," Wolf said. "One of the people from the convention, a local op named Jim Lauterbach, was hanging around that bungalow. I got the feeling he was also interested in Timmy and his mother."

"Lauterbach. I met him. He's kind of seedy, originally from Detroit. Wore a bright red shirt."

"Yeah, that's the one. I tried to find out where he has his agency, but it wasn't listed in the directory."

"That's because he took over a friend's operation. The Owens Agency, I think he said."

Wolf nodded. "I guess I should tell Knowles about all this."

"You'd better. We don't want *you* in trouble too."

His look told me he didn't appreciate my attempt at humor. After a moment he said, "You're not going to keep on poking your nose into this business, are you?"

"Of course I am."

"Sharon—"

"Look, you yourself think that Elaine's death might not have been an accident. It certainly wasn't a suicide; people who are going to kill themselves don't usually make appointments to review their tax situations — or write letters to their attorneys to protect themselves from being implicated in illegal situations. Something is going on at that hotel."

"Yeah, and the sheriff's department will find out what it is. I'll talk to Knowles—"

"I've got a feeling that Knowles isn't going to probe that deeply. Plus, Elaine's death might not have anything to do with what's going on at the Casa del Rey. There could be a more personal motive."

"Like?"

"Like that Rich fellow, for instance — the one who accosted her in the bar. Tell me again what he looked like."

"Good-looking, wavy brown hair, funny gray-blue eyes. Younger than her, maybe in his late twenties. Sharp dresser — Madras jacket and white slacks. You know the type."

"How were his eyes funny?"

"Well, they had odd little lights in them — like fires, only down deep so you couldn't really pinpoint them. Why are you asking all this?"

"Because even if Rich didn't have anything to do with Elaine's death, it occurred to me that if he were her boyfriend, she might have told him what was going on at Casa del Rey."

"Possibly."

"And if I find him, it might be a shortcut to getting that information."

I told Wolf which exit to take and directed him up F Street toward Elaine's

153

house. When he turned the car onto Hilltop Drive, he said, "How do you expect to find Rich, with just a first name and a description?"

"Oh, stop — there's my car." I unhooked my seat belt and started to get out. "Thanks so much for rescuing me, Wolf."

"Hold on a second." He put a hand on my arm. "How do you expect to find this guy Rich?"

"Well . . . it stands to reason she'd have her boyfriend's name in her address book."

"You're not going back in that house?"

"Certainly not."

"Then how—?"

"I've got her address book in my purse."

He stared at me.

"Let me explain before you go getting stuffy and paternal again," I said. "One of the first things Knowles said was that he was going to search my purse to see if I'd taken anything from the house. I said that wouldn't be necessary, that I'd give him what I'd taken. And I did — the letter and also a love note I found crumpled up in the wastebasket."

"A love note?"

"Yes." I told him what the note said. He looked thoughtful, but didn't comment. "Anyway. Knowles has both letters now. But

154

I was confused, and I forgot about the address book."

"Uh-huh. But you remembered later, so why didn't you give it to him then?"

"Because after I'd leveled with him and turned over the other stuff, he still insisted on pawing through my purse. He dumped everything out on the seat of his car and then tossed the stuff that was obviously mine back in. I guess he figured the address book belonged to me."

"And you didn't tell him otherwise."

"No. It wasn't really withholding evidence. And after what he did, I just didn't feel like cooperating anymore."

Wolf frowned, looking genuinely puzzled. "I don't see why not."

"Obviously you don't know anything about women and their purses." My hands curved protectively around mine, just thinking about Knowles's treatment of it. "Purses are very private property. We keep all sorts of stuff in them, stuff we wouldn't want anyone else to see."

"Like what?"

"Well, in mine I keep a rock."

"A rock."

"Yes, a rock that an old boyfriend picked up and gave to me at the beach. And a piece of coral from a trip to Hawaii."

·"McCone the romantic."

"I guess I am sort of sentimental. Anyway, who the hell wants some dumb cop looking at her piece of coral? I mean, it's embarrassing."

Wolf was grinning.

"What's so funny?"

"Once, when I was first seeing Kerry, I fumbled around in her purse, looking for this little bottle opener she carries. And she yelled at me, told me to keep my hands out of there."

"Of course. Maybe she hauls rocks around too."

Wolf looked thoughtful, drumming his fingers on the steering wheel. "She lets me rummage in her purse any time I want now," he said. "That's a good sign, huh?"

"Very good." Before he could bring the conversation back to the subject of my future plans, I opened the door and got out of the car. Leaning in, I said, "Wolf, for someone your age, you really don't understand women very well."

"Yeah, I know," he said ruefully. "I never have."

I thanked him again for helping me out, shut the door, and went to my car. Then I took out Elaine's address book. I would check the two men called Rich, as well as the one called Rick, on the off chance that Wolf had misheard the name.

I figured when I found the right one, I'd know him by those funny eyes.

14: "Wolf"

It was after seven when I got back to the Casa del Rey. The talk with McCone had cheered me somewhat; now that I had additional confirmation that peculiar things were going on at the hotel, I would call Tom Knowles, tell him about Timmy and his mother, and then quit worrying and try to enjoy what was left of this so-called mini-vacation. I wished McCone would do the same thing. She was too stubborn and head-strong for her own good — and too young to respect the letter of the law as much as she should. But she'd learn eventually. The hard way, if she kept on creating and compounding felonies whenever it suited her.

There was a different clerk on the desk now, older and not quite as spiffily dressed as the other one. Along with my key, he delivered a couple of messages. One was from Charley Valdene; he wanted me to call him about our movie date tomorrow afternoon. The other one was from somebody I had never heard of, June Paxton. It said: *Can we talk about Elaine Picard? I'll be on the terrace bar for a while. Chubby woman, midfifties, dressed in black.* Below that was her name and the time the note had been written: *6:15.*

I asked the clerk, "Would you know a woman named June Paxton?"

"Yes, sir," he said. "Ms. Paxton is an officer of the Professional Women's Forum."

"What's that?"

He gave me an arch look and said patiently, as if explaining something obvious to an idiot, "An organization of professional women. They meet here regularly."

"What sort of profession is Ms. Paxton in?"

"She is a certified public accountant, I believe."

"Was she a friend of Elaine Picard's?"

"Yes, sir."

"Too bad about Miss Picard, isn't it?"

A pained look this time, but it was more professional than genuine. "A terrible accident," he said in a voice like a bad actor playing an undertaker. "Terrible."

"Yeah. All that bad publicity."

"I beg your pardon?"

"Never mind."

I left him looking puzzled and went through the Cantina Sin Nombre and out on the terrace bar. It was moderately crowded with conventioneers, Japanese tourists, and other people who liked fresh air, ocean views, and sunsets. Especially sunsets. There was an elegant one brewing out over the Pacific — dark reds, oranges, a little shading of lemon yellow, and some cloud wisps that were blackening at the edges like pieces of paper that had just been set afire.

June Paxton wasn't hard to find. She was sitting by herself off to one side, and she was the only person there who was wearing mourning black. Chubby was a good word to describe her; another was homely, and a third was sad. At some other time, she might have resembled a graying Betty Boop. Now, hunched over something in a pineapple shell with two straws sticking out of it, she looked exactly like what she was: somebody who had just lost a close friend.

I stopped at her table and said, "Ms. Paxton?" and she looked up at me out of blue eyes that had a glazed sheen, like pottery fresh from baking in a kiln. Whatever the pineapple-shell concoction was, she'd had more than one of them. I told her who

I was, and she nodded bleakly and said, "Sit down," and then proceeded to study me while I got myself into the chair across from her.

Pretty soon she said, "You don't know who I am, I guess. I mean, we've never met. I'd remember you if we had."

"Would you?"

"Oh, sure. Big men are my weakness. Always have been."

"Well, the desk clerk told me who you are."

"Him," she said. "He's a faggot. Not that I've got anything against faggots, you understand, unless they're obnoxious like that one. One of Elaine's and my best friends is bisexual."

"Yes, ma'am."

"Karyn Sugarman. You know Karyn?"

"No, I don't."

A waiter came by and I told him I'd have a Miller Lite. June Paxton ordered another of the pineapple things; then she rummaged around in a fat black purse and got out some cigarettes and lit one awkwardly. Out over the ocean, the sunset colors had begun to shift and blend together, and the cloud wisps were darker at the edges and backlit as if by flames.

"I quit smoking four years ago," she said.

"Not a single goddamn coffin nail until this afternoon. As soon as I heard . . . I wanted a cigarette. Isn't that funny? One of your best friends dies and all of a sudden you start craving nicotine."

I didn't say anything. What can you say?

She said, "I'm getting drunk. You don't mind, do you?"

"No, ma'am."

"Stop calling me ma'am. Do I look like a ma'am? My name is June." She blew smoke toward the beach, and her lower lip quivered, and I thought for a moment she might burst into tears. But she held her control and said, "Damn," in an empty little voice. Then she said, "You saw it happen. That's what they said on the TV newscast I heard."

"I saw it. I wish I hadn't."

"They said it was an apparent accident. 'Apparent.' What's that mean? Was it an accident or wasn't it? That's why I want to talk to you."

"Do you think it might have been something else?"

"I don't know," she said. "I wasn't there, I didn't see it happen. *Was* it an accident?"

"It might have been. But the way she came over the railing . . . well, she could have jumped. She could even have been pushed."

"Damn," June Paxton said in that same

162

empty little voice. She scrubbed out her cigarette in a clamshell ashtray and immediately lit another. "She killed herself. That's what happened, she threw herself out of that tower."

"Why do you say that?"

"She wasn't herself lately. Just wasn't the same."

"How do you mean?"

"Moody. Unhappy. And she hadn't been sleeping — you can tell when a person's not sleeping. Kept to herself, wouldn't socialize much. She was always private, you know, never said much about her personal life, but lately . . . if anyone asked her a personal question she'd just close up."

"How long had this been going on?"

"Weeks. A long time."

"Any idea what was bothering her?"

"A man, I suppose. Isn't it always a man?"

"Not always. Sometimes it's other things — like a job."

"No, not with Elaine. She liked her job."

"She got along with Lloyd Beddoes, then?"

"More or less. He's a hunk, but . . . who knows? I've never seen him with a woman. Maybe *he's* a faggot too."

"Did she get along with Victor Ibarcena?"

"Definitely a faggot, that one. And a

163

twerp. 'Yes, sir, no, sir.' A twerpy faggot. Whole place is probably full of 'em."

"So there was no trouble between Elaine and either Beddoes or Ibarcena?"

"Doesn't matter, does it? She killed herself."

"And you think it might have been over a man."

"Sure. Always a damned man."

"Any particular man?"

June Paxton frowned, and you could see her thinking it over. The waiter came back with my Miller Lite and another of the pineapple things for her. I tried to pay him, but she wouldn't have any of it; she shoved a twenty-dollar bill at the waiter and shooed him away. Then she took a slug of her drink, shuddered, and went after her cigarette again.

"Rich, maybe," she said. "God knows why."

"Rich who?"

"Don't know his last name. But I don't like him."

"Boyfriend of Elaine's?"

"What else? She wouldn't talk about him."

"Young guy, wavy hair, odd blue eyes?"

"That's him. You know him?"

"I met him yesterday," I said. "Why

wouldn't Elaine talk about him?"

She shrugged. "Ashamed because he was so much younger than her, I suppose. Twenty years' difference in their ages."

"How long had she been seeing him?"

Another shrug. "I only saw them together once."

"Where was that?"

"Borrego Springs. Casa del Zorro, six weeks ago." I gave her a blank look and she said, "Borrego Springs is a town out in the desert. Casa del Zorro's their fanciest spa. Lady friend and I went out there for the weekend, ran into Elaine and Rich having dinner."

"Did you talk to them?"

"You bet. I went right up and said hello. Elaine was embarrassed — she didn't say ten words to me. Him neither. Just sat there looking like a fox in the henhouse."

"You said you didn't like him. Why?"

"His eyes. Kind that make you feel crawly."

"Did Elaine ever tell you anything about him?"

"No. I asked her later, but she wouldn't talk. As much as told me to mind my own business."

"Is there anybody else she might have confided in?"

"Well, Karyn — Karyn Sugarman. But if she did, Karyn wouldn't say. So it had to be professionally."

"Professionally?"

"Karyn's a shrink. Elaine did the couch trip a few times. Don't know why. Nobody tells me anything anymore."

"So you don't have any idea what this Rich does for a living?"

"Probably a damned gigolo. God, that's the kind if I ever saw one — kind that makes a woman do crazy things. *He'd* be the one she'd kill herself over. Not somebody like Henry."

"Who would Henry be?"

"Henry Nyland. Been after her to marry him for months."

Henry Nyland. That was the name of the guy Charley Valdene and I had had the brief run-in with in the parking lot Friday night. I said, "Is he the politician, the one running in the special election for city councilman?"

She nodded. "Retired admiral with plenty of money, inherited it from his wife when she died five years ago. Good-looking too. Not a bad catch, but Elaine didn't see it that way."

"How come?"

"Who knows? Didn't love him, I guess."

"Was Nyland upset by her rejection?"

166

She said, "Who knows?" again, and then belted down some more of her pineapple drink. She squinted at me over the straw, using it like a gunsight. "I guess you're married, huh?" she asked.

"Uh, no. No, I'm not."

"Got a lady friend, though?"

"Yes."

"Sure. Figures. I'm too fat anyway. Too fat and too old and too drunk."

Uh-oh, I thought, she'd going to get sloppy and maudlin. But she wasn't that kind at all. She pushed the drink away, saying, "No more for me. Any more and I'll fall on my face. Or wrap my car around a pole somewhere. One death today's enough." She squinted at me again. "Thanks for talking to me. I wish it'd been an accident."

"So do I, June."

She put the cigarettes into her purse and hoisted herself out of her chair. She was a little unsteady, but it didn't look as though she were in any danger of falling over. I said, "You want me to walk you out?" and she said, "No, I'm okay. Just need to be alone for a while. Walk on the beach'll sober me up." She patted my hand, gave me a melancholy smile, and went away across the terrace to a gate in the side wall, moving carefully and with dignity.

I stayed where I was, watching her waddle through the white sand toward the water. The angle of her passage made it look as if she were walking off into that elegant sunset — walking straight into the dying fire of the sun.

15: McCone

The first person in Elaine's address book I tried to call was her lawyer, Alan Thorburn. I reached an answering service, and the operator told me Mr. Thorburn was out of town until Monday morning. Was there any way I could reach him? I asked. Well, he was out on his boat, but due to call in sometime this evening, or perhaps tomorrow. . . . I left my name and my parents' number, hoping Counselor Thorburn would indeed check with his service.

Then I examined the addresses for Rich Woodall, Rich James, and the man listed only as Rick. Rich James's was the closest to the shopping area near Elaine's house where my phone booth was located, but his telephone had been disconnected. I decided to drive over and see if he was home.

The address turned out to be a decaying apartment house right on Imperial Beach, south of the Silver Strand. Built in the garish architecture of the fifties, it had a gigantic pink-and-turquoise mosaic peacock on the end wall by the parking area. A number of the tiles had fallen away, including those that formed the bird's left eye, so he appeared to be a molting old peacock with a cataract.

I left my car in the lot and went around to the beach side of the building. Although it was late — close to seven o'clock — the heat had not let up and the sand was still crowded. The sun was low, and flamelike color spread across the water, reducing the people who strolled in the surf to purple-gray silhouettes. Here and there a barbecue fire sent smoke skyward, and a few diehard athletes tossed Frisbees and volleyballs around.

The apartment building was two-tiered, with iron balconies over which a number of beach towels were draped. I went up a concrete stairway at one end and along the top floor, avoiding a tricycle, a surfboard, and an assortment of sand toys, to the apartment number that had been noted in Elaine's book. Already I'd begun to doubt that Rich James was the man Wolf had seen with my friend in the Cantina Sin Nombre. This place had a seedy air that didn't match the sharp dresser he'd described.

The door to the apartment stood open, and from inside I could hear the dull beat of rock music. I pounded on the doorframe and a few seconds later, a young man with a fluffy blond beard appeared. He wore cutoff jeans and had a dishtowel tucked into his belt.

"I'm looking for Rich James," I said.

"Sure. Hi. That's me."

Disappointed, I said, "I'm Sharon McCone, a friend of Elaine Picard's—"

"Oh, yeah, Elaine. Look, can you come in?" Without waiting for my answer he turned and disappeared into the gloom beyond the door.

I followed him into a sparsely furnished living room. The drapes were pulled against the sunset's glare and two little boys, around six or seven, sat on a lumpy rattan couch watching a TV program whose sound competed with the stereo. Newspapers were scattered on the threadbare carpeting, and pop and beer cans sat on every available surface. When the little boys saw me, they stared for a moment, then exchanged a solemn, knowing look. One of them said, "Daddy, we're hungry."

"Supper's coming up any minute now. It's just got to heat." To me, he added, "Come

171

on out to the kitchen. I'm cooking. Weekend father, you know."

I followed him into the kitchen, a tiny, airless room at the rear of the apartment, on the side that faced the street. He picked up a can and dumped its contents into a pot on the stove. "Franco-American spaghetti," he said, holding up the can. "It's not much, but I never learned to cook. Mama didn't tell me it would be like this."

I glanced around, noting the dirty dishes and the trash that overflowed the wastebasket. A pizza box sat on the counter, full of gnawed crusts. Mama hadn't taught him to clean up, either. Mentally I shuddered, thinking of my brother John. Would it be like this when he got his own place and took the kids on weekends? What if, by some strange quirk, he managed to get permanent custody of them? Would they live like this all the time?

"So you're a friend of Elaine's?" Rich James asked, extending a beer can toward me.

"Yes." I took the can, eyeing it suspiciously and wishing there were a polite way of wiping off its top before drinking from it.

"What's wrong this time — the water heater?"

"Huh?"

172

"Well, the last time she called, it was on the fritz. I replaced the pressure valve, but you never know with these cheapo things they're installing these days."

I frowned, beginning to understand.

"She *did* send you about something for me to fix around the house, didn't she? I told her I'd had the phone taken out." He smiled disarmingly. "I'm a compulsive caller, especially when I've had a few. And everybody I want to call seems to be long-distance. So I had the thing disconnected."

"You're Elaine's handyman," I said.

"Yeah." Now it was his turn to frown. "Who'd you think I was?"

"I take it you haven't seen the news."

"Nope. The kids like to watch reruns of *Cannon* and *Quincy* on Saturday. That station doesn't have news until seven. What about it?"

"Elaine's dead. She fell from one of the towers at the Casa del Rey this morning."

His face went slack with surprise. "Jesus, that's terrible!"

"Yes, it is. I'm locating her friends, trying to find one in particular, named Rich. Your name was in her address book."

"Friends? I wouldn't say we were exactly that. I'm a buddy of her nephew Jim's. We lived in the same apartment complex over in

Lemon Grove, until the wife booted me out. When I moved over here, Jim suggested maybe Elaine could use someone to help around her new house. And she sure could — water heater, electrical, plumbing, you name it — everything went wrong. That lady sure knew how to pick them."

"I guess you spent a lot of time over there, then. Did you ever meet any of her friends?"

He shook his head. "Elaine didn't seem to have many. Oh, there was this blonde fox that came around sometimes, Karyn somebody-or-other. But no men, if that's what you mean."

"I see. Was Elaine close to your friend Jim?"

"Not really. I mean, he liked her and all, but he thought she was strange, the way she kept to herself. I doubt if he knew her any better than I did."

"And you don't know anyone else named Rich whom she might have been close to?"

"Sorry, I don't—" There was a bubbling noise on the stove, and the spaghetti boiled over. "Damn!" Rich snatched the dishtowel from his belt and began mopping at the orange-colored mess.

"I'd better be going," I said, setting my unopened beer on the counter. "It looks like you've got your work cut out for you."

"Yeah. Let me tell you, I never appreciated what my mother went through all those years. Thanks for telling me about Elaine. I'm sorry she's dead. She was kind of strange, but she was a real nice lady."

"I thought so too." When he started to follow me to the door, I added, "Don't bother, I can let myself out."

As I passed through the shabby living room, the boys looked up in surprise, and after I'd gone outside, I heard one say, "She's not staying. They always stay, don't they?"

Again I shuddered at what might be in store for my brother's kids. Much as I loved John, I knew he was as ill prepared for the role of single father as Rich James was.

The next address, for the Rick listed in Elaine's red book, was downtown on Seventh Avenue, between Broadway and C Street. It was a fairly nice section, with a number of the new high-rise buildings that all seemed to contain banks, and smaller structures housing specialty shops that catered to the daytime population of office workers. The number I was looking for turned out to be a renovated brick storefront sandwiched between a delicatessen and a hairdressing salon. A stylistically lettered sign announced it to be the HOUSE OF SLEN-DERIZING AND MASSAGE.

Of course, I thought, remembering the stationary bicycle and set of weights in Elaine's TV room. She hadn't stayed in such good shape without a great deal of effort. Probably she'd come over here to work out. But why, I wondered, had she come all the way downtown, rather than to an establishment closer to the Casa del Rey or her home in Chula Vista? Surely they had health clubs there.

And, more important, who was Rich? A masseur? Her exercise instructor? I supposed, from the description Wolf had given me, that the man in the bar at the Casa del Rey could have been either. But since the health club had a CLOSED sign in the window, I wasn't going to get any answers to my questions tonight.

I waited at the curb in front of the place, hoping someone might be inside in spite of the sign, but couldn't make out any lights. Then I took out the red book and looked up the address for my last prospect, Rich Woodall. He lived quite far out of town, north of El Cajon, near Lakeside, but I decided to check on him anyway.

The area near Lakeside was full of rocky, barren hills and tree-covered hillocks, all of which looked deserted and uninviting in the rapidly fading light. Woodall's street, Lost Canyon Drive, was a winding, unpaved road that led up onto a heavily wooded hillside. I followed it for about a quarter of a mile before I spotted a Spanish-style stucco house surrounded by palm trees and partially screened by a big pyracantha hedge covered with red berries.

I parked close to the hedge and went up the walk, my hopes fading when I saw there were no lights on inside the house. In spite of that, I rang the bell, but it chimed emptily and there was no answer. Squinting at my watch, I saw that it was already nine. I was reluctant to give up and go home after coming all this way, but it seemed I had no choice. I'd have to return tomorrow.

Suddenly there was a loud rattling sound. It reminded me of those old-fashioned noisemakers we used to have at Halloween — tin cans that wound up on a handle and, when released, gave off a hollow clacking. The noise was repeated and then the night became still again.

As near as I could tell, the sound came from behind the house. There was a driveway that ran alongside, and I followed it, reminding myself of what trouble I'd got into the last time I'd strayed into a backyard.

Still, it had been a strange sound, and for all I knew something could be wrong back there.

The two-car garage was straight ahead, its door closed. To the left, where I assumed the yard should be, was total darkness. I reached into my purse and took out my small flashlight. Switching it on, I shined it around until it illuminated a stucco wall with pieces of jagged glass embedded in its top and a partially open gate. I went over and pushed on the gate.

It swung inward to blackness that was even thicker than in the driveway. I waited for my eyes to adjust, and finally made out several large rectangular shapes, perhaps the outline of a grape arbor like the one in my family's yard. Stepping through the gate, I shined the light around again. Startled yellow eyes glared at me.

There was a swift snarling noise. I shrank back against the wall, almost dropping the flash. The snarling went on, and then the rattling noise began again. I heard a flapping, like wings, and then from my other side came a whining, feral and dangerous. I felt a prickling at the nape of my neck, and my heart began to race. Getting ready to run, I jerked the light over there.

The whiner had beady eyes and a big

black nose. An animal that resembled a raccoon, but wasn't, enclosed in a sturdy iron mesh cage. It froze when the light hit it.

I laughed weakly and swung the flash back to where the yellow eyes had been. They belonged to a cat — but one that hardly resembled the fat, docile housecat named Watney that graced my home. This one was sinewy and sleek and, from what I'd seen in zoos, probably full grown. Its cage — like the one that housed the thing that resembled a raccoon — looked sturdy.

The cat flattened in a crouch as I held the light on him, and kept growling. The rattling and flapping sounds increased. Wondering what else was here, I turned the light toward the source of the flapping sounds and found a cage of exotic-looking birds. I shook my head in amazement. Apparently I'd stumbled onto a miniaturized version of the San Diego Zoo.

Curious to see what other kinds of animals Woodall was harboring, I swept the light around the yard. There were a number of other cages, one containing more of the raccoonlike animals, another holding two more big cats. There were some lynxes — I recognized them by their lack of tails — and a bunch of foxes, white ones that looked as if they'd been bleached. Another cage held large snakes that I didn't recognize. I shuddered, staring at their sleek, patterned coils.

Yes, I thought, it was a zoo, and not such a small one at that. But what was Woodall doing, keeping it here in his backyard? Weren't there laws about what kinds of animals you could have in your backyard? As I recalled, even the ducks my parents had had — the ones the coyotes had eaten — had been illegal.

And why, for heaven's sake, hadn't the gate been locked? Big cats were dangerous beasts, and if these got loose there was no telling what kind of damage they might do.

I went over to the gate, fumbled around for the latch, and found a chain with a padlock attached to it. Shining the light on it, I saw that the chain had been broken forcibly. There were marks, as if someone had used a hacksaw on it.

Lights flashed suddenly in the driveway, illuminating the garage door. A motor purred, and a small car came into view. Before I could step back, the lights swept over me.

The car jerked to a stop, and a man sprang from the driver's seat. Then he was running toward me, yelling, "Hey! What the hell are you doing there?"

16: "Wolf"

I ate supper in the hotel coffee shop and then went up to my room and tried to call Kerry. No answer. So then I tried to call Eberhardt. No answer. So then I tried to call Charley Valdene, and *he* wasn't home either. Feeling lonely and unwanted, I switched on the television and found something to watch — a 1943 film labeled an "Inner Sanctum Mystery" and carrying the sedate title of *Calling Dr. Death.*

The movie was pretty awful, but I managed to stick with it for close to an hour. Until J. Carroll Naish, playing a cop, said to Lon Chaney Jr., playing a neurologist in one of the all-time great pieces of miscasting, "You've gone beyond life, doctor — *into the brain!*" At which point I got up and shut the thing off.

Time to go beyond the brain, I thought,

into something even greater and more desirable: the realm of sleep.

I went to bed.

17: McCone

The glare of the headlights illuminated the man who was running up the driveway toward me. He had wavy brown hair like the man Wolf had described, and his handsome face was contorted in anger. He reached out to grab me, but I stepped back, deciding to take the offensive.

"What do you mean, going off and leaving this gate unlocked?" I said. "Don't you know that's dangerous?"

He stopped, momentarily taken aback.

"What if kids or somebody got in and let those big cats out? What would happen then?" I shined my flashlight on him.

He stood there, arms hanging at his sides, anger turning to wariness. I looked into his eyes, and confirmed that this was the man who had accosted Elaine in the Cantina Sin Nombre. Wolf had been right about those eyes: they were very, very odd. Something burned deep down in them, something changeable that I couldn't quite make out.

Finally he said, "Are you a cop?"

"No, but I've conducted plenty of investigations in cooperation with them. And I know enough to realize that this menagerie is in violation of a whole bunch of ordinances. For one thing, it's an attractive nuisance—"

Recognition had started up in his eyes when I'd mentioned investigations. Now he said, "Wait a minute — you're from that convention at the Casa del Rey. I saw you in the bar with Elaine Picard."

"Right."

"What are you doing in my backyard?"

"Originally I came looking for you. But then those birds started up, and I found myself in the middle of a zoo. Why wasn't the gate padlocked?"

Woodall glanced at it, troubled. "That's what I'd like to know."

"What does that mean?"

"I came home an hour ago and found that somebody had sawed through the chain. None of the animals had been disturbed, as far as I could tell. I went right out to get a new chain, but you can imagine how hard it is to find a hardware store open on a Saturday night."

He went back to the car and got a paper

bag, then took out a chain and set about fastening it with the padlock. When he was done, he turned to me. "Are you here about Elaine?"

"You've heard she's dead, then."

"It was on the news." He said it flatly, as if he were talking about a baseball score he'd heard. "But why are you coming to me about it?"

I hadn't said Elaine was the reason I was here; why did he assume it? "Look, can we go inside and talk?"

He looked uncertain. "You haven't told me your name."

"Sharon McCone. I'm a friend of Elaine's from San Francisco."

He nodded. "Rich Woodall. But you must know that, since you came all the way out here."

"Yes."

"Well," he said reluctantly. "I guess we might as well go inside." Giving the padlock a final tug, he turned and led me down the driveway. After turning off his car's headlights, he unlocked a side door to the house, reached inside, flicked on a light switch, and motioned me to enter.

I stepped into a large kitchen and dining area. At the far end was a round oak table in front of a two-sided brick fireplace that also opened into a formal living room. Woodall motioned at the table and went into the kitchen.

"I feel like having a glass of wine," he said. "Will you join me?" His manner had changed subtly, and his voice modulated to a sort of soft slyness. As he spoke, he adjusted the hang of his well-tailored sport coat.

Much as it put me off, I decided to play along with his unpleasantly seductive manner. "Sure," I said, smiling. "Thank you."

He went to a cupboard, took out stemware, and busied himself with a corkscrew. "Red okay?"

"Perfect. Tell me, what are you doing with all those animals? Are they pets?"

"Not exactly. I'm a zoologist — in public relations with the zoo. Unfortunately, the job's strictly administrative and doesn't allow me much opportunity to keep my hand in at my specialty, so I've set up my own little zoo here at home."

"But you're aware it's illegal — keeping those kinds of animals in your yard."

He came toward me, carrying the glasses of wine. His odd eyes appraised me, and when he spoke it was teasingly. "Oh, come on, you wouldn't tell on me, would you?"

I took the glass he extended. "I don't know."

"The poor animals aren't hurting anybody."

"They could."

Abruptly, his manner changed again. "Well, don't worry about it, dearheart. The animals are well looked after — and even without the gate locked, those cages are plenty sturdy. Besides, it isn't illegal — this is an unincorporated area."

"Oh. Don't your neighbors object, though?"

"The nearest house is half a mile away. The people around here like their privacy." He sat next to me, uncomfortably close, and raised his glass in a brief toast. The wine was good — rich and full-flavored — and when I held it to the light, it seemed to burn with secret fires, like Rich Woodall's eyes.

I decided not to let Woodall know I had heard about the scene in the Cantina Sin Nombre yesterday. I said, "Did you talk to Elaine after I left the bar?"

For a moment he looked blank.

"I mean yesterday afternoon, when you saw us together."

"Oh. Oh, no."

His first mistake. "I'm surprised. The two of you were pretty close, weren't you?"

"Elaine and me?" His eyes moved from side to side, calculatingly. "Not really."

"Oh, I thought . . ."

"What did you think?"

"For some reason, I had the impression you were seeing one another."

"How did you get that?"

I frowned. "Why, now that you mention it, I don't know."

"Did she say something about me?"

"I honestly don't remember where I got the idea."

He watched me for a moment, then said, "Actually, Elaine and I have had dinner a few times. She's a member of our Adopt-an-Animal Program."

"Your what?"

"It's a P.R. and fund-raising device the zoo has. People are encouraged to make donations, and in return they become the adoptive parents of one of the animals."

"Which one was Elaine mother to?"

"A gorilla. Named Fred."

"Good Lord." But it didn't sound right. As I recalled, Elaine didn't like animals, wouldn't even have a cat in the house. "What does an adoptive parent do?"

"Some of them visit the animals regularly. Show them off to their friends."

"I can just see Elaine telling her friends, 'There's my son the gorilla.' "

He smiled — in a restrained way, as befitted a person talking about a dead friend. "I don't think she was that big on parenthood. But she was a strong supporter of the zoo. And, of course, it made a good tax deduction."

I'd have to check with Elaine's accountant, if I could locate him. "Of course, now the gorilla is motherless."

Woodall's face became somber. I had the feeling that he always tried to come across with the appropriate response, in spite of what he really felt about a given situation. "Her death is a shame. A real tragedy. Elaine was a lovely woman."

And that, I thought, was why you roughed her up in the bar yesterday. "So you only knew her through the zoo."

"Yes." He got up and went to fetch the wine bottle.

"Do you know any of her other friends?" I asked.

"Sorry, I don't."

"What about someone named Rick?"

"Rick?" An odd look passed over his face and he turned to refill our glasses. "Can't say as I do."

"He either belonged to or worked for the club."

Woodall set the bottle down. "What club?"

"The health club downtown that she belonged to."

"Oh, that. Elaine was very conscious of her body. Liked to keep in good shape."

"But you don't know Rick."

"No." There was an edge to his voice. "Look, I'm getting tired of all these questions about Elaine. I've had a hard day. I go into work on a Saturday to plan the spring promo, I get home expecting to relax the rest of the evening, only to find my gate has been tampered with and I have to rush out to find another chain . . ." He was complaining like a small, peevish boy.

"Yes, what about that? Who would want to break into your yard anyway?"

"I don't know." His mouth twisted. "But I'll tell you, it's lucky for him I wasn't here, because if I had been, I wouldn't have thought twice. I'd have blown him away." He motioned toward the formal living room. Through the two-sided fireplace, I could see a rack of hunting rifles mounted on one wall.

"That's strange," I said.

"What is?"

"A man who loves animals being a hunter."

Woodall gave me a look that suggested women shouldn't attempt to talk about such things. "You have to keep the herds thinned out," he said. "But I'm not going to explain the balance of nature to you at this hour."

I sipped wine, just as glad he wasn't going to bother to trot out that old overworked argument.

"So why are you here, exactly?" Woodall asked. "You didn't drop by to commiserate with me on my loss of Elaine."

"No. I'm merely checking all the people in her address book. It's the only lead I have."

He went a little pale at that and took a hefty gulp of wine. "You're a private detective, aren't you?"

"Yes."

"Who hired you to look into this?"

"I'm sorry, I don't give out the names of my clients except to the police."

"Did your client give you my name?"

I shook my head in a way that could have been either yes or no.

Woodall looked petulant. "What did he say about me?"

"Who?"

"Your client."

"I didn't say that he told me about you."

"Then who—"

"Rich," I said, "did Elaine mention anything to you about something being wrong at the Casa del Rey?"

Whatever he had expected me to ask him, that wasn't it, and in a way it seemed to put him at ease. "No. But as I told you, I hardly knew the woman."

Their relationship had deteriorated markedly in the time I'd been talking to him. I started to phrase yet another question, but Woodall stood up. "I'm sorry," he said, "but I'll have to ask you to leave now. I have . . . a lady coming over in a little while."

His resistance was pretty high now; I'd get no more from him tonight. Nodding, I got to my feet. He led me through the tastefully appointed living room, past the gun rack, to the front door.

By the time I'd stepped out onto the walk, Woodall had recovered his poise. "I wish I could have helped more," he said, spreading his hands in a helpless gesture and smiling. "But you know how it is."

"Yes, I know how it is."

And how it was was pretty damned suspicious.

18: "Wolf"

On Sunday morning, things at the Casa del Rey took an abrupt twist. And not for the better, either.

I went down about eight-thirty, on my way to breakfast, and detoured by the desk to drop off my key. The *Esquire* fashion-ad clerk was back on duty. He looked at me as if I had suddenly turned into a minor V.I.P. and said, "Excuse me, sir. Aren't you the gentleman who asked about Bungalow Six yesterday?"

"That's right. Why?"

"Well, sir, I really must apologize. I was under the impression that Bungalow Six had been empty, but that wasn't the case at all."

"It wasn't, huh?"

"No, sir. A young woman and her son *were* staying there; you were absolutely right about that. Mrs. Nancy Clark and Timmy. One of our assistants checked them in and failed to fill out a registration card or notify any other member of the staff."

I looked at him for a time without saying anything. He looked right back at me; he was somebody you wouldn't want to play poker with, not unless you had a .38 cocked in your lap. Pretty soon I said, "What about the maid?"

"Sir?"

"I talked to the maid who was cleaning Bungalow Six yesterday afternoon. She also said it was empty, hadn't been occupied for a week."

"A heavyset black woman? Middle-aged?"

"Yes."

"Well, I must apologize for her too. We've had trouble with her before. She's not very friendly with guests and sometimes tells lies when she doesn't want to be bothered. Mr. Beddoes intends to dismiss her."

"Uh-huh," I said. "All right, where did Nancy and Timmy Clark go in such a hurry? And how come they didn't check out first?"

"Oh, they did check out, sir. With Mr. Ibarcena, who is a personal friend of Mrs. Clark's. They had a plane to catch and he drove them to the airport."

"A plane to where?"

"I don't know, sir."

"So Mr. Ibarcena must have known they

were staying in Bungalow Six. How come *he* didn't say anything to anybody about it?"

"He had no reason to, sir. Until this morning, when I happened to mention to him that you'd been asking about Bungalow Six."

Nice, I thought. They've got it all worked out nice and pat. I said. "How about if I talk to Mr. Ibarcena? Or is he off again on another errand?"

"As a matter of fact, he has left the hotel. But if you'd care to talk to Mr. Beddoes I'm sure that can be arranged."

"Mr. Beddoes said it was all right, did he?"

"Why, yes, sir, he did. Would you like to see him?"

"Sure. I'd like it a whole bunch."

"If you'll just wait here for a moment . . ."

He came around from behind the desk and went through a door to the left marked PRIVATE. Two minutes later he reappeared and gestured to me, and I went past him and into an anteroom that might have been a waiting area in some sort of penitentiary: gray carpeting, flat white walls, gray steel file cabinets, and a desk with a frumpy-looking young woman behind it. There were three doors leading off the anteroom, two of them closed and one open. In the open doorway

195

was Lloyd Beddoes, smiling at me. But the smile was a little off-center, like a tough warden welcoming a member of the Prison Reform League.

"Come in," he said, "come in, won't you?"

I went in. His office was bigger than the anteroom and a little less institutional, with windows that looked out toward the ocean on one side and the gardens on the other. The air conditioner was on and turned up high; it was like walking into a cold-storage locker. Beddoes shut the door, waved me to a chair, and went behind his desk and sat down when I did. The smile was still in place and still crooked. He had a tense, worried look about him, similar to the one he'd worn yesterday while Knowles and his men were on the grounds.

"Now, then," he said. "Mr. Scott explained about the misunderstanding with Bungalow Six?"

"He explained it."

"You seem, ah, a bit skeptical."

"Why should I be skeptical?"

"No reason. None at all."

"I'm just curious," I said. "I ran into Timmy Clark and his mother yesterday, not long before Elaine Picard's death, and we had a talk. The boy indicated they'd be staying on here another day or two. Then all of a

196

sudden they disappeared. You can see how that would make me wonder."

Beddoes plucked nervously at a wing of his blond hair. "Oh yes," he said, "of course. Perfectly understandable."

"How come?"

"I don't . . . Oh, you mean how come they left so suddenly. Well, I believe it had to do with a family emergency of some kind. You'd have to ask Mr. Ibarcena."

"I'll do that. I don't suppose you know where they went?"

"No, I'm afraid I don't. Perhaps Mr. Ibarcena—"

"But you *can* tell me where they live."

"Where they live? Why do you want to know that?"

"We kind of hit it off, the three of us," I lied. "Talked about getting together later on. So I'd like to get in touch with them. Pretty woman like Mrs. Clark . . . you know how it is."

He nodded a little jerkily; his smile wasn't much at all now. I wondered if he'd turned the air conditioner up so high on purpose, just before I came in, to keep himself from sweating during our little interview.

He said, "I'm afraid I can't give out that information."

"Why not? You've got a record of it, haven't you?"

"Of course. But the law forbids us to divulge personal data about our guests."

"Well, we wouldn't want to break the law, would we." I started to get up, pretended to change my mind, and sat down and leaned toward him. "Any word yet on Elaine Picard?"

He blinked at me. "Word? I don't know what—"

"About her fall yesterday. Whether it was an accident or what."

"Oh. No. No word."

"You haven't talked to the sheriff's department since then?"

"I . . . no, I haven't talked to them."

"Well, what's *your* opinion, Mr. Beddoes? Did she fall or jump? Or was she pushed?"

"Pushed?" he said. His hands twitched; he folded them together to keep them still. "What makes you think she might have been pushed?"

"I didn't say that's what I thought. But it *is* a possibility, wouldn't you say?"

"No, I wouldn't. Who would want to — to murder Ms. Picard?"

"Seems you might have some ideas about that."

"Well, I don't. Why should I?"

"She worked for you; she was your chief of security. Any sort of security or police work can be high risk at times."

"Not at the Casa del Rey. We've never had any serious security problems."

"I heard you tell Lieutenant Knowles that she was distraught the last time you saw her. Extremely distraught, I think you said. That didn't have anything to do with her work here?"

"Absolutely not."

"Do you know what was bothering her?"

"I have no idea. None."

"But you did know her personally, didn't you?"

He twitched again; the question seemed to make him even more nervous. "No," he said. "No, I didn't know her well at all. We certainly didn't socialize, if that's what you're implying."

"I'm not implying anything, Mr. Beddoes. Did you know any of her friends? A young guy with wavy brown hair named Rich, for instance?"

"The only friends of Ms. Picard's I'm acquainted with," he said stiffly, "are the members of the Professional Women's Forum. Why are you asking all these questions? What right do you have to interfere in this matter?"

"I saw her die — remember?"

"Still, that doesn't give you . . . For God's sake, she either threw herself out of the tower or she fell accidentally. There's nothing — sinister about it. It happened and now it's finished, there isn't any more to it."

"Isn't there, Mr. Beddoes? I wouldn't be too sure about that if I were you." I got on my feet. "Have a nice day."

I left him sitting there looking a little pale around the gills. When I came out into the lobby I had a half-formed notion to head for the coffee shop instead of the hotel dining room. I had no appetite for breakfast now; all I wanted was a cup of coffee. But one of the people threading their way through a confusion of loaded luggage carts and departing guests was McCone, and that changed my mind. I detoured over to her, caught her arm.

"Wolf," she said, "you're just the person I wanted to see."

"Ditto. Let's go talk."

"Where? The coffee shop?"

"No. Outside somewhere, away from any big ears."

We went out through the side entrance, into the gardens. But there were a bunch of Japanese tourists there, taking photographs of the tropical flora and of each other, so I steered McCone down onto the beach. It was hot already, and there were people sprawled out on the sand and splashing around in the light surf. Out where the deep blue water met the paler blue of the sky, a couple of naval vessels moved like sluggish gray reminders that all this was illusion and the world wasn't such a peaceful place after all.

McCone stopped and took off her sandals. As we started off again she said, "Okay, what's up? You seem kind of grim this morning."

"I feel kind of grim. I just had a talk with Lloyd Beddoes." And I told her about that, and about the sudden switch in official hotel position on Nancy and Timmy Clark.

"Sounds fishy," McCone said. "How do you figure it?"

"The same way you're figuring it. Beddoes is running some kind of scam with the hotel as cover. Ibarcena's probably in on it too. The desk clerk Scott, too, maybe, but more likely he's just doing what he's told. Same with the maid."

"What kind of scam?"

"I don't know yet. But Beddoes and Ibarcena are scared to death the police will find it out. That's what made them so nervous yesterday after Elaine's death, and it must be why Ibarcena hustled the Clarks out of here so fast. Then you found that letter Elaine wrote to her lawyer and gave it to Knowles, and he must have gone after Beddoes right away, talked to him sometime last night. Beddoes covered up somehow — pleaded ignorance, or maybe tried to discredit Elaine as a paranoid and probable suicide — but that wouldn't have made him feel much safer."

"And then this morning," McCone said, picking it up, "he came in and Scott told him you'd been asking questions about Bungalow Six. So Beddoes cooked up that story about the Clark family and told the clerk to pass it on to you as soon as he saw you."

"Right."

"But the thing I don't get," she said, "is what sort of illegal activity could involve a seven-year-old kid traveling with his mother."

"Neither do I. Not yet."

We walked along in silence for a few seconds. We were down close to the water, where the sand was wet and packed and the footing was better. Little wavelets rolled in and lapped at McCone's bare feet; she didn't pay any attention. I don't like feet much — a foot fetish is one of those quirks

202

I've never been able to figure out — but hers were small and well shaped. It made me feel a little silly to have noticed them and to be thinking about them. The human mind is a funny instrument sometimes.

She said, "I found the guy named Rich last night. And you were right — he's strange."

"How did you manage to track him down?"

She gave me one of her little smiles. "Detective work. I'm good at it, too, you know."

"Mmm. Who is he?"

"His last name's Woodall and he's a zoologist — does public relations for the San Diego Zoo. He also keeps a private zoo in his backyard."

"A what?"

"A private zoo. Big cats, birds, foxes, snakes, some other things. Right before I got there, he found that someone had broken into his yard where the cages are — sawed through the chain. Can you imagine what might have happened if his menagerie had gotten loose?"

"If he lives here in the city, it could have been pretty bad."

"Actually he's in a secluded area north of El Cajon, near Lakeside. No close neighbors, and he tells me the area is un-incorporated, so there aren't any laws prohibiting what he's doing. Still, he'd have been in trouble if his zoo had scattered. He was really upset about the break-in. He said if he'd caught the person who did it, he'd have blown him away."

"That kind, huh?"

"Yes. He keeps a rack of guns in his living room. I can't reconcile it — an animal lover also being a hunter. But maybe that's just me."

"Did you get anything out of him about Elaine?"

"Not much," she said. "I pretended ignorance of what happened in the bar on Friday, and he didn't mention it either. He said he wasn't Elaine's boyfriend and didn't see her socially. According to him, they were just casual friends who got acquainted when she adopted an animal at the San Diego Zoo. One of those sponsorship deals — a gorilla. But I think that's a lie."

"How come?"

"When I knew Elaine she didn't like animals. Wouldn't own a pet, wouldn't have anything to do with them."

"I can give you another reason Woodall might be lying. One of Elaine's friends, a woman named June Paxton, told me last

night that she saw Elaine and Woodall together in a place called Borrego Springs six
weeks ago. Having dinner at some hotel
there — the Casa del Zorro."

McCone gave that some thought. One of
the patrol planes from North Island came
zooming over. When it was gone and the
beach was quiet again she said, "How'd you
happen to meet June Paxton?"

I told her. When I started to explain who
June Paxton was, she broke in, saying, "I've
met her. Yesterday morning in Elaine's office. She seemed like a nice person."

"I thought so too. She was taking Elaine's
death pretty hard."

"Did she think it was an accident or
what?"

"Suicide. Because Elaine hadn't been herself recently."

"She have any idea why?"

"No definite idea. She thinks it was man
trouble."

"Rich Woodall?"

I nodded. "But she said there was another
man in Elaine's life too."

"Oh? Who?"

"Guy named Henry Nyland. A retired admiral and budding right-wing politico.
Seems he'd been trying to get Elaine to
marry him and she kept turning him down."

McCone looked thoughtful again. "I've heard of Nyland. He's running for city council on what amounts to a Moral Majority ticket. God knows why Elaine would get mixed up with somebody like that."

I said, "I had a little brush with the man on Friday night," and told her about it. "He seemed to be a pretty unpleasant type."

"I wonder if he came here to see Elaine," she said. Then she said, "That love note I found. Nyland must have sent it to her."

"Sounds likely."

"It said they met at some club. Probably a health club downtown — the House of Slenderizing and Massage. She had their address in her book."

Another plane went over. When the sound of it faded, McCone asked, "Did you find out anything else from June Paxton?"

"Not much. Except that one of her and Elaine's friends is bisexual, if that means anything."

"Which one?"

"A woman named Karyn Sugarman. She's a shrink — might have been seeing Elaine professionally."

McCone looked surprised. "I met her too. I wouldn't have thought she was the type to go both ways."

"You never know these days," I said. "Everybody's got some kink or other, it seems," and I found myself thinking again, stupidly, of foot fetishes and McCone's feet.

"Well, Sugarman is one of the people I'm planning to talk to," she said. "June Paxton too. Now I'll have to add Henry Nyland to the list." She paused. "What are you going to do?"

"Something I should have done yesterday: call Tom Knowles and tell him about the Clarks. That'll clear my conscience. Then I think I'll talk to Lauterbach, see what he knows. After that . . . we'll see."

She stopped walking and put a hand on my arm. "Wolf, we've sort of been working together on this and we ought to continue — keep each other informed of what we're doing and what we find out. Don't you think?"

"Yeah. But if you do any more breaking and entering, or pull off some other kind of felony, I don't want to hear about it."

"You'll be the last person I tell," she said, and damned if she didn't lean up and kiss me on the cheek like a damn daughter.

19: McCone

I hurried back to the hotel lobby feeling faintly embarrassed. What on earth had possessed me to kiss Wolf on the cheek? I am not an overly demonstrative person; it was the sort of thing I would only do to a lover — and Wolf certainly was not that — or to my own father. Well, that must be it. Wolf *did* have a tendency to fatherize.

The Casa del Rey was humming this morning, with people checking in and out, and all the phone booths were occupied. While I waited, I debated trying to call Elaine's lawyer, Thorburn, once more, but decided that since he hadn't returned the message I'd left with his service, he must still be out on his boat. Then I consulted Elaine's address book and found a listing for Karyn Sugarman but none for Henry Nyland. June Paxton's name was there, but the address and number had been crossed out and no new ones entered.

A fat woman in a muumuu, whom I'd been seeing off and on since the convention had started, squeezed out of the phone booth nearest me, catching her voluminous garment on the door. I helped her free herself, then slipped inside, leaving the door open so the scent of her heavy perfume would dissipate.

Karyn Sugarman answered my call on the first ring. Her husky voice held undertones of weariness, and at first she didn't remember who I was. When I reminded her of our meeting in Elaine's office and asked if I might see her today, she hesitated. "I'll be at my office," she said finally. "I keep Sunday hours for a few patients whose schedules won't permit appointments during the week. I suppose you could come there." She directed me to an address in the Old Town area and said she could see me in fifteen minutes.

I got in my car and started off, my mind only half on driving. Mostly I was puzzling over what Wolf had told me about the little boy and his mother who had disappeared from the Casa del Rey. It sounded suspicious, all right, but I couldn't imagine it being anything so major that Elaine would have been killed over it. And yet . . .

I was certain Wolf would get nothing more about the Clarks from either Beddoes or Ibarcena. Their guard was up now. And even after he reported what he knew to Knowles, I doubted the lieutenant would find out anything, since the people at the hotel would have had a good bit of time to prepare for him. Perhaps, however, I could learn something. I'd have to try to see both Beddoes and his assistant manager today. And I wanted to track down Henry Nyland. It wouldn't hurt to talk to June Paxton, either, or to see Rich Woodall again.

And where, I asked myself, do you get any time for yourself? I'd planned this next week after the convention as a vacation. I was supposed to relax and enjoy my family and try to talk my brother John into looking at his custody situation realistically. Hell, at the rate I was going, I wouldn't even have time for dinner with that lie-detector salesman. In fact, I'd even forgotten to call Don in San Francisco, to see how he was doing in my absence.

The address Karyn Sugarman had given me was a two-story Spanish-style structure built around a little courtyard. The entrance was guarded by wrought-iron gates and, looking in, I could see a tiled fountain, benches, and lots of dwarf citrus trees in pots. The names on the directory were mainly doctors and dentists, and each had a doorbell beside it. I rang Sugarman's and received an answering buzz that tripped the lock on the gates.

I stepped into the courtyard and looked around, unsure where to go. Sugarman's voice called out from the second-story gallery, near the rear. She was standing at the railing, dressed casually in white pants and a brown tunic top. "The stairway's over here," she said. "Come on up."

I climbed up there and followed her into a light, airy reception room. The walls, carpets, and upholstery were white; the wood was blond; and in startling contrast to the room's modernity, the walls were covered with old-fashioned black-and-white photographs.

Sugarman's walk seemed a little hurried and nervous. Once inside, she turned to me and said, "I'm on the phone right now — a client with a crisis — but it shouldn't be much longer. Make yourself at home, and I'll be with you as soon as possible." She went though a door into an adjoining room, shutting it behind her.

Since one of my interests is photography, I went over and took a look at the pictures. Some were quite old sepia prints that apparently had been touched up and could have been of members of Sugarman's family — women in long dresses and bonnets, men sporting goatees and watch chains. Farther on were pictures that might have been taken in the twenties — people at the beach in heavy, dark bathing costumes, the women even wearing shoes and stockings. Finally there were photos that recalled the fifties and early sixties. One was a group of girls, all attired in the same type of white blouse and dark skirt, all in variations of the same bouffant hairdo, all smiling, all with their hands clasped in their laps. A gold crest and Greek letters were emblazoned in the lower righthand corner of the print, and I translated them as Mu Omega Sigma.

So Sugarman and Elaine had been members of the same college sorority, I thought, remembering the paddle in Elaine's "crazy closet." That would make it a long friendship indeed, spanning over twenty years. I examined the picture more closely and found Sugarman in the third row, her blond hair poufed and teased and smoothed to make her a washed-out Jackie Kennedy. I didn't see anyone who looked like Elaine, but she would have been several years older than these girls. Perhaps she'd been Sugarman's big sister, or an alumna adviser.

"All's under control." Sugarman's voice came from behind me. She sounded less tense now, and I guessed the crisis she'd mentioned hadn't been too serious.

I turned and said, "I was admiring your pictures. Are you a photographer yourself?"

She shook her head. "I don't have time for hobbies. But then you know how that goes, since you knew Elaine."

"I didn't know her all that well." I followed Sugarman into an office that was furnished in the same style as the waiting room.

"Oh?" She looked surprised and motioned at a pair of easy chairs. "I had the impression you were good friends."

I sat down, and she took the chair next to me. "From whom?"

"Elaine. She was very pleased you were here and said something about looking forward to having a long talk with you."

That was odd, I thought. On Friday afternoon, Elaine had confined our conversation to a casual chat over drinks. But we'd always been able to talk easily and at considerable depth; maybe after that initial meeting she'd decided to confide in me about what was bothering her.

"I take it you didn't have that talk, then?" Sugarman asked.

"No," I said regretfully. Maybe if we had,

I could have prevented Elaine's death. If she'd wanted to talk to me, it was because I was also a professional investigator and could help her deal with a threatening situation.

Sugarman was watching me with keen, evaluative eyes. Her gaze reminded me she was a therapist and made me slightly edgy. "When I said I didn't know Elaine all that well, I didn't mean that we weren't friends," I said. "It's just that I don't have much idea of what her life was like these past years."

Sugarman stretched her long legs and leaned back in her chair. It wasn't the same catlike motion I'd seen her make yesterday morning in Elaine's office, but more of an effort to ease some sort of discomfort. Her eyes were deeply shadowed, as if she'd had a bad night — and probably she had. Like June Paxton, she was taking Elaine's death hard. "Well, Elaine's life was pretty much like mine," she said. "In fact, we had very similar interests."

"And what were those?"

"Our work, the Women's Forum." She reached for a pack of cigarettes on the table between us. "When you're trying to build a career, it comes first. Many times it doesn't even allow for personal relationships."

I thought of Rich Woodall and Henry

Nyland, then asked, "Do you have any idea what Elaine wanted to talk over with me?"

"I'm sorry, she didn't confide in me."

"Well, I do know something was bothering her. I keep hearing how she wasn't herself lately, that she might have committed suicide. I thought you'd be a good person to discuss that with, on account of your work."

"I don't understand."

"I wonder if you know the cause of her depression."

"You mean, was I her therapist?"

"That wasn't my specific question, but the thought has crossed my mind."

Sugarman exhaled smoke, made a face, and crushed the cigarette out. "God, everything tastes terrible today. To answer your question — no, Elaine wasn't one of my clients, although she'd seen different therapists from time to time. But my practice is mainly with lesbian or bisexual women. Elaine didn't go either way." She hesitated. "Perhaps that was part of her problem."

She seemed to be saying this last more to herself than to me, but I asked, "What do you mean?"

She shook her head. "I shouldn't have said that. It's merely a personal evaluation and has no bearing on her suicide."

"You believe it was suicide, then?"

"What else? One doesn't trip and fall over a three-foot railing."

I nodded, unwilling to bring up the possibility of murder yet. "Did Elaine say anything to you about a problem at the hotel?"

"Plenty. Lloyd Beddoes isn't the easiest man to work for."

"Maybe that was what she wanted to talk to me about. What exactly did she say about the situation there?"

"Oh, the usual on-the-job carping. Not that I blame her. Lloyd can be a petty bastard if there ever was one."

"You know him well, then?"

She leaned forward and reached for another cigarette, her tawny hair falling forward across her cheek. "Only through Elaine, but that was enough."

"What about Rich Woodall?"

She stopped, match halfway to the cigarette. "Rich Woodall. What about him?"

"Then you *do* know him."

"Only slightly." The match burned her fingers and she dropped it in the ashtray. "You'll have to forgive me — bad nerves today. What about Woodall?"

"Apparently, Elaine was seeing him, or had been. There was an unpleasant scene in the bar at the Casa del Rey Friday afternoon. A friend of mine saw it. Woodall seemed to be threatening Elaine, and he grabbed her. Later he claimed to me that he hadn't even spoken to her."

"God! That disgusting little I.P.!" Sugarman finally got the cigarette lit and flung the match into the ashtray.

"I.P.?"

"It's a psychological term. Stands for Inadequate Personality. They're people without much inside; no interior sense of self. They don't do well in relationships because they aren't really capable of caring about another person beyond what that person can do for them, even though they appear very sincere. If they're intelligent, they realize they're lacking. To cover, they spend their lives running around acquiring things and indulging in a lot of frantic activity. Put on a lot of front. Often they're quite successful in a worldly way — many of our richest men and most influential politicians are I.P.s, for instance."

"And that's your diagnosis of Rich Woodall?"

"I don't diagnose people I don't know. It's just what he seems like, from what Elaine told me. He maintains a private zoo, not because he likes animals but because they're exotic, good for show. He owns two expensive cars, and worries excessively about his appearance. That kind of thing."

For someone who didn't know the man, she certainly was vehement about him. But if someone like that had been bothering a close friend of mine, I supposed I would have been too. "But why would Woodall come on to Elaine in public like that?"

"He'd been doing it a lot lately. Elaine had gone out with him a few times—"

"Wasn't he a little young for her? There must have been twenty years' difference in their ages."

She gave me a withering look, as if to say I'd grow up someday. "Many women prefer younger men. Anyway, Elaine caught on to Woodall's false charm quite quickly, and refused to continue seeing him. He construed it as an extreme rejection — and if there's one thing an I.P. can't stand, it's rejection."

"How do they react?"

"With attention-seeking tactics. They can't stand to be ignored, so they seek attention of any kind — good or bad. While a normal person is merely regretful that a relationship hasn't worked out, an I.P. will pull all sorts of tricks, from suicide attempts to what Rich Woodall did."

"Bothering Elaine in the bar at the hotel where she worked?"

"Oh, that was extreme. In fact, he started

off pretty subtly. He'd follow her when she went out shopping and park his car next to hers. Or follow her when she went out to lunch or dinner and sit at a nearby table staring at her. Then it went on to phone calls. God knows where it would have ended up. . . ."

Or did end up, I thought. In the east tower at Casa del Rey? "Where did Elaine meet Woodall?" I asked.

Sugarman's eyes were on the long ash of her cigarette. She crushed it out in the ashtray, then got up and carried it and her cigarette package to the desk on the opposite side of the room. "No more of these for me. My nerves are shot as is, and I've a client coming soon."

"You were going to tell me where Elaine and Rich met," I said.

"I was? You know, I'm not really sure."

I thought of Woodall's explanation, about the zoo. It hadn't had an authentic ring to me, so I made a guess and asked, "Could it have been at the club?"

Sugarman turned to face me. "What club?"

"The health club she belonged to, downtown. I got that impression from Woodall—"

"Yes, you're probably right. He *would* be a fanatic about his body."

We were both silent for a moment, Sugarman leaning against the edge of her desk. Then I asked, "And that's all you know about Woodall and Elaine?"

"Yes. What's all this leading up to?"

"I'll explain in a minute. What do you know about Henry Nyland?"

"Nyland. Henry Nyland. He's a politician, running for city council, I believe."

"Did you know he was interested in Elaine?"

"No, I didn't even know she knew him."

"Apparently he wanted to marry her, but she kept turning him down." For a moment I considered telling her about the love note I'd found, but decided some things should be allowed to remain private. "I gather he met her at this same club where she met Woodall. That must be some place to work out, with all these proposals — decent and indecent — coming out of it."

Sugarman didn't seem to see the humor in the remark. Her eyes were far away, hands knotted together. Finally she said, "Poor Elaine."

"How do you mean?"

"Everybody wanted her, but she didn't want any of them."

"Was this a pattern with her, that men she didn't care for fell in love with her?"

"All her life," Sugarman said. She looked at her watch. "I'm afraid that's all the time I can let you have. I'm going to have to review my client's file before she gets here. I'm sorry I can't be of more help to you. Elaine and I were friends, but I really didn't know much about her personal life."

I stood up, then remembered June Paxton. "Do you have June's address, by any chance? It was crossed out of Elaine's address book."

"That's because she just moved." Sugarman went to her desk, looked it up, and wrote it down on a scratch pad for me.

She followed me out, saying I should call if I had further questions. I went down the stairs from the gallery, past the tinkling little fountain, and out to my car.

The trouble with talking with Elaine's friends, I thought, was that the kind of constrained relationships she had formed hadn't permitted any intimacy. Karyn Sugarman had told me nothing I hadn't known before — except for a bit of interesting psychological analysis of Rich Woodall.

Still, it was odd that Sugarman hadn't repeated her question about what I was leading up to. Perhaps the kinds of things I had asked her had made it unnecessary.

20: "Wolf"

I called the sheriff's department from the telephone in my room, but Tom Knowles wasn't in and wasn't expected: it was his day off. I left a message for him to get in touch with me in the morning. So much for that and so much for my conscience.

The telephone directory gave me Jim Lauterbach's home address in National City; and downstairs at the desk, the fashion-plate clerk, Scott, gave me a map of the area. I went out and got into the rental clunker and took it back through Coronado, onto the long curving bridge to the mainland. National City was a short distance south on Highway 5 — a place full of industrial complexes, evidence that it had once been a rail center, and what seemed to be a large number of old Victorian houses. I stopped at a Union 76 station and got directions to Division Street, which was close to the freeway.

The address turned out to be a trailer court, and a rundown one at that. I drove in and stopped at a weed-choked mobile home with a sign in front that said MANAGER. A thin, lemon-haired woman in an ancient pair of pedal pushers confirmed that the Jim Lauterbach who lived there was a private detective and said that his trailer was on Lot 12, toward the rear. I went back there on foot, through brown grass and dust and heat, and found 12: a tarnished silver Airstream, with a tattered awning along the front and some cactus growing at the back. There was no car parked near it, and when I went up and banged on the door, nobody answered.

Wild-goose chase, I thought. I moved over to a side window that had grayish chintz curtains pulled together on the inside. By standing on my toes and chinning myself a little on the sill, I could look past the curtains and inside. There wasn't much to see. The interior of the trailer was a mess: dirty dishes, clothing strewn around, a dozen or so empty and crushed beer cans, an overflowing garbage pail. Lauterbach was a slob — but then so was I. You can't condemn a man for sloppy housekeeping habits.

I went back to the door, looked at the latch, remembered all my preaching at

McCone, and tried it anyway. Locked. Well, that made it easy to walk away. I never had been any good at picking locks or jimmying windows.

I turned and came out from under the awning, and a bulky guy in a T-shirt that said "Charger Power" on it was standing in front of the next trailer, watching me. He said suspiciously, "You looking for somebody?"

"Jim Lauterbach. You wouldn't happen to know when he'll be back?"

"Nope."

"Or where I might find him?"

"Nope. You a friend of that peckerhead's?"

"Not exactly. Why is he a peckerhead?"

"He's a private cop. All cops are peckerheads."

"I'm a cop," I said.

We looked at each other for about five seconds. Then he spat on his brown grass, turned around, and went inside his trailer and slammed the door. Score one for the peckerheads.

When I got back to my car, I drove around until I located a 7-11 store that had a pay telephone in its parking lot. The directory hanging under the phone yielded the number of the Owens Detective Agency, plus an address on Sixth Avenue in San Diego. I found a couple of nickels in my pocket and dialed the number and let it ring a dozen times. Nobody answered.

So maybe he's back at the hotel, I thought. The convention's still going on; he could still be hanging around.

I drove back across the bridge, paid a dollar and twenty cents to get through the toll plaza, and battled the Sunday traffic on Coronado to the Casa del Rey. People were gathered on the mezzanine, waiting for the last panel to start, but Lauterbach wasn't among them. I spotted Charley Valdene, again minus the stock private-eye getup, lurking outside the meeting room, and took him aside and asked him if he'd seen the drunk we'd ministered to on Friday night.

"Not today, no," he said. "And I've been here since ten o'clock. How come you're looking for him?"

"Personal business."

"Nothing I can help you with, I guess?"

"No."

"You're still coming out this afternoon, aren't you?" he asked. "For *Sleepers West*?"

"I don't know, Charley. Some things have come up; I'll have to see how they develop."

He looked a little hangdog, but he nodded and let it go at that. He'd be here at the hotel until about three, he said. I told him I'd let him know by then.

Upstairs in my room, I called Eberhardt's home number and this time he was in. I said. "You're a hard man to get hold of. I called last night and Friday night both."

"Yeah, well, I been busy."

"Doing what?"

"Making time."

"What?"

"Making time," he said, and there was something that sounded like a smirk in his voice. "I met a lady Friday night."

"Yeah? Where?"

"Grocery store near here. We were both buying some cutup chickens and I dropped my package on her foot."

"How romantic," I said.

"Yeah. Her name's Wanda."

"What does she do?"

"You mean for a living?"

"What else would I mean?"

"She's a clerk at Macy's downtown. Women's footwear."

"Uh-huh."

"We been together all weekend," he said, with some more smirk. "Getting to know each other."

"I'll bet."

"She's here right now. Out in the kitchen."

"Cooking up the chicken you dropped on her foot, no doubt."

". . . How'd you know that?"

"I've got mystic powers," I said.

"She's a looker, paisan," he said. "Wait'll you meet her. Knock your eye out. We'll all have dinner when you get back — you and Kerry, me and Wanda. Maybe tomorrow night."

"Not tomorrow night. I don't know if I'll be back tomorrow. I may stay over here a day or two."

"Ah? Don't tell me *you* met somebody too?"

"No."

"So why stay over? You having a good time at the convention in spite of all your grumbling?"

"I'm having a lousy time," I said. "There're some things going on around this hotel that I don't like."

"Oh, Christ, don't tell me you're working?"

"More or less."

"What does that mean? You got a client?"

"No client. I'm sort of hooked up with Sharon McCone."

"The female P.I. from here? So that's it. A looker like Wanda, as I remember. Only Wanda's a blonde."

"Don't go getting ideas. It's strictly business."

"What business? What's going on there that you don't like?"

I told him: Elaine Picard's death, the disappearance of Nancy and Timmy Clark, the cover-up. He groaned a little. "Leave it to you. You go off to a convention and in two days you get yourself ass deep in trouble."

"I'm not in trouble. I'm just poking around a little."

"You and McCone. What a pair."

"Eb, do me a favor. Call up one of your pals at the Hall of Justice and run a check on some people for me."

He sighed. "I might have known. All right, who are they?"

"Private detective named Jim Lauterbach, for starters. That's L-a-u-t-e-r-b-a-c-h. Originally from Detroit, came to San Diego a while back to take over the Owens Agency here. I need to know if he's got a clean record or if he might be an angle player."

"Who else?"

"Lloyd Beddoes and Victor Ibarcena, manager and assistant manager of the Casa del Rey." I spelled both those names for him too. "Any felony record on either man. Same for Rich Woodall — works in P.R. for the San Diego Zoo."

"The zoo, huh? That figures."

"How long you figure it'll take?"

"Depends on who's working at the Hall today. Few hours, probably. You want me to call you back?"

"I don't know if I'll be here. Why don't I call you. Or are you and Wanda going to get to know each other some more?"

"You're jealous," he said, "that's what you are. Wait'll you see her. Man, is she something!"

"Can I call you or not?"

"Sure, call. If there's no answer, just try back a little later."

"Yeah," I said. "You old dog, you."

I rang off. All right, now what? Well, maybe Lauterbach had come home. I called his number, and the line buzzed and nobody answered. I tried his office number again; no one there, either.

I sat down on the bed and shuffled through the directory and found a listing for Victor Ibarcena in Ocean Beach. Same thing: nobody home.

Sundays, I thought. McCone's got things to do; everybody's got things to do except me.

I put in a long-distance call to Kerry's number in San Francisco. And *she* wasn't home. That damn dog-food commercial must be taking more time than she'd thought. Bowzer Bits. For Christ's sake, who would buy a product called Bowzer Bits? They could film a *hundred* commercials and the lousy stuff would still sit there on grocers' shelves gathering mold.

Maybe I ought to try to hunt up Henry Nyland. But McCone had said she was planning to see him. There wasn't anything to be gained in the two of us stumbling over each other, double-talking to people.

What else, then? Nancy and Timmy Clark — where had Ibarcena taken them yesterday afternoon? If he'd put them on a plane, where to? Mexico? Possible. What was it Timmy had said about the place where his father lived? "A town on the water with monkeys in it." Well, maybe there was a lead in that.

I went down to the gift shop off the lobby and bought the most comprehensive map of Mexico they had. A rack of travel and guide books stood against one wall, and I rummaged through those and found one on Mexico and Baja California and bought that too. I took the map and the guide into the Cantina Sin Nombre, got a Lite beer, and sat at one of the tables to familiarize myself with the geography south of the border.

Twenty minutes later I knew exactly the

same as when I'd started, which was nothing. I concentrated on Baja and on the mainland coast of the Sea of Cortez, because there was plenty of jungle along there and where you had jungle you had monkeys, but that brilliant deduction got me nowhere. There were a lot of towns large and small along both coasts, towns with names like La Paz, Puerto Vallarta, Cabo San Lucas, Mazatlán, Culiacán, Los Mochis, Los Monos, Topolobampo — but none of them seemed to have anything worth mentioning to do with simians. Ditto any of the inland towns that were on lakes and rivers.

So much for that idea.

I looked at my watch. Two o'clock — the whole empty afternoon still lay ahead of me. I couldn't just sit around here doing nothing all day; I'd be a Valium case by sunset.

Charley Valdene, I thought.

Well, why not? It wouldn't be working, but then I had no work to do. A few hours at Valdene's house would appease him, relax me, and maybe kill enough time for Lauterbach to show up at his trailer or office or here at the hotel, and for Eberhardt to come up with the background information I'd requested.

Valdene was still lurking on the mezzanine, standing with an ear cocked near the partially open door to one of the meeting rooms. The last of the panels was going on inside, the jazzy one called "Seidenbaum's Method of Directive Interrogation: A Creative Debate"; somebody was taking Seidenbaum's name in vain, whoever the hell Seidenbaum was, as I approached. Valdene seemed happy to see me, and happier still when I told him the movie date was still on and suggested we get to it right away. He offered to drive me out and back, but I said no, I'd better take my rental. That way I could come back early.

I followed him out to his house in Pacific Beach. He got beers for us and set up his projector and put on his videotape of *Sleepers West*. It took me a few minutes to get into it, through no fault of the film, but then it held my interest. Lloyd Nolan was an underrated actor and made a pretty good detective. Most of the action took place on a train; I'm a sucker for trains. And the story was based on a novel called *Sleepers East* — leave it to Hollywood to turn things ass backward — by Frederick Nebel, one of my favorite pulp writers.

It helped to relax me, all right. So did the beer: I accepted Valdene's offer of a final one before I headed back to the Casa del Rey. He got it for me, and when he sat down again he said, making conversation, "You find that fellow Lauterbach?"

"Not yet."

"Well, he'll probably be at the banquet tonight."

"Maybe. I'll look for him."

"Sure wish I could go," he said wistfully. "You know, I'm kind of surprised they didn't cancel it, after what happened to that Picard woman yesterday."

"Nobody pays much attention to death anymore, Charley."

"I guess not. All those people outside after it happened, staring at the body . . . it was pretty gruesome."

"Yeah."

"That guy who manages the hotel . . . what's his name, Beddoes? He sure seemed upset. You hear him yelling at people to break it up?"

"I heard him. Look, Charley . . ."

"He's weird, that guy. I mean *weird.*"

I had been about to ask him to drop the subject, but there was something in the way he said the word "weird" that made me change my mind. "How do you mean?"

"I ran into him once in a place out by Balboa Park, a couple of months ago. He was there when I got there, buying some stuff."

"What's weird about that?"

"This place . . . well, it's a specialty shop. I mean, *real* specialty items. Exotic stuff. You know what I mean?"

"Pornography?"

"Right. But high class. Books, mostly, but also artwork — statues and paintings and curios." He looked a little sheepish. "I'm not into that kind of thing, in case you're wondering. The guy who runs the place, Max Littlejohn, is a friend of a friend and he got me some pornographic private-eye books. I didn't even know they existed, but Max told me about 'em and I had to have 'em for my collection."

I nodded. "What was Beddoes buying?"

"Some books. Looked pretty old. But the really weird thing was this carved statue of a bunch of naked people, guys and women, all tangled up together . . . you know, having an orgy. It was made out of marble or something. Christ, it didn't leave anything to the imagination."

"You're sure the man was Beddoes?"

"Positive. The way he and Max talked, I figured he was a regular customer. Like I said — a weird guy."

In more ways than one, I thought.

And then I thought, Pornography. Now what, if anything, could that mean?

Lauterbach didn't show up for the Society banquet that night. I hung around on the mezzanine during the cocktail hour, talking to Brock Callahan and Miles Jacoby and an old friend from Hollywood, Ben Chadwick, just to make sure. McCone was also a no-show. I wondered if she was finding out anything useful.

There was no way I was going to sit through the rubber chicken and the speeches and the awards ceremony, not to mention the postprandial champagne party and the Latin melodies of the Mexican Bandit Band. I went away as soon as the banquet started, ate a hamburger in the coffee shop, and then retreated to my room to call Eberhardt.

He still sounded smirky and pleased with himself — he'd probably got laid again by Wanda the Footwear Queen since we'd last talked — but he had the information I wanted. Lauterbach was pretty much the type of operative I had pegged him to be: an angle player, skirting the edges of the law, no doubt working petty scams whenever he could. He'd come close to having his ticket pulled twice in Michigan, once on a divorce case before the no-fault law was adopted, once on a shakedown involving electronic bugging. Lack of evidence had saved his bacon in both cases. He'd had a little difficulty getting a California ticket, but his friend Jack Owens, the guy whose agency he'd taken over, had gone to bat for him and the State Board had finally granted him one on a contingency basis. So far, he'd kept his nose clean in San Diego.

With the other three I drew a blank. Neither Beddoes nor Ibarcena nor Rich Woodall had been convicted of a felony in California or anywhere else in the U.S. Woodall *had* been arrested three years ago on suspicion of selling animals in violation of the federal Endangered Species Act, but lack of evidence had kept him from being indicted.

When Eberhardt and I were done talking, I gave Kerry's number another try. No answer. Without much hope I dialed Lauterbach's home and office numbers one last time. No answer at either place. Scratch him until tomorrow.

Scratch me until tomorrow too. I took one of the issues of *Dime Detective* I'd got from Charley Valdene into the bathroom and into the tub. H. H. Stinson's "Rancho El Maniac" was just what I needed to cap a perfect day.

21: McCone

I found a phone booth in a shopping arcade not far from Karyn Sugarman's office and tried to call June Paxton. Her line was busy. Next I looked up Henry Nyland in the directory; he lived on Coronado. A woman whose voice held the professional tones of a housekeeper informed me he had gone to campaign headquarters and then would be meeting with party officials all afternoon. I got the address of his headquarters downtown and drove there.

The headquarters were in a storefront that looked as if it might once have been an auto dealership. Red, white, and blue banners draped the large plate-glass windows — excessively patriotic, I thought, for a campaign for city council. I tried the door and found it locked, then peered inside. There were desks covered with envelopes and literature, numerous phones, and the obligatory coffee urn for weary volunteers, but no people. Nyland must already be on the way to his meeting. That eliminated the possibility of seeing him, at least until evening.

I found another phone booth and tried to call June Paxton again. Her line was still busy. Lloyd Beddoes and Victor Ibarcena were both absent from the Casa del Rey — Ibarcena's day off and Beddoes temporarily unavailable, the switchboard said. I wondered who minded the store while they were gone.

Beddoes's home number was in Elaine's book. I called it, and listened while it rang ten times. Ibarcena, I found, was listed in the directory at an Ocean Beach address. No answer there either. I tried Paxton again: still busy.

I was running out of people to call and starting to get frustrated. It was steaming hot in the booth, and I propped the door open, trying to decide what to do next. This was a rotten way to spend a Sunday, a rotten way to spend a vacation. I wished I was home in San Francisco, with Don.

Don. Good Lord. I had called him the night I'd arrived, promised to call again in a couple of days. And then I'd totally forgotten to do so.

I fished out my phone company credit

card, stuck my well-used dime in the slot, and placed a call to his home number. A woman answered and said to hold on, Don was in the shower.

The temperature in the phone booth must have risen thirty degrees while I waited. When Don's cheerful voice came on the line, I snarled, "Who was that?"

"It's not what you think."

"What am I supposed to think? There's a woman in your apartment, answering your phone while you're in the shower."

"Right. It's, uh, my cousin Laura from Tacoma. We used to play doctor together, so I hardly think my taking a shower in the same apartment with her is anything new or shocking."

That gave me pause. Don *did* have a cousin in Tacoma.

"Laura's in town for the week," he went on. "She wants to meet you. When are you coming back?"

"I don't know." Briefly I outlined what was happening down here.

"Busman's holiday, huh?" he said when I was finished.

"Sort of. I wish I were home."

"So do I. I was worried when you didn't call."

"I meant to, but . . ."

"I know."

We went on for a little while, exchanging the small mundane facts that close relationships thrive on. There had been a power failure and Don's freezer had defrosted. Did I think he should refreeze the squid he'd had in there? (No.) The mailman had got drunk again and dumped all the mail at the bottom of the steps instead of putting it in the boxes. Should he complain? (Yes.) A celebrity had got mad at him on the talk show and used the F word before they could bleep him. Don had a tape of it for me to hear. (Good.) When we hung up, I felt the warm glow that talking to him always gave me.

Until I remembered that the name of his cousin in Tacoma was Patricia, not Laura.

The day went on in the same frustrating fashion. I kept getting a busy signal at June Paxton's number — along with her address, I now had it memorized — and decided to drive down to Chula West to see her. When I arrived at her neat frame house on a street not far from Elaine's, she had gone out. I called Beddoes a couple of times, both at home and at the hotel, but with no luck. Ibarcena continued to elude me. I checked with Henry Nyland's housekeeper; he was still in his meeting, as far as she knew. I tried to drop in on Rich Woodall, but he wasn't home, and the animals were locked up tight.

About four o'clock, I remembered I'd forgotten to eat and stopped at a burrito stand. I ordered one with chorizo and hot sauce, took it to my car, and the damned thing fell apart in my lap.

When I went to home to change my grease-and-sauce-splattered jeans, Charlene's kids were tearing the playroom apart, Charlene was lying down and totally ignoring them, my mother was slamming pots and pans around the kitchen and casting her dark looks at all who entered, and my father was singing up a bawdy storm in the garage. I didn't even ask where John and Joey were — I didn't want to know.

I changed, took three aspirin, and headed back to the Casa del Rey, hoping to buy Wolf a drink and see if he'd found out anything from Jim Lauterbach. But Wolf wasn't at the hotel, and the convivial conventioneers who were warming up for the banquet only depressed me. I had a solitary drink on the terrace outside the Cantina Sin Nombre, brooding about Don, then called Ibarcena's home number and received a busy signal. With a sense of relief at having something concrete to do, I set out for Ocean Beach.

Ibarcena lived in a large redwood-shingled apartment complex not far from the beach. To get to his unit, I had to go through a central courtyard where there was a swimming pool and a putting green, then along a side walkway screened from the adjoining building by tall junipers. There was no one at the pool, in spite of the late-afternoon heat.

I pushed Ibarcena's bell and heard his voice call, "I will answer that." He opened the door, wearing a light bathrobe open almost to the waist. His eyes widened when he saw me, and he started to shut the door.

I stepped forward, wedging my foot between the door and the frame. "Hello, Mr. Ibarcena," I said. "You remember me — Sharon McCone, Elaine Picard's friend?"

"Yes, what is it you want?"

"I need to talk to you about Elaine—"

Behind him the phone rang. He made an annoyed sound and stepped back. I moved inside the apartment. Ibarcena gave me an irritated look and went to the phone. When he said "Yes?" his voice crackled with impatience.

I looked around the room. It was small, with charcoal-gray walls that made it seem even smaller. The furnishings were spare, modern pieces, and the colors were all red and gold and gray — very trendy high-tech. When I looked back at Ibarcena, he was placing the receiver none too gently in its cradle.

"Who was that?" The voice came from a door in the far wall. I glanced over and saw a young man who couldn't have been more than sixteen. He was dressed in a skimpy, tight bathing suit, and held a tray containing two iced drinks and a bowl of peanuts.

Ibarcena made the annoyed sound again. "Lloyd, of course."

"Is he still threatening to come over?"

"Yes. He is all upset—" Ibarcena paused, glancing at me.

"Lloyd Beddoes?" I said. "What's he upset about?"

The boy seemed to notice me for the first time. He set the tray on a chrome-and-glass coffee table and retreated toward the door.

"Don't leave, Roger," Ibarcena said. "This will not take long."

The boy remained by the door, poised for flight. I was beginning to see what was going on here; Ibarcena was gay — a fact that didn't really surprise me, given his appearance and mannerisms — and obviously had a penchant for young men. I'd interrupted a romantic interlude.

"Why is Beddoes upset?" I asked again.

Ibarcena sat down on the red couch, drawing his robe closer around him. "He has been under a very great strain since Elaine Picard's unfortunate death."

"Haven't we all." I sat down uninvited on the chair across from him. Behind me, Roger moved restively.

"Just what is it you want, Ms. McCone?" Ibarcena asked.

"I need to talk to you about Elaine. It seems she had discovered some illegal goings-on at the Casa del Rey shortly before her death. She'd written a letter to her lawyer."

Ibarcena's eyes narrowed and he leaned forward. "What was in that letter?"

"She detailed the things that were going on," I lied.

"And what were they?"

"Things about Nancy and Timmy Clark, for instance."

Ibarcena paled under his tan and drew back. His eyes darted from me to Roger, and he ran his tongue over his lips.

When he didn't speak, I added, "It was very convenient for you and Lloyd Beddoes that Elaine was killed when she was, wasn't it?"

Roger gave a sort of squeak. Ibarcena glanced anxiously at him. In a moment, he

244

cleared his throat and said, "Is what you are saying that Mr. Beddoes or I had something to do with Ms. Picard's accident?" His accent had become thicker and he stumbled over the question.

"For an accident, it was very good timing."

Ibarcena stiffened and stood up. "I do not like what you are hinting at, Ms. McCone. And I do not feel that I owe you any answer whatsoever. But to clear your mind of these suspicions, I think I should tell you that Mr. Beddoes and I were together in his office at the time of Ms. Picard's accident."

I remained sitting. "Again, it's convenient."

"Our secretary has confirmed this to the sheriff's men."

"Then you're in the clear."

"'There is nothing to be 'in the clear' about. Ms. Picard either threw herself off that tower or fell by accident."

"Tell me about Nancy and Timmy Clark, Mr. Ibarcena."

His face went red and he made a move as if to pull me to my feet, but at that moment footsteps sounded outside on the walkway. Lloyd Beddoes's voice called Ibarcena's name, and then Beddoes began pounding on the door.

Ibarcena flung out his arms in a gesture of despair. Behind me, Roger said, "It's the old switch-hitter himself."

"Be quiet." Ibarcena went to the door and opened it. Beddoes stood there, looking disheveled and hot. His thick blond hair was rumpled, as if he'd been clawing at it with his fingers.

"Come in, Lloyd," Ibarcena said calmly. "Do not try to break the door."

Beddoes half stumbled into the room. First he caught sight of me and he gaped. Then he spotted Roger. He turned to Ibarcena, shaking his head from side to side. "How could you, Victor? After everything? After all we've been?"

"Get Mr. Beddoes a drink, Roger," Ibarcena said. "It will calm him."

Roger started toward the tray he'd brought in earlier, but a furious look from Beddoes stopped him. The young man glanced around, as if looking for a place to hide, and then he stood still.

"Lloyd," Ibarcena said, "you must sit down and try to relax. Scenes like this are not good for your heart."

"There's nothing wrong with my heart."

"At your age . . ." Ibarcena shrugged.

I was amazed that Beddoes — the "fine figure" of a man, as June Paxton had said —

was gay. Or was he? Roger had called him a "switch-hitter." But what really surprised me was the change in Victor Ibarcena. A moment ago, he'd practically been cringing under my none-too-subtle accusations. Now he was cool, totally in control. A nasty light glinted in his eyes as he looked at Beddoes — something almost sadistic. He'd been Beddoes's lover, and now he was relishing the idea of casting him off for a mere boy.

Beddoes remained standing. "After all we've been to one another, I can't believe you'd take on this . . ."

"After all we've been, Lloyd?" Ibarcena's voice was cutting, and he smiled."You make yourself sound the model of fidelity. Must I remind you of your jaunts to that house of ill repute? At least *I* didn't go with a woman."

Beddoes backed up, blinking. "That wasn't—"

"Wasn't what?" Now Ibarcena advanced on him.

"It's only . . . It doesn't mean . . ."

"Do not tell me what it means. You have been having it both ways too long, Lloyd. And I am sick of it." Ibarcena glanced back at Roger, who still stood frozen. "Now I will not have to put up with you any longer."

Beddoes's face crumpled, and for a moment I thought he might cry. He made a strangled sound, then turned and fled from the room.

Ibarcena looked at me. "I suggest you follow him, Ms. McCone."

"So you and Beddoes were lovers. How's this going to affect your job?"

He came at me suddenly, grabbing my arm with bruising fingers. "I said, get out!"

He dragged me toward the door and shoved me through it, his face contorted with fury. I stumbled over the sill and almost fell into the juniper hedge. Ibarcena slammed the door, and the dead bolt turned. Inside, his voice was raised in wordless ranting.

I stood rubbing my arm. The man was certainly subject to sudden mood shifts. I was willing to bet poor Roger was still standing there as if he were playing Statues. And Lloyd Beddoes was nowhere to be seen.

22: *"Wolf"*

When I woke up on Monday morning, there was no longer any question that I would be staying on for at least one more day. So first thing after I got out of the shower, even though it wasn't eight yet, I called Kerry. She was always up by seven-thirty at the latest; and I missed her and wanted to hear her voice.

She sounded grouchy, and when I asked her how she was she said, "Crappy. That damn dog-food commercial."

"It didn't go well, huh?"

"No. We didn't finish shooting until last night."

"How come?"

"Trouble with the dogs."

"What dogs?"

"The goddamn mutts they brought in to eat Bowzer Bits. Don't be dense."

"What happened?"

"One of them bit Al Douglas, the director. Then it bit me."

"What? Are you all right?"

"I'll live. It was just a nip. But it still hurts."

"Where did you get nipped?"

"Never mind where."

"Not on your—"

"I said never mind."

"Poor baby. I'll kiss it and make it better when I get home."

"Like fun you will," she said. "And how was *your* weekend?"

"Also crappy. But I'm going to stick around here another day or two, just the same."

"What for?"

I told her what for. She didn't like it; she never likes it when I get involved in homicide cases. Which is all right, because I don't like it either.

"So you're working with that McCone woman," Kerry said. "She's attractive, isn't she."

"So are you."

"No fooling around?"

"Hell. She's young enough to be my daughter."

"So am I. That didn't stop you with me."

"Cut it out," I said. "Desist. You can worry

250

about my health, that's okay. But you don't have to worry about my virtue."

"Mmm. Take care of yourself, will you?"

I said I would. Then I told her that I missed her, and told her some other things, and she said maybe she'd let me kiss her dog bite and make it better, after all. I was smiling when I rang off and I thought she probably was too.

It was after eight by then. I called the airline and canceled my one-o'clock return flight and got an open reservation instead. While I had the directory out, I flipped open the Yellow Pages to "Investigators" to see if the Owens Detective Agency carried an ad. It did, a small one that said it opened for business "promptly at 9 a.m., Monday thru Friday."

I had a quick cup of coffee in the coffee shop and then took my rental car across the Coronado Bridge and downtown. The building that housed the Owens Agency was on Sixth Avenue between Broadway and E Street, a block that just missed being shabby. It was flanked on one side by a transient hotel and on the other by an out-of-business Mexican cafe. The lobby was empty except for a couple of potted plants and a big sand-filled urn. The elevator was old and cranky and made grumbling noises to itself, but it got me to the third and top floor in under five minutes.

I went down a hallway past a door marked LAVORATORY, another one marked DUTTON DESIGN & MANUFACTURING CO., a third that said K. M. ARDRY, ATTORNEY-AT-LAW — DIVORCE SPECIALIST. There didn't seem to be much going on behind the last two doors. Most people probably hadn't shown up for work yet.

The Owens Agency was at the far end. I tried the knob, half expecting to find it locked, but it turned under my hand and let me into an anteroom large enough for three cane-bottom chairs and two small tables. Nobody was in it. Opposite, bisecting the room, was a floor-to-ceiling partition made out of wallboard to waist level and old-fashioned pebbled glass the rest of the way up; a doorframe and a door were set in the middle of it, the door standing open, and on the other side I could see the rest of the office. I went over and poked my head through for a closer look. That part was empty too.

So maybe he's down in the john, I thought. I backed up to one of the cane-bottom chairs and sat down to wait.

Ten minutes went by. There weren't any magazines around; nothing at all on the tables except a lone ashtray. I sat there. But

I don't sit well without something to do with my hands or something to occupy my mind. I began to fidget, to cross and uncross my legs, to squirm my fanny around on the chair. I had quit smoking years ago and had no desire to start up again, but at times like this I found myself developing a vague hunger for a cigarette. At least smoking one would have been an activity.

From out in the hallway I heard footsteps, voices — but none of them came this far down. Other people arriving for work. And where the hell was Lauterbach? The air in the anteroom was warm and stuffy and smelled of stale cigarette smoke. You'd have thought the first thing anybody would do on a Monday morning would be to open a window, air the place out a little.

Well, maybe Lauterbach *hadn't* come in yet. But then why was the door unlocked? Was he that careless — go off on Friday or Saturday and forget to secure his office? Could be. Lots of people are careless. And he might have been in a hurry, distracted — even drunk, given Lauterbach's apparent taste for the sauce.

Another five minutes of just sitting was all I could take. I got up and tried to pace, but the anteroom was too small for that. All right, what the hell: I went through the open door into the back half of the office.

Old kneehole desk that looked as if it had come out of a cheap secondhand store. Windows behind it that looked out on Sixth Avenue and a parking lot across the street. Bank of file cabinets, the top drawer of one pulled open. A table with stacks of police-science brochures, F.B.I. flyers, electronics magazines, and bulletins from the National Society of Investigators. A smaller table containing a hot plate, a coffeepot, a jar of coffee, a jar of peanut butter, a package of crackers, a box of sugar, an almost empty fifth of Ten High bourbon, a dirty knife, a dirty coffee cup, a dirty glass with a cigarette butt lying on the bottom like a dead bug, and a sifting of crumbs. The walls were bare except for a framed photostat of Lauterbach's California license and another of his Michigan license. And that was all there was to see. No electronic equipment, which struck me as a little odd, considering Lauterbach's apparent fondness for the stuff. But then maybe he kept whatever he had in his trailer or locked in the trunk of his car.

I wandered over to the desk, letting myself feel annoyed at Lauterbach's absence so I would have an excuse to snoop. The desktop was cluttered but not half as sloppy as the inside of his trailer; if it hadn't been for the remains of his lunch or breakfast or whatever, the office would have been moderately neat. Telephone, pens and pencils, typing paper, a notepad, part of last Friday's *San Diego Union* — that was all.

Two of the desk drawers were pulled out a little; I went around behind the desk with the idea of opening them a little more, so I could see what they contained. As I bent toward the lower one my foot snagged one leg of the chair, which was pushed up into the kneehole, and scraped the thing back a few inches. Inside the kneehole something fell over with a small plopping sound. I moved the chair the rest of the way out and bent down to peer under there. A briefcase. It had been propped against the inside of the kneehole — a sort of semihiding place, I supposed, where a man like Lauterbach would put something large that he didn't want out in plain sight.

I didn't move for a couple of seconds, looking at the briefcase and listening. There wasn't anything to hear except muted traffic sounds from the street and the distant clacking of somebody's typewriter. So then I dragged the case out and put it on the desk and opened it. The only item inside was a thick manila file folder with a typed name on the tag at its top.

Well, well, I thought. Sometimes it pays to be as clumsy as I am: you stumble on the damnedest things.

I flipped open the folder with my fore-finger. The first thing I saw was a 5" x 7" photograph, in color, clipped to a sheaf of papers. There were two people and a boat in the photo. The boat was the yacht variety, small and sleek with gleaming brightwork. The woman was Elaine Picard, wearing slacks and a tank top and a windblown look, smiling at the camera. The man, dressed in white ducks and a blue blazer and a yacht-ing cap, was the same gray-haired military type I'd seen in the hotel parking lot on Friday night — Henry Nyland.

I unclipped the photo and turned it over. There wasn't anything written on the re-verse. I put it back and shuffled through the sheaf of papers. The first few were from the desk notepad or one like it, a lot of hen scratches and what I took to be a personal code; but the gist of it was clear enough; Henry Nyland had hired Lauterbach six weeks ago to investigate Elaine Picard. And he'd done it because he suspected there was another man in her life, and because he was afraid she was involved in "something bizarre." If he had speculated about what that something might be, Lauterbach hadn't written it down.

The rest of the papers were carbons of reports he'd sent to Nyland at an address on Coronado, and notes scribbled to himself at various points of his investigation. There wasn't much in the reports. According to what Lauterbach had told Nyland, Elaine's behavior had been normal and above reproach; as far as he'd been able to determine, she hadn't had any clandestine dealings with men.

But the scribbled notes seemed to tell a different story. Most of them were indecipherable — the personal shorthand again — but there were some references to Rich Woodall, who had evidently bothered Elaine while she was eating lunch in a restaurant one day and whose name Lauterbach had got by checking the license number of Woodall's car through the D.M.V. Other references told me that Elaine regularly spent time at or near Borrego Springs, at some sort of club. On one sheet was a list of names, a few of which had check marks in front of them. I recognized three: Woodall, Lloyd Beddoes, and Karyn Sugarman.

At the bottom of the folder was a plain white business-size envelope. When I opened it, I found half a dozen black-and-

257

white photographs taken with a wide-angle lens. A couple of them were off-center and the rest were not quite in focus, as if they'd been hurriedly snapped; but you could see that all of them were of a big, odd-looking house somewhere in the desert, a sort of free-form thing that blended into the jumble of high, jagged rocks against which it had been built. Parked in front of the house were a number of cars. In one of the photos, more of the desert itself was visible — an open part that contained the usual vegetation and what looked to be the remains of an old spur railroad track, a decaying water tower, and a dilapidated loading platform of some kind. None of the photographs bore any written notations.

I couldn't find any significance in them. They just weren't very good or very clear, which made me wonder if maybe there were more, if these were culls from an entire roll of film. If so, the rest weren't in the folder and they probably weren't anywhere in the office.

Then again, I thought, it wouldn't hurt to look.

I put the photos back in the envelope, the envelope back under the papers, the folder back into the briefcase, and the case back inside the kneehole. The two partly open desk drawers didn't contain any photographs or further information on Elaine Picard; neither did the other two drawers. Nothing of interest at all, unless you considered a rolled pair of socks an interesting thing to keep in a desk drawer.

I shut the last one and turned toward the file cabinets. Maybe there was something enlightening in there. Something on Nancy and Timmy Clark, for instance —

Out in the hallway, a woman screamed.

The cry came again and kept on coming, cutting through the walls like a knife through sponge cake. I wheeled around with my scalp prickling and ran out through the anteroom, yanked the door open, and lumbered into the hall. She was down at the far end near the elevator, backed up against the wall, pointing and yowling. I started to run toward her, but men and women were spilling out of the offices of the Dutton Design & Manufacturing Co. and K. M. Ardry, Divorce Specialist, and they got in my way.

One of the men grabbed the screaming woman, a fortyish secretarial type with glasses hanging on a chain over her flat chest. "What is it, Millie? For God's sake, what's happened?"

"In there!" she said, screeching the words.

She was still pointing, not at the elevator, as I'd first thought, but at the door to the lavatory. "In there, in there!"

The guy started toward the john, but I got to the door ahead of him and shoved inside. I didn't see anything wrong at first, not until I got to where I could look into the open stall to one side. There was a dead man inside it, one leg hooked over the toilet and the rest of him wedged back against the wall. One of his eyes was wide open; the other was now a black-edged hole full of dried blood. Shot. Not once, at least four times: there were also bloody holes in his chest, in his neck, in his right arm.

I had finally caught up with Jim Lauterbach. And from the way the body looked, he'd been dead most of the time I had been trying to find him.

23: McCone

At nine-thirty Monday morning I called Elaine's lawyer, Alan Thorburn. At first he was reluctant even to see me — Elaine's affairs were confidential, he insisted — but when I mentioned I worked for All Souls, he allowed as how he had gone to school with our tax attorney, Anne-Marie Altman. Could he get back to me in a few minutes? he asked.

I waited, knowing Thorburn was calling Anne-Marie to check me out. I wondered if she would guess I'd stumbled onto an unofficial investigation. Probably; she'd been with the co-op as long as I had and had been watching me do just that for years.

After about fifteen minutes Thorburn called back, sounding considerably more friendly. He could see me at eleven-thirty, he said, and gave me a suite number in one of the newer high-rises downtown.

Since I had time to kill, I went to the kitchen to see if there was any coffee. A couple of cups remained in the percolator, so I poured myself one and sat down in the breakfast nook to think. The house was quiet; my mother was off at Safeway, Pa was out on a job, and Charlene and the kids had gone back to L.A. the previous evening. Joey was at work, his latest attempt at a career being a supervisory position at a MacDonald's. John, as far as I knew, was still asleep.

After I'd left Ibarcena's apartment late yesterday afternoon, I'd tried to hunt up Beddoes, but with no luck. Either he hadn't gone home or he wasn't answering his phone or his door. Then I'd gone back down my list of other people to talk to, but had similar bad fortune. I didn't know what they did, but the people Elaine had known must have made the most of their Sundays. Finally, at around eight o'clock, I'd taken myself back to my parents' house.

John had been the only one home, and I'd joined him in the living room to watch an old movie on TV and drink a couple of beers. We'd said little until about ten-thirty, when, during one of the long commercial breaks, he'd again brought up the subject of getting custody of his kids.

Maybe it was the general frustration of the

day, or maybe it was the nagging worry in the back of my mind about Don and his so-called cousin, but whatever caused it, I became very stuffy with John. "You know," I said, "before you start any expensive court proceedings, you might consider going back to work and finding your own place to live."

"I'll get to that."

"Like hell you will. How long has it been since she threw you out?"

"A couple of months is all."

"And how long since you worked?"

He shrugged.

"Also a couple of months. John, you've got that contractor's license. If you don't want to work for yourself, there are lots of firms that would hire you."

Nothing from him but the sound of a pull-top popping on a beer can.

"If you really want custody of those kids, you'll have to prove to the court that you can support them — and give them a decent home."

"Ma—"

"Ma's already raised her family."

"She said she'd help."

"Sure, help. But not raise them. Besides, no judge is going to take the kids away from their natural mother under circumstances like these."

"Since when are you a lawyer?"

"I don't have to be a lawyer to know that."

He turned to face me, his long chin jutting out defiantly. "I want those kids, Shar."

"Do you? Maybe you just like to talk about it. Because it makes people feel sorry for you."

And at that he got up and stalked out of the room. And I had watched the rest of the movie feeling stuffy and selfrighteous and ashamed, because I loved him and I'd hurt him.

Now I sat in the sunny breakfast nook, drinking my coffee and wondering what I was really accomplishing here. I'd missed the whole convention, and instead of spending time with my family as I'd planned, I was chasing all over San Diego trying to prove Elaine Picard hadn't killed herself or fallen from that tower by accident. And why? She had been a friend, but not a close one, and that friendship had been put on hold years ago. There were lots of people here I'd been closer to, including the women who'd acted scared of me at the party the other night. Why all this frantic activity over Elaine?

Because, I told myself, you're an investigator. Not somebody who just works at it nine to five, but a person who lives it every hour, every day. You can't escape it; it's in your blood.

Besides, I added, there's something illegal going on at the Casa del Rey, something involving the little boy Wolf met, and you want to get to the bottom of it. And you keep seeing Elaine's pensive face, with the little lines of tension and shadows under her eyes — strain that was probably caused by her awareness of the illegal goings-on.

And, finally, I kept on thinking that if only we'd had the talk Sugarman had said Elaine had wanted — a real talk rather than superficial chat about houses and boyfriends — she might not have died the other day. . . .

I looked at my watch and realized I'd just have time to get downtown for my eleven-thirty appointment.

Alan Thorburn's office was plush and modern, with a fine view of the bridge and Coronado Island. Thorburn himself surprised me. He was young-looking, bespectacled, and saved from being homely only by a boyish, almost bumbling charm. I wondered how he could afford such offices; surely anyone of his appearance could not attract the high-paying clients necessary to foot the bills. But when I shook his hand, I saw the wrinkles that the boyish manner had at first made me overlook and I caught the gleam of keen intelligence in his eyes. Alan Thorburn was neither young nor incompetent; his mannerisms had probably fooled a good many people — and fooled them to his advantage.

We sat down and I explained my relationship to Elaine and my suspicions about her death. Thorburn listened quietly, only reacting when I mentioned the carbon of her letter to him and the clipping she'd supposedly enclosed. "I guess," I said, "that the sheriff's department will be calling on you soon, wanting to see that clipping. But I'd like to get a look at it too."

He thought a moment, then reached over and pressed a button on his intercom. When a woman's voice answered, he said, "Linda, has anyone from the sheriff's department asked to see me regarding Elaine Picard this morning?"

"No one."

He glanced at me. "That shows how strong their interest in her death is."

"I'm sorry?" the voice on the intercom said.

"Never mind. Will you bring me her file, please?"

In a moment the secretary entered and placed a large manila folder on Thorburn's desk. He looked though the papers in it, then extended a newspaper clipping to me. "Maybe it will make sense to you. Frankly, it's had me puzzled, and I'd be glad of an explanation."

The clipping was from the *San Diego Union,* dated on a Thursday about six weeks before, and headlined MYSTERY DISAPPEARANCE OF LA JOLLA FINANCIER. I read on.

Oilman and financier Roland Deveer, 56, was reported missing from his La Jolla home yesterday by his wife, Celia.

Deveer, whose financial empire includes interests in Alaskan and South American oil drilling ventures, was last seen leaving his home at 4 p.m. on Tuesday, presumably to attend a meeting at his company's downtown San Diego headquarters. His 1984 Cadillac Seville was later found abandoned in a loading zone at Lindbergh Field. Checks with the airlines have indicated Deveer did not take any commercial flight from the airport.

Mrs. Deveer states that she knows of no reason why her husband would disappear voluntarily. . . .

I turned the clipping over, just to make sure there wasn't something on the other side that was more relevant to Elaine's letter, but found only part of an ad for men's suits. I reread the clipping, but could make no sense of it. What did a missing oilman have to do with the illegal activities at Casa del Rey? Or with Elaine?

When I looked up, Thorburn was watching me expectantly. "This doesn't mean a thing to me, either," I said. "Did Elaine know this Roland Deveer?"

"I'm not sure, although I doubt they traveled in the same circles — Deveer is married to a socially prominent woman and active in high-toned civic causes. But then I didn't know much about Elaine's personal life."

"Apparently no one did." I remembered Rich Woodall and his claim that Elaine was mother to a gorilla named Fred. "Do you know anything about her tax situation?"

"A little."

"Had Elaine made any large donations to the San Diego Zoo in the last year or so?"

"The zoo?"

"Their Adopt-an-Animal Program. The adoptee may have been a gorilla."

Thorburn smiled faintly. "I doubt it. She and I met semiannually with her tax practitioner, Hugh Katz. I'm certain that kind of deduction would have come in for some humorous comment."

"I guess so. May I have a copy of this clipping?"

Thorburn nodded and took it out to the reception area, then returned in a minute with a Xerox copy. "Do you intend to pursue this unofficial investigation?" he asked.

I put the clipping in my purse and stood up. "What makes you think it's unofficial?"

"Something Anne-Marie said when I called her."

I smiled. "She knows me too well. But in answer to your question — yes, I do."

"Well, I suppose you know the dangers of that. If you need any legal advice, call me. And let me know what you find out."

I thanked him and assured him I'd be in touch — only to report my findings, I hoped. But on the other hand, it was nice to know who to call if I got arrested again.

I stopped at a phone booth down the street and called Roland Deveer's wife in La Jolla. She agreed to see me as soon as I could get there. If anything, the woman, who spoke in a low, cultured voice, seemed overly eager to talk with a total stranger who had merely identified herself as a private investigator interested in Mr. Deveer's disappearance. Perhaps I would find out something useful from her.

★★★

The Deveer home was English Tudor, set well back on a pristine lawn. A uniformed maid answered my knock and led me through a large hallway and across a sun porch to a terrace paved with old-fashioned flagstones. A tall, thin woman rose from one of the wicker porch chairs and came forward to greet me.

"I'm Celia Deveer," she said, extending her hand. "You must be Ms. McCone."

"Yes. Thank you for taking the time to see me."

"I'm glad to meet with anyone who may have information concerning my husband's disappearance. May I offer you some coffee?"

"That sounds good."

She nodded at the maid, and the woman went back in the house. As we sat down on the wicker chairs, I studied Celia Deveer. She was almost painfully thin, with coiffed dark hair and a long, angular face that was too sharp-featured to be really attractive. Though her beige pants suit was expensively tailored, the overall impression she gave was not of money but of good breeding. As a girl, she would have attended private schools, had riding lessons at the hunt club, gone to summer drama camp, and acquitted herself nicely in piano recitals. And because she was so unattractive, she would have been the debutante whom the organizers of the Cotillion had worried about, the one they'd despaired of ever finding a suitable match for. Looking at her, I wondered what Roland Deveer was like.

The terrace where we sat was at the top of a hill that sloped gently to a formal garden. A Mexican man, wearing a straw hat against the heat of the sun, was at work down there, edging the lawn around the flower beds. I said, "You have a lovely home. It's refreshingly old-fashioned, compared to so many places in this area."

"Thank you." She helped the maid settle a tray onto the table between us, then poured coffee into delicate white cups. "It was my family's home, and I was glad to move back into it after my father died. Mr. Deveer didn't care for it, I'm afraid. He would have preferred a modern house in the hills, or perhaps a place at the beach. Although he never said so, of course."

Why "of course"? I wondered.

Celia Deveer handed me my coffee. "Now tell me, what information do you have concerning my husband?"

"It's not much to go on, but you may be able to tell me something that will give it

271

more significance. Did Mr. Deveer have any connection with the Casa del Rey hotel?"

"You mean on the Silver Strand?"

"Yes."

"Not that I know of. Oh, we'd attended the usual functions there from time to time. I came out in its ballroom, in fact. Why?"

"Their security chief, who died last weekend, seemed to think there was some connection."

She sipped her coffee, looking meditatively off at the garden. "I can't think what it would be. My husband was nowhere near the Casa del Rey when he disappeared."

"They found his car at the airport?"

"Yes. But he didn't take a flight out — at least not a commercial flight. That, however, means very little. Roland had a number of friends and associates with private planes. He could have left on any of them."

"But surely the police have checked that."

"Yes, they did. No one with any connection to my husband filed a flight plan that day. But again, that doesn't mean much."

"Why not?"

She smiled bitterly. "For a price, almost any pilot can be persuaded not to file a flight plan."

I paused, unsure how to ask the next question. Finally I just plunged ahead. "In

272

the newspaper account I read, you said you didn't know of any reason your husband would disappear voluntarily. Now you seem to have changed your mind."

The bitter lines around her mouth deepened. "Yes, I have, because certain things have come to light since his disappearance. Roland's business enterprises were quite far-flung and complicated. A few months ago, he mentioned there might be some tax complications, something to do with our personal tax affairs having become mixed up with those of one of his holding companies. I was not to worry, he said, but I might be required to sign some forms."

"And did you?"

"No."

"So perhaps the trouble amounted to nothing."

"Or perhaps Roland didn't want me to know how bad it was." She set her cup down and turned to face me, anger plain on her face. "You see, Ms. McCone, my husband attempted to shield me from the crude realities of his business whenever possible. I was to keep the home, raise the children, and amuse myself in typical genteel ways. But the home keeps itself, the children are grown, and I've never been contented with bridge or with volunteer work. I begged

Roland to give me a more active part in his business affairs, but he flatly refused. I'm not a stupid woman, though, and I've done a fair amount of reading about finance. I know when something is wrong."

"Did you ever broach the subject again, after the first time he mentioned it?"

"Yes. He told me not to trouble myself about it. I wasn't equipped, he said, to understand." She smiled, a caricature of mirth. "I find his assumption highly amusing. After all, I was the one who put Roland Deveer where he is today. Or where he was before he disappeared. *I* was the one who forced him to success. It was my money that founded his empire and kept it going through those first rough years. It was my prodding that kept *him* going. Roland Deveer was nobody when I married him. Nobody. And now he's gone off and left. . . ."

She paused, looking embarrassed. Ladies of her class didn't blurt out their anger and resentments in front of strangers. Quickly I said, "I understand. So often it's the woman who is responsible for the man's success. But the man gets all the credit."

"Yes. That was exactly the way it was with Roland and me. And now . . ."

"Now?"

"Now I don't know. Something had to be terribly wrong for him to disappear the way he did. And I'm afraid that when it all comes out, it will be left for me to clear it up. But after his betrayal of me, I'm not sure I have the strength. Or the resources."

"You mean financially?"

"Yes, Ms. McCone, financially. One of the things I've discovered in this last month is that Roland closed out all of our joint accounts, and liquidated a number of assets."

"Is there any logical reason for that? Is he a gambler, for instance?"

"No, Roland was very strongly opposed to any sort of gambling. He felt it brought out man's latent stupidity."

"What about foul play? Could he have taken the cash out for some sort of business deal and been murdered by someone who knew he was carrying it?"

"His business arrangements seldom involved cash — and certainly not in that amount."

"Then he disappeared with a substantial amount of money?"

"Very substantial."

To a woman of Celia Deveer's background, I imagined, "very substantial" would be large indeed. "Mrs. Deveer," I said, "did your husband have an office here at home? Somewhere he might keep personal papers?"

"His study, yes. But I've been through it, and so have the police."

"Would you allow me to go through it? It's possible something in there might have some other significance to me than either to you or the police."

She hesitated. Her instinct for privacy seemed to be fighting with her anger at her husband. Anger won out. "Yes, Ms. McCone, I believe I will allow that. Come this way."

We went inside and back across the hall to a door at its far end. Unlike the other doors leading off there, it was closed, as if Celia Deveer were attempting to shut off all reminders of her husband. She opened it and motioned for me to go in.

The room was paneled in dark wood, with built-in floor-to-ceiling bookcases. The volumes in them looked old and well-read. On the floor was a worn Oriental carpet, and a large mahogany desk stood in a recess by the windows.

"This was originally my father's study," Celia Deveer said. "Roland has not improved the library by so much as one book."

I went over to the desk and began going through its drawers. The center one yielded the usual paper clips and pens and pencils. The top one on the right contained stationery, some printed with the address in La Jolla and some with Deveer Enterprises' address downtown. In the drawer below that, I found a handgun — a .22, fully loaded and well oiled. I held it up questioningly.

Mrs. Deveer said, "Roland had a terrible fear of burglars, even though the house is wired with an alarm system."

I nodded and put the gun back in the drawer. The other drawers held supplies and back copies of annual reports and other business publications.

On the desktop was a blotter, an onyx pen-and-pencil holder, and the standard desk calendar you'd find in any office. There was nothing written on the blotter, or hidden under it. Finally I started through the calendar, beginning a few months ago, when Mrs. Deveer said he had first mentioned possible financial problems to her, and continuing up to the day he disappeared. It contained the usual notations of social and business appointments, including the meeting he'd supposedly left to attend the afternoon he'd last been seen.

There was nothing I could see that was out of the ordinary in the calendar or the desk. I planned to continue searching, of course, taking out each drawer to see if anything was taped to its bottom or had fallen behind it, shaking out the pages of each book on the shelves. But I doubted I'd find anything of significance.

I kept flipping through the calendar, looking at appointments Deveer had made and never kept. There were plenty, but that didn't mean anything; he could have put them down to make his disappearance seem unintentional. But there, on September 18th, was a notation that did mean something to me: the familiar phone number of the Casa del Rey. Above it was the word "arrangements." And below it was another number with a familiar look.

Reaching in my bag for Elaine's address book, I said, "Mrs. Deveer, is the date September eighteenth significant to your husband in any way?"

"Yes, it's his birthday."

His birthday. What better place to note something down where he could easily find it but where others would not be likely to look?

I took out the address book, looked up Lloyd Beddoes's home phone number, and compared it with the second one on the calendar. They matched.

24: "Wolf"

I spent better than two hours in and around Lauterbach's office while the S.D.P.D. homicide boys went about their grim business. The cop in charge was named Gunderson. I told him everything I knew, but I didn't get into any of the suspicions about Elaine Picard's death, the disappearance of Nancy and Timmy Clark, or illegal activities on the part of Lloyd Beddoes and Victor Ibarcena. For one thing, despite Lauterbach's connection to Elaine and to the Clarks, none of those matters might relate to his murder. And for another thing, the sheriff's department was handling the Picard case and the hotel was their jurisdiction; Tom Knowles was the man to talk to on those fronts.

By keeping my ears open during the time I was on the scene, I found out that Lauterbach had been dead close to twenty-four hours — since Sunday noon at the latest. The first person to try to use the lavatory this morning was the screaming woman who'd found him, K. M. Ardry's flat-chested secretary. He had been shot with a small-caliber weapon at close range; two of the entry holes bore the scorching, cruciate tears, and powder tattooing that mark contact and near-contact wounds. The murder weapon hadn't been in the lavatory and apparently wasn't anywhere else in the building. A search of Lauterbach's office revealed nothing directly linked to the shooting. Nor did the people from Dutton Design & Manufacturing and the divorce specialist's office know anything useful; none of them had been in the building the day before. They also didn't know if Lauterbach was in the habit of coming in to his office on Sundays — but he could have done it easily enough, in any case, because each tenant had a key to the front entrance.

Not much in any of that, except that it provided a rough fix as to the time of death. The coroner would probably be able to pare it down closer at the postmortem.

When Gunderson finally said I could leave, I had every intention of talking to Knowles first thing. The problem was, he wasn't in when I got to the sheriff's department on West C Street and nobody could tell me just when he'd be back. The best estimation was "sometime this afternoon" from another plainclothes officer.

On my way to where I'd parked the rental car, I did some brooding about Lauterbach's death. Why had he been killed? Because he was investigating Elaine Picard? Well, maybe. But if he'd found out anything that made him a candidate for homicide, I hadn't been able to see it in his notes. It was also possible that there was a connection between his murder and whatever was going on at the Casa del Rey, and with Elaine Picard's death. But if that was it, I couldn't even guess what it might be. And where did Rich Woodall and a place called Borrego Springs and a house somewhere in the desert fit in?

I gave it up for the time being and considered stopping somewhere for coffee and a sandwich. Only I had no appetite; Lauterbach's blood-caked face, the bullet hole where his left eye had once been, had seen to that. I wondered if I should look up Henry Nyland, to ask him why he'd hired Lauterbach to investigate Elaine, but I decided against it. That was Tom Knowles's prerogative, and Gunderson's. And if there was anything else to be found out, anything

Nyland might not tell the authorities, McCone could probably get at it better than I could. She had more of a vested interest in all of this than I did.

A few blocks from the sheriff's department I stopped for a traffic light. There was a secondhand bookshop across the street, with a big sign that caught my eye — and it reminded me of what Charley Valdene had told me about Beddoes's interest in pornography. Not much of an angle in that, maybe, but I could check out the shop where Valdene had run into Beddoes; Charley had given me the name and address. It was something to do, at least, until I could connect with Knowles.

When I reached the address, out past Balboa Park near University Avenue, I found myself at a newish, boxy, five-story office building, with a realtor's sign out front that said OFFICE SPACE FOR RENT. The occupied space seemed to belong mostly to lawyers, architects, and other professional people: all very upper middle class and proper. I wondered as I scanned the lobby directory if Valdene might have made a mistake with the address. But he hadn't; I found the listing near the bottom — PRIAPUS BOOKS AND CURIOS, 5E.

The elevator deposited me on the fifth

floor. I went down a carpeted hallway until I came to 5E. Except for a tiny magnifying-glass peephole, the numeral and the letter were all that was on the door; but on the jamb, above an inlaid bell button, was a fancy scrolled business card tucked into a metal frame. It read:

PRIAPUS

Books and Curios

MAXWELL LITTLEJOHN   ADULTS ONLY

I pushed the inlaid button. Nothing happened for a time, but I got the feeling I was being studied through the peephole. I tried to look like a guy with an interest in erotica instead of what I was, and I must have managed all right; there was the sound of a lock snicking free and the door popped open and the guy standing there said pleasantly, "Yes? May I help you?"

He looked like somebody's kindly grandfather. He was about sixty-five, he had wispy white hair and a wispy white mustache and polished-apple cheeks, and he was decked out in a conservative three-piece gray suit and a bow tie. He didn't surprise me much. Purveyors of pornographic art, like everybody else, come in all shapes, sizes, ages, and dispositions.

I said, "Mr. Littlejohn?"

"At your service. I don't believe I know you, sir."

"Ah, no, you don't. I've never been here before."

"May I ask how you learned of Priapus?"

"You were recommended by a friend — Lloyd Beddoes."

He beamed at me. "Yes, of course, Mr. Beddoes is one of my most valued customers. And your name, sir?"

"Wade. Ivan Wade."

"Come in, Mr. Wade. Please come in."

He stepped back and I went into an area carpeted in plush wine — red, softly lighted, and outfitted as a showroom. There were glass cases along three of the four walls, another in the middle of the room. The cases were full of books and carvings and things, none of which appeared to be particularly erotic when I got close enough to see what they were. The same was true of the paintings, pen-and-ink sketches, and woodcuts illuminated on the walls. It all might have been pretty hot stuff thirty years ago, but in this permissive age it wouldn't stimulate anyone — except maybe a sheltered old maid or a member of the Moral Majority.

Littlejohn watched me browse for a couple of minutes. Then he asked, "Did you have anything particular in mind, Mr. Wade?"

"Well, something a little more — you know, graphic."

"Books? Art?"

"I'm not sure. Is this all you have?"

"Oh no. This room is for my more conservative clientele. I have another that might prove more suitable. Priapus wouldn't be worthy of the name if it didn't offer something for the taste of every connoisseur."

"It wouldn't?"

"Ah, you're not familiar with the mythological reference?"

"No, I'm afraid not."

"In Greek mythology, Priapus was the son of Dionysus, best loved son of Zeus, and the god of wine and pleasure. Priapus was the god of virility and procreation; his symbol was an erect penis."

"Oh," I said.

"Will you follow me, Mr. Wade?"

I followed him — into another room, much larger than the first one but similarly appointed. There was also a desk unobtrusively tucked into one corner, and beside it a portable bar that appeared to be well stocked. Littlejohn asked me if I cared for an aperitif; I said no thanks. Then we got down to the real stuff, the most erotic and no doubt most expensive items in Littlejohn's stock.

First he showed me what he called "Dionysian literature": old books, many of them beautifully bound in leather — copies of the *Chin P'ing Mei* from China, *Harlot's Dialogues* from Italy, *Fanny Hill* from England, Sade's *Justine* and *Juliette*. Then it was Rajput miniatures from India, delicate Chinese Ming scrolls, small screen blocks and painted scrolls and two-hundred-year-old folding paper fans from Japan; wooden statues and carvings from Madagascar, Central Africa, the Philippines, silver figurines from Peru, bronze figurines from the Ivory Coast, a humorous phallic demon from Bali; paintings and sketches, both primitive and modern, from all over Europe and from the United States. Some of the stuff was downright obscene, but in the main it was highly sensual. I found myself thinking that it was a good thing I'd come here and not McCone; a few of the items made *me* blush. But that was my paternal streak again. McCone was a grown woman, as she'd tartly reminded me. For all I knew, she might have enjoyed all of this much more than I did.

Littlejohn gave me a running commentary on each of the objects we looked at, beaming on them in a paternal way of his own. "Erotica from every culture has passed through Priapus," he said. "Think of it, Mr. Wade. Every culture of man! The human animal has always been fascinated by matters of the flesh, always paid tribute to his desires."

"Uh-huh. Tell me, what kind of erotica fascinates Lloyd Beddoes the most?"

He looked mildly surprised. "You haven't seen his collection?"

"Ah . . . well, no, not his recent acquisitions. I've been out of the country for a while. On business."

It was flimsy, but all he said was "What business are you in, Mr. Wade?"

"Oil exploration."

"Very lucrative, that sort of thing, isn't it?"

"I do pretty well," I said.

"Yes, of course. Well, Mr. Beddoes prefers items with homosexual and S and M themes, naturally."

"Why 'naturally'?"

This time Littlejohn frowned. "You really don't know Mr. Beddoes very well, do you?"

"Not really, no. He's — a friend of a friend."

"Indeed? May I ask who that is?"

I had backed myself into a corner. Trying to get out of it, I said the first thing that came to my mind, "A fellow in Borrego Springs. He, ah, belongs to the club out there."

It was the right thing to say, even though I had no idea why. Littlejohn beamed again and said, "Mr. Darrow?"

Darrow was one of the names that had been on the list among Lauterbach's notes, one of those with a check mark in front of it. I said, "That's right. Arthur Darrow. You know him, then?"

"Oh, yes. He and his charming wife both. Lovely people. They buy from me occasionally, you know."

"I didn't know that. The same sort of items Beddoes is interested in?"

"Somewhat. Although their tastes generally run more to the heterosexual."

I pretended to study a complicated Oriental silk painting. "Does Beddoes come in often?"

"Oh, yes," Littlejohn said. "Every week or two."

"Does he buy much?"

"Well, I do consider him one of my best customers. He has a very large collection."

"All homosexual and S and M stuff?"

"For the most part. Just last week I found a marvelous whipping statuette from Germany for him. And before that, a rare first edition of *Teleny, or the Reverse of the Medal* — one of the earliest and best of the homosexual erotic novels, published in 1893 and quite probably written by Oscar Wilde." Littlejohn beamed again, but there was a glint of avarice in his eyes. He was telling me all this because he thought I had money to spend and that I would be impressed by his ability to satisfy his customers. I was impressed, all right. But not the way he thought.

I said, "Items like that rare first edition must be pretty expensive."

"One must always pay well for the rare and the unusual. Don't you agree, Mr. Wade?"

"Sure. Always."

"And may I ask what you've seen that strikes *your* fancy?"

I hesitated. I wanted to ask him some more questions about Beddoes, and about the Darrows of Borrego Springs, but I couldn't figure a way to do it without arousing his suspicions. And if his suspicions got aroused, he'd be on the phone thirty seconds after I walked out the door, telling Beddoes and the Darrows all about my visit.

The smart thing for me to do was to back off and be satisfied, for now, with what I had already learned.

To make it look as if my hesitation had been over one of his offerings, I reached out and picked up an item at random. "What would this set me back?"

"Ah," Littlejohn said. His smile got wider and the gleam in his eyes got brighter. "An excellent choice, sir. A truly excellent choice. That figure is from the third or fourth century B.C., of Mexican origin. Note the simplicity of the design, the superior condition of the terra-cotta. A rare work of art. I know of only three others like it in existence."

"How much?"

"I could let you have it for five thousand."

"*How* much?"

"Five thousand dollars. A bargain at that price, Mr. Wade. A bargain."

I took a closer look at the thing in my hand. And then put it down in a hurry. "Well, uh, I'll have to think it over, Mr. Littlejohn. Five thousand might be a little out of my price range."

But it wasn't the price that made me put the figure down so fast. It was what the thing was — for all I knew, a statuette of old Priapus himself. The guy it depicted was

290

naked and grinning, probably because he had the biggest jutting phallus you ever saw. And *that*, for God's sake, was what I had been holding it by.

25: McCone

Lloyd Beddoes looked terrible. He sat hunched on the edge of his couch, wearing a blue shirt and pants that he must have slept in. Yesterday afternoon his hair had had the appearance of having been clawed at; now it looked like someone had been working on it with a rake. His face was pale and drawn, his eyes red. I couldn't decide if he'd been crying or had a bad hangover — or both.

I'd spent a while longer at the Deveer place, making a thorough search of the office and Deveer's personal belongings, in the hopes of turning up a more concrete link between the financier and Beddoes, but nothing had materialized. Then I'd called to see if Beddoes was at home and, on hearing his subdued voice, had hung up without speaking and driven to his shingle-and-glass home perched high on a bluff in Point Loma. To my surprise, he'd admitted me without a protest, almost indifferently, and now he was trying to ignore my presence.

In spite of his wretched appearance, I had an irresistible urge to needle him. "Are you feeling okay, Mr. Beddoes?" I asked, sitting down on the other end of the couch.

He gave me a baleful sidelong look. "What do you think?"

"That was a nasty scene yesterday at Victor Ibarcena's."

"No more than I should have expected from the little faggot. But surely you didn't come here to talk about my emotional life. What is it?"

I got up and began moving around the room. It was expensively furnished, in nubby brown-and-white fabrics and good teakwood, and had a panoramic view of the sea. The walls were covered with abstract prints and drawings, and several of the glass-fronted cabinets contained what looked to be valuable curios.

Beddoes's eyes followed me slowly, as if the effort hurt. When I didn't answer, he said, "This is what I get for allowing a convention of private investigators to meet at my hotel. First my head of security dies violently, and then I'm beset by detectives."

"Who else besides me?"

"A big Italian-looking fellow who's staying

at the hotel. I forget his name."

Wolf. I pretended ignorance and asked, "Why is he bothering you?"

Beddoes waved a weary hand. "He seems to be finding fault with our establishment in every way possible. I won't go into it."

I continued to pace around the room. Beddoes was in bad shape, and even a small amount of pressure might make him crack and tell me more than he wished to. I stopped in front of a large ink drawing — sweeping lines that at a distance made no sense. Leaning closer, I examined the patterns they made, then drew back in surprise. It represented three, or maybe four, people engaged in various kinds of sexual activity with various parts of one another's bodies. Whips too. And ropes.

I looked at some of the other drawings. They were definitely interesting — and I supposed a couple of them could have been arousing, if I hadn't been here for reasons far removed from looking at high-class porn. One thing I found significant was that few were strictly homosexual in content — bearing out young Roger's comment about the "old switch-hitter."

When I looked back at Beddoes, he was staring blankly out the window at the sea. I went to the nearest curio cabinet and checked out the statuettes displayed there. They were of the same ilk as the drawings; the one that held my attention was a Mexican pottery rendition of the classical three monkeys — see no evil, hear no evil, speak no evil. These weren't seeing, hearing, or speaking, but they sure were *doing,* in every way their little monkey brains could possibly have thought up.

Beddoes was still looking away from me. I went back to the couch, sat down again, and said, "What about Roland Deveer, Mr. Beddoes?"

He twitched convulsively, glanced at me, and then covered up by propping his elbows on his knees and lowering his face into his hands. After a moment, he said, "Who?"

"Roland Deveer, the La Jolla businessman who disappeared six weeks ago."

"I've never heard of him. I don't know anything about any disappearance."

"Oh, come on, Mr. Beddoes. It was front-page news."

"I don't read the papers."

"Mr. Beddoes, Roland Deveer had your phone number, as well as that of the Casa del Rey, in his desk calendar. And above it he'd written the word 'arrangements.' "

He rolled his head against his palms and looked at me with one bloodshot eye. "So?

Perhaps he was planning a function at the hotel. Needed something catered. You say he was a businessman? Maybe he was arranging an office party."

"With you personally? Why wouldn't he just deal with the catering department?"

"My management style is very hands-on, Ms. McCone. Our guests and other customers are free to get in touch with me personally, day or night. The staff have all been given instructions about that."

Sure, I thought; that's why Wolf had such an easy time getting hold of you. I said, "Was that true of the Clarks?"

Now he lifted his head and looked at me with both eyes. "The who?"

"The Clarks. The woman and little boy who were staying in Bungalow Six — only, according to some of your staff, they weren't there at all."

Beddoes let out a protracted sigh. "Now I see what this is all about. You've been talking to what's-his-name, that Italian fellow. He ran into the Clark woman and built up the fact that the clerk had forgotten to register them into a big thing. I tried to explain it, but apparently he — and you — want to create some sort of mystery around it. Just like you want to create a mystery around Elaine Picard's death."

"Isn't there one?"

"No! The woman was distraught. She took her own life. It's unfortunate, but that's what happened."

"Is it?"

"Yes!"

"You sound as if you were there."

"What?"

"You sound as if you were in that tower watching her."

He stood up, then put his fingers to his temples, pressing hard. "Ms. McCone," he said, "I was nowhere near the tower. I was in my office with Victor Ibarcena, going over the monthly accounts. I have told this to the sheriff's department. Victor has told them. Our secretary has told them. What more do you need?"

Obviously they were standing firm on the alibi, in spite of yesterday's falling-out. I was beginning to wonder if it wasn't true after all.

Beddoes went to the window and drew the heavy white draperies against the late-afternoon glare. His movements were slow and pained.

"Mr. Beddoes, what's going to happen with you and Victor, after your argument yesterday?"

"What do you mean?"

"It sounded pretty final."

He was silent for a moment. "Yes, I suppose it was."

"Will you fire him?"

He laughed harshly. "I doubt I'll get the opportunity."

"What do you mean?"

"If I know Victor, he's already—" Beddoes broke off.

"Already what?"

"Never mind."

"Making plans to run and leave you holding the bag? That's what you were going to say, isn't it?"

He turned slowly, his face reddening. His hands were clenched into fists, and for a moment I thought he was going to rush at me. Then he seemed to deflate. The fists unclenched, and he crossed his arms, clutching each elbow with the opposite hand. He looked at me quietly, his eyes growing bleak and dead, as if some inner resource had finally been depleted. Then he said, "You'd better go, Ms. McCone."

"You know, if you went to the sheriff now, you wouldn't be stuck holding that bag."

He shook his head. "There's nothing to go to the sheriff about."

"Sooner or later it will all come out about Roland Deveer."

"Will you please go!"

I finally complied. I would get nothing out of him by continuing the pressure. People are funny when they're at the end of that proverbial rope. Some will break down and tell you everything in a gush of relief; others will cling to their lies because that's all they have left.

26: "Wolf"

Lieutenant Tom Knowles was a hard man to connect with. When I left Priapus Books and Curios, I drove back downtown to the sheriff's department, but he still hadn't returned. And probably wouldn't until late, if he came in at all today, the deputy I talked to said; he was somewhere up in Escondido on a case. The deputy wouldn't tell me if it was the Elaine Picard case or not.

So all right. That left me with nothing more to do for the time being — until I talked to McCone and we could compare notes. There was a chance she wanted to get in touch with me, too, and that she'd left a message at the Casa del Rey. If not, maybe I could reach her through her parents; she'd told me she was staying with them, in an area of the city near Old Town, so I figured they'd be listed in the phone book.

It was almost four by the time I got back

to the hotel. There weren't any messages. In my room I looked up the McCone name in the directory: only one listing, and it turned out to be the right one. The man who answered said he was Sharon's father, but that she wasn't there and he hadn't seen or heard from her since early morning. I left a message for her to call me and he said he'd see that she got it.

I switched on the TV, looking for an early newscast that might give me some additional information on Lauterbach's murder. There wasn't one; I would probably have to wait until five o'clock. I left the thing on, with the sound turned off, and got out the map of Mexico and the Mexico guidebook, just to have something to do, and went over them again for some hint of that "town on the water with monkeys in it" where Timmy Clark's father lived. I was still getting nowhere when the telephone rang.

McCone. "That was quick," I said.

"Quick?"

"I called your parents' house not ten minutes ago and left the message."

"Message? Oh," she said. "No, I didn't get it. I'm up in Point Loma. I just thought I'd check in with you. What's up?"

"You already know if you've been listening to your car radio."

"I haven't. What—?"

"Jim Lauterbach's been murdered. Shot sometime yesterday morning in the lavatory down the hall from his office. I happened to be there this morning when he was found."

She breathed in my ear for a time. Then she said, "Any idea who did it?"

"None I'd want to go on record with."

"Wolf, a second killing this soon . . . It has to be connected with Elaine's death."

"Looks that way, yeah," I agreed. "And there's a definite connection between Lauterbach and Elaine. I was in Lauterbach's office for a while before a secretary stumbled on his body, and I did a little snooping. His briefcase was hidden under his desk, with a file folder in it — seems Henry Nyland hired Lauterbach to investigate Elaine."

"He did? Why?"

"Couple of reasons. He thought she was seeing another man. And he thought she was involved in quote something bizarre unquote."

"Such as what?"

"If he had an idea, it wasn't in Lauterbach's notes. Have you talked to Nyland yet?"

"No. I'm on my way to do that now. When did he hire Lauterbach?"

"Six weeks ago."

"What'd Lauterbach find out?"

I filled her in on the details of the file. "Looked to me like he held back some of the stuff from Nyland for his own purposes — blackmail, maybe. But I couldn't make enough sense of the notes to figure out exactly what he'd uncovered."

"Well, there might be something in that club angle. Nyland mentioned a club in the love note I found in Elaine's house. And Rich Woodall had a funny reaction when I mentioned the club to him."

"What kind of club is it?"

"The one I told you about yesterday, I think. The House of Slenderizing and Massage, downtown."

"Is there a branch in Borrego Springs?"

"I don't know. Why?"

"One of Lauterbach's notes indicated Elaine spent time at some club out there. And June Paxton saw her in Borrego Springs with Rich Woodall, remember. There's another connection too. Does the name Darrow mean anything to you? Arthur Darrow?"

"No. Who's he?"

"Somebody who lives in Borrego Springs. Somebody who knows Beddoes and who's connected with the club there. I got his name from a pornographic art dealer named Maxwell Littlejohn."

"Pornographic art?"

"The high-quality type," I said, and explained how I'd got Littlejohn's name and what I'd found out at Priapus Books and Curios. The only thing I omitted was a detailed description of Littlejohn's stock.

McCone said, "I don't quite see how pornography fits in. But Beddoes does collect the stuff; I just came from his house and I saw part of his collection." She paused. "Come to think of it, Karyn Sugarman mentioned his quirk on Saturday morning, in Elaine's office. I didn't pay much attention at the time."

"Did Elaine have any interests along those lines?"

"Not that I know about. She didn't have any porn in her house."

"Any of the other people you've talked to?"

"No. Dammit, Wolf, this is all so confusing."

"Yeah. What've *you* turned up?"

"Well, I went to see Elaine's lawyer, Thorburn, and he showed me the clipping she mentioned in her letter to him. It was about the disappearance of a financier, a man named Roland Deveer, some six weeks ago."

"What sort of disappearance?"

"The kind that might be deliberate. I looked up Mrs. Deveer and had a talk with her. She thinks her husband deserted her and she hates him for it, so she let me go through his papers. Deveer had the telephone numbers of the Casa del Rey and Beddoes's home written down on his calendar."

Now it was my turn for some silent ruminating. At length I said, "Could there be any link between Deveer and the Clarks?"

"I doubt it. The only link seems to be Beddoes and the Casa del Rey."

"Some kind of operation to get people out of the country, maybe — people who want to vanish for one reason or another."

"Makes sense that way."

"Except for one thing. Why would Nancy and Timmy Clark want to disappear?"

"Could be they're running away," McCone said. "From something or somebody."

"Yeah, could be. Did Elaine give her lawyer any details about what she'd found out?"

"No. All her note to Thorburn said was that she was afraid something illegal was going on and she was writing the letter to him to protect herself. She wouldn't talk about what it was and she wouldn't mention any names. She wanted more information first, she said."

"Would she have confided in any of her friends?"

"I don't think so. She kept pretty much to herself."

"How about Karyn Sugarman? Was Elaine seeing her professionally?"

"Sugarman says no. She couldn't, or wouldn't, tell me anything about Elaine's problems."

"Uh-huh. Well, I wish I knew what Tom Knowles has found out. Maybe he's got more than we have and we're beating our heads against a wall for nothing."

"Haven't you been in touch with him?"

"No. He was off yesterday and he's been out of town all day today."

"I'll bet he knows even less than we do," she said. "As far as I know, the only person he's talked to so far is Beddoes."

"You're probably right."

"It's up to us, Wolf. And we'll get to the bottom of it, too, if we can just find the motive for Elaine's murder."

"If she was murdered," I said.

"She *was*, I'm sure of it. I'd like to believe it was because she found out about the hotel scam, but I can't anymore. I just don't see

Beddoes as a murderer. Ibarcena is capable of it, but he says he was with Beddoes when she died, and the way things are between them now, he wouldn't stick to that story if it wasn't true."

"The two of them have some sort of falling-out?"

"A personal one. They were lovers, but Ibarcena's taken up with somebody else and he and Beddoes had it out over that. I think Beddoes is afraid Ibarcena is going to run off and leave him holding the bag."

"He could be right."

"I think so too. Ibarcena was born in Mexico; he could jump over the border, bribe some people here and there, and disappear without much trouble."

"How's Beddoes holding up?"

"Not very well. But he still wouldn't admit anything when I threw Deveer's name at him, even though it shook him up." She made a wry chuckling sound. "See no evil, hear no evil, speak no evil."

"What?"

"The three wise monkeys. He's got an obscene Mexican statuette of the little *monos*. I was just thinking how ironic that is."

I said sharply, "What did you just say?"

"That I was thinking how ironic—"

"No, no. You used a word, a Spanish word."

307

"*Mono?*"

"Yeah. What does it mean?"

"It means monkey. Wolf, what—?"

"Sure, that's it. That's got to be it."

"*What's* got to be it?"

"I think I know where Nancy and Timmy Clark might be."

"Where?"

"A town on the Mexican seacoast. Hang on a minute, I want to check the map."

I put the receiver down, hauled the map over, and spread it out on the bed. And there it was, the small town on the Bahia Topolobampo that I'd noticed before: Los Monos. The Monkeys. But not real monkeys; seven-year-old kids aren't nearly as precise as adults, I should have known that. Just the *word*, the word in Spanish. Los Monos — "a town on the water with monkeys in it."

I caught up the receiver again. "Sharon? Got it. It's a place a couple of hundred miles north of Mazatlán. Los Monos."

"Are you sure that's where they are?"

"No. But from what Timmy Clark told me, it's a pretty good bet."

"What are you going to do?"

"I'm not sure yet. Turn the information over to Knowles, I suppose. Maybe he'll be able to turn up something on who the Clarks are."

"And if he doesn't?"

"I'll cross that bridge when I come to it. Listen, if I need to talk to you again, can I reach you through your folks?"

"Yes. I'll check in there as often as I can."

"Okay. And I should be here tonight if you need me."

We rang off. I opened the guidebook and looked up Los Monos. It was a fishing village not far from the town of Topolobampo, on the bay of the same name — one of the best spots on the Sea of Cortez for billfish, marlin, sailfish, yellowfin tuna, and other big-game fish. There wasn't much there otherwise to attract tourists: a couple of small hotels, a shrimp cannery, a boatworks, housing and supply stores for the local fishermen, and "a few spacious villas for those from Mexico and the United States who enjoy a combination of privacy and primitive beauty." The population was under a thousand, which meant that if the Clarks *were* there, they could be found easily enough.

I got on the horn again and called the sheriff's department, but Knowles still wasn't in. I left another message — he had to pick up his damn messages sometime — and started to get up and pace while I did some thinking. But the TV, which was still on, caught my eye: it must have been five o'clock because a newscast was just starting. I leaned over to turn up the sound, then sat back down again.

The Lauterbach murder was one of the day's top stories, at least on this channel. The newscaster made plenty of the fact that Lauterbach was the "second local private eye to die under mysterious circumstances" in as many days; he also made reference to the convention and allowed as how the real world of the private investigator didn't seem so far removed from the fictional one, after all. But he didn't tell me anything I didn't already know — not until he mentioned a woman from Michigan named Ruth Ferguson, and hinted that there might be a possible link between Lauterbach's death and "a personal tragedy" she'd recently suffered.

Then I was looking at Ruth Ferguson herself, in an interview with one of the station's roving reporters: a thin, beautifully dressed, beautifully made-up woman with icy good looks and an unpleasant way of speaking. She said Lauterbach had called her at the Bloomfield Hills home yesterday morning, identifying himself as a San Diego private detective who had once worked for her ex-husband and who had information on the whereabouts of her seven-year-old son: the boy had been kidnapped — probably by his father, she said with heavy bitterness — from his school in the Detroit suburb one week ago. Lauterbach had urged her to fly to San Diego and she had done so, arriving this morning to discover that he'd been murdered. And then a photograph of Ruth Ferguson's son appeared on the screen, and I saw what Lauterbach had been up to at the Casa del Rey, I saw the false assumption I'd been operating under from the beginning.

The boy in the photograph was Timmy Clark.

27: McCone

I sat in the phone booth I'd called Wolf from, contemplating the graffiti scrawled on its wall. *Fuck the devil,* it said. And underneath: *God is love, and if you don't believe me, I'll kill you.* At any other time it would have made me smile wryly. Now it just brought up questions about the mentality of the average American — questions I'd just as soon avoid thinking on.

Now that Jim Lauterbach had been murdered, it seemed certain that Elaine had been killed to cover up something. The illegal activities at Casa del Rey? lbarcena and Beddoes both had an alibi, backed up by their secretary. Beddoes, even disintegrating emotionally as he was, had stuck to the story, which meant it was probably true.

Once again I considered a personal motive, one stemming from a romantic relationship. There was Rich Woodall, of course, and I would want to talk with him again. But more important, there was Henry Nyland, who had hired Lauterbach to investigate Elaine. Nyland was connected with both murders, and my first priority should be to talk to him. I'd been intending to do that anyway.

I dialed Nyland's home on Coronado, and the housekeeper told me he would be at campaign headquarters from seven o'clock on. After I hung up, I looked at my watch. Ten after five, It would take me a while to get to downtown San Diego and Nyland's headquarters, but not two hours. That left time for a stop at the House of Slenderizing and Massage, where Elaine presumably had met both the retired admiral and Woodall.

When I parked across the street from the renovated brick storefront, an enormously fat woman was going in. I crossed and followed her, but was forced aside by two even fatter women who were coming out, grumbling cheerfully about something called a Nautilus machine.

Good Lord, I thought, the folks who run this place have their work cut out for them.

Directly inside the door was a lobby with muted lighting and mirrors all around. I glanced at my reflection and found myself possessed of a gazellelike slimness I'd never noticed before. Trick mirrors, not as exaggerated as those in a fun-house, but enough to make a person look ten pounds lighter.

A young woman with dark hair piled high on her head sat behind a reception desk working on a bookkeeping ledger. I went up to her and asked to see the manager. She smiled cordially and said, "You've found her. Our regular receptionist is out sick today, so I'm wearing two hats. What can I do for you?"

"Do you have an employee named Rick?"

She sat up a little straighter and pursed her lips. "Mr. MacNelly is no longer with us."

"How long has it been since he left?"

"More than two months."

"Is there any way I can get in touch with him?"

She gave me a look as if I'd just committed an indecent act. "I'm afraid I can't give out that information."

Something was wrong here if the mere mention of the man's name could make her freeze me out this way. I said, "Look, I'm a private investigator, trying to locate Mr. MacNelly in connection with a case."

She relaxed slightly, and then her eyes took on a thoughtful look. "Do you have any identification?"

I got out the photostat of my license and showed it to her. She nodded, a nasty smile beginning to play on her lips. "I do hope Rick's not in any trouble."

Since she so obviously *did* hope so, I said, "Not yet. I take it he didn't leave under pleasant circumstances."

"I fired him."

"Why?"

"Moral reasons. Rick had been soliciting some of the ladies for sexual favors — his favors, to be paid for by them. Apparently he had quite a bit of luck before anyone complained."

"I see." Had one of those ladies been Elaine? "Who was it that complained?"

"Mrs. Abbot." She motioned at the door behind her. "She came in just before you did."

The huge fat one. Good Lord.

The woman went on, "If she hadn't complained, God knows what would have happened. We just opened six months ago, and we're trying to build a reputation as a decent spa, a place where the ladies can go right downtown near their offices. We certainly don't need a scandal. I put a lot of money into this franchise—"

"Do you know where I can reach Mr. MacNelly now?"

"In San Francisco. I have the address where I sent his final paycheck."

I copied it down, an apartment house on Sanchez Street, not far from where I lived. I'd use it as a last resort, if all my leads here came to nothing. "You mentioned ladies a couple of times. Do you have male members as well?"

She shook her head. "Most of our ladies are quite heavy. They would be uncomfortable displaying their bodies in front of the opposite sex."

I frowned. "But Rick MacNelly is a male."

"A masseur. That's different."

This couldn't be the place where Elaine had met Woodall or Nyland, then. "Does your club have a branch in Borrego Springs, by any chance?" I asked.

"No. This is the only branch in the San Diego area." She paused. "It's odd you should ask, though."

"Why?"

"Rick apparently spent a good bit of time in Borrego Springs. He would mention going out there occasionally."

"Why, do you know?"

She shrugged. "I'd always supposed he was into dune buggies or dirt bikes. They do a lot of that out there in the desert."

Now I felt more at sea than before. "I'd

like to run some names by you, if I might, to see if you recognize any of them."

"Sure, go ahead."

I did, mentioning Elaine, as well as all the principal figures in the case, male and female. She recognized Henry Nyland as running for city council, but to all the others she replied in the negative. I thanked her and started to leave.

"Hey," she called after me, "aren't you going to tell me what Rick's done?"

"Sorry," I said, "it's confidential." I gave my new, gazellelike body a final look and went out into the street.

As I drove toward Henry Nyland's campaign headquarters, I thought about Rick MacNelly, the man who sold himself to women. What on earth had Elaine been doing with the name of such a person in her address book? She hadn't been a member of the club where MacNelly worked. And surely she hadn't had to pay anyone for sex.

The club. It kept cropping up in people's conversations. And Wolf had said that, according to Lauterbach's file, Elaine had spent time at a club in Borrego Springs. *What* club? Maybe Nyland could enlighten me.

Unlike the day before, Nyland's campaign

headquarters bustled with activity. Men and women — most of them around college age — rushed about, waving papers and calling to one another. Several sat at a long table stuffing envelopes, and another group were making phone calls. I recalled from my reading of the local papers that Nyland was running in a special election, to fill the seat of a council member who had died. Balloting was next week, hence this last-minute flurry.

A floppy-haired young man tried to recruit me as a volunteer the instant I came in the door. I said no thanks, and asked to see Nyland. The young man replied that Admiral Nyland was in conference with his campaign manager, and absolutely no one was to interrupt them.

I showed him the photostat of my license. Evidently he didn't know the difference between it and police identification, because he looked perplexed and rushed away, muttering something like "not again."

Of course the police would have seen the same information in Jim Lauterbach's office as Wolf had; they would have talked to Nyland by now. I was covering the same ground as the officials, but, as I'd told Mrs. Deveer in relation to her husband's papers, maybe something that Nyland said would have significance to me that it hadn't to the police. I sat down on a folding chair to wait.

A red, white, and blue banner hanging across one entire wall trumpeted what appeared to be Nyland's campaign slogan: HONESTY, INTEGRITY, NO NONSENSE. The words were laid out as an acrostic on the candidate's full name, Henry Innis Nyland. I looked around at all the fresh-faced, clean-cut volunteers and remembered reading that the campaign had shaped up into a battle between liberals and the Moral Majority. Even if I hadn't read about Nyland and known he was a retired admiral, I would have known which camp this was.

In a couple of minutes, the floppy-haired young man came back, followed by an older man in his fifties. He had iron-gray hair, a stiff military bearing, and was dressed in expensive-looking golf clothes. Normally he would have been handsome, but right now his bushy brows were drawn together, giving his face a downward cast, and his mustache twitched with irritation.

"Is this the one?" he asked the young man, gesturing at me.

"Yes, sir."

"Then you're dismissed. I'll handle it."

The young man scurried away, and his

companion came up to me, folded his arms across his chest, and planted his feet widely apart. "I'm Henry Nyland," he said. "What's the meaning of this interruption?"

"I'd like to talk to you about Elaine Picard."

It wasn't the answer he'd expected. He glanced around, as if to see if anyone was within earshot.

"And Jim Lauterbach," I added.

"I've already spoken to another policeman. And a man from the sheriff's department."

I hesitated. It was the perfect opening; I could let him go on thinking I was with one of the law enforcement agencies. But this was a powerful man, doubtless with friends in high places. I couldn't risk a charge of impersonating an officer.

"Admiral Nyland, could we go someplace more private?"

Again he glanced around. "Very well. This way." He led me through a maze of desks and tables to a cubicle at the back of the room, one of several that had probably been used by salesmen for closing their deals when this was an automobile showroom. Once inside, he seated himself behind a cluttered desk and motioned me to a chair on the other side of it.

I sat and got out my identification. "I'm not with the police or sheriff's department, Admiral Nyland," I said. "I'm a private investigator, a friend of Elaine's."

He took the I.D. and looked at it. When he handed it back to me, his irritation had faded, and his gray eyes were puzzled. "I don't understand. Elaine died in an accident. According to my sources, there's no question of that."

"Perhaps not officially, but I was Elaine's friend, Admiral. And I think she was murdered."

He started, and the color faded from his face, leaving it with a grayish clayey look. "Why?"

"There are a number of reasons."

"No." He shook his head. "No one would want to kill Elaine. She was lovely, good . . ." But a worried expression had come into his eyes, as if he too were thinking of possible reasons. After a moment, he said, "Are you conducting your own investigation into her death?"

"A personal one."

"I see." He stared down at the desktop, drumming his thick fingers on a sheet of computer printout. "I can appreciate why you're doing this — I cared for Elaine a great deal. If anything, she was the love of my life. And if someone killed her, I want to see him punished. But I don't know what I can tell you."

"You may be able to shed light on some of the things that are puzzling me. When did you last see Elaine?"

"Several weeks ago. I'd tried to reach her since then, the last time being Friday night. I went to the Casa del Rey, hoping to talk, but the clerk said she'd already gone home. I doubted his story because her car was still in the lot. Probably she'd asked him to lie for her."

"Why wouldn't she want to see you?"

"That is personal."

I tried another tack. "Where did you meet Elaine?"

"At the Casa del Rey. The party held a fund-raiser there last spring. There was some trouble, and the security people were called in. Elaine was efficient, very take-charge. I appreciate that in a woman, so I asked to see her again."

"Trouble? What kind?"

"Nothing serious. A bunch of young punks — radicals — setting off fireworks outside the banquet room."

"And this was the first time you'd seen Elaine?"

"Yes. Why do you ask?"

"I had the impression you'd met her at a club."

"Well, I took her to the Officers' Club — both at North Island and Miramar — a number of times. But no, I didn't meet her there."

That was not what I'd hoped to hear. "Admiral Nyland, I don't mean to pry into your personal affairs, but did you ever write Elaine a love note mentioning a club?"

"A *love note?* My dear young woman, I have better things to do with my time!" He seemed genuinely affronted, as if I'd questioned his manhood.

"Can you think of any club she might have belonged to?"

"Club? What is this about a club?"

"Please, can you think of any?"

He paused. "No."

"What about in Borrego Springs?"

"Not that I know of."

"Do you know of any friend of hers named Darrow? Arthur Darrow?"

"I've never heard the name. Would you mind telling me what this is leading to?"

"Apparently, Elaine spent a good deal of time at some club in Borrego Springs, and she knew the Darrow person from there."

His eyebrows drew together in a frown. "If she did, she never told me about it." I could tell he was seriously upset now; he didn't like the idea of Elaine having had a part of her life she had kept back from him. "How do you know all this, Miss McCone?"

"Jim Lauterbach had discovered it. Hadn't he reported any of this to you?"

"No. He'd reported nothing of significance."

"Well, he'd uncovered that much."

"The police didn't tell me that. By all rights, that information belongs to me."

"You'll have to take it up with them. Why did you hire Jim Lauterbach, Admiral Nyland?"

His posture went ramrod stiff.

I added, "Didn't the police ask you that?"

"They did, and I told them. But I don't feel the necessity to go into it again. So if you'll excuse me . . ."

I'd known men like Nyland all my life — Navy types with rough exteriors, used to having their own way. My father had been like that before he'd retired and mellowed to the point of singing folk ballads. So I put on a downcast, little-girl look and reached out one hand in a supplicating gesture. "Please, sir, Elaine was my friend. I'm awfully upset about what happened to her, and I need to know . . ."

He looked down at me, his face softening.

"I understand. Her death has hit me hard too. The only way I've managed is to carry on with the campaign as if nothing had happened."

"Then please won't you tell me why you hired Lauterbach?"

"All right." He sat again, straightening the computer sheets on the desk and aligning their edges with those of the blotter. "I hired Lauterbach because Elaine wouldn't marry me and I couldn't understand her reasons. I'm well off, respected in the community. I was giving her the opportunity to share my life, be my helpmeet. But she repeatedly turned me down."

"Why, do you think?"

"Because the woman was a damned fool, that's why."

"But you didn't need a private detective to tell you that."

"Of course not. There had to be a reason for her foolishness, however, and I assumed it was another man. I needed to know who it was, what he was like, in order to talk her out of it."

"You told Lauterbach you thought Elaine was involved in something bizarre."

His face lost its softness and became a protective blank. "Where did you hear that?"

"It was in his file, the one I suppose the police have now."

"No one has a right to see that!"

I was silent.

"By all rights, they should have turned that file over to me. I paid for Lauterbach's services in advance."

"What was the bizarre thing, Admiral Nyland?"

He paused, trying to calm himself. "Nothing, really. I was making too much of some little things she said once when we'd both had too much to drink. We won't discuss it."

I sat contemplating framed copies of the Pledge of Allegiance and the Lord's Prayer on the wall above Nyland's head. I knew Navy people; they came in as many types as the population as a whole. But with old-school officers like Nyland, the things a great many of them wouldn't discuss were sex and drugs.

Had Elaine been using drugs? I doubted it. She couldn't have handled her demanding job if she had been addicted. Well, she *could* if she'd been using uppers. But Elaine had acted too tired to be availing herself of such measures.

What about sex? What would Nyland have considered bizarre? Homosexuality. But no less an authority than Karyn Sugarman had been certain Elaine's orientation was heterosexual. So it couldn't be that, either.

"Admiral Nyland—" The young man with the floppy hair stuck his head into the cubicle. "Admiral, we've only got half an hour before we have to tape that show for Channel Eight."

Nyland had been staring at the blotter, and it took a few seconds for him to rouse himself. He looked at the young man as if he had forgotten why he was taping a show.

The aide held up his wrist and pointed to his watch.

Nyland stood up slowly. "I'll be with you in a minute." To me, he added, "I'm sorry, Miss McCone, but I must keep to my schedule."

I got up and followed him across the large room to the door. "You run a tight campaign ship, Admiral."

He looked at me curiously. "Were you a Navy brat?"

"Yes, sir. My father was a chief. Thirty-year man."

He looked around the room — at the envelope stuffers and the phone canvassers, and at the red, white, and blue banner. Something seemed to have gone out of him, as if my visit had recalled images of Elaine too vividly. He stared blankly at the banner, then shook his handsome gray head. "Then you know what we're trying to do here," he said with an effort. "The godlessness we're dedicated to fighting."

"Yessir, I do."

And although I wouldn't put it in religious terms, I knew far better than he, for all his years and experience. I'd been out there in the middle of the filth and the crime and the violence, while Henry Nyland had only viewed it from his lofty and protected perch. Unlike him, I didn't have the slightest idea how to fight it, except on a slow, day-to-day basis. But I did know his way wouldn't work.

28: "Wolf"

I stared at the television screen, at the woman named Ruth Ferguson. She was talking about her son again, her son Timmy. An unidentified woman in her midthirties with short dark hair had enticed him away from his school in Bloomfield Hills — probably someone hired by her ex-husband, she said. The ex-husband was named Carlton Ferguson and he was a design and structural engineer who had divorced her two years ago and then vanished after a bitter custody fight that had left Timmy in her charge. She thought he might have gone to South America, where he'd once spent a year "building bridges or something," but investigators she herself had hired in the Detroit area after Timmy's kidnapping had thus far been unable to trace him. She was offering a five-thousand-dollar reward, she said, for information leading to the whereabouts and safe return of her son — money she had been prepared to pay to Jim Lauterbach.

Then she was gone, and the newscaster said that anyone with any information on either the death of Lauterbach or the whereabouts of Timmy Ferguson should contact the San Diego police or the channel's newsroom. Then he went on to something else, and I reached over and shut him off.

I sat there. Five thousand dollars. If I was right about where Timmy was, all I had to do was call the cops or the TV station and the money would be mine — half mine, because McCone was entitled to fifty percent of it. All the investigating we'd done wouldn't be for free after all. And I'd have done my good deed for the year.

But I didn't move. I kept seeing Ruth Ferguson's beautiful, cold face, kept hearing that voice of hers, emotionless except for the bitter edge, as if, instead of her son, she'd been talking about a piece of rather valuable property that had been stolen from her. She hadn't seemed to care much about whether or not Timmy was all right; she hadn't seemed to care at all that Lauterbach was dead, only that he'd died before he could tell her what he knew. And all I could think of was what Timmy had said to me about his mother — not the woman I knew as Nancy

Clark, but his natural mother, Ruth Ferguson.

I don't like my mother. She makes me afraid.

Why? I thought. Why does she make him afraid?

I got up and paced the room for a time. But I needed more space than that, more activity. I took the elevator down to the lobby, went outside, and walked along the edge of the beach.

Maybe I ought to go talk to Ruth Ferguson, I thought, see what kind of impression she makes in person. But I had no idea where she was staying and I couldn't get to her through the police or through the TV station without telling them why I wanted to see her. I could try canvassing the hotels in the area by phone, but that was a tall order; and even if I did find her that way, and I saw her and didn't like her any better face-to-face than I had on television, she'd know right away that I knew something about Timmy's disappearance.

All right, what about the boy's father? He must have arranged the snatch, just as Ruth Ferguson thought, since she hadn't mentioned any sort of ransom demand. What kind of father kidnaps his own son? A worried one, maybe, who cares more about the boy than his ex-wife does. Or one just as bitter and cold as she — a bastard who wants only to get back at a woman he hates. For all I knew, Carlton Ferguson could have killed Lauterbach: he might have come to San Diego, too, and Lauterbach got in touch with him somehow and tried blackmail, and Ferguson had paid him off with four bullets instead of cash.

I left the beach and walked up into the gardens, across in front of Bungalow 6. All this speculation . . . what the hell good was it? There was no way I could judge what kind of man Ferguson was, because I didn't know anything about him. And I couldn't talk to him any more than I could talk to the boy's mother. . . .

Why couldn't I?

I stopped walking. Fly down to Mexico, confront Ferguson, see what was what, and *then* make a decision what to do about Timmy. In Ferguson's case I wouldn't have to worry about letting on what I knew; I'd *want* him to know I was onto the truth, so I could gauge his reaction. Another thing: I might be able to get the full story of the operation Beddoes and Ibarcena were running here. Ferguson would know some of the details, at least.

But hell, it was an off-the-wall idea. I wasn't certain that Los Monos was where

Carlton Ferguson lived, or that that was where Timmy was now; it could easily turn out to be a wild-goose chase — an expensive one. It would cost plenty to get to a semi-isolated place like Topolobampo Bay.

Stupid idea. Forget it. Call the cops instead, turn it over to them, let them get Timmy back to his mother where he belongs.

She makes me afraid. . . .

Damn it, he's just a kid. Kids make up things about their parents, kids exaggerate. She's probably a terrific mother, gives him cake and ice cream and crap like that whenever he wants it.

But what if she isn't? What if she really does make him afraid? What if she abuses him in some way?

The thoughts kept running around inside my head, scrimmaging with each other like a bunch of nervous football players. All the way to Mexico, for Christ's sake, on a piece of guesswork and an impression of a woman based on a kid's remark and a one-minute TV interview. I must be losing my grip on sanity even to be considering it. That was probably what McCone would say if I told her about it. You're nuts, Wolf, she'd say. Five thousand bucks, twenty-five-hundred apiece, and you want to maybe throw it away by hopping down to Mexico on a hunch and a prayer. Yeah, you're nuts, all right.

I went back through the gardens and into the Cantina Sin Nombre and drank two bottles of Miller Lite. I was still nuts when I was done. So I went upstairs and called McCone's parents' house and asked the man who answered — Sharon's brother, he said — to have her call me as soon as she checked in. Then I rang Room Service and asked them to send me up a sandwich. Then I called two different airlines and found out that it would cost me close to four hundred bucks for a round trip, via Mazatlán, to the closest city with an airport to Topolobampo Bay, a place called Los Mochis; transportation to and from Los Monos and incidental expenses would no doubt bring the final tab to over five hundred.

But I was still nuts even when I was done talking to the airlines. And I stayed nuts, so that when McCone called a while later, as I was eating my sandwich, I came right out and told her what I was thinking of doing.

"I think you ought to go, Wolf," she said. "The kid's welfare is more important than the reward. And besides, if the father turns out to be a bastard we'll end up with the five thousand anyway."

She was nuts too. We were both nuts.

Tomorrow morning, on the first available flight, I was going to Mexico — to the town on the water with monkeys in it.

29: McCone

I hung up the receiver of the kitchen wall phone and perched on the edge of the counter to think about what Wolf had found out. Interesting as it was, I couldn't quite tie it to Elaine's death. Well, better to let Wolf take care of the Casa del Rey angle while I continued to concentrate on the personal aspects of Elaine's life.

And I could rest assured he would take care of it, in his own way. The distraught mother of Timmy Clark — no, Timmy Ferguson — was here in town, offering five thousand dollars just for information leading to her son. Wolf had that information, and what was he doing with it? Going to Mexico because he didn't like the looks of the mother. Because of some chance remark the kid had made about being afraid. And who had approved the plan, told him he should go? Me.

Five thousand dollars. Wolf had said he

would split it with me if he ended up claiming the reward. That would mean we'd be compensated for all this investigative work after all. Five thousand dollars. Twenty-five hundred apiece.

But I had the feeling we'd never see a cent of it. Money — unlike trouble and hassles and confusion — rarely made its way to my door. And I suspected it was the same with Wolf.

I got up and looked in the refrigerator for something to eat. That was the reason I'd come back here in the first place — because I couldn't face another greasy burger or burrito. There was some of Ma's caraway potato salad, which I ate right out of the storage dish, standing up at the counter.

Now what? I still didn't think Beddoes or Ibarcena had killed Elaine. Which left me where I had started, with a more personal motive. I needed to find out about the club in Borrego Springs. And the easiest way to do that was to ask the man who had written Elaine that love note.

Rich Woodall. If it wasn't Henry Nyland, then it had to be Woodall.

I set the empty dish in the sink, grabbed up my purse, and headed out to talk to him.

I drove past Woodall's house and parked in the shelter of some palm trees farther down the rutted, unpaved road. As I started back along it, I saw the porch light behind the pyracantha shrubs flash on. Perhaps Woodall was expecting company.

A couple of seconds later, however, I heard the door slam and footsteps sounded on the path. I stopped and watched as Woodall came through the opening in the hedge and got into a convertible parked in the driveway. I hadn't paid any attention to the make of the auto on Saturday night, but now I noticed it was one of those old Porsches — red and shiny, with the top down. The car fit with what Karyn Sugarman had said about people who had inadequate personalities cluttering up their lives with expensive toys, and, coupled with what else I'd seen of him, it confirmed her assessment of Woodall.

He didn't notice me standing there, because he gunned the car out of the driveway and down the road. I ran back and got into my MG and followed him, leaving my lights off until I turned onto the main road into Lakeside. Probably he had a hot date, or maybe he was just going to a movie, but it was worth pursuing him to make sure.

The little red car careened along the road as if it were on a racetrack, and eventually roared onto Highway 67 and then over to Highway 8, heading toward San Diego. I've never trusted Porsche drivers — they tend to be unpredictable and do things they wouldn't behind the wheel of a Toyota, for instance — so I followed cautiously, several car lengths behind. When we got to the exit for Balboa Park and the Porsche's signal light flashed, I realized Woodall was heading for the zoo. Why would he be going to work at this time of night? Maybe one of the animals was sick. No, that wouldn't concern him — Woodall had said his was a strictly administrative capacity.

I followed him along a wide street, past a school, and when he turned right into Zoo Place, once again I switched off the MG's lights. He went along the palm-lined drive and made another abrupt turn directly opposite the zoo's Warner Administration Center. The car's brake lights flashed and then went out.

I stopped on the drive and watched as Woodall crossed to the wood-and-glass building that housed the zoo offices. When he had disappeared into the shadows, I drove on, past where he'd left his car. It was parked in one of the slots reserved for vendors and the media. I coasted along into the vast, empty parking lot and left my car near the perimeter, where it wouldn't be easily noticed.

There was a covered walkway leading from the sidewalk to the front door of the administration center. The lobby was dark and there were no lights to indicate Woodall's presence, but to my left was an iron gate with an entry-code device like a push-button phone mounted beside it. That was probably the way Woodall had gone.

I went over to the gate and touched it, starting when it opened under the pressure of my hand. In his haste, Woodall had neglected to close it completely. I hesitated, looking through the bars at the jungly courtyard beyond. There was a pond, with a bridge to the left, and directly ahead was an archway leading into the zoo itself. The courtyard was illuminated by a shaft of light coming from one of the windows of the administration center.

It wasn't really breaking and entering, I thought, if I walked through an unlocked gate. There was no sign saying to keep out or warning that this gate was for employees only. I cringed mentally, knowing what Wolf would have said to that reasoning. Then I went through the gate.

I moved toward the shaft of light, keeping close to the thickly planted vegetation next to the building. As I neared the window, I paused for a moment. Behind me it was quiet, but in the distance I could hear indistinct noises — animal noises, an occasional birdcall. The wind rustled through the leaves of the tall palm trees, and the moon shone in the dark sky behind them. In spite of the night's warmth, I shivered.

Crouching, I went closer to the window and stopped just outside the beam of light. Through the glass I could see an office with four desks. Woodall stood at a file cabinet, the kind with small drawers that hold 3" x 5" cards. His back was to me and he was reaching into one of the drawers.

He turned, a white card in his hand, and I hunched lower. He went to one of the desks, pulled the plastic cover off a typewriter, and inserted the card. Still standing, he began to type.

After about thirty seconds, he pulled the card from the typewriter, went to a different drawer in the file, and flipped through the cards until he found the place he wanted to insert the one he had in his hand. Then he shut the drawer and looked around the office, an expression of satisfaction on his face.

I started to inch closer, to see if I could make out the label on the file drawer. Woodall stared directly out the window at the place where I was and I froze, even though I knew he couldn't see me. He remained standing there for a few seconds, then turned and went through a door behind him. A second light flashed on.

I moved closer, crawling through the plants until I was below the window, then stood up and peered through the glass.

The file had little blue labels on each drawer. They were alphabetical — *A* to *C*, and so on. The top drawer of the cabinet, however, had a longer notation. I strained my eyes and made out the words *Adopt-an-Animal Program*. Quickly I ducked back down and squatted behind a rubber tree plant.

So Woodall had been adding a card to the file of people who sponsored zoo animals. And as near as I could tell, the drawer he'd added it to was *P* to *R*. *P* for Picard. The 3" x 5" card undoubtedly listed her as the proud mother of a gorilla named Fred.

Woodall had lied to me about how he knew Elaine. And now he'd manufactured evidence to back up the falsehood. But why, I wondered, hadn't he merely filled out the card when he was at work?

Well, for one thing, the card file was in an office with four desks. It would have been hard for Woodall to get to without someone observing him. And secondly, he might not have felt it important until today. After all, there had been another murder —

I heard a noise in the zoo proper, outside the archway. Standing up, I slipped back toward the gate. A silhouette appeared in the archway, swinging a flashlight. I looked around, saw the little footbridge to my right, and tiptoed across it into the darkness beyond.

Ahead of me were tall shapes that reminded me of a bandstand. A path sloped downward and I took it, not thinking, just wanting to get away from what was surely a security guard. After a moment I looked back to see if his light was gone, but found the path had turned and I could no longer see the bridge or the courtyard.

I doubled back, came to a fork in the path, and took the left-hand branch of it. After a few seconds, I realized I couldn't see the administration center at all. I'd taken the wrong branch, and it was leading me farther away, into the zoo itself.

Now what? I thought, stopping and looking around. I could see nothing but dark vegetation and hear nothing but the distant animal sounds and the overhead drone of a plane heading for Lindbergh Field. Closing my eyes, I tried to picture the zoo as I remembered it from dozens of past visits. But that didn't help much; I'd always come in through the visitors' gate.

Where were the guards? How often did they patrol? The one I'd seen had probably checked the courtyard; if he'd noticed the open gate and locked it, I was in real trouble. Or had he seen the light in the office and gone in to see who was working late? There was no way of telling until I got back there. *If* I got back there.

I went back up the path, took another fork, but found it wasn't the right one either. At this rate, I could wander all night. The zoo covers a hundred acres of canyons and mesas in the northwestern reaches of Balboa Park. The animals live in relative freedom in natural habitats, which are separated from visitors by low walls and moats rather than barred cages. I supposed if I came to something I recognized, the bear den or monkey island, I could find my way to the main gate. And that was just down from the administration center—

Off to my right something screamed.

I almost screamed back at it. Then I leaped off the path, heading for the cover of the shrubbery. Whatever it was yelled again, and then a great ruckus started, with all sorts of shrieks and flapping.

Birds. I must be near where they kept the

big birds — ostriches and emus and God knows what else.

Had I caused this uproar? Or did it happen frequently? Would the guards come to investigate, or just ignore it as a matter of course? I crouched in the shrubbery, waiting.

Birds. That didn't help me one damn bit. The things were everywhere, all over the zoo. I'd have to figure out some other way to get my bearings.

But how? It was dark, and I didn't dare use my flashlight. . . .

Dummy, I thought. The moon. The moon is out tonight. You can fix your position by it, like a good little Girl Scout.

The birds were quieting down now, and I didn't hear any footsteps coming to investigate the commotion. I stepped out from the cover of the bushes and looked up at the sky. The moon was there all right. I took a mental reading, figured out which way was which, and soon was on the right path, heading for the little bridge and the gate beyond.

At the bridge, I paused, looking around and listening. The light was still on in the office, but all was quiet. Probably the guard had checked to see who was there, and now Woodall really was working late, to back up whatever story he'd given security. I slipped across the bridge and grasped the iron bars of the gate. It was still open.

I went through it fast, breathing hard, and hurried down the walk and across Zoo Drive to where Woodall's car was still parked. From here I'd be able to hear him close the gate if he left, so I decided to take the opportunity to examine the car. It would be easy to do, since the convertible top was down.

I slipped into the driver's seat. The car smelled of leather and more faintly of cigarette smoke. I opened the glove compartment and found it empty except for the registration and a San Diego map. The ashtray was full of butts, and a side pocket on the door was stuffed with odd bits of paper. I pulled them out and went through them.

There were credit card slips from gasoline stations, mostly Union Oil; a crumpled bill from an auto repair shop; an empty matchbook from an Italian restaurant; ticket stubs for the symphony; several business cards. I looked carefully at each card. One was from a New York Life Insurance salesman; another from the alterations department of a downtown men's store; still another from a lawyer, Newell Dunlap.

And one from Arthur Darrow.

I looked closer at Darrow's card. It was ragged, seemed old. Probably it had been in the side pocket a long time. It gave Darrow's occupation as an investment counselor, and showed both business and office addresses and phone numbers in Borrego Springs.

Turning it over, I found a notation in a thin, spidery hand: *9 p.m., Les Club.*

Les Club. French for "The Club," I supposed — but if that was so, it was bad French. It should have been *Le* Club, instead of the plural *Les*. In any case, a utilitarian label with a Continental flare.

But for what? It sounded as if it could be a restaurant. Or a bar. A fancy nightspot, perhaps. Or even a health club, as I'd first supposed.

Well, whatever it was, I'd now found a link connecting Woodall with Arthur Darrow. Darrow, who was connected to Elaine by Jim Lauterbach's file. Lauterbach, who had been hired by Henry Nyland. Nyland, who suspected Elaine had been involved with another man — another man who had to be Woodall. Woodall, whom Karyn Sugarman had classified as an Inadequate Personality. Sugarman, who . . .

Everybody seemed connected. Loosely connected, to be sure, but all linked by something called Les Club.

347

30: "Wolf"

My Western Airlines flight on Tuesday morning went *north* out of San Diego, to L.A. to pick up a bunch of noisy tourists, and then turned around and proceeded on down to Mazatlán. I took that as an omen of things to come. And I wasn't far wrong.

In Mazatlán it was hot and so humid the air had a wet drippy consistency that made it difficult to breathe. There was no air conditioning in the waiting area for the feeder flight to Los Mochis; I sat there for an hour with my jacket off and my shirt unbuttoned halfway down my belly, simmering in my own sweat. The plane, when I finally boarded it, was small and cramped and even hotter than the waiting area; and the pilot handled it on takeoff, in the air, and on landing with a kind of wild nonchalance that scared the hell out of me. None of the other five passengers, all of whom were Mexican, seemed bothered in the slightest.

Los Mochis was a modern little city in the middle of El Fuerte Valley, surrounded by rice fields and canebrakes and sugar mills. It took me fifteen minutes to recover from the flight, which was all right because it took the airline people fifteen minutes to find my missing bag. The first three taxi-men I talked to either didn't speak English or had no interest in driving me all the way to Topolobampo Bay; the fourth guy, whose name was Hernando and who said proudly that he was a Tarahumara Indian, agreed to do the honors. Which was too bad for me, because he drove with the same kind of wild nonchalance exhibited by the feeder pilot — only worse, like somebody who had just escaped from an asylum. I didn't get to see half the countryside we passed through, on account of I had my eyes shut most of the time.

Near the Bahia Ohuira we entered a stretch of heavy jungle, vivid green and spotted with bright-colored flowers. It was even hotter and more humid in there, which made the interior of the taxi — a twenty-year-old Dodge sans air conditioning — feel like the interior of a stewpot. We couldn't even open the windows for a breath of air because, Hernando said, the jungle was home of "oh so many millions of mosquitoes who will gladly suck out every drop of our blood." The land around the village of Topolobampo, not far ahead, had remained uninhabited until recent years because of the mosquitoes, he said. Malaria, he said. But the disease had been wiped out, he said, except in rare cases, and then only tourists were afflicted.

Topolobampo was an old village with a cluster of new-looking hotels spread out along the narrows where Bahia Ohuira became Bahia Topolobampo and where there was a confusion of mangrove islands and dark estuaries. We went through the town, southwest toward the Sea of Cortez. And a little while later, in midafternoon and in the middle of a hot windstorm, we finally rolled into the town on the water with monkeys in it.

Los Monos was down near the mouth of the bay, tucked in between the water and a series of low jungly hills — maybe fifty buildings in all, most of them old, built around a central plaza with a fountain in its middle and a church at one end. At the other end was the shrimp cannery and a network of little piers and boat moorage, where three or four dozen fishing vessels writhed under the lash of the wind; the bay and the sea beyond were a dazzling blue laced with whitecaps. What looked to be the only hotel was on the west side of the square, a three-story tile-roofed adobe structure painted pink and called El Cabrillo.

The place looked like a ghost town: there wasn't another human being in sight, nothing moving anywhere except a lot of dust and leaves and things swirled up by the wind. It gave me a vague eerie feeling, until I remembered that the afternoon siesta was practically a second religion in Mexico. That was where everybody was, inside out of the heat and that hammering wind, having themselves a short snooze. It seemed like a pretty good idea. But not as good as a cold *cerveza*, if they had cold beer in Los Monos, and a bucket of water to douse my head with.

Hernando slammed the Dodge to a quivering stop in front of the hotel. My legs felt a little weak when I got out; it had been some wild ride. I paid him the price we'd agreed on, plus a tip, and asked him to wait. If Carlton Ferguson didn't live here I wanted a ride straight back to Los Mochis, even if it meant another hour and a half of fear and trembling. And if Ferguson *did* live here I might need a ride to wherever his house was. Hernando was cheerfully agreeable, and when I left him he was about to attack the contents of a huge straw lunch basket.

The lobby of El Cabrillo was small, hot, strewn with sturdy native furniture, and empty except for a round little man dozing in a desk area about as large as an elevator shaft. He didn't speak English, it turned out, but he went and got somebody who did — a middle-aged guy with a Pancho Villa mustache, the fierce effect of which was spoiled by a ready smile and pleasant brown eyes.

"I am Pablo Venegas, owner of this first-class hotel," he said. "You wish a room, señor? Two are available, one on the top floor with a magnificent view of water and jungle—"

"Thanks, but I may not be staying the night. That depends on what you're able to tell me."

"*Por favor?*"

"I'm looking for a man named Carlton Ferguson, an American engineer. Does he live in Los Monos?"

"Ah, Señor Ferguson. Sometimes he comes to have dinner in my first-class restaurant. He is my good friend."

So far, so good, I thought with some relief. "Can you tell me where he lives?"

"On a hill beyond the village," Venegas

said. "Perhaps two kilometers from here. A fine villa. It was formerly owned by a general in the army, but his family moved away after he was blown up by guerrillas."

"Would you know if Ferguson is home?"

He shrugged. "I have not seen him."

"When did you see him last?"

"Perhaps two days ago."

"Did he have a little boy with him? About seven years old, with light-colored hair?"

"Little boy? No, he has no children I know about."

"Does he live alone in his villa?"

"Ah, no. With a woman who is not his wife, I think. A very beautiful woman."

"How do I get there?"

He told me, and the directions seemed simple enough. I wasn't quite ready to leave when I had them straight — I wanted to ask him a few more questions about Ferguson — but he must have thought I was. He said, "You seem hot and tired, señor. Some food before you go? My wife prepares the finest *huachinango* — what you call the red snapper — that you have ever eaten." I started to shake my head, and he said without missing a beat, "A cold *cerveza*, then? Dos Equis. Tres Equis, Tecate, Carta Blanca?"

"Cold?"

"My first-class hotel is equipped with a

gasoline-powered refrigerator. The *cerveza* is very cold indeed."

The inside of my mouth and throat felt like a sandpit; I didn't need any more persuading. I followed Venegas into a little bar, where a pair of ceiling fans stirred the air with sluggish monotony and gave free rides to a colony of flies as big as bees. The bottle of Dos Equis he sold me was as cold as advertised.

"Tell me, Señor Venegas," I said, "what sort of man is Carlton Ferguson?"

"You do not know him?"

"No. I'm here to see him on a private matter."

"Ah, he is a fine man. He gave the padre ten thousand pesos to fix the roof of the church."

"A generous man, then?"

"Yes. Very generous."

"How long has he lived here?"

"For almost one year."

"And what does he do?"

"Do, señor?"

"For a living. How does he make his money?"

"Ah. He is a very great engineer. He works on the government project to improve the port of Topolobampo."

"Would you say he's well liked?"

"Oh, yes. Everyone likes him."

"So there's been no trouble with him since he came to Los Monos."

"None," Venegas said. He was frowning now, so that his mustache bristled and he looked a bit more like a bandit. "Why do you ask these questions, señor? They are very odd questions."

"A private matter, like I said."

He lowered his voice, even though there was no one else around. "You are *policia?*"

"In a way," I said.

"Ah," he said. "A matter of seriousness, señor?"

"No. It's nothing for you to concern yourself about. You can just forget I was ever here."

"Of course," he said solemnly. He had misunderstood: he thought I was some sort of government official, from the State Department or maybe even from the C.I.A. He was very impressed. He said, "If you desire to have a room later on, I will see to it that you are accommodated to the utmost. The finest room in El Cabrillo — I guarantee it."

I thanked him and went back outside. Hernando was asleep on the front seat of the Dodge, which he had moved over into the shade of a date palm. I woke him up, climbed into the back seat, repeated Venegas's directions, and off we went in a screech and a roar.

Beyond the church, an unpaved road climbed up into the low hills that flanked the bay to the north. That road connected with another one, and we climbed higher through lush jungle, an open area dotted with papaya trees, then more jungle, toward the crest of one of the hills. Here and there, high stucco walls with wooden gates marked the location of villas hidden among the vegetation. We passed three of these; the fourth we came to was almost invisible behind a screen of mango trees that had pink-flowered tropical vines climbing through them. This, according to Venegas, was where I would find the villa that belonged to Carlton Ferguson.

Hernando skidded the car over under the mangoes, narrowly missing their trunks, and braked to a stop about an inch from one of the gateposts. I asked him again to wait, and he nodded and smiled and lay down on the seat to continue his siesta. I got out, went over to the gate. It wasn't nearly so windy up here, but it was just as hot and more humid; the air had that wet drippy feel I was beginning to hate.

You couldn't see anything through the gates because they were made of solid wood.

And you couldn't see anything over the wall because it was a good eight feet high. I looked for a bell or something for a visitor to announce himself, but there wasn't anything at all. So now what? I thought. Climb the wall like one of the *monos?* Beat the gate down? Stand around and wait until somebody comes out? Start yelling? Use my private-eye cunning?

Cunning was what solved the problem for me: I reached down and tried the gate latch, and it wasn't locked, and I opened it and walked in. *Norteamericano* mentality. People down here didn't have to put bolts and locks and chains on their property, like we did up in the civilized world.

A gravel drive led through a jungle garden of palms, banana trees, flowering shrubs, and mosquitoes that kept trying to bite my neck. Behind the screen of vegetation I had glimpses of the villa; then the drive jogged to the left and widened into a clearing, and I could see all of the house. It was perched at the edge of a downslope, no doubt to take advantage of an impressive view of the bay and the Sea of Cortez in the distance. It had three wings, all of them white stucco with red tile roofs, framing a central courtyard that contained more trees and shrubs and the inevitable mosaic-tile fountain. To one side of the clearing was a carport with two cars parked under it — a dusty black Mercedes and a small Japanese compact.

I went toward the courtyard. When I got close enough, I could see that a tunnel-like passageway led through the villa's back wing, so that you could go straight from the courtyard onto what appeared to be a large terrace. From the terrace, carried on the dying wind, came the sound of voices. And one of them was the piping voice of a child.

A couple of paces inside the courtyard, I paused to consider how I would handle things with Carlton Ferguson. I was still considering when a door to the wing on my left opened and a woman came out. She saw me and stopped, and we stood there staring at each other for about five seconds before she said in a low anguished voice, "Oh my God."

She was the woman who had kidnapped Timmy, the woman I knew as Nancy Clark.

31: McCone

Sun was streaming into the room when I woke on Tuesday morning. I sat up and looked at the clock. A few minutes after ten. I'd overslept.

Then, because the damage had been done and a few more minutes wouldn't hurt, I lay back down again.

The room was the one I'd occupied my whole life before I moved north to go to school at Berkeley. It was a pleasant place, with pale yellow walls and flowered curtains, but it bore no traces of my former occupancy. The McCone family was too big and the grandchildren were too numerous to preserve shrines to departed members, and soon after I'd left home, my remaining possessions had been relegated to the attic. It was just as well: I really didn't want to have to look at high-school pennants, pictures of old boyfriends, and snapshots of me in my cheerleading costume and prom dresses. About the only thing I missed was the red plush kangaroo with a baby in its pouch that had been my constant companion until a disgracefully advanced age. Roo-Roo had taken the place of dolls; I had *hated* to play with dolls.

My thoughts quickly turned from the kangaroo to more troubling things. Don, for one. I ought to call him again but, frankly, I was afraid the woman named Laura would answer the phone. Laura, who in no way was his cousin from Tacoma. Don had lied to me — something he had never done before. . . .

Think about something else, I told myself. Think about what you plan to do today, about Borrego Springs and Les Club.

That club connected several people — maybe more than I'd thought of last night. I ought to drive out to Borrego Springs, see what it was. But before I did that, I'd better make a few phone calls.

I got up, showered, and dressed in a hurry, then took out Elaine's address book. Since I could hear Ma rattling around in the kitchen, I used the phone in the living room. First I called Sugarman, only to be told by her secretary that she was out of town. On an impulse, I asked, "Is she in Borrego Springs?"

"Possibly. She didn't say where she was going."

"But she does go to Borrego Springs frequently? She does know people there?"

There was a pause. "I'm afraid you'll have to ask Ms. Sugarman about that." Which probably meant the answer was yes to both questions.

I took Arthur Darrow's business card from my pocket. He was an investment counselor — although I wondered how much business he did in a desert community like Borrego Springs — and likely to be in his office at this hour. But when I dialed the business number on the card, the answering-service operator said he was out of town.

Next I called the home number, hoping to speak to Mrs. Darrow — if there was one — or some other member of the family. The phone rang several times, and then a woman's voice said, "Darrow residence."

"Is Arthur Darrow in?"

"I'm sorry, he's unavailable."

"Is this Mrs. Darrow?"

"This is their housekeeper."

"When will Mr. Darrow be available?"

"Not for several days."

"Is he on vacation?"

"I'm sorry, I can't give out that informa-

361

tion. I'll be glad to take a message, if you like."

"Is Mr. Darrow at Les Club?"

There was a pause. "Where?"

"Les Club."

"I'm sorry, but I don't know what you're talking about. If you'll leave a message—"

"Thank you. I'll call back."

I hung up and began looking through the address book for June Paxton's number, then remembered it wasn't there. Even though I'd dialed it many times since Karyn Sugarman had given it to me, the intervening period had wiped it from my mind. I'd have to find the piece of paper Sugarman had written it on, which should be somewhere in my purse, but first a cup of coffee would help.

I went down the hall to the kitchen, where I found Ma kneading bread. She is an expert baker — one of the few talents I've inherited from her. She frowned when she saw me.

"Are you on your way out again?"

"Yes, Ma." I went and got a cup of coffee from the percolator.

"You've been mighty busy this visit."

"Well, the convention takes a lot of time."

"I thought that was over Sunday."

I hesitated. Ma worried about me; I'd never been able to fool her into thinking my job

362

wasn't dangerous. If she knew I was conducting an investigation, it would only upset her at a time when — given John's problems — she didn't need any more aggravation. Finally I said, "I have to admit it. I've met a man."

Her eyebrows rose. "A man? At the convention?"

"Yes."

"He's not another detective, is he? The one with the Italian name who called?" Ma had not approved of my relationship with the homicide cop Greg Marcus, because she'd been afraid he'd involve me in more of what she called "those terrible things you poke your nose into." She hadn't met Don, but I sensed she thought his work as a disc jockey too frivolous to qualify him as a proper suitor. And I was afraid that she would heartily disapprove of another investigator.

"No," I said, remembering Wally and the date we were supposed to make, "he's a lie-detector salesman."

She looked relieved. "A lie-detector salesman. Do they make good money?"

"Probably. I think they work on commission."

"Hmm." She gave the bread a final punch and popped it into a bowl to rise. "Are you seeing him today?"

"We're supposed to have dinner."

"That doesn't explain why you're going out now."

I set my coffee cup in the sink. "Well, if I go to dinner, I have to have something nice to wear."

"You're going shopping?"

"Yes." Eventually, in the course of the next few months, I supposed I *would* go shopping. But since picking out a dress couldn't possibly take all day, and the trip to Borrego Springs would, I added, "And then I thought I might take a drive out into the desert."

She looked skeptical about that idea, but merely said, "Have you made any headway with your brother?" She has a way of switching subjects that only those who understand how her mind works can follow.

"Not much. He's as stubborn as the rest of us."

"Try again, will you please?"

"Yes, Ma." I kissed her lightly on the cheek and started out.

"Sharon," she said.

I turned.

"Be careful, while you're . . . uh, shopping."

I have never been able to fool my mother. Never.

★★★

The first thing I did was drive downtown to the phone company to check their directory for Borrego Springs. Since no one was home at Arthur Darrow's house, I needed more to go on than just his address. There was no listing for Les Club, or anything other than the town's two country clubs. Somehow I doubted either of them was it.

Then I went over to the recorder's office in the county courthouse and asked a few questions of the white-haired old man behind the desk. He was friendly, with bright blue eyes that twinkled like a man's half his age, and he flirted a little as he showed me how to search for property listings. Soon I was ensconced at a long table with a big registry for the Anza-Borrego desert area.

And about an hour later I had the location of a piece of property listed in the name of Les Club, Inc.

So it was incorporated. That meant the state would have a listing of the corporation's officers, and, given enough time, I could find out who was behind it. The trouble was, I had no time to spare.

I went back to the desk and asked the man if he could help me figure out the property's exact location. He came over and explained about tracts and lot numbers, then sketched a rough map on a piece of scratch paper.

I thanked him and hurried off to find out about Les Club.

32: "Wolf"

Neither Nancy Clark nor I moved for another few seconds after she spoke. I could feel the sweat trickling down my face, down from my armpits; the hot Mexican sun burned against the back of my neck. From out on the terrace, the little boy's voice rose in a shrill excited cry — a sound that some tropical bird hidden nearby mimicked with surprising accuracy.

I wanted her to move first, to break the tableau, because I wanted to see what she'd do. She didn't do much. Just came toward me in a herky-jerky stride, with her long legs flashing in the sunlight and shadow. She was wearing a two-piece black bathing suit that didn't cover much territory and her skin was browned to the color of toast; but when she got up close I could see that her face had gone pale under the tan. Her eyes had a stricken look.

"Who are you?" she said. "What do you want?"

"I came looking for Timmy."

"How did you find us?"

"Something the boy said when I talked to him in San Diego."

"Why? What do you want with Timmy?"

"That depends. His mother's in San Diego now, you know."

Her mouth opened a little; her tongue flicked out like a cat's to lick away a droplet of sweat from her upper lip. The stricken look stayed in her eyes, but it had been joined by smoldering anger.

She said, "What are you, some kind of detective?"

"Yes, ma'am. The private kind."

"Did Lauterbach send you? Is that it?"

"No."

The negative seemed to throw her off-balance for a moment. Then she said, "That bitch, then. Did *she* send you?"

"You mean Mrs. Ferguson?"

"Who else would I mean? Well, I'll tell you this, mister — you're not taking Timmy back to her. He belongs here with his father."

"That's not what the courts in Michigan decided."

"The courts in Michigan don't know what a nasty cunt Ruth Ferguson is. If they did they wouldn't have granted her custody of a dog, much less a child."

"Meaning what, Miss . . . Clark's not your real name, is it?"

"It's Pollard, and I don't give a damn if you know it."

"Meaning what about Ruth Ferguson, Miss Pollard?"

"Meaning just what I said. She abused Timmy. You don't know that, do you? Well, it's true."

"Abused him how?"

"Whipped him. Locked him in a dark closet for hours at a time, without food, when she decided he'd been naughty. God, what I'd like to do to that woman!"

"How do you know all this?"

"Carl found it out. She's not the only one who can hire detectives."

"So you snatched Timmy and brought him here. Kidnapping is a major crime, Miss Pollard. You can get twenty years in jail for it."

"I don't care about that. Don't you understand? We had to get Timmy away from his mother before she really did something ugly to him."

" 'We?' " I said. "What's your relationship to Carlton Ferguson?"

"I live with him. I have ever since he

369

divorced that bitch and moved down here."

Which made her the "very beautiful woman" Pablo Venegas had told me about, the one who shared this villa with Ferguson. Yeah, that figured. Having her grab the kid out of his school was better, safer than hiring somebody. The fewer people who knew where Timmy was being taken, the slimmer the odds that he could be traced. Keep it in the family, I thought cynically, that's the best way to do it.

"Aunt Nancy! Hey, where are you?"

We both turned. Timmy came running out of the tunnel in the back wing — a white streak in a pair of flowered swim trunks, wet blond hair flattened down on his head. He slowed when he saw us, stopped altogether when he recognized me. But then he smiled and came the rest of the way to where we were; he seemed pleased to see me, the way kids are when they get an unexpected visit from an adult who was nice to them.

"You're the man from San Diego," he said. "The man with the funny name."

I nodded. "How are you, Timmy?"

"Great! My dad's got a neat pool."

"He does, huh?"

"Yeah. Aunt Nancy wouldn't let me go swimming any of the other places, but ever since we got here I can swim all I want."

"Good for you."

"I'm getting a tan too. See?"

He turned around so I could see that the white skin of his back was reddened with a light sunburn. But I could also see something else, something that brought a tightness into my chest and made my hands flex involuntarily. Down low on the boy's back were a series of horizontal, all-but-healed marks that looked to have been lacerations — the kind you get when somebody lays a stick across your hide.

I glanced at Nancy Pollard. She knew I'd noticed the marks, and her mouth was set in a thin, tight line. Her expression said: "There, you see?

Timmy was facing me again. "Did you come here to see my dad?" he asked.

"Yes. But I wanted to see you too."

"You did? Really?"

"Really. Is your dad here now?"

"Sure, he's out by the pool. Come on, I'll show you." He wheeled and ran a little way and then stopped to see if we were following. "Come on! You too, Aunt Nancy!" Then he was off again, into the shadows of the tunnel.

I went after him, not hurrying; Nancy Pollard fell in alongside, walking in a stiff-backed way, eyes straight ahead. When we emerged onto the terrace I saw that it was about the size of a football field, floored in squares of colored tile, with a waist-high stone parapet all around. The pool was on the left, an L-shaped job made out of gray stone, without the usual diving board and chromium ladders, so that it resembled a pond. A couple of wooden walls had been erected on the inner sides, to help support a clear Plexiglas roof; the other two sides were open and had pole supports and rolls of mosquito netting — a nifty arrangement that would allow you to drop the netting and swim at night without getting gnawed on.

Near the pool was a palm tree to provide shade, and under its fronds, on one of several pieces of dark wood deck furniture, was a brawny guy in trunks and huaraches and a pair of wraparound sunglasses, reading a magazine. He glanced up as Timmy raced toward him shouting something about a visitor, and when he saw me he got up on his feet. It was like watching a bear get up. He had enough hair on his chest and shoulders and arms to make a winter coat for a midget.

Timmy ran to him and he put his arm around the boy. He wore an expression of mild puzzlement, but that changed when Nancy Pollard nodded at me and said,

"Carl, he's a detective," in a flat warning voice. His face closed up hard, his eyes got dark with anger and something else — resolve, maybe. You could see the muscles tensing up and down his body.

I stopped and Nancy Pollard stopped, and we all looked at each other in heavy silence. I didn't want to talk in front of the boy, and neither did Ferguson. He said, "Timmy."

"Yes, Dad?"

"Go inside and ask Maria-Elena to bring three bottles of cold beer and some snacks. Stay there and help her get everything together."

"Do I have to?"

"Yes. Go on, now. Be a good boy."

"Can I have another of those mango drinks?"

"Tell Maria I said it was okay."

Timmy nodded, gave me a shy smile, and was off again. Nancy Pollard moved to stand next to Ferguson; the two of them were like a barrier between the running boy and me. None of us said anything until Timmy was out of sight. Then Ferguson said, controlling the words, "You're not taking him. Not unless you've got a platoon of Mexican *policia* waiting outside."

"I didn't come here for that, Mr. Ferguson."

"No? Then why did you come?"

"To meet you. And to find out some things."

"What things? Who the hell are you?"

"He's a private detective," Nancy Pollard said. "He was at the hotel in San Diego. He's the one I caught talking to Timmy before that woman died."

Ferguson said to me, "Who are you working for? Lauterbach? Or my ex-wife?"

"Neither one. I'm here on my own."

His mouth took on a bent, bitter look; he thought he had me pegged now. He said contemptuously, "Blackmail."

"Wrong. But it might have worked out that way if Lauterbach hadn't been murdered."

Both of them reacted to that, with surprise that seemed genuine enough. "What happened to him?" Ferguson asked. He sounded puzzled again. "How was he killed?"

"Somebody shot him Sunday morning. In his office building."

Nancy Pollard caught her breath — a second reaction almost as sharp as the first. When I looked at her, she wouldn't meet my eyes; she turned a little to one side to make avoiding them easier.

I said, "You know something about

Lauterbach's murder, Miss Pollard?"

"No, of course not."

"When did you and Timmy arrive here?"

"That's none of your business."

"Nancy," Ferguson said. "Let's get to the bottom of this." Then, to me, "They arrived yesterday morning around ten."

"Were you here to meet them?"

"Certainly."

"Were you here all weekend?"

"Yes. Are you trying to imply that Nancy or I had something to do with Lauterbach's death?"

"The thought crossed my mind," I said. "He recognized Timmy somehow, at the Casa del Rey hotel, and put two and two together. One of the things he did was call your ex-wife and tell her he could find the boy for her. She's put up a five-thousand-dollar reward for Timmy's return. Or maybe you already know about that."

He didn't say anything.

I said, "Lauterbach could've traced you, gotten in touch, and tried to blackmail you for more than the five thousand."

"Well, he didn't. I didn't even know he'd moved away from Detroit until—" Abruptly he broke off.

"Until what? Until Miss Pollard told you she saw him at the Casa del Rey?"

They exchanged glances.

"Yeah," I said. "*She's* the one he tried to put the bite on, isn't she?"

Ferguson said, "Neither Nancy nor I is a murderer. Believe that or not, but it's the truth."

"Let's say I believe it. I still want to know what happened between her and Lauterbach."

Nancy Pollard glanced at Ferguson again, wet her lips, and said, "All right. Friday night was the first time I saw him. He and some other men from the convention were drunk. Timmy heard them singing and went outside when my back was turned — he's a very curious little boy."

"What happened then?"

"I ran out and got Timmy, and Lauterbach saw me too. I didn't know who he was; I'd never seen him before. He went away with the others and I didn't think any-thing more about it until Saturday morning. Then he showed up at our bungalow, alone."

"Demanding money?"

"Yes. I was terrified that he'd call the au-thorities and they'd arrest me and take Timmy back to his mother. I told him I'd call Carl, try to raise some money. He wanted to stay there while I made the call but I wouldn't let him. It was obvious he didn't know where Carl was and I wasn't about to let him find out. He said I'd better not try to run away because he'd be watching the bungalow, and finally he left."

"And what did you do?"

"Tried to call Carl, but the telephone service down here isn't very good and I couldn't get through. Then Timmy slipped out again and I found him talking to you. I thought you were working for Lauterbach, that he'd hired you to keep tabs on us. I was half frantic by then. I tried calling Carl again, still couldn't get through. I was still on the phone when the assistant manager, Ibarcena, came and said there'd been an accident, a woman had been killed. We weren't supposed to leave the hotel until Sunday morning but he wanted us to go immediately."

I asked, "Did you see Lauterbach around anywhere when you left?"

"No."

"Where did Ibarcena take you?"

"To a motel on the edge of the Mexican quarter."

"He left you and Timmy alone there?"

"Yes. That's where we spent Saturday night."

"Did you see or talk to Lauterbach again

before you left San Diego?"

"I . . . no."

"Try to get in touch with him at all?"

She hesitated. "Why would I do that?"

"You might have been afraid he'd think you left the Casa del Rey because of his blackmail demand. Afraid he'd be angry enough to call the authorities. *Did* you try to contact him, Miss Pollard?"

Another glance at Ferguson, who nodded slightly. She said, "You might as well know it all. I tried to call him several times at his home and at his office, both on Saturday night and early Sunday morning. Carl told me to keep trying; I'd finally got through to him late Saturday. We both felt I had to talk to Lauterbach before Timmy and I left for Mexico."

"And?"

"He answered his office phone about ten-thirty Sunday morning. He was angry, abusive; he wanted to know where Timmy and I were. I wouldn't tell him. He said that unless I came to his office inside an hour he'd call the police."

"Did you go?"

"I had no choice. But he wasn't there. That's the truth — I swear it. His office was unlocked and Timmy and I sat there for over an hour waiting, but he didn't come. I didn't know what to think. It never occurred to me that he might be somewhere in the building, dead. But I couldn't wait any longer. Ibarcena was picking us up at one o'clock. I had to take the chance that neither Lauterbach nor the authorities would be able to stop us from leaving the country, and that they wouldn't be able to find us down here."

"What time was it that you got to Lauterbach's office?" I asked her.

"After eleven sometime."

"Did you see anyone on his floor when you arrived?"

"No, no one."

"Anyone in the building?"

"Well . . . a man bumped into me in the lobby, coming out of the elevator just after we got there. I was standing in front of the doors when they opened and there he was."

"What did he look like, this man?"

"I don't know, I didn't pay much attention to him. He was just a man carrying a machine under one arm."

"What kind of machine?"

"It looked like a tape recorder, one of those small ones. I noticed that because a corner of it dug into my arm when he bumped me."

"Can you remember anything about him?

The color of his hair, his size, what kind of clothes he was wearing?"

"No. It was just one of those things that happen in two or three seconds. We ran into each other, he said, 'Excuse me, dear,' or 'sweetheart,' something like that, and then he was gone and Timmy and I were in the elevator."

"You don't have any impression of him at all?"

"No. I was too nervous and worried."

"Any chance you'd recognize him if you saw him again?"

"I don't think so."

The man had to be Lauterbach's killer, I thought. The time element was right, the tape recorder under his arm was right. He must have taken the recorder from Lauterbach's office after the shooting; I remembered that I hadn't seen any electronic equipment in there on Monday morning, and how odd that had seemed considering Lauterbach's past record and the stuff I'd noticed in his car on Friday night. Whatever had been taped on that machine figured to be the motive, or part of the motive, for his murder.

Not much of a lead without some clue to the man's identity, but a small lead was better than none. I would pass it on to the cop in charge of the case, Gunderson, as soon as I got back to San Diego.

I said to Ferguson, "Let's back up a little. How did Lauterbach know Timmy by sight?"

"I once made the mistake of hiring him, earlier this year in Detroit."

"To do what?"

"Confirm what a friend from Bloomfield Hills told me — that my ex-wife was abusing Timmy."

"And did he confirm it?"

"To my satisfaction, yes. But he tried to gouge me for more money and I fired him and brought another detective into it."

"Who also confirmed the abuse?"

"That's right."

"Why didn't you go to the authorities? Why kidnap the boy?"

"It was the only choice I had. The proof my detectives found is inconclusive in the eyes of the law. Timmy wouldn't have been taken away from my ex-wife immediately, not without an official investigation. And the boy is terrified of her — she threatened to beat him bloody if he ever told anyone how she treated him. She'd have done it too. She might have done it anyway, even if he hadn't told the truth. She hates Timmy because he's my son, a part of me. When she hits him she's really hitting me. Can you understand that?"

"I can," I said, "if it's true."

"You saw Timmy's back," Nancy Pollard said. "Isn't that enough proof for you?"

"Not necessarily. It doesn't prove his mother was the one who put those marks on him."

"Ask him. Just ask him."

"I guess I'll have to do that."

"I have the detectives' reports," Ferguson said. "I'll show you those too, if I have to. But why should I? I still don't know who you are or what you're doing here. Or how you found us." He turned to Nancy Pollard. "How could he find us with all that maneuvering around they put you through?"

"I don't know," she said. "Something Timmy said to him when they talked in San Diego . . . I don't know."

"What maneuvering?" I asked her. "And who's 'they'?"

She didn't answer. But Ferguson said tiredly, "The people I made arrangements with to get Nancy and Timmy from Bloomfield Hills down here."

"You mean Lloyd Beddoes and Victor Ibarcena?"

His expression went blank. "Who?"

Nancy Pollard said, "No, they were only

382

the ones at the last stop. It was somebody else Carl talked to, somebody in Chicago."

"I won't give you his name unless I have to," Ferguson said.

"Let me get this straight. This guy in Chicago runs some sort of escape network, is that it?"

"Runs it, or handles arrangements for it — I don't know which. I got his name through channels. It took me weeks and everyone was extra cautious."

"I'll bet. How does it work?"

"I'm not sure, exactly. But there are a number of different people involved. Nancy and Timmy were shunted over half the country last week."

She said, "They took us by car from one city to another and put us up in a hotel for a day or two. Kansas City, Denver, San Francisco, and then San Diego."

I nodded; I was getting it now. "The idea being to make it impossible for anyone to trace you and Timmy."

"That was the idea," Ferguson said bitterly. "Only you seem to have done it without much trouble."

"I got lucky." I turned back to Nancy Pollard. "Where were you taken from San Diego on Sunday?"

"A private airfield out in the desert somewhere. I don't know where. Ibarcena made us put on blindfolds. We waited there for hours before the plane came."

"And then you were flown down here?"

"To another airstrip somewhere in Mexico. Then we were blindfolded again and taken by car to a third airstrip. The plane from there brought us to Los Mochis."

So now the whole operation was clear, at least as far as the Casa del Rey was concerned. Beddoes and Ibarcena were little spokes in a big wheel — opportunists recruited to turn their hotel into a way station for fugitives on the move through the network, fugitives like Roland Deveer, the missing financier. Whenever they'd put somebody up in one of the bungalows, they had probably told selected members of the staff that the person was some sort of V.I.P. who desired anonymity, so no registration forms were to be filled out and they were to act as if the bungalow was empty. Elaine Picard was one of the staff members they'd have had to tell, because of her role as chief of security, and she'd doped out the truth — maybe seen Deveer and recognized him. That would account for the newspaper clipping Elaine had sent to her lawyer.

I considered pushing Ferguson for the

name of the man in Chicago, but I didn't believe it was necessary. Once Beddoes cracked — and he would, sooner or later — the identity of the ringleaders would come out. Yank one of the bricks out of the foundation of an organization like this and the whole shebang would collapse.

Ferguson said, "All right, now you know everything. Suppose you tell us just what it is you're investigating? Timmy's disappearance? Lauterbach's murder? The hotel men in San Diego?"

"All of those, in one way or another."

"And you don't have a client? You paid your own way down here?" He seemed incredulous. "What kind of detective are you?"

"Sometimes I wonder myself."

"Why didn't you just contact my ex-wife, if you knew where to find us? You said she's offering a five-thousand-dollar reward."

"I could have contacted her — she's in San Diego now, called in by Lauterbach, and I saw her on the TV news last night. But I didn't much like the way she talked about Timmy, as if he were a piece of property. And I remembered him telling me that he didn't like her because she made him afraid."

Ferguson nodded slowly. He no longer

seemed angry; a kind of wary hopefulness had come into his expression. "So you came to Los Monos to see if I might have had just cause to kidnap him. If I might be a more fit parent than his mother."

"Something like that."

"And? What have you decided, now that you know the whole story?"

I didn't say anything. Beyond Ferguson and Nancy Pollard, a door to the rear wing of the villa opened and Timmy came out ahead of a middle-aged Mexican woman carrying a huge tray. Ferguson saw me looking in that direction, glanced over his shoulder, and then put his gaze back on me.

"What are you going to do?" he said.

I still didn't say anything. But I didn't have to this time; it was there in my face. Ferguson read it, and let out a heavy breath, and Nancy Pollard read him, and then all three of us knew what I was going to do. They didn't speak either. We just stood there, waiting, and the only sound in the hot stillness was Timmy's voice as he ran toward us shouting, "Dad! Aunt Nancy! Wait'll you see what Maria-Elena made for us to eat!"

33: McCone

I took Interstate 8 east as if I were going to Woodall's house, turned north on Route 67 at El Cajon, and finally east again on Route 78. At the little town of Julian — a Western-style tourist town full of motorcycles, which was far too cute for my taste — I stopped and bought some chilled Calistoga Water as protection against the mounting heat. There were seven miles of sharp curves down Banner Grade from Julian, and then the landscape abruptly changed to desert.

The road lay before me, covered by shimmering pools of illusionary water that kept receding into the distance. The dry heat grew even more intense, making my skin feel papery, the membranes of my nose and mouth dry. Periodically I drank from the sweat-beaded bottle of water.

The land around me was sandy and flat, dotted with spiny jumping cholla and desert sagebrush. Smoke trees and lifeless-looking ironwood trees grew down in the washes. I thought of my childhood excursions to the desert, when I'd learned the names of these plants. The trips were supposed to delight, but in reality had only given me my first inkling of man's insignificance and inherent loneliness.

And then I ceased to think of anything much at all; the desert has that numbing effect on those who drive across it.

The only other vehicles on the road seemed to be campers, pickups, and motorcycles. An occasional truck hauled a dune buggy. The sky was starkly blue, and hawks wheeled across it. I kept going, over San Felipe Creek, where tamarisk trees and desert willows grew in abundance, toward the turnoff for Borrego Springs.

Named for the bighorn sheep that live high in the surrounding mountains, Borrego Springs is an oasis in the Colorado Desert. The gateway to the Anza-Borrego Desert Region, it sprawls in a valley, a palm-shaded little town with two country clubs and a small shopping area. The thought of getting out of the car and sitting in the shade — maybe getting something to eat — appealed to me, and I was about to turn north on Yaqui Pass Road when I thought to stop and check the map that the man in the recorder's office had drawn for me.

The map indicated I should continue on Highway 78 to the village of Ocotillo Wells. So much for a brief interlude under a palm tree. I put the car in gear and went on, past rocky washes and land where the vegetation became more and more sparse.

As I approached Ocotillo Wells, groups of campers and tents began to appear on the barren land on either side of the road. The village itself consisted of a café, store, and Mobil station. Its one dubious claim to fame is being the "dune buggy capital of the world," because of its proximity to the Ocotillo Wells State Vehicular Recreation Area. I smiled wryly as I drove in, thinking, What if Elaine came out here to roar around in a dune buggy? What if Les Club is nothing more than a bunch of motorized maniacs?

Somehow I knew that wasn't it.

From Ocotillo Wells, the map showed I should take Split Mountain Road south toward the former site of Little Borrego, but I decided to ask directions anyway. Maybe someone here would know of Les Club and simplify matters for me. I pulled into the gas station, where a few scruffy-looking young men stood drinking beer around a dune buggy. I parked to one side, and went into the office. A sun-browned teenage boy came out of the garage area, wiping greasy hands on a rag.

"Help you, ma'am?"

"Yes. I'm looking for a place near here called Les Club."

He looked blank. "Never heard of it."

"I have a map."

He took it gingerly, trying not to smear it with grease. "Oh, yeah. I see. What you do is take Split Mountain Road, the one right next to the station here, almost to where it ends at the big gypsum mine. There's a rutted road that branches off to the south. You follow it about seven miles up to the foothills. Part of it's pretty badly rutted, so be careful in that little car. The old Matthews place is at the end of it."

"What kind of place is it?"

"You never been there before?"

"No."

He grinned. "Then you'll see. I don't want to spoil the surprise." He turned and went back into the garage.

I drove down Split Mountain Road, past the Elephant Tree Ranger Station. At first I saw dune buggies running alongside the roadside, but soon they disappeared, and by the time I got to the turnoff, I felt as if I were the only person for miles around. Within sight of the entrance to the U.S. Gypsum Mine, I turned right, onto a washboard surface, and bumped along toward the foothills.

It seemed a funny place for a club — or for anything else. There was nothing out here but sand, sagebrush, and thorny ocotillo. As the boy had said, the last couple of miles the road was badly rutted, and I had to put the car in first gear. The road snaked through a wash, then up a steep rise toward where the eroded, wrinkled hills rose. At the top, I slammed on the brakes and stared.

It looked like no club I'd ever seen before in my life. I couldn't imagine what activities the members could have engaged in out here in the barren desert, much less inside such an odd structure. And the place was no less strange for the fact that I had heard it described by Wolf when he was talking about the pictures he'd seen in the file in Jim Lauterbach's office.

The house was low, built of adobe and native stone, whose color blended into the landscape. It was composed of curved, windowless walls and numerous cylindrical shapes, and the front door resembled the opening to a kiln. On its roof perched three giant air conditioners, known as swamp coolers, a type frequently used in desert climates. Even from where I sat in the car, I could hear their noisy rattling.

The house stood out against the heat-hazed hills and was surrounded by dark green greasewood bushes and the ashy-white shrubs known as burroweed. To the right, at a fair distance, were the remains of an old water tower and a loading platform that apparently had once served a spur railway. The sections of track that were still there were badly rusted. In front of the house was a large parking area with one car in it — an orange Datsun.

Well, at least there was someone here. Maybe now I'd get some answers to my questions.

I continued downward from the rise and parked next to the Datsun. Getting out of my car, I watched the house for a moment, and when no one came out, I went around the other car and checked the glove compartment for its registration.

The Datsun belonged to Karyn Sugarman.

I stared at the house again, my eyes narrowed against the sun's glare, then went up to the door. The rattle of the swamp coolers was very loud, and I could smell the resiny sweet odor of the greasewood trees. I looked around for a doorbell, then noticed that the door stood open several inches.

Knocking on the frame, I called out, "Karyn? It's Sharon McCone." There was no answer. After a moment, I pushed the door open wider and looked in. There was a round entry with a slate floor and adobe walls the same color as the exterior of the house. No one was in sight.

I stepped through the door, calling out again. It was chill inside — and very quiet. The roar of the swamp coolers was muted by the thick walls and roof.

The curving wall of the entry was broken by five archways. The largest, straight ahead, led into a sunken living room crammed with brown modular couches that were strewn with lighter brown pillows. In the center was a round pit fireplace with a copper hood. I went down the three steps and stood looking around. The room was quite dark, because of the lack of windows, but I noticed track lighting on the ceiling. At the far side was a wet bar and on it stood a half-full bottle of Scotch.

A living room? What people in the seventies used to call a "conversation pit"? I spied a glass on the edge of the fireplace, about a quarter full of amber liquid and small fragments of ice. I went over and lifted it gingerly, sniffed its contents. Scotch, like the bottle on the bar. Someone had been sitting here with a pretty hefty drink — and not all that long ago.

Who? Sugarman? Probably. But then why hadn't she answered my call?

I went back to the entry and through the next archway, calling out again. It opened into a formal dining room, replete with a huge table and silver candelabra. The table, however, was only two feet off the ground and surrounded by mats and pillows, It would have reminded me of a traditional Japanese restaurant, except the decor — ornate red and gold and black — was distinctly non-Oriental.

A swinging door led from the dining room to a kitchen full of stainless steel, butcher-block wood, a huge range, and three refrigerators. It had a sterile appearance, as if it hadn't been used in a while. Retracing my steps through the dining room, I headed for the entry to try another of the archways. This time I didn't call out; something about the silence in the house told me no one was here, in spite of Sugarman's car.

The archway I chose led into a hall with six doors leading off it. I opened one and saw a round room — one of the cylindrical shapes I'd noticed from the front of the house — equipped with a water bed. There was clothing in the dresser drawers and in the closet — both men's and women's — but not more than one would need for a weekend. A connecting bath also contained only the necessities. I went through the door on the other side of it and stepped into a room with a king-sized bed.

A woman's tan leather purse lay on the bed, next to a halfpacked overnight case. I picked up the purse, rummaged inside it, and found a wallet containing Karyn Sugarman's driver's license and credit cards.

She wouldn't have gone away and left both her purse and her car. Unless she was out walking in the desert . . .

In this heat? She'd have to be crazy.

I looked more closely at the overnight case. It was partially filled with underthings, and one drawer of the dresser stood open. From the way the clothing was jumbled in the case, I guessed she had been packing rather than unpacking.

Why? I wondered. From what her secretary had implied, she'd only gone out of town this morning. Had she arrived here, unpacked and then changed her mind about staying? If so, what had caused that change? Or had she come here for the purpose of reclaiming these things?

Again — if that was the case — why? Because they provided a link between her and this place? Because something was wrong here and she didn't want that connection made?

Hastily I went through three more bedrooms. Two contained water beds, another a conventional king-size. All had various personal effects stored in them, but not enough to indicate anyone lived here permanently. I hurried down the hall to the last door, stepped in, and recoiled at a sudden movement nearby. Then I realized what I'd seen was myself.

The room — round like the others, but much larger — was all mirrors. They covered the walls and the ceiling. The floor space was taken up by the most enormous round bed I'd ever seen, covered by an equally enormous fur spread.

I stared around and caught my wondering expression reflected over and over, everywhere I looked. And as the knowledge of what this room — indeed this whole house — was used for finally dawned on me, my expression became rueful.

Les Club. *Not* bad French — a pun. L-e-s was pronounced "lay." Lay Club.

God, you're innocent not to have figured it out before this, I told myself. You must have teddy bears in your brain.

I hurried back to the entry and tried the next archway. Inside was a projection room, equipped once again with modular furniture and throw pillows. A screen was pulled down across from the projection booth, and I went in there and examined the titles on the cans of film.

Skinkicks . . . The Licentious Landlord . . . Saturnaha . . . Carousal on the Carousel . . . Master of the Whip . . . Bottoms Up . . . Three's a Sandwich . . .

I didn't have to look at the films themselves to know what they were about.

I rushed out of the projection room, crossed the entry, and went through the last archway. There was a door just inside it, heavy and carved, hung on huge iron hinges, with a big key in an old-fashioned lock. I grasped the knob and pulled it open.

The inside was bathed in a bloodlike gloom. I looked up and saw the source of the red glow: spots set into the ceiling. They were probably on a rheostat that had been turned down but not completely out. I felt around the door for the switch and pushed it up.

And found myself looking at a medieval dungeon.

"Jesus," I said aloud.

It was like nothing I'd ever seen before in my life. An honest-to-God dungeon, with dark stone walls and chains hanging off them, and a rack of whips. Hooks stuck out from the walls at intervals, and on them were ropes and cat-o'-nine-tails and hoods like those worn during the Spanish Inquisition. There were handcuffs and masks and blindfolds and paddles . . .

Paddles. I remembered the sorority paddle in Elaine's closet, the one that had surprised me because I hadn't known she'd gone to college. And the handcuffs and leather thongs in her dresser drawer.

"Jesus," I said again. Sado-masochism. Or perhaps the new, sanitized version — Domination and Submission — that they were now writing feature articles and pseudopsychological books about. D and S had turned into a big business recently. In San Francisco, there was a place that gave workshops in it; publications dealing with the joys of what its adherents called "imaginative sex" had sprung up all over. But call it S and M, or D and S — what did it matter? It was all the same, differing only in degree.

I stepped back, leaning against the wall next to the door, and my hand brushed its surface. The stone wall was vinyl. Vinyl wallpaper.

It would have been funny if what I was looking at hadn't been so disgusting. Disgusting and pathetic and sad.

I stood there, my eyes adjusting to the bloody light. Then I noticed that the room, unlike the others in the house, was not round but L-shaped. Mentally shuddering at what strange apparatus I might find there, I went over and peered around the corner into the other part of the ell.

It was smaller and more dimly lit. I could see more hooks with S and M paraphernalia. And elaborate three-foot-high sconces, also fitted with red bulbs. And on the far wall, a cross, made of sturdy pieces of wood nailed together.

Tied to the cross with heavy ropes was a figure. A long slender female figure whose head lolled to one side, its features obscured by a fall of light hair. . . .

I drew in a shuddering breath and moved forward. The cross was set low on the wall, and her head was only a couple of feet above mine. I reached up, brushed the hair back. And stared into the contorted, blood-suffused face of Karyn Sugarman.

There were vicious bruises on her broken neck. Blood had flowed from her nostrils but was now dry. Her eyes stared blankly at some point in eternity.

There was a ringing in my ears, and my vision blurred. I stepped back, letting her hair cover her mottled features again. My stomach lurched and I fought for control.

Got to get out of here, I thought. Get to a phone, call the police. Get help . . .

Behind me, in the other arm of the ell, I heard a noise. My stomach lurched again. I whirled and ran back along the wall and around the corner.

No one was in sight. But the door to the dungeon was shut and somebody was turning the key in the latch.

34: "Wolf"

The detectives' reports Carlton Ferguson had told me about — one set from Jim Lauterbach and the other from a large Detroit agency that had a name I recognized and a good reputation in the industry — pretty much corroborated the fact that Ruth Ferguson was an abusive mother. Talks with neighbors in Bloomfield Hills, tapes from bugs planted in the Ferguson house, the statement of a doctor who'd treated Timmy for a badly twisted arm and lacerations he'd received "in a fight with some other boys" — all that and more. Inconclusive in a legal sense, maybe, and some of it evidence illegally gathered and inadmissible in court, but enough for me. Not that I needed any more confirmation: what I'd seen and heard here, and my gut instinct, had already cemented my decision. You learn to trust gut instincts after a while; they're like old and reliable friends.

When I was done reading the reports, Ferguson and Nancy Pollard and I sat on the terrace, drinking cold bottles of Carta Blanca and talking, while Timmy splashed around in the pool out of earshot. I found myself liking the two of them. I don't condone kidnapping, even in extreme cases like this one, but people — good people — get driven to desperate measures sometimes, and they don't always use the best judgment.

I found myself liking Ferguson even more when he offered to reimburse me for my plane fare and expenses — and didn't insult me by offering any payment beyond that. I didn't say no to the plane fare and expenses; I figured I was entitled, since I had just blown the five-thousand-dollar reward for McCone and me. I also didn't say no when he offered to put me up for the night and to arrange a private flight straight back to San Diego first thing in the morning. He knew somebody in Los Mochis who made regular trips to Los Angeles twice a week — one of the days being Wednesday — and wouldn't be averse to delivering me on the way. And Ferguson was willing to drive me to Los Mochis himself, if I had no objection to getting up at four A.M. I had plenty of objection to being awake at that hour, but this time I waived it. He went in and made a call and came back to say that it was all set.

The Mexican servant, Maria-Elena, went out and sent Hernando on his way. A little later, she served us dinner on the terrace — *pescado espada al horno,* which was swordfish baked with olive oil and sprinkled with green onions and which was good enough to make even a confirmed fish-hater like me revise his opinion. Afterward we drank thick dark coffee and Mexican brandy and watched the sunset colors out over Topolobampo Bay and the Sea of Cortez. It was the kind of night you wanted to linger outside long after dark, to enjoy the stars and the lights along the coast and on the night fishers out on the bay, but the mosquitoes wouldn't allow that. Swarms of them drove us inside before it was full dark.

I said good night to Timmy in the big private room they'd given him. I didn't ask him if his mother had abused him; there wasn't any need to now, and he'd had enough pain as it was. But I did ask him if he was happy here, living with his dad and his Aunt Nancy. And he said, "Sure!" with considerable enthusiasm. "I wish my dad had sent for me a long time ago."

"What about your school?"

"Aunt Nancy was a teacher once. She's going to make me study. But that's okay. I like to read books."

"You don't want to go back to Bloomfield Hills? To your friends . . . your mother?"

"Uh-uh. I don't have any friends there — she never let me have any. And I don't want to see *her* again. Not ever."

Before I left him, I also asked if he could tell me anything about the man who had bumped into his Aunt Nancy in the lobby of Lauterbach's building on Sunday morning. He couldn't. Kids' memories are selective at his age; he didn't remember the man at all.

In my fan-cooled guest room I got undressed and lay down on the bed under its canopy of mosquito netting. I was pretty tired and I should have been able to sleep right away, but I didn't. It was still muggy in there, despite the fan, and all I could do was doze, hanging on the edge of sleep — that kind of half wakefulness where thoughts keep running around inside your head, some of them over and over, like the words to a song or to an intrusive little jingle.

Dear . . . sweetheart . . . dear . . . sweetheart . . . dear . . .

sweet . . . heart . . . dear . . . heart . . . dear-heart . . .

And all at once I was wide awake, sitting

up in bed. Then I was out of it, out from under the mosquito netting and into my pants and on my way through the quiet villa. There were lights on in the living room: Ferguson and Nancy Pollard were still up, sitting in front of the terrace windows, sipping a last snifter of brandy before bed.

They were surprised to see me up again, and even more surprised when I said to Nancy, "That man you saw in Lauterbach's building Sunday morning. You said he spoke to you after you collided outside the elevator. Something like 'Excuse me, dear,' or 'sweetheart,' you said. Do you remember the exact term he used?"

She blinked at me. "No, not exactly . . ."

"Was it dear? Or sweetheart?"

"Neither one. Something that sounded like one or the other."

"Dearheart?"

"That's it," she said. "Dearheart. 'Excuse me, dearheart.' Does that mean something to you?"

I nodded. I'd only heard the term used once that I could remember, and that had been last Friday afternoon in the Cantina Sin Nombre, by the man who had been annoying Elaine Picard.

Woodall. Rich Woodall.

35: McCone

I ran to the door, turned the knob franti-
cally. It wouldn't budge. I rattled it, then
pounded and shouted.

"Let me out of here!"

Silence on the other side of the door.

"Let me out, dammit!"

Nothing.

Then I heard a sound that might have
been the key being dropped on the floor,
and footsteps going away. They were pon-
derous, heavy. I kicked the door, shouting
again, but the footsteps faded and were
gone. I was alone. Alone with Karyn
Sugarman's corpse.

I let go of the knob. And then I began to
shake. The shakes turned into body-
wrenching shudders. I grasped my mid-
section and bent over, knowing I was on the
way to a real attack of hysterics if I didn't get
myself under control. Finally the near-

convulsions subsided and I sat down on the floor. The bloody light cast weird shadows and I closed my eyes to block it out.

Someone else must have been in the house all along — or arrived immediately after I came in here. Who? In all likelihood, Sugarman's killer.

But *who?*

That didn't matter now. What mattered was getting out of here.

I crept back to the door and crouched, listening. There was no sound out there. Had the person left, or was he in some other part of the house? Would he leave me here to starve? Or come back and kill me? There was no way of knowing. I had to chance trying to pick the lock on the door.

That type of lock wasn't going to yield to my favorite implement, the credit card. I looked around for something to use, wishing there were some way to tone down that blood-red glare without plunging myself into total darkness. Then I noticed that — quite incredibly — I still carried my purse, hanging now from the crook of my elbow rather than my shoulder. I thought of the Swiss Army knife Don had given me a couple of months ago — a decidedly unromantic gift by most people's standards, but one that suited both of us — and I reached inside the rear pocket of the bag. The knife caught on something and I gave it a vicious tug to get it out. Then I went to work on the latch.

After what seemed like an hour, I had to admit there was no way I was going to pick the lock. I flung the knife down in frustration, got off my knees, and started to pace the room — avoiding the ell where Sugarman's body hung.

In any other house there would have been some way out besides the door. Other houses had windows, heating ducts, air vents. But this place defied all normal concepts of construction. Or did it?

I began at the door and worked slowly toward the outside wall, tapping against the vinyl stones with the hilt of the knife. It was a large room and it took me a long while to cover it; I became accustomed to my surroundings and even the red light ceased to bother me. I tapped exhaustively, everywhere I could reach, but each tap struck solid adobe. There were no hollow-sounding spots, no open spaces that had been covered over by the wallpaper.

My lack of success only made me more determined. I went on, even along the wall where Sugarman's body hung. When I went by it, I kept my eyes averted.

What if I were stuck in here for days? I thought. Sugarman's killer hadn't come back; there was no reason to suppose he would now. What if nobody ever came and I died in here?

My stomach lurched again, and I fled the ell for the other part of the room. I sank to the floor, my back against the wall, breathing hard. I sat there for a long time before I roused myself and looked at my watch.

It seemed an eternity since I'd started tapping the walls, and indeed it was after ten. When had I been locked in here? Five o'clock? Six? I'd lost all track of time.

After a moment I told myself I had to resume tapping in the ell; it was the only chance I had. But somehow I couldn't bring myself to get up off the floor and go back in there by the body.

Look, I told myself, your life depends on this.

And somewhere inside me, a voice replied: I can't do it.

Yes, you can. Don't think about the body. Just do it!

I did it. But the effort was futile — the walls in the ell were also uniformly solid.

What now? I thought, sitting back down on the floor where I'd been before. Wait for someone to come? *Will* someone come, someone other than Sugarman's killer?

For some inexplicable reason I had a sudden sharp hunger pang. I remembered I hadn't eaten since the potato salad I'd gobbled out of the refrigerator last night. I never ate breakfast, and I hadn't been hungry later on because of the desert heat: I *shouldn't* be hungry now, not under this stress, but I was. Also I was thirsty. It had been a long time since I'd finished the bottle of Calistoga Water.

Well, hunger I could do something about, and maybe eating would distract me for a moment from the awful situation I was in. As a chocaholic, I always carry a couple of Hershey bars in my purse. I crawled over to where I'd left it in the middle of the floor and felt around where the candy usually was.

It wasn't there.

This was impossible! I always—

And then I remembered that a few days ago, two of Charlene's kids had been beating the hell out of each other and I'd bribed them to be good with the last remaining squares of chocolate. Charlene had been furious with me and had given me a big lecture on child-rearing.

Hunger was the least of my problems, however. I could live without food for quite a while. Water was a more serious deprivation. And what about air? How well was this room ventilated? How long would the oxygen supply hold out?

In response to that thought, I began to feel light-headed and leaned my head forward against my knees.

"Stop it, Sharon," I said aloud, sitting erect. "You've been in worse situations before."

Oh, yeah? the small voice answered.

"Yeah. Remember when that murderer had the knife at your throat? How about when you were almost trapped in that burning Victorian? And don't forget when you were locked in the storeroom of the old winery, with all those lunatics with guns outside."

There could be a lunatic with a gun here too.

"Don't think about that."

Then I realized I was talking to myself, and put my fingers to my lips. All I'd need was to sit here babbling like some wino on a Mission Street bus, while I should be thinking my way out of here. Logic dictated there must be *some* way. . . .

But I was tired and, try as I might to think, my mind wandered. Finally I looked at my watch again, then stared at it in amazement. It was well after midnight. I'd been here six hours, maybe seven. I slumped against the wall, looking despondently at a piece of crumpled paper—

Paper? I didn't remember seeing it when I'd come in. Probably, like the note Alice had found in one of my favorite childhood tales, it would say "Drink me."

I giggled at that. "Drink me." As if paper would assuage my thirst.

"Sharon, you're getting giddy," I said sternly. "And I don't care if I'm talking to myself, because there's no one to hear me and think I'm odd." Then I crawled forward, picked up the paper, and smoothed it out.

It was the piece of scratch paper on which Sugarman had written June Paxton's address and phone number on Sunday morning. Probably it had fallen from my purse when I yanked out the Swiss Army knife. June Paxton's name, written in bold, strong letters. Black felt tip on white; both now bathed in that bloody glow. Forceful letters, full of life . . .

And then I was suddenly alert, staring at them. My mind cleared. I sat back on my heels, holding the paper in both hands. And stayed there, frozen for a long time, while I began to put it all together. . . .

I got up and went into the ell where Sugarman's body hung. I stared at it without the pity and horror I'd felt earlier. And then, knowing I sounded half cracked — probably was half cracked — but not giving a damn, I began to talk to her.

"You loved Elaine, didn't you?" I said. "I know you did because I found that note at her house, in your handwriting. You said you couldn't get her out of your mind ever since that night at the club. *This* club. Isn't that right?"

I paused as if waiting for an answer, then went on.

"Which one of you introduced the other to Les Club? You, probably. You and Elaine had become friends, and you sensed she was ripe for a double life. The kind of double life you and all the other members of Les Club led. But she was heterosexual, not bisexual like you. What attracted *her* to a wide-open sex club? Lots of men, with no strings attached? Bondage? S and M?

"Sure, I bet that was it. She liked that sort of kinky stuff, just like you did. I should have realized that — you both seemed to know something about Beddoes and his porn collection, which is definitely oriented that way. More than you would have known if he'd been merely Elaine's employer. I'm willing to bet he's a member here too. And then Elaine had that paddle in her closet — a paddle with the insignia of the sorority *you* belonged to. I remember now — Elaine never went to college. We talked about that when she urged me to go — she told me how she regretted it. *You* gave her the paddle, didn't you? It was a joke. Some joke, Karyn."

I sat down on the floor, cross-legged, and resumed my monologue.

"But then things stopped being so funny, didn't they? Something happened out here. What? Well, that's easy to imagine, even for an innocent like me. Lots of people messing around in that living room — high on booze or grass or coke. Who? You, Elaine, Beddoes, maybe Rich Woodall. Or Rick, the masseur from that health club who wasn't above selling his body on the side. Who knows? It doesn't matter. What matters is what happened with Elaine and you. There you were — all ending up on that round bed in the room with the mirrors. And who does what — and to whom? What's the difference what sex they are?

"Elaine was probably horrified by what she'd done with you. That would partly explain her very noticeable depression. And

414

she also must have realized she'd gotten in over her head with Les Club. After all, Rich Woodall had started bothering her. Her life was no longer contained, compartmentalized.

"So what did she do about it? I think she probably quit coming here. I found all those slinky, sexy clothes exiled in the back of her closet, the handcuffs and thongs stuffed in a bottom drawer, your paddle tossed in with her mementos. I think she decided to get out while she still could. But she found she couldn't get away from it — not even at work. After all, her boss was a member of Les Club. I bet she got her job because she met him here. And he knew he could control his chief of security — because he had something on her."

My voice was growing hoarse from thirst and talking too much. But I kept on; I had to work this out.

"Okay, when Elaine quit coming here, what did you do? Probably not much at first. Continued to see her. Lunches, committee meetings for the Women's Forum. Little dinners. You thought you could win her over. You thought she'd be better off with you. Remember what you said to me about Elaine's sexual orientation? That she wasn't bisexual or lesbian and perhaps that was her problem. So you decided to court her. And when she still resisted, you wrote that note.

"And she crumpled it and tossed it away. She rejected you and your offer of love. When she didn't respond to the note, you tried to talk to her. I think you'd been trying for some days before she died. You must have been frantic — you knew you were going to lose her."

I knew I was going a little crazy, holding a conversation with a dead woman, but it seemed so normal to be confronting her with it all.

"I think you gave it one last try, Karyn, that morning after the breakfast meeting in her office at Casa del Rey. Remember how you told her you were going to escort June to her car so she'd leave Lloyd Beddoes alone? And on your way out to the door, you looked back and said — ever so meaning-fully — 'And remember — we have to talk about that other matter.' And Elaine nodded — ever so wearily — and said, 'Yes, I know.' "

I leaned back, propping myself on my el-bows, tired of sitting erect.

"There may be no way I can prove it, Karyn, but I think you came back to the of-fice after you escorted June to her car. You waited until Elaine came out of the meeting

416

with Beddoes and Ibarcena. And you had that talk. Why didn't you have it in the office? Because there were too many people around, and besides Elaine was due to chair a panel at the convention soon. So you went upstairs and into the tower, where it was secluded and quiet.

"Did you go up there with the intention of killing her if she rejected you? I don't think so. I think going there might even have been her suggestion — just a quiet, out-of-the-way place. Did you beg her? Plead with her? I guess you must have. And once again she turned you down.

"And that was it for Elaine Picard. Jealousy and rage made you shove her, and over the rail she went."

I paused. The words rang with such finality in the empty room.

"In a way," I went on after a moment, "it was also the end for you. Because somebody figured it out just as I have. Somebody who belonged to Les Club, probably. Somebody who cared for Elaine. He got you out here, and he killed you. I won't know who or why or how until I get out of here and find him."

If I get out of here, my inner voice said.

"*When* I get out of here," I said.

There was still a lot I didn't understand, however. I lay back on the floor, closing my

417

eyes. For one thing, I didn't see where Jim Lauterbach's murder fit. He couldn't have known that Sugarman had killed Elaine — or could he? Well, maybe. And maybe not. And what about Roland Deveer? And Timmy Ferguson? And Beddoes's and Ibarcena's scheme? Were all these things connected with Elaine's death? Or were they merely confusing side issues?

And then I slept, the heavy sleep of the truly exhausted. Slept on and on, wasting precious time. . . .

36: "Wolf"

The guy who flew me to San Diego from Los Mochis was an American named Bradley. He regaled me with an endless string of ribald stories in a buttery Southern drawl, some of them pretty funny, which helped to ease my terror at being up in his small, cramped, and speedy Beechcraft. But he was a good pilot — a professional who operated a full-time shuttle service — and we didn't run into any bad weather or other airplanes en route. So it wasn't a bad trip, all things considered. And he had me back on U.S. soil before noon.

I went through Customs in less than five minutes. Out on the concourse I spotted a bank of public telephones and started in that direction. The first person I wanted to talk to was McCone — to tell her that I'd soft-hearted us out of Ruth Ferguson's reward money, to find out if she'd learned anything, and to confer with her on my suspicions about Rich Woodall. She might have more information that I could arm myself with when I went to see the San Diego cops, something more concrete that would nail down Woodall as the murderer of Jim Lauterbach; if so, I would have an easier time keeping Timmy and Carlton Ferguson and Nancy Pollard out of it.

But I didn't get to the telephones immediately. What delayed me was a guy sitting in one of the waiting areas, reading a copy of the *San Diego Union* that he held wide open in front of him so the front page faced outward. I glanced at it as I went by, the way you do, and one of the larger headlines caught my attention and held it. I stopped and stared at the headline for a couple of seconds. Then I went on a quick hunt for a newspaper-vending machine. When I had my own copy of the *Union,* I sat down with it to read the story on page 1.

The headline said: HOTEL MANAGER IN MYSTERIOUS SUICIDE. And the story under it began:

The body of Lloyd R. Beddoes, 48, manager of the fashionable Casa del Rey on the Silver Strand, was found in his Point Loma home late last night, an apparent victim of suicide.

An empty bottle of sleeping pills and a suicide note were found nearby. County sheriff's investigators would not reveal the contents of the note pending the outcome of their investigation.

The mysterious death of Beddoes comes less than one week after Elaine Picard, Casa del Rey's chief of security, fell to her death from one of the hotel towers. Lieutenant Thomas J. Knowles, the officer in charge of both cases, refused to speculate as to a possible connection between the two. . . .

There wasn't much in the rest of the story. No mention of Victor Ibarcena; Beddoes's body had been discovered by a neighbor. The reporter did bring in the shooting of Jim Lauterbach, as "a third unexplained death in the past week," and hinted that it, too, might be connected to Beddoes's suicide. He also managed to deepen the mystery and hint at a bizarre angle by mentioning Beddoes's penchant for erotic art.

I put the paper down. Murder? Maybe; his death was no less suspect, on the basis of the skimpy information given in the news story, than Elaine Picard's. But I remembered

McCone's assessment of Beddoes, that he knew his world was coming apart and that he seemed to be coming apart with it. That type — weak, afraid of losing everything that mattered to him, afraid of prison — was a prime candidate for self-destruction. The odds were that he'd taken the easy way out.

But where did that leave the sheriff's-department investigation into the illegal goings-on at the Casa del Rey? Had Beddoes confessed his part in the escape network in his suicide note? Had Ibarcena been taken into custody or had he cut and run, as McCone had believed he might? I wouldn't know the answers until I talked to Tom Knowles. And if he *didn't* know about the escape network, then I would have to tell him; I couldn't withhold information like that from the authorities. The tricky part, again, would be finding a way to do it without revealing the whereabouts of Timmy Ferguson and my own peripheral involvement in his kidnapping.

Knotty problems. But there wasn't any point in worrying about it now; I would just have to see how things stood when I conferred with Knowles. And hope I didn't make a mistake that cost me my license again: I'd lost it once, through a set of circumstances that weren't really my fault, and if I lost it a second time I'd never get it back.

Meanwhile, there was McCone. Maybe *she* knew something about Beddoes's suicide. I hurried to the telephone and called her parents' house.

Her mother answered. "Sharon's not here," she said. There was both annoyance and concern in her voice. "I don't know where she is. She didn't come home last night."

"Didn't come home?"

"She said she was going out on a date with some man she met at the convention. A lie-detector salesman. If she'd been hooked up to his machine when she told me that, it would have gone crazy."

"You mean she lied to you?"

"Right in my face. The salesman called up here last night looking for her. He hadn't even talked to her since Saturday."

"Do you have any idea where she might be?"

"No. All I get from that girl is lies and double-talk. She makes *me* crazy sometimes. What she needs is a husband."

"When did you last see her, Mrs. McCone?"

"Yesterday morning. Around eleven."

"Did she say where she was going?"

"Yes, but I didn't believe her. More lies and

423

double-talk. 'I'm going shopping,' she said. 'If I go to dinner, I have to have something nice to wear.' Then she said, 'I might take a drive out into the desert,' and off she went."

Borrego Springs, I thought. "Did she say anything about a man named Arthur Darrow?"

"No."

"How about Rich Woodall?"

"No. Who are these men?"

"People in the case we're investigating," I said. "But don't worry, Mrs. McCone. She probably got hung up somewhere and couldn't get back home. Car trouble or something."

"Then why didn't she call?"

"Would she actually call in a situation like that?"

"Usually, yes. I'll say that much for her. She's not a bad girl, she's just too inquisitive for her own good."

So why *didn't* she call? I thought.

"Running around playing cops-and-robbers," Mrs. McCone said. "What kind of life is that for a young woman? Getting shot at, rubbing elbows with criminals and hookers and God knows what other riffraff. She ought to get married, settle down—"

"Thanks, Mrs. McCone," I said and hung up on her.

I hustled out to the car-rental booths in the main lobby. I had turned in the other clunker when I left for Mexico because I hadn't known how long I would be down there and I hadn't figured to need a car anymore when I got back. Well, I needed one now. It was a long way to where Rich Woodall lived. And an even longer way to Borrego Springs.

I was reasonably sure that Woodall had killed Jim Lauterbach, and it was possible that McCone had figured it out, too, and gone to brace him about it yesterday; she was just headstrong enough to do that without calling in the authorities first. The second possibility was that she'd gone to check out Arthur Darrow and something had happened to her in the desert. Both of those possibilities, coupled with Lloyd Beddoes's apparent suicide, made me worried and uneasy. There had been too many deaths the past few days, one right after the other — and McCone had her nose poked smack in the middle of them all.

37: McCone

I was aware of turning over on the hard floor of the dungeon a few times, of trying to pillow my head on my arms. Then I began to stir. I thought I had heard a noise, but it must have been part of a dream.

I sat up, stiff all over, and looked at my watch. It had stopped. Stupid of me not to have wound it. I wasn't hungry anymore, or even very thirsty. Long deprivation had almost made those senses dormant. I stretched my cramped body, then went over and sat by the outside wall — ignoring the dead woman because, after having slept, the craziness that had permitted me to deal with her the night before was gone.

I closed my eyes, trying once more to think of a way out of the dungeon. And then I heard a faint rattling sound, the sound I'd heard before that I'd thought was only part of a dream.

It came from directly above me, a noise from one of those swamp coolers I'd seen perched on the roof of the house. Why hadn't I noticed it last night? Probably because they operated on some sort of automatic timer, coming on and going off only when the heat was most intense. That would make sense; there were no power lines to the house and running the coolers all the time would only sap the generator.

I tried to dredge up what I knew about swamp coolers. They used water, usually from a hose from some outside source. And there had to be some sort of venting arrangement, sometimes as simple as an open window. I had a friend who lived in Phoenix who had a swamp cooler, and she'd complained of having to leave a window open and thus creating an invitation to burglars.

If this cooler was running, there had to be a vent. And the vent had to be close by.

Then why hadn't I found it during all that tapping I'd done last night?

Because it was someplace I couldn't reach. Like up near the ceiling.

Well, that was just great. Because I couldn't get up there to check.

Or *could* I?

I eyed the two ornate sconces, still burning

with red light. They were massive, sturdy. If I unplugged them, took the light bulbs out, and used each as a sort of stilt . . .

I rushed over and yanked their cords out of the wall socket. The bulbs were hot, but I ignored the pain as I unscrewed them. Listening carefully, I located the position of the cooler, then placed the sconces by the wall closest to it. Mounting them was a tricky proposition. Finally I stood up, my legs shaking, the sconces wobbling.

I began tapping the wall close to the ceiling. I had to move the sconces twice, but eventually I struck a hollow place. A large hollow place.

Dull excitement stirred inside of me. I climbed down, got my purse and the Swiss Army knife. After climbing back up again, I ripped at the vinyl wallpaper with the knife. It came off easily, and soon I was looking at a hole with rubber hoses poking through it. And beyond that was bright daylight, which half blinded me after the long hours in that hellish red glow.

Daylight. How long had I been in here anyway? Twelve hours? Eighteen?

I wrenched at the hoses, and they came free of the cooler above me. Water dripped down on my head as I pushed them out the hole, leaned forward, and squinted through it. I could see sand and rocks and ocotillo. In the distance was the old water tower. The sun glared down; it must be late morning.

The hole was big enough for me to slide through — if only I had the strength to hoist myself up to it. On the first try, my right foot slipped on the sconce. It clattered to the floor and I pitched downward after it. I landed on my side, tears of pain coming to my eyes. Brushing them away, I got up and righted the sconce.

This time I was more careful, getting a firm grip on the edge of the opening and pulling myself up slowly. I slipped partway into the space, wriggled forward, and poked my head out, estimating the distance to the ground. It was a good eight feet — but I'd fallen almost that far only minutes ago.

I wriggled farther forward. My purse caught on the edge of the opening; I gave it an angry tug. It came loose, and I curled in a ball, trying to get my feet out the opening. One heel caught on the purse strap.

I decided to abandon the bag. The only important thing in it was my car keys, and I kept an extra set in a little magnetic case under the dash. I gave the purse a kick and heard it drop onto the floor of the dungeon. Then I slid my feet the rest of the way through, pushed off, and fell to the sandy ground.

I lay there for a moment, stunned and blinded by the glaring light. The sun was well overhead, moving either toward or away from its meridian. Finally I got to my feet, wincing with pain, and ran around the house, toward the front where I'd left my car.

But my car was gone. So was Sugarman's. And in their place was a long white Cadillac.

38: "Wolf"

I had no trouble finding Lost Canyon Drive, the unpaved dead-end street Rich Woodall lived on out near Lakeside. The map I'd got at the airport car-rental booth was a good one, and the route up to this sparsely populated residential area from Highway 67 wasn't complicated. I parked in front of his house, a tile-roofed Spanish job set well back from the street, screened by palms and a big hedge full of red berries. His nearest neighbor had to be a half mile away. Some house for a man who earned his living doing P.R. for a public institution. . . .

I went along the front walk. The driveway that paralleled it was empty; I could see the garage toward the rear of the house, backed up against a brushy slope, but the doors were closed and I couldn't tell if there was a car in it or not.

Ringing the bell got me nothing but the

echoes of distant chimes. I went around to the rear and alongside the garage, to where a grimy window gave me a blurred view of the interior. An old red Porsche convertible sat there alone. But it was a two-car garage and there was a fresh-looking oil spot on the unoccupied side: Woodall probably owned a pair of cars and had gone off in the second one.

A seven-foot-high stucco wall with pieces of jagged glass embedded along its top barred access into the backyard; the gate in the wall sported a new chain and padlock. From the other side I could hear the sounds of animals moving around, the throaty cry of some kind of cat.

I looked around for something to stand on so I could see into the yard. There wasn't anything. Well, maybe I wasn't too old or out of shape to do a little climbing. I moved over to the gate, got one foot on the padlocked latch, and managed to hoist myself up. The broken glass took away any chance of my getting all the way inside, but at least I could see the cages and the animals that were in them: the yard wasn't big and everything was more or less grouped in close to the wall.

Badgers, a bobcat, a lynx, a couple of arctic foxes, some exotic birds I couldn't identify. And a glass cage full of snakes that looked uncommon. An odd assortment, I thought. Much odder than your average private menagerie.

I hung there a little longer, even though my bad left arm, the one that had never quite healed properly after I'd been shot over a year ago, was beginning to cramp up. I had had a job a while back that involved the theft of a variety of creatures from the San Francisco Zoo, so I knew something about endangered species. Badgers and lynx and bobcats and arctic foxes were all endangered animals. They were also the kind that unscrupulous people made coats, hats, and stoles out of. And the birds and snakes looked to be the sort coveted for expensive purses, shoes, and hats.

I knew some other things too. I knew that Woodall's P.R. job would put him in contact with all sorts of people who dealt with animals, including a supplier or two who might not be above making an illegal dollar now and then. I knew from what Eberhardt had told me that Woodall had once been arrested on suspicion of selling animals in violation of the federal Endangered Species Act. I knew from Woodall himself, via McCone, that somebody had broken in here a few days ago. I knew that Jim Lauterbach had been a blackmailer, and that there had been a list of check-marked names in his file on Elaine Picard — a list of potential shake-down victims, probably — and that one of those names had been Woodall's. And I knew, or was fairly certain, that Woodall had murdered Lauterbach.

Put all of that together and what did you get? You got Woodall still selling endangered creatures to the manufacturers of garments for rich and uncaring consumers, and Lauterbach breaking in here and finding out about it. You got Lauterbach trying to black-mail Woodall, and out of that you got at least part of Woodall's motive for blowing him away.

There were still plenty of loose ends. Such as: Why did Lauterbach break in here in the first place? What had he found out about Woodall and the others on that list that made them candidates for blackmail? And what was on the tape recorder Woodall had made off with after the shooting? One or more of the answers might lie in whether or not Woodall had also killed Elaine Picard. If he had, and Lauterbach found that out, too, Woodall's motive for murdering him would have been doubled.

I dropped down off the gate, massaged the stiffness out of my left arm and shoulder, and went back out to the rental car. Had McCone tumbled to all of this too? And if she had, had she tried to brace Woodall herself? The uneasiness was sharp in me now, and mingled with it were the stirrings of fear.

The nearest service station was half a mile from Woodall's house; I pulled in there and telephoned the administration office at the San Diego Zoo. The woman I spoke to said Woodall wasn't there, he hadn't come to work today. Hadn't called in, either. She had no idea where he was.

He wasn't home, he wasn't at work — where the hell was he?

And where was McCone?

39: McCone

I stepped around the dark green branches of a greasewood bush, out of the sun's glare, and stared at the place where my car had been. It wasn't difficult to figure out what had happened. Sugarman's murderer had found the magnetic key case under the dash and had driven the MG, as well as Sugarman's Datsun, off someplace — probably not too far away or he wouldn't have been able to walk back. The Cadillac must belong to him, and I was certain he hadn't been so foolish as to leave the keys in the ignition.

Still, its windows were open and I could get inside. And that was all I needed, since I possessed valuable, though untested, knowledge — I knew how to go about hot-wiring a car. It was something I'd picked up years ago from my brothers, who, while they never stole cars themselves, had traveled in a set where the ability to hot-wire was looked upon in the same way society people appreciate a low golf handicap.

I moved away from the protection of the greasewood bush and studied the front of the house. The door was shut and, owing to the lack of windows, I felt reasonably safe about going over to the car. Nonetheless, I hurried across the parking area in a crouch and slipped into the Cadillac on the passenger's side, which faced away from the house. Wriggling across the hot black leather seat, I checked the ignition. No keys.

I lay down on the seat and reached under the dash for the ignition wires. When I located them, I started to put them together, then realized I needed a way to hold them in place once the car was started. My brothers had advocated always carrying a stick of chewing gum for this purpose, but I had nothing on me but the Swiss Army knife — and that certainly wouldn't do the job. Glancing around the car, I spotted a paper clip on the floor and snatched it up.

Quickly I aligned the proper wires and pressed them together while I touched one foot to the gas pedal. The car started with a roar. I slipped the paper clip onto the wires and was about to sit up and put the car in gear when the engine died.

Damn! It must have something to do with

the paper clip. Something to do with metal shorting out the current. I ducked down and tried again. The engine started — and died.

Somewhere outside I heard a noise. Sitting up, I peered over the seat back and through the rear window. The door of the house was open and a man was coming out.

The glare of sun bouncing off the trunk lid and onto the rear window blinded me, so the only thing I could tell about him was that he was big — and running toward the car.

I pounded my fist on the seat in frustration, then ducked down and moved back across to the passenger's door. I slid out to the ground and threw a glance back along the road toward the rise. The sound of the man's footsteps came closer.

I hated to run, but in my weakened condition there was no way I could stay and fight. I looked to the left and spotted the ruins of the water tower and loading platform, about three football fields away across the hard-packed, rocky sand. As the man closed in on the other side of the car, I stood up and plunged off toward the tower.

The footsteps came after me. A spurt of adrenaline enabled me to speed up, in spite of a wrenching pain in the side I'd fallen on earlier. My breath came in gasps; about halfway there I faltered and looked back over my shoulder, expecting to see the man gaining on me.

But he had turned, and now was running back toward the house. He wore blue pants, a white shirt, and had lightish hair. His gait was shambling and erratic.

It both surprised and relieved me; the man must be old or ill or out of shape. But I knew that this might only be a temporary reprieve. He was probably going back to get a gun.

I ran on, finally reaching the shed and skidding around it. I slammed into the wall, and there was a stinging in my bare arm. Glancing down, I saw splinters and bloody scrapes. A nail had caught my blouse and ripped it along the side.

I gritted my teeth in pain and irritation, leaning on the wall for a moment. If I could get to the road, I could make it to the Elephant Tree Ranger Station — and help. But if I tried to run along the road I would be an easy target for a man in a car; that was why I'd come this way in the first place. It was better to find shelter in the desert and then double back to the road later — under cover of night, if necessary.

About a hundred yards away was an outcropping of rock, and beyond it the desert sloped downward from the foothills. I started running toward it, but when I crossed the remains of the spur track, my foot caught and I fell. Scrabbling to my knees, I looked back toward the house. The man had not reappeared.

I got up and kept running.

The rocks were sandstone, steep and crumbly. I went up them on all fours, clawing for handholds. At the top I flattened to the ground, panting, and then began inching along. After about five feet I came to a drop-off that ended in a drift of rock and sand. I rolled down it, the fine powder filling my shoes and caking my nostrils, the rocks cutting into my skin. Then I struggled to my feet.

The desert spread before me, ripply and wrinkled, with occasional outcroppings before it merged with more of the low, eroded hills. The sky above was relentlessly blue and clear. As far as I could see, everything was tan, dotted with dead-looking scrub vegetation, hazed with shimmering heat. There was nowhere to hide nearby. Nowhere to escape Sugarman's killer or the cruel rays of the sun.

I pivoted to the right and then the left, finally spotting a wash full of thorny underbrush. It was hundreds of yards away, across

440

open country where I could easily be sighted, but it was my only chance.

Once again I ran.

The sand was not so rocky here, and I felt as if I were running in slow motion. The intense heat seared my lungs. Every step brought wrenching pain to my side; my tongue was so dry it felt swollen. For moments it seemed as if I were running on an endless tan treadmill, but then the wash grew closer, and closer . . .

It was deep and rocky, full of mesquite and dead-looking cheesebush. I barely broke stride at its edge, sliding and tumbling down to the bottom. The rocks cut into my skin, tore at my clothing. I rolled to a stop against a low, rounded chuparosa bush, its thorny branches poking into my side.

There had been no sign of the man as I crossed the open sand, but that didn't mean I was safe. This wash, with its tall mesquite trees, was probably the only shelter within miles; it wouldn't take the man long to figure out I'd run for it. And it might be sheltering other things than me: there might be rattlesnakes; they went for shade in the heat of the day. I couldn't stay here.

Looking around for snakes, I got up and moved under the nearest mesquite, temporarily out of the sun, and looked off along the wash. It curved away for a long distance, becoming rockier, with sparser vegetation.

Not promising, I thought, but I'll have to follow it.

I felt a trickling on my upper arm and looked down. Blood oozed from a deep cut. Funny — the blood didn't feel warm, the way it usually did when you cut yourself. But of course, my skin was heated to a degree far higher than ninety-eight point six. I brushed the blood away, wiped my hand on my jeans. Then I started along the wash.

It curved and branched, as unpredictable as the flash floods that had helped to form it. I followed the branches that afforded the most protection from the sun, ever alert for the presence of snakes, trying at the same time to maintain my mental fix on the direction of the road. If the wash eventually came out closer to it, I would chance moving into open country and going for help.

The terrain kept getting rougher. After a while I was stumbling over large rocks, then clambering over boulders. Periodically I glanced over my shoulder and up at the rim of the wash, but there was no sign of a man with a gun. Gradually the wash narrowed, and finally it ended in a rough V of sandstone.

The V created shade, and I slumped down

in it. My head was pounding, my tongue swollen. Sweat came out on my body, but dried almost immediately. Even the matted hair at the nape of my neck was barely damp. Dust caked my nostrils, making it difficult to breathe.

Got to have water, I thought.

A wave of dizziness swept over me, and I closed my eyes and leaned my head back against the sandstone.

Can't stay here without water, I thought. I'll die without it.

I thought of Don. His familiar, swarthy face swam in the darkness behind my eyelids. A couple of days ago I'd been worried because of an unknown woman named Laura, a lie he'd told me. Now I was worried I'd never see Don again. And what of my family? Or Wolf? What about my other friends, and the folks at All Souls?

I pictured them all, and then the images blurred and were gone. The dizziness passed, and I opened my eyes. I was looking at the sharply sloping side of the wash above me.

You've got to climb it, I told myself. You're boxed in down here.

I struggled to my feet and started up.

There were very few hand or toe holds, and I kept slipping backward. For minutes it seemed I lost more ground than I gained. The knees of my jeans tore out and my already sunburned skin became scraped and bloody. Sliding on my stomach, I finally gained the rim of the wash.

I lay there gasping, looking around. No one was in sight, and all around stretched the barren, sun-washed desert. It was dotted with spiny cactus, sand verbena, and ocotillo, but otherwise there were no signs of life. None of the little animals that lived out there were stirring, and there wasn't even a jeep track to show that anyone had been here before me.

I couldn't see the house or the water tower. I couldn't see the road to Les Club, or Split Mountain Road, or the utility lines that stretched along it. If those lines had been visible, I could have got to the ranger station and help. But they were nowhere in sight.

I stared bleakly into the distance, realizing I was lost.

I'd lost all sense of direction while following the curving, branching wash. The hills ranged around me, but I couldn't tell if the ones I was looking at were the same I'd seen earlier as I'd lain on top of the sandstone outcropping within sight of the old water tower. I stood up and searched for a landmark, but saw nothing.

How far had I come from the house? I wondered. How long had I been out here? Hours, it must be. My tongue clogged my mouth, my eyes were dry and sandpapery. How much longer could I last? I didn't even know which direction to take to get to civilization.

Direction. I could figure direction from the sun — the damned sun. It beat down on me in pulsing waves. I glanced up, shading my eyes, and noted its position.

The unpaved road to Les Club — whatever its name was — ran southwest. Southwest. But that didn't matter now. I needed shelter. And water.

Once again I scanned the horizon, my eyes burning. There had to be something. . . .

And then I saw a gray-green haze. Clouds of smoke some distance away. Smoke? I strained my eyes. The clouds swam into focus.

Trees. Smoke trees, named for the illusion I'd just witnessed. And other trees — tamarisks, and what could be desert willows. Trees that grew near water holes . . .

They seemed an infinity away, across an endless stretch of rocky sand. How far? I wondered. Half a mile? More? It didn't matter. Those trees meant shade — water.

I began moving again.

I went more slowly this time, to conserve my flagging strength. My breath wheezed in my throat, and wherever there was a little shade, I stopped and rested. Still my heart felt as if it would explode. My skin felt as if it might begin to bubble. I stumbled a number of times, fell twice. But I kept going, gasping and clutching my side, and thinking of water. The trees loomed larger, and then I reached them and plunged into them, down a rocky incline, to the bottom where the water would be.

I fell flat, the shade of the trees coming between me and the wicked sun rays. I lay there for a moment, then pulled myself up and crawled on all fours to the water hole. Leaned forward, toward the precious water.

Only it wasn't there.

At another time of the year it would be. But not in August. Not in the hottest month of the year.

My throat constricted and a whine came from my lips. I crouched there, staring into the sun-cracked bottom of the water hole. My sight blurred and visions started to dance before me.

Sugarman hanging on the cross . . . Elaine's broken body . . . Others, out of the past: bodies with strangled faces . . . bloodied heads . . . stab wounds . . . bullet holes . . .

I would join them — all of them, this legion of the dead.

Then the visions were gone. I lowered my head to the ground. And lost consciousness.

40: "Wolf"

It was bloody damned hot in the desert. It hadn't been so bad in the San Diego area, after that liquid humidity of the Mexican coast, but out here the temperature must have been up over a hundred. Heat shimmered off the highway, glared off the metal surfaces of other cars, made the stark countryside look sere and fiery, and blew inside the rental heap like the breath of Old Nick himself. The car had air conditioning but it had conked out coming down the steep Banner Grade. Which figured. If I hadn't insisted on the cheapest rental the National agency had, this sort of thing wouldn't have happened. And I wouldn't be roasting and dripping like a chicken under a broiler.

The turn for Borrego Springs, off Highway 78, was called Yaqui Pass Road. It climbed, steep and winding, up a sagebrush-strewn hill, and from where it crested you had a pretty awesome view of empty desert spread out to the southwest. A short while later, I had my first look at Borrego Springs. The town was scattered over the floor of a brown, beige, and dull green valley, with massive, barren mountains ringing it in the distance. This entire area was part of the Anza–Borrego Desert Region — several hundred miles of state park that stretched almost to the Salton Sea on the east, almost to the Mexican border on the south.

I was here because I didn't want to believe McCone had gone to see Woodall yesterday, that he'd done something to her. And because I had nowhere else to look for her. Nowhere else to go period, except back to San Diego to see Tom Knowles. Which was what Knowles wanted me to do. I'd finally got in touch with him, by phone from the service station near Woodall's house, and told him what I suspected. But I was in no mood for sitting around doing nothing while he made up his mind whether or not to put out an APB on Woodall and on McCone. When he'd told me to come in and talk to him in person I had pretended that there was something wrong with the line and hung up on him.

Down in the valley I passed La Casa del Zorro, the resort hotel where June Paxton had seen Elaine Picard and Rich Woodall having dinner; but I couldn't see much of it because it was hidden inside a grove of densely grown palms and tamarisk trees. The town, some distance beyond, wasn't much to look at: plain desert-style buildings, most of them designed to cater to tourists and to the horde of motorcycle riders and dune-buggy drivers who clogged a central green called Christmas Circle. I looped around the circle, drove past the Road Runner Realty Company, and stopped at a Union 76 station.

Arthur Darrow was listed in the local telephone directory — a number on Pointing Rock Road. Darrow was the only lead I had out here; if McCone *had* come to Borrego Springs yesterday, she'd probably have looked him up. The station attendant told me how to get to Pointing Rock Road. He also told me that as far as he knew, there was no House of Slenderizing and Massage or any other health club in town. No clubs of any kind, he said, except for the De Anza Country Club and the new Ram's Hill Country Club.

The Darrow house turned out to be nestled up against the De Anza Country Club's golf course, with its backside abutting one of the greens. It wasn't quite what I'd expected, somehow: a smallish hacienda-style place, with a low brick wall in front that sported a couple of old wagon wheels for decoration. The yard behind the wall had a patch of lawn, some dwarf palms and yucca trees, a lot of prickly-pear cactus, and two orange trees heavy with fruit. Still, the place had the look of money. Whoever Arthur Darrow was, he didn't have to worry about where his next meal was coming from.

I parked the rental car in front. In the adjacent driveway was a newish Chevy pickup with the words MILNE GARDENING SERVICE painted on its door; a big man wearing a blue shirt with the same words on its back was kneeling in front of one of the orange trees, trimming the grass around it with a pair of hand clippers. I went up the path past him to the narrow front porch and rang the bell. Nobody answered. I rang it again, waited awhile longer, and then turned and went down the path and over to the gardener. He hadn't paid attention to me up to then, and he didn't pay much to me now.

"Afternoon," I said. "I'm looking for Arthur Darrow. Or his wife. Would you know where I could find either of them?"

He stood up, dragged a handkerchief out of his back pocket, and mopped his sweaty face. He was in his sixties, sun-creased and in better physical condition than I was. A pair of mild gray eyes gave me a brief appraising look. "You don't look like one of their friends," he said. He didn't seem to mean it as an insult.

"I'm not. It's a business matter."

"They're not here," he said.

"So I gathered. Can you tell—"

"Hawaii," he said.

"Pardon?"

"They're in Hawaii. Another vacation."

"When did they leave?"

"Last week. They go to places like that three or four times a year — stay a month. Must be nice to have money."

"I wouldn't know," I said.

"Neither would I."

There was something in his tone that indicated he didn't like his employers much. Maybe because Darrow was rich; maybe for some other reason. Which was probably why he was so willing to tell a stranger — who might be Raffles, the international jewel thief, for all he knew — that the Darrows were away in Hawaii on an extended visit.

I asked him, "Did you happen to be working here yesterday? I'm also trying to find a young woman who might have stopped by . . ."

"Nope," he said. "Wednesdays and Saturdays are my days."

"I see."

"Ask Mrs. Flowers."

"Who would she be?"

"Housekeeper. Lives in. She knows everything." He didn't like Mrs. Flowers much either.

"She's not here now," I said.

"No. Went shopping or something."

"Any idea when she'll be back?"

"Nope. Maybe she took the day off."

"When the cats are away," I said.

"Huh?" he said.

I left him and went back to the rental car and sat there for a time. So the Darrows were in Hawaii and had been for a week; if McCone had come here yesterday, she'd probably have discovered the same thing. So then what would she have done? Hung around to check out that club angle, probably. But *what* club? Not the country club over there, or the other one in town; she'd seemed to think the club Beddoes and the Darrows belonged to was some kind of health spa. Only there wasn't a health club in Borrego Springs, according to the gas station attendant. . . .

I kept sitting there, looking at the house. And pretty soon I realized why it wasn't what I'd expected: those photographs I'd found in Jim Lauterbach's office, in his file on Elaine Picard. An odd-looking house in the desert, at least semi-isolated, with an old spur track and the remains of a water tower and a loading dock not far away. When Darrow's name came up, along with the fact that he lived in Borrego Springs, I had made the same kind of false assumption I'd made about Nancy Pollard being Timmy's mother — that the house in the photos must be Darrow's house.

All right, it wasn't. Then whose was it?

I got out of the car again and went back through the front gate to where the gardener was. He wasn't happy to see me back; but then he wasn't unhappy either. He looked blank when I asked him about the place in the photos — until I mentioned the spur track and the ruins nearby. Then he rubbed at his creased face and began to nod.

"You must mean the old Matthews place," he said. "Funny-looking house, looks like a big toadstool grew up out of the ground after a rain?"

"Something like that. You say somebody named Matthews owns it?"

"Not anymore. Leonard Matthews built it back in the thirties. Crazy as a coot. Owned the Matthews Gypsum Mine not far away,

454

up in the foothills; built the spur track, too, to get his ore to Plaster City — it used to connect with the old Gypsum Mining Railroad that runs down there. Mine petered out after the war, but Matthews stayed on until he died. Must have been thirty years ago, about."

"Who owns the house now?"

"Nobody, far as I know. Sits up in the middle of nowhere, looks like a toadstool. Who'd want it? Not many people as crazy as old Matthews was, even these days."

"Where is it, exactly?"

"You know where the U.S. Gypsum Mine is?"

"No."

"How about Split Mountain Road?"

"No."

"Well, you can't miss Split Mountain; it's smack in the middle of Ocotillo Wells. You know where *that* is?"

"Not far from here on Highway 78, isn't it?"

"That's right. You take Split Mountain past the Elephant Tree Ranger Station, almost to where it ends at the U.S. Gypsum Mine. There's a dirt road branches off it to the south, up into the foothills. Follow that about seven miles and you'll be at the old Matthews place."

"Thanks."

"You planning to go out there this time of day?" he asked.

"Yes. Why?"

"Better take some water with you, just in case," he said. "That's empty desert up around there and hotter'n the hinges of hell. Something happens and you get caught without water, you might not come back alive."

41: McCone

I was lying on my right side, arm folded under me. Sharp objects poked into my flesh. My arm tingled painfully. I moved off it, moaning with the effort, and opened my eyes.

My cheek was pressed against the sandy ground. I was staring at the roots of a low green shrub that had a whitish sheen, as if it had been dusted with flour. I tried to push myself up and found my arm was nearly numb. Rolling over on my back, I looked up through tree branches at the sky. It was clear blue, and little patterns of sunlight shone through the dark tracery. Sunlight that slanted from the left.

My lips were badly cracked and dry. I opened my mouth and tried to lick them, but my tongue was even dryer. It was very hot, and I hurt all over. What had happened?

Images flickered in my mind. Sand . . . a

rocky wash . . . a high outcropping . . . hills . . . trees in the distance . . .

The desert. I had run across the desert in the blazing heat. And got lost.

Something rustled in the dry shrubbery near me. A rattlesnake? Alarmed, I sat up, my body aching, and looked around. I was lying at the edge of a dry water hole in the shade of a clump of stunted desert willows. Their branches were gray and brittle-looking, because there was no water. . . .

My thirst came back full force, along with a dull pounding in my head. My eyes ached as I studied my surroundings.

I was at the bottom of a shallow wash filled with dormant vegetation. The water hole's bottom was sun-cracked, without even a trickle of moisture. It was very hot, but nothing like what I'd experienced running through the sand. The slight drop in temperature and the shade from the trees had probably saved my life, slowing the rate of my dehydration so I'd regained consciousness.

From the angle of the sun's rays, I could tell it was sinking. The desert would cool off after dark. Perhaps then I could cross the wastes once more and find my way to civilization.

But there was not much chance of that.

For one thing, I knew I couldn't travel any farther without water. For another, when it was dark I would run the risk of becoming even more disoriented. I knew nothing about the moon or constellations that would help me chart my course. My only real chance was to get to high ground now, while it was still light, to see if I could spot the water tower and the road. That was what I should have done before, but fear, exhaustion, and thirst had clouded my thinking.

Shakily I got to my feet and moved up the slope to the rim of the wash. About a hundred yards off to the west was a rocky outcropping. If I could get to the top of it and pinpoint the old water tower or the utility lines along Split Mountain Road, I could move in the straightest line to Elephant Tree Ranger Station.

A sudden wave of dizziness swept over me. I closed my eyes, waiting for it to pass. And knew beyond a doubt that I'd never get to those rocks if I didn't have water.

When I opened my eyes, I began looking at the plants around me, trying to remember my high-school biology field trips. This vegetation might look dead, but in actuality it was only dormant, waiting for the return of life-giving moisture. Many plants stored water. But did any of these? No.

What I needed was a barrel cactus. And what I saw, on the other side of the wash, leaning toward a path of sun that streamed through the tree branches, was one of the cylindrical, spine-studded plants. To me, it was as good as finding a lake.

I got up and stumbled over to the cactus, running my hand over its trunk, not caring that the thorns scratched my skin. It was a small one — around three feet high — but large enough to contain enough liquid to refresh me and get me back to civilization. Reaching into the pocket of my jeans, I found the Swiss Army nnife. Thank God I'd stuffed it in there before I'd jumped out of the vent from the dungeon.

I opened the knife to the largest blade and began sawing at the cactus a few inches below its crown. It was tough and fibrous, and the knife cut slowly. I gave in to my impatience and hacked at it. In a few minutes I yanked the crown off like the lid of a pot.

Dropping the crown, I reached inside the cactus and scooped out a handful of the wet pulp. I pressed it to my mouth, sucking and gulping, feeling the moisture trickle down my face and throat and under my blouse. I reached in for more pulp, cupping my hands carefully now so I wouldn't waste any. It was sticky and bitter-tasting and heavenly.

My stomach gave a sudden contraction, and I warned myself to take it easy. There was nothing in it — hadn't been for almost two days now — and I didn't want to dehydrate myself further by getting sick. I took my time sucking the pulp and resting, and when I felt stronger, I cut out chunks of the cactus and stuffed them in my pockets. They would provide extra moisture in my trek back across the desert.

Then I began moving toward the nearby outcropping of rock. I went slowly this time, telling myself that my earlier panic had cost me valuable strength and energy. Sugarman's killer was not out here looking for me; he'd have been beating the brush in that wash long before this if he were. In all likelihood, he was waiting at the house, thinking I'd eventually double back that way.

I climbed the rocky outcropping and stood shading my eyes and peering around. At first I saw nothing but the brush — dotted sand stretching to the hills. But then I made out a leaning black spire with a dark square next to it. And behind it, a series of lumps. It had to be the outlines of the water tower, the loading platform, and the house.

I looked up at the sun, taking a fix on my position. Since the house was southeast of here, I'd be walking with the sun more or less at my back. It would beat down on my head and shoulders, but at least I wouldn't be blinded by it.

Scrambling down off the rocks, I began my long trek. I moved carefully, stopping in what shade I found to suck on the chunks of cactus I carried. The sun sank lower and its rays were less punishing. I judged the time to be about five o'clock.

After what must have been an hour, I finally reached the sandstone outcropping several hundreds of yards away from the water tower. I paused beyond it, resting and sucking moisture from my last piece of cactus. Then I started up the steep, sandy slope and, when I had reached it, cautiously poked my head over the top.

In the distance, the house lay quiet in the afternoon heat. The Cadillac was still parked in front. And beyond it now was a maroon car — some sort of compact. My spirits rose slightly. It *could* be help. If I could get to the shed beside the loading dock, I could watch and wait. And after dark, if nothing else happened, I could walk to the ranger station — maybe hitch a ride, if there was some traffic out this way — and summon the law.

I stood, ready to drop to the ground if I heard any sound. All remained quiet. I slid down the other side of the outcropping, the rocks scraping my already battered flesh, and staggered toward the shed.

I was about twenty yards away from it when the man stepped out from behind it with a gun in his hand and opened fire at me.

A buzzing noise whined close to my ear, and then the shot cracked. Panic ripped through me. I whirled and ran back toward the outcropping, my feet churning on the rocky ground.

A second buzzing noise. A second crack. My goal was too far away. I knew I wouldn't make it—

I felt a jarring impact in the middle of my body. It staggered me and pitched me forward as I heard the third shot. My face hit the sand. Numbness spread through me; the heat seemed suddenly gone, replaced by an icy, enveloping cold.

I thought, My God, I'm going to die. . . .

42: "Wolf"

The private road that led in and up to what the Darrows' gardener had called the old Matthews place was full of ruts and holes and dislodged rocks, the product of countless winter rains and maybe a flash flood or two. The rental car had a lousy suspension system, so that I had to drive at a crawl in order to keep from banging the top of my skull on the headliner at each bump. It was a little like being inside a big box that somebody was shaking up and down, none too gently.

After better than seven miles of this, I came up out of a dry wash to the top of a rise and saw the house. It was the one in Lauterbach's photographs, all right, and an even weirder sight in reality. No wonder the gardener had called Leonard Matthews crazy as a coot; the place looked as if it had been designed and built by one of the mad characters in the old Shudder Pulps.

There was a car parked on the big flat area in front and to one side, a dusty white Cadillac. Beyond it, in the empty desert that fell away to the northwest, I could see the remains of the water tower and the loading dock. The railroad spur track too: broken up by time and the elements, pieces missing, ties missing, parts of it hidden by sagebrush and greasewood, making a snaky line toward the eroded, humpbacked hills that rose behind the house. I drove on down toward the house and parked next to the Caddy. My mouth was dry and dusty; before I got out, I drank some of the bottled water I'd bought in Borrego Springs on the advice of the gardener. It had been good advice: this definitely was not a place you'd ever want to be caught in without water.

Nobody came out of the house. But then, if the Caddy's owner was inside, he might not have heard me drive up; there were some big things on the roof that looked like air-conditioning units and they were making a hell of a racket. In contrast, the high rocks and the sun-blasted desert were silent, motionless, empty.

I went over to the Cadillac and looked through the driver's window. The first thing I saw were wires hanging down from under the wheel — ignition wires, as if somebody had been trying to hot-wire the car. On impulse I tried the door. It was unlocked, and I opened it and leaned inside. The interior didn't contain anything interesting that I could see. Neither did the glove box: no registration, nothing that told me who the Caddy belonged to.

I continued on to the house. The front door was recessed in an opening that looked like the mouth of a cave, and it was standing wide open. I poked my head inside and called out a greeting.

No answer.

"Is anybody here?"

No answer.

I went into a wide foyer that had five archways opening off it. I took the one straight ahead and found myself in a sunken living room with a fireplace in the middle. The Darrows' gardener had said the house was abandoned, but all the parked cars in Lauterbach's photographs had indicated otherwise; and this room, full of expensive furniture and artwork, confirmed that people either lived or spent a fair amount of time here.

When I didn't get an answer to another hail, I went prowling through the place. And it didn't take me long, once I saw the other rooms, to figure out just what kind of place it was. A mirrored bedroom gave me the first hint, a room fixed up for the screening of what were clearly pornographic films expanded the idea, and a series of other bedrooms containing different personal belongings fleshed it out completely. The club McCone and I had kept hearing about wasn't anything so mundane as a health spa; it was a private sex club, a place where a bunch of kinky people got together to look at X-rated movies and to hold orgies. People like Elaine Picard, Lloyd Beddoes, the Darrows, Karyn Sugarman, Rich Woodall.

That Cadillac out front, I thought. Woodall's?

The last of the five foyer archways led to a closed and locked door that might have been rescued from a medieval English castle: thick black oak, ironbound, with an old-fashioned latch and keyhole. On the floor nearby was a big brass key that looked as if it would fit the lock; I picked it up and tried it, and it worked, all right. I opened the door and went inside.

It was like walking onto a stage set for a film about the Spanish Inquisition. Imitation-stone walls hung with chains, racks of whips and paddles and cats-o'-nine-tails, other stuff I didn't recognize — all of it lit in a reddish glow from bulbs recessed in the ceiling. I could feel my flesh start to crawl. These people were into more than just orgies; they were into bondage and sado-masochism as well.

The room was L-shaped, and I moved ahead to where I could see what was around of the ell. More of the same . . . and a cross on the wall with a female figure hanging from it, a figure I thought at first was a dummy and then realized was human — had been human. In that bloody light I couldn't tell the color of her hair or see her face, because the hair covered it, and I thought with a surge of horror that it was McCone. I ran back there but it wasn't McCone; it was a woman I'd never seen be-fore. Strangled. Dead a long time. Crucified with heavy rope in lieu of nails.

But McCone *had* been here. There was a purse lying on the floor, and when I grabbed it up and rummaged through it I found her identification. Torn strips of wallpaper lay on the floor too. And high up on the wall, near the ceiling, sunlight streamed in through a hole that led to the outside.

The whole scene was like a warped and distorted religious painting from the Middle Ages — the crucified body, the bondage-and-torture implements, the shaft of sunshine like a divine light cutting through the bloody pagan darkness. Chills skittered along my back. I tasted bile and gagged it down, backing away.

McCone — where was she now?

I turned and ran out of the room, out of the house and into the broiling desert heat. The windows and hood of the Cadillac blazed with reflected sun rays. McCone must have been the one who'd tried to hot-wire it, I thought. But she'd failed for some reason. And then what?

I started toward the Caddy, to give it a more thorough search. I was thinking of McCone locked for God knew how long in that simulated dungeon with the woman's body. It was the stuff of madness. What if she—

Somewhere on the desert below, there was the dull echoing crack of a gunshot.

It brought me up short, with my head jerking this way and that; sound carries in open spaces, gets distorted by distance so you can't always tell which direction it comes from. I ran ahead, beyond the Cadillac and my rental car, past a clump of greasewood to where I had a better view of the buff-colored landscape spread out below. Nothing moved that I could see, but the sun glare was intense; it burned painfully against the retinas of my eyes, blurred the edges of everything more than a couple of hundred yards away.

The gun cracked a second time. Hand weapon, I thought; it didn't have the resonance of a rifle or a shotgun. But I still couldn't place its source. I thought it might have come from over by the ruins of the water tower and loading dock, but I was looking that way when the third shot came. This time I saw movement, somebody running out in that direction. Five seconds later the figure was gone again, hidden from my view behind the dock and its adjacent shed.

Without thinking what I was doing, I started to run. The ground was hard-packed for the most part, rocky, but there were sandy patches and clusters of spiny cholla cactus and greasewood and sagebrush, so that I had to take a weaving course instead of going in a straight line. There weren't any more shots. No further movement either; but the dock and the shed were directly ahead of me — the person I'd seen was still somewhere behind them.

I had covered half the distance, with the hot dry air like fire in my lungs, before it registered that I was unarmed and had no idea of what might be waiting for me. But it might be McCone I'd seen — that was the thing that kept me running. She'd escaped the house, she hadn't been able to start the Cadillac . . . where else was there for her to go except into the desert?

The half-collapsed framework of the water tower loomed on my left, its tank stays canted at odd angles like a pattern of crooked bars against the bright hot sky. I was within a hundred yards of it now; through the shimmering heat waves I could see that the ground ahead was strewn with pieces of splintered boarding, lengths of iron and steel, the crumbling segments of a wooden duct. Still no movement out there. And no sounds either, except for the thin scrape of my steps and the labored rasp of my breathing.

The heat had begun to sap my strength; as I went past the tower I could feel myself starting to falter, slowing down at the same time I was trying to run faster. I kept waiting for the sound of another shot — and not hearing it, kept thinking that the target of those first three had been hit, killed, so that another bullet wasn't necessary.

I skirted what was left of a platform that had once housed the tower's water pump. Ahead, the loading dock was nothing more than a decaying skeleton, but the shed alongside it was still more or less whole. I veered toward the shed, and when I finally reached it there was a stitch in my side and I was out of breath. I leaned against the sagging wall, struggling to take in air. There were gaps in the siding big enough for a man to squeeze through; I rubbed my eyes clear and peered through to the desert beyond.

A man stood twenty to twenty-five yards distant, half turned away from me and bent a little at the waist, a pair of binoculars hanging from around his neck. He was peering at a huddled mass on the ground. A woman — I could see the long dark hair fanned out around her head. McCone.

I could also see the squarish snout of the automatic in the man's hand. He was pointing it straight down at her.

A kind of desperate rage settled into me. I got my breathing under control; shoved away from the wall and around the side of the shed, picking my way through another litter of splintered wood and pieces of eroded metal. When I got to the front corner I had a better look at the man. Rumpled iron-gray hair, stiff military bearing. Not who I'd expected to see, not Rich Woodall —

Henry Nyland.

McCone wasn't moving. There was blood on her; I could see it glistening bright crimson in the hard white sunlight. Sounds came to me, like whispers at first, disjointed and indistinct. Then they got louder, and I realized Nyland was talking to her: "I didn't want to do this. Don't you understand? I didn't want to do anything to you. It was the other one, that Sugarman bitch — she killed Elaine, she was evil. I had to kill *her*, didn't I? For Elaine?" And all the while he kept aiming the automatic at Sharon's unmoving head.

Better than twenty yards separated us — too far, too damned far. If I made a rush at him, he'd hear me coming and have all the time he'd need to turn and set himself, and blow me away too. I could try to cat-foot it out there while he was still focused on McCone, but the risk would be the same. . . .

Do *something*, for Christ's sake!

Hurriedly I scanned the ground where I stood, then picked up a chunk of sandstone about the size of a baseball and stepped away from the shed with it. Nyland was still babbling to McCone, saying now, "I'll bury you out here. Both of you. They'll never find your bodies. What choice do I have? You see that I don't have any choice, don't you?"

Hit him in the head, I thought, knock his frigging head off — and I threw the rock with all the force I could muster.

473

It missed him by ten feet, but he heard it go by and spun around jerkily with the automatic swinging up in front of him. I was moving by then, and he saw me and yelled something and fired. I went down, hugged the ground alongside the shed, but the shot was wild, not even close. On hands and knees I scrambled around to the rear, came up and looked through one of the gaps. Nyland was running toward the shed. Even at a distance I could see the wildness in him, the look of a man out of control.

I stumbled around to the other side, dodged out far enough to let him see me again. He fired on the run, as I'd hoped he would, and that one missed badly too. Three shots at McCone, two at me; most automatics had six-bullet clips: one shot left. Maybe.

Back against the shed wall, I yelled at him, "Nyland! You'll have to kill me too!"

No answer. But I heard him running; he was close to the shed now. I backpedaled fast, jumped over a jumble of rusted pulleys and cables, and ran in a crouch toward the loading dock. Over my shoulder I saw Nyland come into view alongside the shed, saw him slow when he spotted me and raise the gun. I threw myself sideways onto a patch of barren sand; the gun cracked as I landed bouncing and sliding and banged my chin and hand against more abandoned machinery. Another miss. Then I was scrambling around, coming up, and Nyland was a dozen yards away, still running with the gun out at arm's length.

If I'd been wrong about the number of bullets in the automatic's clip, I would have been a dead man. But I wasn't wrong. I heard the empty click of the hammer; heard it twice more. I was up on my feet by then, and I saw him hurl the gun away in frustration. But he was still moving, closing the gap between us — hands out in front of his body now, the fingers wiggling like fat white worms. Except for the way his eyes bulged, there was a kind of terrible blank calm about him.

We were both a couple of old military men, which meant we'd both had training in hand-to-hand self-defense, but for all I knew he had superior strength and skill. I wasn't about to try slugging it out with him.

I could only think of one other thing to do. I started toward him, brandishing my fists like Muhammad Ali coming out of his corner at the bell, yelling, "I'll smash your face in, Nyland!" Some ten feet separated us. I moved sideways a couple of steps, and he did the same thing, and now there were five feet between us — and I stumbled, grimaced, grunted as if in sudden pain, and clutched my chest and went down hard to my knees. It wasn't much of an acting job, but he was half out of his head and not alert to tricks: it froze him for an instant, just long enough for me to catch up the short length of warped strap iron I'd been angling for and swing it sideways in the same motion, down low at his legs.

The piece of metal struck him beside the left knee with enough force to knock him off his feet. He cried out, came down hard on his shoulder, and started to roll over. I swung the strap iron again and this time it connected with the side of his head, made a dull crunching noise and came loose from my grip and flew away to one side. But that didn't matter; I didn't need it anymore. Nyland had quit moving and was lying on his back with a bloody gash across one temple, his eyes half open and part of the whites showing.

I crawled closer to him, felt his neck: he was still alive. Not that I gave a good goddamn about that at the moment. The way his eyes looked, I'd hit him hard enough to give him a concussion. He wasn't going to be any more trouble.

Wobbling a little, I got up on my feet and went to where he'd thrown the gun and picked it up on the move, put it into my pocket. The lowering sun was right in my eyes as I ran out past the shed to where McCone lay; the harsh glare of it half blinded me, so that I couldn't see her clearly until I was just a few feet from her.

She was moving. Making little groaning noises and clawing at the sandy earth, trying to get up.

My knees went weak with relief; I sank down at her side. There wasn't as much blood on her as I'd imagined from a distance, and I could make out the wound where she'd been shot. It wasn't in a vital area. Her jeans and blouse were torn in a dozen other places, her skin was scratched, her face and arms were burned raw by the sun, and her lips were split and blood-caked. A feeling of tenderness moved through me; I took hold of her, to help her sit up.

Her body went rigid at my touch. She made an animal sound in her throat and tried to pull away. I said, "Sharon, it's me, it's Wolf," and her head twisted and her eyes focused on me and she said, "Oh my God, Wolf," in a cracked voice that had disbelief in it, as if she couldn't quite assimilate the fact that I was actually beside her. She went limp. I hoisted her up onto her left side, held her clinging against me.

After a few seconds she said, "Nyland . . ."

"Don't worry about him. He's out of it now."

She pulled back from me a little, wincing. "I think he shot me," she said. "Part of my right side's numb."

"He shot you, all right. But it doesn't look too bad."

"Where did he—?" She felt herself, clenching her teeth against the pain, and a look of indignant horror spread over her face. "The dirty son of a bitch!" she said.

"Yeah," I said.

"He shot me in the ass!"

I couldn't help it — I burst out laughing. It was a release of tension more than anything else, and once I got started I couldn't stop. McCone dug her nails into my arm — and then she started to laugh, too, painfully but just as crazily.

It was a good thing nobody but Nyland was around. Hanging on to each other the way we were, yukking it up like a couple of deranged hyenas, we must have been some sight to behold.

43: McCone

I was lying on my parents' living-room couch wearing a long green caftan — the only garment I had with me that was loose enough to be comfortable and still be what my mother deemed "suitable to be seen by a gentleman caller." I had to rest on my left side because the bullet wound in my right hip hurt like hell, even though it was superficial. My face was gunked up with burn cream and there was red antiseptic smeared on my cuts and scratches. I must have been a sight.

Wolf didn't seem to mind, however. He sat across from me in my father's favorite armchair and smiled. "What's that smell coming from the kitchen?" he asked.

"Crab cioppino. It's being made in your honor."

"That's nice."

"Well, it *is*, isn't it?" The words came out

grumpily, and Wolf looked surprised. I grinned to show I wasn't annoyed with him — a painful smile because my mouth hurt every time I moved it.

I *was* annoyed with my mother. She'd already come in twice, foisting beers off on Wolf and fluttering and smiling. I knew what was going through her head. She was sizing him up as prospective-husband material, the way she'd been sizing up practically every man I'd so much as spoken to for years. And I was getting sick of it.

I certainly couldn't feel any annoyance at Wolf, though. He'd saved my life and then had taken charge — getting me to the emergency hospital in Borrego Springs, dealing with the law both there and in San Diego, and when I'd flatly refused to spend the night in the hospital, he'd got me home with a minimum of hassle. When he'd arrived here today, half an hour ago, he'd brought the news that Henry Nyland had confessed to Karyn Sugarman's murder.

The way Nyland told it, my visit to him at campaign headquarters had started him thinking that Elaine might have been murdered. And since he felt Jim Lauterbach's file on Elaine was rightfully his property, he'd used his extensive contacts in city administration to obtain copies of both the file and the photographs of the house in the desert. Those photographs had immediately meant more to Nyland than they had to Wolf, because he'd met Karyn Sugarman a few times at Elaine's house and knew what kind of car Sugarman drove — the Datsun that, in the photos, was parked among the others in front of Les Club.

On Monday night, Nyland had called Sugarman to ask about the house. Sugarman had denied knowing of it or ever having been there. This made Nyland all the more suspicious and he decided to check it out on Tuesday. He'd driven out to Borrego Springs in the morning and shown the photos to some of the residents. Because the old Matthews place was known to old-timers, one of them had readily identified it.

When Nyland arrived, he found Sugarman packing her things. Wolf and I speculated that Nyland's call to Sugarman the night before had panicked her and sent her out there to remove all traces of her presence. But whatever the reason, she was there, and it hadn't taken Nyland long to figure out what kind of place it was — and what Sugarman's and Elaine's connection with it had been.

Nyland had flown into a rage, and Sugarman had tried to calm him down.

Doubtless she had used counseling techniques and psychological jargon — but her kind of counseling only inflamed him more. He went on a rampage, storming through the house, and they finally ended up in the dungeon. The sight of it totally unhinged him; he attacked Sugarman, slapping her until she admitted she had killed Elaine. Her reason, as she'd told it to Nyland, was much the same as I'd worked out that night in the dungeon room.

Originally, Nyland's rage at Sugarman had been because she'd introduced Elaine to Les Club. But once he found out she'd also killed Elaine, he went wild and strangled her. And then he'd tied her to the cross, out of some warped religious fervor.

Nyland had then gone back to the living room, had a couple of stiff drinks, and left. But after driving several miles, he'd calmed down enough to remember Sugarman's car. And he also knew he'd left clear evidence of his presence, in the form of fingerprints on the glass and Scotch bottle. He turned back, and in the meantime I'd arrived.

After he'd locked me in the room with Sugarman's body, Nyland went to work packing the rest of her possessions, putting them and her purse in her car, and then driving the car into a hidden part of the desert.

He walked back, got rid of my car — it has since been returned to me — walked back again, and then sat down to decide what to do with me. He had an automatic along, one that he always carried in his glove compartment; killing me would be a simple thing. Fortunately for me, guilt drove him back to the bottle and eventually he passed out and slept well into the next day, when he heard me trying to start his Cadillac. After I escaped into the desert, he waited near the house, watching for me with his binoculars, so he could kill me if the desert didn't.

Last night at the emergency hospital, Wolf had also told me how he'd figured out Rich Woodall had killed Jim Lauterbach. Now I asked, "Did the police finally arrest Woodall?"

"Late last night, at his house. He'd been down in Mexico all day, apparently. At a jai-alai game, he said, but Knowles figured he was down there making arrangements to sell off those animals of his."

"Did he confess to Lauterbach's murder?"

"No, he's stonewalling on that and on the animal-selling too."

I nodded. That seemed consistent with what I knew of the man.

"But the D.A. doesn't need a confession to convict him," Wolf added. "Knowles found Lauterbach's tape recorder in the trunk of his car. Apparently, Woodall got rid of the murder gun, but the damned fool hung on to the recorder."

"What was on it?"

"A lot of stuff you wouldn't want to hear. Evidently, Lauterbach not only took those photographs of the outside of Les Club, but also got inside the house and bugged it. Woodall's voice is on the tape. So are a lot of other members', including Elaine's."

"Why do you think Lauterbach broke into Woodall's yard?"

"Looking for more blackmail evidence, probably. And he found it when he saw those animals. He must have demanded a big payoff from Woodall to keep both his activities in Les Club and his animal-dealing quiet. Instead he bought himself four bullets."

"I wonder if Woodall planned the murder or not."

"I'd say not. Maybe he went down to Lauterbach's office Sunday and tried to scare him off. If my reading on Lauterbach is right, he wasn't the type to scare — he probably ignored Woodall."

"And if there's one thing that'll send that type into a rage, it's being ignored."

"Right. He either followed Lauterbach

down to the john right then or went out, got himself worked up, and then came back and found Lauterbach in the stall."

"What about Beddoes and Ibarcena?" I asked. "Does Knowles think Beddoes really did kill himself?"

"There doesn't seem to be any question of that. He just couldn't stand the idea of shame and prison, I guess. As for Ibarcena, you called that right. He's skipped town, taking his young boyfriend with him. Back to Mexico, probably. As far as I'm concerned, he can stay disappeared. If the authorities don't find him, I doubt if Timmy Ferguson's mother will be able to trace the boy, reward or no reward. That part of this mess will have a happy ending, at least."

"At least. One last thing, Wolf — what about Les Club? Who really owned that house?"

"Darrow and his wife. State records show them as officers of the corporation. They probably incorporated for tax reasons and then charged the other members dues."

"Tax reasons. Good Lord. I'm glad I never met the Darrows."

"Me too."

I was silent for a moment. "You know," I finally said, "everything was like a chain reaction, with one catalyst setting off three separate but connected personal explosions."

"The murders."

"Yes. The catalyst could have been Elaine's death, but actually I think it goes back further than that, to the night Sugarman fell in love with Elaine and let things get out of hand."

"Or even further, to when Sugarman introduced Elaine to the club."

"You're right. The club probably would have gone along as usual if it hadn't been for Elaine joining. But because she did, Sugarman couldn't handle her emotions, and that explosion ended in Elaine's death."

"And Woodall blew up at Lauterbach — who wouldn't have known anything about Les Club, much less Woodall's animal farm, if Nyland hadn't hired him to find out about the 'bizarre thing' Elaine was involved in," Wolf said. "And chances are Nyland never would have killed anyone if he hadn't found out Sugarman had brought Elaine into the club and then killed *her*."

"It makes me think of that old saw about evil begetting evil," I said. "And more evil than just what was going on at Les Club. All these people with all their little scams that they didn't want exposed — like a lot of people these days, I guess. Beddoes and Ibarcena had their fugitive-smuggling operation. Lauterbach was a blackmailer. Woodall had his illegal animal sales. Even Henry Nyland had a scam."

Wolf looked at me with interest. "How do you figure that?"

"Reactionary politics. In a way, it's the most dangerous scam of them all."

My mother came into the room, smiling. "Cioppino's almost done," she said cheerfully. "But before we eat, your brother John wants to talk to you, Sharon. I'll just take your friend into the kitchen for a nice little chat of our own."

"John wants to talk to *me?*"

"Yes, he's in the canyon—"

"Huh. He probably plans to murder me out there and leave me for the coyotes to eat."

"Sharon!"

"Well, face it, Ma, I'm not John's favorite person today."

"You were awfully hard on him last night."

"I couldn't help it."

"Well, go see him anyway. He asked me to tell you—"

"I'll go! I'll go!" I got up slowly and reached for the cane I'd been using. It was my father's, bought when he'd sprained his ankle dancing the polka — of all things — at a friend's daughter's wedding a few years ago.

My mother looked at the cane and frowned. "I don't know why John can't talk in the house. Are you sure you'll be all right, climbing down those steps?"

"Yes!" I left them and went outside. Pa was humming loudly as he repotted plants under the grape arbor; I waved to him and made my way across to the canyon.

I *had* been rough on John last night, but I'd been half out of my head with exhaustion and pain, and when he'd come into my bedroom — ostensibly to see how *I* was doing — and started whining about *his* troubles, I'd let him have it. I'd told him about Timmy Ferguson and the whip marks Wolf had seen on his back. I'd told him about Elaine's handyman — the guy down at the beach with the two little boys and the pizza crusts on the kitchen counter. I'd told him how difficult it was to be a single parent if you weren't prepared; how anger and frustration can lead to child abuse; how he'd better be damned sure he could handle custody before he went out and tried to get it. And then I'd told him to grow up.

What made me feel so damned high and mighty? I wondered as I climbed down the canyon steps, holding up my caftan so I wouldn't trip, going slowly in deference to my sore rear. I wasn't a parent, hadn't the slightest idea what it was like. But maybe one didn't have to be. Maybe all it took was common sense. . . .

I spotted John, sitting on his usual log. He turned and looked at me. And then he smiled.

Surprised and somewhat encouraged, I kept going. "You wanted to see me, John?"

"Yeah. I've got something to tell you. I went to see the kids' mother this morning."

The kids' mother, I noted, not "that bitch." John's ex-wife was coming up in the world. "And?"

"And I told her all the things you said last night. She agreed. She said she's been having trouble being a single parent herself. She got mad and slapped Johnny the other day."

"So what do you intend to do?"

"Well, we talked it over and we decided on joint custody — they'll spend half the time with each of us. It's easier that way. Only we're not going to drag them back and forth and disrupt their lives."

"How do you plan to accomplish that?"

"The kids will stay in the house. When it's her turn to have custody, she'll live there with them. When it's mine, I'll live there. We'll both keep small places of our own for the time when we don't have the kids." He paused to open a beer, then added, "It's kind of a new concept, but it's been written up a lot lately, and it seems to work. And it's better for the kids. They're who counts, you know."

"I know." I felt a rush of pride and affection for my big brother, who just might grow up after all. "Listen, Ma says the cioppino's almost ready. Are you coming up for some?"

"Nope. I'll stay here and drink. It's my last chance — tomorrow I look for a job."

I thought of Charley Valdene, the private-eye enthusiast Wolf had been staying with. Valdene was also a painting contractor, Wolf had told me. "I may have a lead on a job for you," I said. "Talk to me when you're sober."

"Tomorrow."

I grinned and started up the steps, thinking about how funny male-female relationships could be sometimes. Now that they were divorced, John and his wife would probably end up being better friends than when they were married. And then there was Don and me. . . .

He'd called last night after he'd heard about me on the news — the hourly broadcast after his talk show, no less. Ma hadn't let him talk to me, though, so I'd called him back this morning. Don had been anxious, solicitous, and had offered to fly right down. I said no, he shouldn't; I didn't want him to see me in this condition. Then I remembered unfinished business and said, "Besides, how can you leave Laura?"

"Who?"

"Laura. Your cousin."

There was a long silence. "Oh, that. Babe, I've got a confession to make."

I waited.

"I don't have a cousin Laura."

"I know. So who was that on the phone the other day?"

"Well . . . promise you won't get mad?"

I didn't say anything.

"I know how you disapprove of this kind of thing. I know you think a man should be self-sufficient and all that. You've always said you would never need anyone to—"

"Don, get to the point."

"Well, I waited until you were out of town and then sneaked out and did it. I'm not proud of that. I — I hired a cleaning woman."

"You *what?*"

"I know I should be able to take care of a one-bedroom apartment by myself, but it had gotten to be such a pit."

"That doesn't explain why you were in the shower while she was there."

"That's the worst part of it."

"Go on."

"Laura isn't a very good cleaning woman. She couldn't get the hang of scooping the ashes out of the fireplace, so I had to show her. And I got all dirty."

I believed him. Nobody — especially Don — could make up a story like that. I started to laugh, and so did he. We must have laughed away a good half-minute of my parents' long-distance money. Then I said, "Look, Don, I don't care if you need somebody to clean for you — as long as it's not me. If Laura's no good, I'll help you find somebody better when I get back."

"Yeah?"

"Yes. Maybe we can find somebody to work for both of us — cheap."

"Great. Terrific. But one thing . . ."

"Yes?"

"Will *you* tell Laura she's fired?"

Still grinning at the memory of our conversation, I stepped over the broken-down fence of the canyon and crossed the yard toward the house. Halfway there, I turned and looked back. I'd never liked that canyon, ever since our black cat had disappeared into it, but if you looked at it right, with the birds hopping through the tree branches and the sunlight playing on the leaves, it wasn't so bad after all.

44: "Wolf"

The McCone kitchen was bright and shiny and full of noonday sunshine. It was also full of the rich smell of crab cioppino, and of the cheerful humming of Sharon's father, who was puttering around outside. It was also full of Mrs. McCone, which wasn't quite as pleasant as the sunshine and the crab cioppino and Mr. McCone's humming. Not that I disliked Mrs. McCone; she was a very nice lady. The problem was, she thought I was very nice, too, and not only because I had saved her daughter's life. She kept smiling at me and giving me appraising and speculative looks. She kept asking me questions. And worst of all, she kept talking about how much Sharon needed a husband — "a nice *mature* man who'd take care of her, keep her out of trouble."

I was sitting at the table, where she'd told me to sit, and drinking the bottle of beer she'd put in my hand, and wishing I was outside puttering and humming with Mr. McCone. Or already on my way back to San Francisco and Kerry. Mrs. McCone made me uncomfortable. She reminded me of my own mother, which meant I couldn't be rude to her because my mother had never tolerated rudeness and I had been raised to be obedient and respectful of motherhood. So I sat there and listened and drank and twitched.

"Spending the night with a dead body," Mrs. McCone was saying, "and a crucified body at that. Horrible. And then getting shot. Shot in the . . . *shot*, for heaven's sake. My little girl. Horrible." She did something to the crab cioppino and then looked at me again. "Have *you* ever been shot?"

"Yes, ma am."

"You have? Then why are you still a detective?"

"It's what I do."

"Wouldn't you like to have another job where your life wouldn't be in danger all the time?"

"No, I don't think so."

She sighed. "I suppose that's how Sharon feels too. I suppose she'll keep right on being a detective."

"I suppose she will."

"It wouldn't be so bad if she had a man around to watch out for her," Mrs. McCone said again. "I wouldn't worry so much if she was married."

I hid my tongue behind my teeth and kept it there.

"An older man would be best for her. Not that young disc jockey she's seeing now — Don; he's not stable enough. A mature man is what she needs." Pause. "I've never understood the objection to May-December romances, have you?"

"Mm," I said.

"Sometimes they work out very nicely. It all depends on the man and woman involved."

"Mm," I said.

She did something else to the cioppino. "Sharon tells me you're not married," she said casually.

"Uh, no. I'm not. But I—"

"Ever been married?"

"No."

"You're not a confirmed bachelor, are you?"

"Well, not exactly . . ."

"That's good. I don't trust confirmed bachelors. They have quirks."

"Yes, ma'am."

"How long have you been a detective?" she asked.

"Almost all of my adult life."

"Do you make a good living? Sharon doesn't, you know."

"I get by all right."

"I'll bet you're very successful," Mrs. McCone said, smiling. "I can always tell when a man is successful at what he does."

Outside, Mr. McCone's humming had grown louder and more jaunty. Now he burst into snatches of song that came drifting in through the open kitchen window.

Mrs. McCone said, "Are you Catholic?"

"Ma'am?"

"Catholic. Most Italians are Catholic."

"Well, I was raised a Catholic, yes."

"Mr. McCone and I are Catholics," she said. "Our children — well, they have minds of their own. Or pretend to. But Andy and I are very devout."

Outside, the devout Mr. McCone was singing in a reedy tenor:

"Onan, son of Judah, was a melancholy
   kid;
He'd jerk and jerk and jerk and jerk, and
   that was all he did.
But the Lord got very angry, when
   Onan shunned his mate;

So awfully hipped on self abuse, he wouldn't fornicate."

Mrs. McCone cocked an ear. Then she went to the back door, opened it, stuck her head out, and said to Mr. McCone, who had paused for breath, "Andy, I would appreciate it if you would confine your singing to the garage. We have a guest." Then she shut the door and came back to where I was. As if she hadn't moved at all, and Mr. McCone hadn't been singing a song in the backyard about Onan the jerk, she said, "You're fond of Sharon, aren't you? I know she's fond of you."

"Oh, sure. She's like the daughter I never had."

"Daughter?"

"I wish I'd gotten married a long time ago so I could have had a daughter just like her. But I guess it's too late now. I mean, even if my fiancée and I get married next month and have a little girl next spring, I'd be eighty-nine and probably dead by the time she reached Sharon's age."

"Fiancée?"

"We're very much in love," I said solemnly.

Mrs. McCone looked disappointed. "Oh," she said. "I see."

The telephone rang. She went over to the kitchen extension and said hello, paused, and then put the receiver down and announced that the call was for me.

I stood up, thinking that it must be Tom Knowles. I had spent last night in Pacific Beach with Charley Valdene, at his invitation; and when I'd left this morning Valdene, who was taking the day off work, had volunteered to pass along word that I could be reached here at the McCones' in the event either the sheriff's department or the SDPD needed anything further from me.

But it wasn't Knowles or anybody else on the cops. It was Eberhardt. And damned if he didn't sound drunk. "Hiya, paisan," he said. "Hell of a P.I. I am, huh? Tracked you right down."

"What is it, Eb? Something come up?"

"Something came up, all right," he said, and snickered. "Listen, hang on, I got somebody here wants to say hello."

"Eb . . ."

Another voice, a shrill feminine voice that sounded even drunker than Eberhardt's, said in my ear, "Hi! This is Wanda."

"Who?"

"Wanda. You know, Ebbie told you 'bout me. Told me 'bout you too. You must be quite a guy. Can't wait to meet you."

"Uh," I said.

"What a party it's gonna be!" Wanda said. "Boy!"

"Party?"

"Here's Ebbie. He'll tell you."

"Me again, paisan," Eberhardt's voice said. "Ain't she something? Wait'll you meet her."

"Listen, *Ebbie,* what the hell is going on up there? You're not at the office, are you?"

"Nah. Taking the day off."

"You're drunk. What's the idea of calling me like this?"

"Wanted you be the first to know the big news."

"What big news?"

"Wanda and me — we're getting married."

"What!"

"Yeah. I popped the question little while ago and we been celebrating. Champagne, five bucks a bottle. Bet you're surprised, huh?"

I didn't say anything. I couldn't have said anything if I'd wanted to.

"We haven't set the date yet, so don't worry 'bout that," Eberhardt said. "You're gonna be my best man. Wouldn't have anybody else." Whispers and giggles in the background. "Got to go now, paisan. You tell Kerry, huh?

Four of us'll get together real soon. Want you both meet Wanda right away."

He hung up. I hung up, too, and stood there trying to get my mouth closed. Eberhardt and Wanda-from-Macy's. Married. Jesus Christ!

Mrs. McCone was looking at me. "Did you have some bad news?" she asked solicitously.

"I'm not sure yet," I said, "but I think so."

Mr. McCone had begun singing again outside:

"Oh, come all ye laddies and listen to
     me,
And I'll tell you a tale that will fill you
     with glee;
Of a pretty young maiden so fair and so
     tall,
Who married a man who had no balls at
     all!"

Yeah, I thought, and his name sure as hell isn't Eberhardt.

Mrs. McCone frowned and shut the window. Then she said, "Well, I'm sure everything will work out for you. I just hope it does for Sharon. She really does need a man to look after her. Marriage would settle her down—"

"I heard that, Ma," Sharon's voice said from the doorway. She came waddling in on her cane; in spite of the gunk on her blistered face, she looked pretty good for a member of the walking wounded. "Why do you have to keep pushing marriage all the time? I'm not even sure I *want* to get married."

"Marriage is what God meant for all of us," Mrs. McCone said. "Sooner or later."

Even Wanda the Footwear Queen, I thought gloomily.

Sharon went to the refrigerator, poured herself a glass of white wine, then perched gingerly on a chair opposite me. "Has Ma been giving you a hard time, Wolf?" she asked.

"I don't give people a hard time," Mrs. McCone said before I could think of an answer. "You're the one who gives people a hard time. If it weren't for this nice man I'd be getting ready for your funeral right now."

"Ma . . ."

"Why don't you work together, you and him? Go into partnership, I mean. I'll bet *that* would keep you out of trouble."

"Wolf already has a partner. Besides, a partnership is like a marriage, which I've already told you I'm not ready for."

"I still think you'd make a good team,"

501

Mrs. McCone said stubbornly. "You solved all those murders together, didn't you?"

"More or less," I said. "But neither of us made a dime out of it. In fact, we both *lost* money on a week's worth of expenses."

"So you'll never work together again?"

McCone and I looked at each other. "Never," I said, and she said, "Not a chance." And then we both laughed and raised our drinks to each other.

You never know what might happen. If we ever *did* work together again, one thing was certain: it would definitely be interesting. . . .

For Larry Herschenfeld, who first suggested this "meeting of the Eyes"; and for Phyllis Brown, Lewis Burger, and the staff of the Grounds for Murder Bookstore in San Diego, with thanks for their help and encouragement.